KINGS OF INFINITE SPACE

ALSO BY JAMES HYNES

The Lecturer's Tale

Publish and Perish

The Wild Colonial Boy

KINGS OF INFINITE SPACE

——

JAMES

HYNES

——

ST. MARTIN'S PRESS

NEW YORK

www.stmartins.com

Library of Congress Cataloging-in-Publication Data

Hynes, James.
    Kings of infinite space : a novel / by James Hynes.
    p. cm.
    ISBN 0-312-45645-X
    1. Government contractors—Fiction.   2. Temporary employees—Fiction.   3. Technical writing—Fiction.   4. Loss (Psychology)—Fiction.   5. Divorced men—Fiction.   6. Texas—Fiction.   I. Title.

PS3558.Y55K56 2004
813'.54—dc22

2003058563

First Edition: April 2004

10 9 8 7 6 5 4 3 2 1

TO MIKE AND TOM,

A COUPLE OF HARDWORKING GUYS

Not to go on all-Fours; *that* is the Law. Are we not Men?
Not to suck up Drink; *that* is the Law. Are we not Men?
Not to eat Flesh or Fish; *that* is the Law. Are we not Men?
Not to claw Bark of Trees; *that* is the Law. Are we not Men?
Not to chase other Men; *that* is the Law. Are we not Men?

—H. G. Wells, *The Island of Dr. Moreau*

KINGS OF INFINITE SPACE

ONE

ONE BRUTALLY HOT SUMMER'S MORNING, Paul Trilby—
ex-husband, temp typist, cat murderer—slouched sweating in
his t-shirt on his way to work, waiting behind the wheel of his
car for the longest red light in central Texas. He was steeling
himself for a confrontation with his boss, screwing up his nerve
to ask for a raise, but his present circumstances were conspiring
against him. His fourteen-year-old Dodge Colt rattled in place
in the middle of the Travis Street Bridge, hemmed in on all
sides by bulbous, purring pickup trucks and gleaming sport util-
ity vehicles with fat, black tires. The electric blues and greens
of these enormous automobiles reflected the dazzling morning
glare through Paul's cracked and dirty windshield; they radiated
shimmering heat through his open window. Waiting for the
light, the fingers of his left hand drumming the scalding side of
his car, the skin of his forearm baking to leather in the heat,
Paul felt less like a man who deserved more out of life than a
peasant on a mule cart trapped in the middle of an armored
division.

"You're paying me as a typist," Paul said aloud, practicing, "but you're working me as a technical writer."

In the heat, and in the rumble of idling engines, this sounded especially feeble. Paul sighed and peered ahead, where a homeless man was walking through the waves of heat between the lines of hulking trucks and SUVs, turning slowly from side to side as if he were lost in a parking lot looking for his car. Unlike most panhandlers, he didn't carry a hand-lettered sign on a piece of cardboard, telegraphing some tale of woe; even more strange, he wore a white, short-sleeved dress shirt and a tie instead of the usual sun-bleached denims and filthy t-shirt. The bluntness of his large, egg-shaped head was exaggerated by a severe buzz cut and a pair of wire-rim glasses, and his body was egg shaped as well—he looked unusually well fed for a homeless guy. Indeed, in his white shirt and polyester slacks, he looked like a caricature of a middle manager from some draw-this-puppy matchbook school of art, one large oval topped by a smaller one. The shirt and tie are a mistake, Paul thought, he needs a sign—WILL TYPE AND FILE FOR FOOD. But that cut too close to the bone for Paul; he was only a paycheck away from panhandling himself. And anyway, it wasn't his job to offer marketing advice to the homeless. I've got my own problems, he told himself, and he lifted his gaze through the heat shimmering off the trucks ahead and saw, at the far end of the bridge, the time and temperature endlessly chasing each other across the shadow side of the Bank of Texas Building. It was just barely eight o'clock, and already 85 degrees. In the morning glare the bank's brass logo along the sunlit side of the building blazed as if it were burning.

"Bot," said Paul, pronouncing the bank's acronym aloud. "Bee. Oh. Tee." Sweat trickled down his breastbone. Both front windows of his unair-conditioned Colt were rolled down, in the unlikely event of a breeze, and his own dress shirt was tossed on the passenger seat so that he wouldn't sweat through it on the drive to work. A racket like someone violently battering a cookie sheet came from the undercarriage of his unevenly idling car and was reflected back at him by the enormous, neon blue Trooper to his left.

This is not the climate for ambition, Paul thought, and at the edge of his consciousness flickered a retort from his former, more politically engaged persona as a university professor: that this kind of thinking was prejudiced and possibly even racist. Old buzzwords flickered dialectically at the back of his brain like heat lightning along the horizon—colonial/postcolonial; First World/Third World; North/South—but Paul was only barely aware of them. During this moment of distraction, each of the red numerals streaming across the bank at the end of the bridge had grown by one. Now it was 86 degrees and 8:01, and Paul was late for work.

The egg-shaped man had come closer, only a couple of vehicles away. All the other drivers on the bridge sat high up behind their tinted windows, ignoring the man in air-conditioned comfort. Paul had come to think of these more affluent drivers as "the truckoisie," middle-class state employees who faced, at worst, a forty-minute, stop-and-start commute every morning, but who did it in vehicles capable of fording a jungle stream or hauling half a ton of manure. These vehicles had names that bespoke Spartan virtues, a semimilitary asceticism—Explorer and Pathfinder and Samurai—but within, even in the cabs of the pickup trucks, the vehicles were as comfy as suburban living rooms, where the truckoisie drank from huge plastic flagons of specialty coffee, talked on their cell phones, and listened to hyperventilating, drive time DJs on the radio or best-selling self-help books on tape. Paul's own tape player had long since choked to death on a cassette of Jan and Dean's greatest hits, stuck at last on the screeching tires of "Dead Man's Curve," and the FM band on his radio no longer worked, leaving him with only the shrill democracy of AM—jammin' oldies, oompah Tejano accordion music, and Dr. Laura. At this moment he waited with the radio off, his car noisily juddering itself to pieces beneath him, and he sat smelling exhaust, his own sweat, and the nitrous aroma of bat shit rising off the sluggish green river below.

"I'm not a typist," muttered Paul, trying to focus on the matter at hand, "I'm a goddamn tech writer."

Suddenly the egg-shaped man was at the Colt's bumper, swiveling his spectacles in Paul's direction. Paul averted his gaze, trying to avoid eye contact. Too late. The homeless man came up to Paul's window, his eyes huge behind his glasses.

Paul glowered straight ahead, his train of thought derailed. This was a breach of panhandler decorum. The way it was supposed to work was, you waggled your sign, if you had one, and scowled in a guilt-inducing manner; the object of your attentions ignored you; you moved on. Paul sighed ostentatiously and lifted his eyebrows at the traffic light, just barely visible above the tall rear end of the Pathfinder ahead of him. Still red. Over the stink of exhaust and hot metal, he was certain he could already smell the homeless man's riparian scent. But for the heat, Paul would have rolled up his window.

Don't meet his eye, Paul told himself. Pretend he isn't there.

But now Mr. Egg was bent at Paul's window like a highway patrolman. Paul allowed himself only the tiniest roll of his eyeballs to the side and was surprised to note that the man's tie featured some sort of astronomical theme, lines of right ascension and declination and signs of the Zodiac against a background of twilight blue. Still not meeting the man's eye, Paul performed another leftward, double-take bounce of his eyeballs. The tie was faded but tightly knotted and clipped to the man's shirt with a dull, silver tie clip, upon which an eroded engraving read ". . . OF THE YEAR." Paul risked another eyeball bounce at Herr Egg, then another. The white shirt front was smudged, and the narrow points of the man's collar were frayed, but astonishingly in this heat—Paul himself perspired like an overweight prizefighter—there were no sweat stains on the shirt. Monsieur Egg wore two pens; the lower end of one poked through a hole in the bottom of his breast pocket. Across his other breast, inches from Paul's nose, was a smudgy, creased, blue-and-white paper name tag, the sort with a sticky backing that conference goers wear. It read, in blue sans serif and large, block hand lettering:

Hello! My name is

BOY G

Paul twisted sideways in his seat and looked the man in his egg-shaped face. "Go *away*," he demanded.

Señor Egg's face from temple to chin was one long, smooth, hairless curve. His skin—another first for a homeless guy in Texas—was pale as a slug, almost albino. His milky scalp gleamed through his stubbled hair, but even this close to him Paul saw not a drop of sweat. The man—Boy G, why else would he wear a name tag?—had a small mouth and a rounded nose, and his tiny, pale eyes were magnified by the bulbous lenses of his wire rims. He was not looking at Paul, however, but past him, appraising the contents and the state of Paul's automobile. His fishy eyes noted the S-shaped crack in the windshield, the greasy dust on the dashboard, the foamy rents in the upholstery. The driver's side sun visor was long gone, torn off in a rage, and the armrest on the passenger door hung by one screw. Behind the front seat a rising tide of Coke cans, crumpled Taco Bell bags, and empty Big Gulp cups cluttered the foot wells.

Paul stared at the man openmouthed and gripped the steering wheel, his stomach tight with anger. Could this bum be *judging* him? Was it possible that Paul Trilby, B.A., M.A., Ph.D., almost a Fulbright, did not meet the exacting standards of the homeless? Boy G's small mouth curved down at either end, either the beginnings of a smile or a condescending frown, and Paul braced himself for some hoarse obscenity or just an indecipherable grunt. He frantically sought for something cutting to say to forestall this asshole's street witticism.

But Boy G spoke in a whisper, his breath betraying no trace of alcohol nor of anything else for that matter.

"Are we not men?" he said.

Paul's retort caught in his throat. "What?" was all he managed to say.

"Are we not men?" repeated Boy G, with the same ghostly inflection.

The driver of the Ram Truck behind him honked her horn just then, startling Paul, and he glanced in the rearview mirror, then ahead through the windshield glare at the traffic light. It was green, and all the gleaming trucks ahead of him were in motion; a wide gap had opened up between his front bumper and the receding wall of SUVs and pickups. Paul jerked his foot off the brake and the Colt rattled forward. Then he remembered the homeless guy so close to his car, and he hit the brake again. He turned to the window as Ms. Ram Truck leaned on her horn.

"Watch it!" said Paul to Boy G, but there was no one there.

The Ram Truck roared around him and raced through the yellow light. Paul cursed and hit the gas, then jammed the brake almost immediately as the light turned red. His threadbare tires screeched; his arthritic shocks groaned. He lurched against his seat belt, and from the passenger seat his shirt and his lunch slid to the floor; behind him the midden of cans and crumpled bags rustled. Paul pounded the wheel and twisted in his seat, looking right and left, forward and back, for the egg-shaped man. But all he saw were the six sun-baked lanes and the concrete parapet of the bridge, and another fearsome brigade of Troopers and Scouts coming up from behind. Boy G had vanished.

TWO

BY THE TIME PAUL PULLED INTO THE PARKING LOT, all the spaces in the shade next to the General Services Division Building had been taken by trucks and SUVs, lined up along the wall like piglets at the teat. Paul's watch said 8:06, and he drove frantically up and down the lanes looking for a spot, the angry rattle under his car reflected back at him by the rows of vehicles. But all the shady spots were taken, and he was forced to park along the river embankment in the sun. Before the car shuddered and gasped to a stop, he had rolled up the windows and bent with a grunt to snatch his shirt and his bag lunch off the floor. He trotted across the lot in the stifling heat, pulling on the shirt as he ran, his bag lunch dangling from between his teeth.

"Tech writer," he snarled through clenched lips, "not typist."

Preston, the security guard, lifted his eyebrows at the sight of Paul tucking in his shirt as he came breathlessly into the dank air-conditioning of the lobby.

"You oughta get a regular badge." Preston had big shoulders, a steel-grey crew cut, and a massive Joseph Stalin moustache. He stood behind the counter at parade rest, one hand clasping the other wrist below his tight little potbelly, and he unclasped his wrist and leaned forward just enough to turn the sign-in sheet towards Paul with his long fingers. "You been here long enough," he continued, in a thick East Texas accent like a mouth full of grits.

"I'm only here temporarily," Paul gasped. Sweat trickled down his collar. He wrote "7:59" on the sheet and dashed out his signature. "It's a temporary situation."

"Prit' near six weeks." Preston slid a visitor's badge across the desk and returned to parade rest. "Save you a few minutes is all."

But Paul was already jogging down the first-floor hall to the refrigerators outside the cafeteria, where he stashed his lunch amid bulging plastic grocery bags and snap-top containers crammed with last night's casserole. He glanced through the door at the cafeteria's morning trade: large white men with belts cinched up under their bellies purchasing breakfast burritos from squat, buxom Hispanic women in hair nets and white aprons. Paul decided against a burrito—it wouldn't do to have salsa on his breath when he talked to Rick—and hurried around the corner to the tiny elevator. The stairs were faster—the GSD Building only had two floors—but riding the elevator gave Paul a moment to catch his breath, to pretend that he hadn't just dashed in out of the heat. As the door slid shut, he loosened the sticky waistband of his shorts, and, through his shirt, pinched his t-shirt front and back, peeling it away from his humid skin, flapping it like a bellows to cool himself. He tipped his head back against the wall of the car and sighed.

Are we not men? he thought. What does that mean?

At the second floor the elevator itself groaned, a long sigh that sounded as if it were giving up. But the door slid open, and Paul stepped out, turned left past the aluminum can recycling box, and slipped through the doorway into cubeland.

The General Services Division of the Texas Department of General Services—the GSD of TxDoGS—was housed in a wide, low-ceilinged, underlit room in the shape of a hollow square. In the center of the square was a courtyard where a sun-blasted redwood deck surrounded an old live oak, which was fighting a losing battle with oak wilt. The offices along the outer walls, with views of the parking lot and the river, were taken by senior managers. Middle managers had offices along the inner wall with a view of the dying oak tree, and everybody else occupied the honeycomb of cubicles in between, where nearly every vertical surface was grown over as if by moss with stubbly gray fabric. Some enterprising ergonomist for the state of Texas had calculated to the photon the minimum lighting necessary to meet code, and then had removed enough fluorescent bulbs from the suspended ceiling to make the room look candlelit. Everybody works better, went the theory, in the pool of light from his or her own desk lamp. Helps 'em concentrate. The drywall of the outer offices kept any sunlight from reaching the interior, and the amber tint of the courtyard windows filtered the Texas glare. No matter the time of day or the weather, the room always looked the same. It was like working underground, Paul thought.

Just now, across the room, over the cube horizon, Paul saw his boss, Rick McKellar, lope out of his office with his chin lifted like a rooster's and his impressive eyebrows raised as he started up one of the main thoroughfares of the labyrinth of cubes. Paul instantly ducked his head and hunched his shoulders like a soldier dashing from one trench to another, and he scuttled past the empty conference room, then left into the first side street, then immediately left again into his cube. The woman in the cube opposite, Olivia Haddock, was for once looking the other way, and her slave, the dying tech writer in the cube next to Paul's, luckily never lifted his head. Made it, Paul thought, and then saw the latest draft of the RFP on his chair, already emended in Rick's bold, red felt tip. In the beginning Paul had interpreted Rick's huge, brusque lettering as rage, but eventually he understood it as a sign of restlessness and not directed at him in particular. Rick corresponded with all his employees that way.

WATERMARK???? read the scrawl in bright red across the top of the title page. A long, bold, blunt arrow descended to the bottom of the page, and alongside it Rick had dashed, in even larger letters, *GLOBAL!!!!*

"A watermark?" Paul muttered. "He wants a watermark?"

"Mornin'!" Paul heard Rick say to someone, still twenty paces away, and Paul snatched the document off his chair and dropped into his seat, which squeaked like a small animal. Without looking, he was conscious of Olivia's gimlet glance from across the aisle, while from the adjacent cube he heard the Darth Vader wheeze of the dying tech writer's breathing tube. With one hand he turned on the fluorescent light under his cabinet and with the other nudged the mouse of his PC so that the screen saver deactivated. He could hear the crepitation of Rick's shoes on the carpet outside his cube, so he picked up the RFP with both hands and leaned back in his squealing chair.

"You're here!" barked Rick, stepping straight into Paul's cube and looming over him. "D'ja take a look at my glads and happies?" He rested his hand on the top edge of the cube, then nervously plucked it away.

"Um, yeah," Paul drawled, as if he were concentrating hard, and he stuck his thumb at random in the stack of pages and flipped it open over the hinge of the staple, as if he were looking for something specific in the interior of the document. He was desperately hoping to convey by this maneuver that he had been sitting here for some time deep in contemplation of the RFP, that he had not just put his ass in the seat, that he was not still breathing hard from the dash across the parking lot, that he was not sweating like a triathelete. From the corner of his eye he saw Rick's hands twitching at the loose, blousy folds of his dress shirt, which was already coming untucked. Squinting at some indecipherable hieroglyph of Rick's, Paul said, "Hmmm," hoping to convey a degree of awe and intellectual curiosity.

"You know how to do a watermark, right?" Rick went on, in his nasal Texas drawl. But before Paul could respond, Rick executed a jerky little pirouette, during which he revolved a complete 360 degrees on the ball of his foot, thrust his palms deep inside his waistband, completely retucked his shirt, and returned to his original position, hoisting his trousers with his thumbs through a pair of belt loops.

"I'll show you." Rick leaned abruptly across Paul, forcing Paul to wheel back in his chair. Rick splayed one broad hand against the surface of Paul's desk and clutched the mouse with the other, his index finger trembling over the clicker like the unsteady needle of a compass. Nothing made him happier than to demonstrate to Paul some arcana from Microsoft Word. Meanwhile Paul was getting a strong whiff of Rick's aftershave and an intimate look at the tiny hairs like wheat stubble riding the folds at the back of Rick's neck.

"You just click on this cheer," Rick mumbled, as he launched the wrong program from Paul's computer desktop.

"Ah, that's PowerPoint, Rick," Paul said, as the start-up screen blossomed. Rick fumbled with the mouse, driving the cursor all over, trying to find a way to shut it down.

"Way-ul," he muttered, "you can't close the barn door after the chickens have roosted."

Paul knew exactly what would happen next; Rick was as easily distracted as a cat. He turned his head away from the screen to look at Paul. His bushy, semicircular eyebrows glided up and down, his forehead creased and uncreased. He seemed utterly unfazed by the fact that he and Paul were close enough to kiss.

"You finish that presentation I asked you for," Rick said, "for the maintenance managers?"

"I gave you the disk yesterday." Paul tried not to wince at the minty sourness of Rick's mouthwash.

"Didja!" Rick unclutched the mouse and stood erect, his hands twitching at his waist. "Have I looked at it yet?"

"I don't know."

"Fair enough," Rick said, and he pivoted out of the cube.

"Uh, Rick?" Paul half pushed himself to his feet. "Could I, uh, take a minute . . . ?"

Rick pivoted again in the aisle. He rested a hand on the edge of the cube and then snatched it away. He bounced his eyebrows.

"Um, well, not here." Paul's eyes flickered across the aisle, where Olivia perched erect at her computer screen, pretending not to listen. "Could we maybe talk in your office?"

Rick's eyes widened. "You're leaving," he declared with infinite sadness. Rick had gone through three unsuccessful temps before Paul.

"Oh no!" Paul was disgusted to hear his voice shoot up an octave. "I'm not going anywhere. I'm . . ." He dropped his voice to a more commanding register. "I'm happy here. It's just—"

At that moment Rick's beeper buzzed, and he executed another half turn before he managed to yank the little device out of his shirt pocket and peer at the readout.

"Later!" he cried, and sailed off, chin lifted, eyebrows bouncing. Paul felt his shoulders sag.

"So you're not leaving us?" Olivia sang out from across the aisle, hands poised over her keyboard, head cocked over her shoulder. The sharp, blonde hemline of her hair swung just above her shoulder. Her spine was perfectly erect, bolstered by a stiff lumbar pillow at the small of her back like a bustle.

Paul blinked at her. One day, waiting to ask a question of Nolene, the department's chief secretary, Paul had witnessed a virtuoso duel of passive aggression between her and Olivia over the use of the fax machine. The skirmish ended with Olivia's parting shot, with its pert rise in inflection at the end, as if she were asking a question, "Well, it's not how *I'm* used to conducting business?" As Olivia marched away, her back as ramrod straight as a drill instructor's, her hair swinging above her shoulders, Paul simultaneously noted the pep squad switch of her not unattractive bottom and her coarse, middle-aged elbows, as creased as an elephant's knees. To his astonishment, Nolene actually stuck her pink, glistening tongue out at Olivia's retreating backside. Then she swiveled massively in Paul's direction, lifted her plucked eyebrows, and, only because he happened to be standing there, delivered a dismissively annotated rendition of Olivia Haddock's résumé: homecoming queen at Chester W. Nimitz High School in Irving, Texas—big whoop. Head of a championship cheerleading team at SMU—as if I give a shit. Twenty-year veteran of a major energy corporation in Houston—like she's *better* than anybody else! Which transferred her to Lamar and then abruptly downsized her—*serves her right!* Started at the bottom again at TxDoGS as a *temp*—"The wretched of the earth," contributed Paul, under his breath—worked her way onto the permanent staff as a purchaser, and because certain *men* around here, and I'm not naming names, like to watch her *twitching cheerleader ass*, she survived the statewide job cuts in the department five years ago when men with *ten times* her seniority were out on the street after *twenty years. Can you believe it?*

"You know what we call her?" Nolene dropped her voice even lower. "La Cucaracha."

"Because . . . ?" Paul pictured a multilegged Olivia mincing up the aisle, antennae quivering.

"Because *she won't die*," hissed Nolene. "Whatever you do to her, she always survives."

This contrasted with the nickname Olivia had picked for herself: As the purchaser for all of TxDoGS's office supplies statewide, she referred to herself as the Paperclip Queen. For a week or so after he had started at TxDoGS, Paul thought he was being charming and mildly flirtatious by calling her the Toner Czarina or the Duchess of Whiteout or the Binder Clip Contessa. But one morning he had come in to find a Post-it stuck to his computer monitor briskly printed in very sharp pencil:

> *PLEASE DO NOT*
> *DEPRECIATE MY*
> *NICK-NAME. YOU*
> *ARE ONLY A*
> *TEMP AND I AM*
> *A PERMANENT*
> *EMPLOYEE*
> *—O.H.*

"So you're not leaving us?" Olivia was saying now.

"No," breathed Paul, as he watched Rick's head gliding away between the tops of the intervening cubicles. He glanced at her across the aisle; Olivia had a small, very sharp nose and large eyes that widened whenever she spoke to him. Years ago it was a look that had probably driven the defensive line of the Mighty Vikings, or whatever they were called, wild with adolescent longing, but now it meant, *Nothing gets by me, buster.* Paul's worst nightmare was that he, like the hapless, dying tech writer, would end up working for her.

"No," Paul said again, "I'm not leaving," and he turned back to his desk.

THREE

MAKING RICK'S LINE EDITS—his "glads and happies," in
Rick's peculiar usage—took about fifteen minutes, and Paul
burned up another forty or so trying to figure out the watermark function in Microsoft Word. Bored by that, he tried to
kill some time checking his e-mail, but no one in the department had sent him anything this morning, and no one from his
old life kept in touch with him anymore. As a temp, TxDoGS
didn't trust him on the Web, but his browser did allow him to
explore the department's intranet site. Unfortunately, after six
weeks on the job, Paul had the TxDoGS site pretty well mem-
orized—for a Ph.D. in English literature from the once-
prestigious University of the Midwest, he had a surprisingly
thorough knowledge of the hazmat regulations in the state of
Texas—so he switched to the PowerPoint slide show he had
assembled for Rick and idly monkeyed with the backgrounds,
making them marbled or watery or sparkly or adding one of
the program's ready-made animations. On the title slide—

Pilot Project

on

Vehicle Maintenance Outsourcing

Texas Department of General Services

—he introduced a mooing little longhorn that clattered across the bottom of the slide, thrusting its horns this way and that. For the slide that listed the project personnel—

RFP Development Team

- **Rick McKellar, TxDoGS Fleet Manager, General Services Division**
- **Colonel Travis Pentoon, J. J. Toepperwein, and Bob Wier of GSD**
- **Paul Trilby, typist**

—he found a little soldier who marched to the middle of the screen, executed a perfect present arms, and saluted.

Every twenty minutes or so, however, Paul bounded out of his chair, snatched up the RFP as an excuse, and then stopped short in the door of his cube. The upper edge of the gray cubescape came to Paul's cheekbones, and, like most of the men in the office, he could gauge the traffic in the aisles from a distance—or some of it, anyway. It was different for women, both seeing and being seen. Callie the Mail Girl, for example, was tall enough so that you could see the cropped top of her head above the cube horizon as she trundled her cart up the aisle, but Renee—pronounced "Renny," in true Texas fashion, a tiny, hollow-eyed woman who purchased replacement parts for massive earthmoving equipment—was invisible until you were nearly on top of her. Paul was an energetic walker, and no matter how he tried to check himself, he always seemed to be blundering into her. This elicited another angry Post-it on his computer screen:

> Please do not
> walk so fast in
> The Aisle. You
> are not the
> only person
> here.

This note was unsigned, but he knew it was from Renee; the printing did not have Olivia's needle-sharp precision but read rather like a child's, or like someone trying to disguise her right hand by writing with her left.

So now Paul felt that he was running the gauntlet every time he left his cube, as he did now. Clutching the rolled-up RFP in both hands like a club, Paul dipped his head and hurried past the doorway of the dying tech writer, almost superstitiously averting his gaze from the knobs of the man's spine rising out of his frayed cardigan and the deepening groove between the wasting cords of his neck. It was uncharitable, perhaps even cruel, to dwell on it, but this wretched man had starred in an actual nightmare of Paul's in which the dying tech writer had arrived at TxDoGS on his first day as a strapping six footer, as ruddy as a rugby player, only to have his vitality sucked dry by a furious, naked Olivia, reducing him to the shriveled and gray-skinned husk he was now. The imagery for this nightmare came from a space vampire video Paul had seen years ago, but recognition of its provenance couldn't keep him from repressing a shudder every time he passed the man's cube.

Paul turned right down the main aisle, grateful he didn't immediately bowl over Renee as he did two or three times a week, but noting the look of pure hatred she gave him even from the safety of her cube. At the next major intersection he glimpsed Callie the Mail Girl in the "library," which was only a big, open cube with a metal bookcase full of ring binders just inside the door and a photocopier in the corner. Callie was sorting mail at the long worktable across from the copier. As a member of the Building Services staff she was exempt from the regime of business casual, and in jeans and a t-shirt she pressed her belly up against the edge of the table, propped herself on one long arm, and sorted the mail into piles with a flick of her wrist. She had a long, oval face, sharp cheekbones, and reddish hair cropped to within an inch of her pale scalp, which had led to a few sniggering lesbo jokes in Paul's hearing. She was long legged and hippy in a way that Paul found immensely appealing, though he'd never had an occasion to speak to her. Still, even as he flashed by the library doorway, he managed to admire her long neck and the cant of her hip against the worktable and the deep curve in the small of her back. Callie blew out a long, bored sigh and flicked another envelope, and Paul turned left, up the aisle towards Rick's office.

Here he ran another gauntlet, past the cubes of the three purchasers who served on the RFP Development Team. First he passed Joe John Toepperwein, a beetle-browed, slope-shouldered young man who hunched before his computer as if he expected to be clobbered from behind at any moment. Squeezing the mouse as if he wanted to crush it, his eyes flicking angrily back and forth, J. J. pushed the little arrow of the cursor around the screen as if he were trying to stab something. Every time Paul passed, J. J. was switching from one Web page to another; he never seemed to settle on one site, but constantly, restlessly surfed. Yet as each page clicked by, J. J. sat sullenly immobile before the screen like a diorama of early twenty-first-century office work, a tableau non vivant.

Then Paul passed Colonel Travis Pentoon, late of the United States Army, a square-shouldered, broad-chested, crinkly eyed man in his late fifties whose fastidiously creased khakis and dress shirt conceded little to civilian laxity. He had let his military buzz cut grow out a full quarter of an inch, and though he removed his sport coat when sitting at his desk, he kept his cuffs buttoned and his tie cinched tight up under his dewlaps. He was usually typing furiously, his fingers arched, his hands rebounding off the keyboard as energetically as a concert pianist's, and he watched whatever he was typing with a penetrating squint, while the black, polarizing screen across his monitor kept anyone else from seeing what he was working on. When he wasn't typing, he was on the phone, holding the handset lightly between the tips of his blunt fingers as he managed his money market account on the state's time, jotting figures on a pad with his free hand. Today he was multitasking, simultaneously hammering the keyboard and cradling the phone between his cheek and his shoulder. "I hear what you're saying," he was telling his broker in a throaty, George C. Scott rasp, "but we're either on the bus with this one, son, or off the bus."

Finally, Paul passed the orderly cube of Bob Wier, with his color-coded state purchasing manuals and his ring binders arranged in descending order of size. In his desk drawer he kept a can of compressed air, and Paul had often seen him blasting the grit from between the keys of the computer keyboard he never seemed to use. He also kept a spray bottle of Windex to keep spotless the curved screen of his monitor and the glass in his array of family photographs—his dead wife and three well-scrubbed children and an eight-by-ten portrait of a blond, blue-eyed Jesus. Bob wore polo shirts and penny loafers, and he was handball trim and aggressively good-humored, but there was something attenuated about him, as if his skin was stretched too tight over his skull. He never stopped smiling, but his eyes were watery, which Paul attributed to the loss of his wife. As a temp Paul was off the circuit for office lore, but one morning, while Bob was temporarily away from his cube, Nolene had given Paul the highlights on fast forward. Bob's wife had vanished, she said, and most folks thought she had simply run off, but Bob referred to her as his "late wife." "And I reckon he ought to know," Nolene added darkly. He'd sent his kids to live with his sister in Amarillo—"As far away as they could git from Lamar," Nolene whispered, "and still be in the state of Texas"—and he filled his time by trying to sell his coworkers on Chris-

tian speed-reading courses, Christian real estate schemes, and
Christian cleaning products. "He don't know what 'no' means,"
warned Nolene. "You ever hear him mention 'distributed sales,'
run the other way."

But Paul was a temp and luckily out of range of Bob's evan-
gelical salesmanship. Still, Bob Wier was one of the few people
in the office to note Paul's presence. Today Bob sat behind his
desk ostentatiously speed-reading a book, thumbing aside each
page with a crisp *snap* as his JESUS IS LORD! screen saver flowed
endlessly across the bright screen behind him. He glanced up
as Paul passed, and his face pulled in two directions as he gave
Paul his wide, desperate smile and his mournful eyes drooped
to either side. Paul returned the look with a wince, and then
brought himself up short again between the uprights of Rick's
doorway.

But once again he had run the gauntlet uselessly, for Rick
was on the phone. FLEET MANAGER read the plaque on Rick's
door; the privatization project that Paul was the typist for—
whoa, whoa, whoa, make that *tech writer*—was only one of
Rick's many responsibilities. Rick sat tipped back in his chair,
head framed by the brittle branches of the dying tree beyond
the window, feet up on the desk displaying the purple bar code
price tag still pasted to the sole of one new shoe—$89.95 from
Texas Shoe Corral. He was bellowing into the headset of his
phone, his eyebrows bouncing up and down. Paul hovered in
the doorway, the RFP coiled tightly in both hands. Rick beckoned him in with an abrupt curl of his fingers and then continued his phone conversation, his hands fiddling at the folds of
his shirt around his waist.

"Uh-huh. Uh-huh. I hear ya. Uh-huh." He recrossed his
ankles on his desk. "Well, I always say, if you're gonna change
horses, you gotta get 'em all in line. Yessir. Uh-huh."

Paul shifted from foot to foot and silently practiced his
opening. He had decided to take the Socratic approach, presenting the RFP as a visual aid. "Is this not a technical document? Am I not the writer of this document? Then is it not

the case that I am a technical writer?" Paul unrolled the RFP to make sure he had it right side up.

"Yowzah," said Rick into the phone, his eyebrows shooting nearly up to his hairline. "The whole enchilada?"

After a minute or two of shuffling in place, Paul backed out of the office and hovered near the network printer, rolling the RFP between his hands again. Nolene gave him a glance and then ignored him, and Paul faded into the gray fabric of the nearby cube walls and listened to the unseen life of the office around him. Paul was still spooked by the eerie invisibility of most of his coworkers. Spread out before him in the weird, undersea light, the gray metal strips on top of the cube partitions outlined, like a map of itself, the labyrinth of right angles in all directions. A few items stuck up above the cube horizon— a row of fat red ring binders across the top of a filing cabinet, a lonely cactus in a green plastic pot, a schoolbus-yellow hard hat, a softball trophy, a pink plastic pig. What Paul could *not* see from where he stood was another single living human being, yet he heard the clatter of computer keyboards, the rhythmic burr of a ringing phone, the squeaking flex of an office chair. He heard the whirr of the printer and the buzz of the fax machine, the rumble of a drawer sliding out and sliding in. He saw the flash of the copier on the suspended ceiling and heard the beep of its buttons and the whine of its carriage shuttling back and forth. He heard the hard-drive purr of a PC. The clatter of a phone returned to its cradle. A laugh. The thump of a stapler, the snick of a ballpoint, the rattle of paper, the bass crepitation of the mail cart against the carpet. All of it, every rattle, click, and chirrup, without being able to see a soul. It was like being surrounded by ghosts, and Paul knew a thing or two about that.

"Hon?" said a voice in Paul's ear, and he started violently.

Nolene was leaning out of her cube, her pale fingers not quite touching Paul's shoulder. "If you want to go back to your cube," she said, lifting her manicured eyebrows, "I'll let you know when Rick's free. You don't need to keep making the trip."

Paul cleared his throat and strangled the rolled-up document between his hands. "Uh, thanks," he choked, and he ran the gauntlet in the reverse direction, past Bob Wier's miserable smile, the clatter of the Colonel's keyboard, J. J.'s glowering back. Someone else was in the library now, one of the other secretaries, photocopying. As he turned right down the aisle, he glimpsed the top of Callie's bobbing head across the office, as she trundled her mail cart up the aisle like Mother Courage. Renee froze in her doorway, clutching her throat in rage as Paul thundered past, muttering an apology. Then left past the empty cube of the dying tech writer—Where had he gone?—and into his own cube.

"Keeping busy?" sang out Olivia from across the aisle, her wrists cocked over her keyboard.

"Yeah," said Paul, feeling his stomach clench at the sound of her voice. He dropped the RFP, now permanently curled from his grip, and regarded his computer screen. He had been gone long enough for the screen saver to kick in; this, no doubt, had not escaped Olivia's notice. In his time at TxDoGS Paul had tried out a couple of screen saver messages—*The mass of men lead lives of quiet desperation* or *Arbeit macht frei*—and had settled on a line from Shakespeare, red, boldfaced, and italic, streaming across a black background:

I could be bounded in a nutshell and count myself a king of infinite space.

"What's it mean?" Olivia had asked him once, poised at the opening of his cube with her hands clasped and her eyes wide, as if she were about to declaim something.

"Ahhhh," Paul had stalled, staring at the screen, until at last he said, "It means that whatever your station in life, you can, um, accomplish great things." He had added, because he knew it would shut her up, "It's from the Bible."

"Oh!" Olivia had said.

Now Paul watched the line slide endlessly across his blackened screen, and he pivoted sharply and stalked out of his cube. *Were it not that I have bad dreams*, he thought, completing the line as he came into the main hallway of the second floor. On the other side of the glass wall, leaning against the rail on the landing of the outdoor stairway, the dying tech writer was having a smoke. Even in the ninety-something heat, the emaciated little man was bundled in a sweater he had buttoned up to the base of his ropy neck. His throat was wrapped in a gauze bandage, and a little plastic tube protruded just below his Adam's apple. He blocked off the tube with his thumb, lifted his cigarette with his other hand, and inhaled. He blinked his deep-socketed eyes, savoring, then lifted his thumb and blew a stream of smoke out of the tube. Paul shivered at the sight, and, as if to evoke Paul's horror, the elevator suddenly groaned at the top of its climb. Paul bolted around the corner of the hallway and banged through the men's room door.

He nearly groaned to himself in relief: He was alone. He entered the stall at the far end of the room and locked the door. This was Paul's escape hatch, his refuge from the soul-destroying boredom of his cube. Every morning about this time, when he dozed slack jawed in front of his monitor, his whole body Novocain numb, his drooping eyelids dragging his whole head towards his chest, he would rise like one of the living dead, stumble to this particular stall, and take a nap. For verisimilitude, he now dropped his trousers but not his underwear, then sat and planted his feet. He propped his elbow on the toilet paper dispenser, planted his cheek in his palm, and closed his eyes. All he heard was the nasal hiss of his own breath and the subliminal hum of the fluorescent lights. He tried to steady his breathing, but he could feel his pulse racing in his wrist and in his temples. Calm down, he told himself. You don't work for Olivia. No space vampire's gonna get you.

Usually he was able to drift off for a restorative minute or two, but today he was aware of the chill of the air-conditioning on his knees, of the hard plastic under his thighs. The insides of his eyelids glowed red with the bright light of the men's room, and he was sure he could see the blood beating through his capillaries. No sleep today, pal. Today, like it or not, was an occasion for self-laceration. How had he wound up here? How could this have happened? He was smarter than anybody in a hundred-yard radius; he was better read; he was wittier; he was—by God!—a better writer. He had a Ph.D. from a well-regarded university; he had won *awards*, for chrissake. He had been a finalist for a Guggenheim! *He'd almost been a Fulbright!*

And then he'd fumbled the ball. Screwed the pooch. Pissed it away. The litany of Paul's mistakes made up his own stations of the cross: He'd picked the wrong postdoc. Hadn't finished his book. Kissed the wrong asses and hadn't kissed the right ones. Married the wrong woman. Then blew that all to hell by sleeping with another wrong woman. Then followed *her* to Texas. Ran up his credit cards. Got a job he hated and lost it. Started another book and hadn't finished it. Gained weight. Lost the woman he'd followed to Texas to a weatherman. Ended up in state government. Started out as a player and ended up as a temp, making eight dollars an hour, sweating blood, pulse pounding as he worked up the nerve to ask for a raise to eleven.

And all because of Charlotte. All because of that motherfucking cat. That devious, cocksucking, motherfucking, bitch whore cunt of a cat. The biggest mistake I ever made. It all starts there, and it all goes downhill. I should have fed Her Royal Fucking Highness on albacore and sweet cream and all the fishy fishy fish snacks she could stuff down her fucking throat. I should have kept the apartment ankle deep in catnip, knee-high in cat toys. I should have stuffed her in her fucking carrier and put her on the bus to Chicago. I should have rented her a fucking limo and driven her to fucking Chicago and dropped her on Elizabeth's fucking doorstep, safe and sound, washed my hands of her, good fucking riddance. So long, suckah. But that's not what you did, is it, moron? Is it, asshole? Is it, you *dumb motherfucker?* No, instead you . . . instead . . .

Something scraped and Paul jerked his head up, sitting up

straight on the toilet seat. Was I talking to myself? he thought. Did I say any of that out loud? He heard another scrape, accompanied by a kind of creak, and he cleared his throat and pulled off a handful of toilet paper. But the little spindle didn't squeak enough for authenticity, so he rattled the dispenser for good measure. He must have fallen asleep because someone was in the men's room with him, and he hadn't heard the telltale thump of the swinging door. God, I hope I wasn't snoring. I hope I wasn't mumbling to myself.

The scrape came again, closer now, almost a sort of *slither.* Paul froze at the sound, a coil of toilet paper slung between his hands. The sound wasn't coming from the center of the men's room. It was coming from above. It was coming from the ceiling.

The door to the men's room banged open, once, then again. Paul pulled the toilet paper taut between his hands and snapped it in two. He heard two sets of footsteps shuffling up to the urinals, heard one man clear his throat, heard the other cough. He heard the creak above him again, and he lifted his eyes to the suspended ceiling. Did that panel *move?*

One of the urinating men cleared his throat again and said, "D'ja get that file I sent you?"

"Yeah," said the other man. "It's cute."

"Have you seen the alien yet?" said the first man.

"What alien?" said the second.

"After the sheep get taken up into the ship."

"No."

"There's a little alien."

"I haven't seen that."

"He waves his arms and legs and his little, whattayacallem, his little antenna around."

"I haven't seen that."

"Then he cuts the field up into little squares and disappears."

"Who, the sheep?"

"No, the alien. He cuts the field up into little squares, and then he disappears."

"I haven't seen him yet."

"Have you seen the black sheep?"

"What black sheep?"

"The black sheep. He butts heads with the little alien."

"I haven't seen the alien yet."

Throughout this illuminating exchange Paul sat perfectly still, his eyes searching the section of ceiling he could see from the stall. The scrape, the moving tile—it couldn't be a rat or a snake, even the tightfisted state of Texas wouldn't stint on vermin control. But the possibility of vermin didn't even occur to Paul. More than anyone else in the building, he had experience with odd sounds when they were least expected, and the thought of what it could be made his skin tighten all over his body, goose pimpling the bare flesh of his legs, tightening his scrotum, making his scalp crawl. He was keenly aware of his own vulnerability, his pants around his ankles, his loins practically exposed. It *can't* be her, he thought, it *couldn't* be. Her absence during the day was the only reason he looked forward to coming to work; the only reason he could stand the daily humiliation was because he knew he'd be free for nine hours of the ammoniac stink of his carpet, of the brittle click of her claws on the kitchen floor. He wouldn't feel the freezing, clammy drafts around his ankles in the night or the rub of her bristling fur. He wouldn't be awakened from his sleep—as he was every morning, half an hour before his alarm—by her icy little teeth biting his toes.

"*Charlotte?*" he whispered in a kind of squeak.

One of the men at the urinals hawked and spat, and both men zipped up and moved around the privacy barrier to the sinks, where Paul lost track of what they were saying. He took advantage of the commotion to stand, keeping an eye on the ceiling panels above. As scared as he was, he didn't want his coworkers to know that he came in here every day at the same time and for what purpose. While the faucets hissed and the men laughed, he hauled up his trousers. But he waited until he heard the door open and the men's voices echo down the hall before he let himself out of the stall and hurried to the sinks.

He watched the ceiling behind him in the mirror as he washed his hands. It's *not* her, he told himself. I was *dreaming*. But his hands shook as he dried them with a length of paper towel, and with one last, nervous glance at the panels overhead, he fled.

FOUR

By LUNCHTIME PAUL HAD managed to convince himself that the creaking he'd heard in the men's room ceiling was a product of his imagination brought on by his anxiety; no doubt he'd simply dozed for a moment and dreamed the noise. In the meantime he'd come back to his cube to find Olivia Haddock in the middle of a tense exchange with the dying tech writer. Paul could not see the poor man, could only hear the wheeze of his breath, but as he slipped into his own cube he got a good look at Olivia posed in the tech writer's doorway, one foot slightly behind the other, her hands clasped palm to palm just below her breasts. It was a stance from her college cheerleading days, no doubt, taught to her by a dance instructor or a drama coach. She looked ready to fill her lungs and deliver a soliloquy or launch into a pirouette, but instead she aimed her wide-eyed gaze down her sharp nose at the tech writer.

"I don't see what the difficulty is," she sang, as Paul lowered himself gingerly into his squeaking seat. "I read the contract to mean that you work until the job is done."

From the other side of the partition came an extra long, extra loud wheeze from the dying tech writer.

"That's not how it works," he said in a ragged, froggy rumble that was exhausting to listen to no matter how many times Paul heard it. The tech writer drew an even longer breath through his tube. "My agent books me for a fixed period of time." Another long, whistling breath. "If I work past that time, I'm not being paid."

The next few words dropped below Paul's hearing as the tech writer ran out of breath. Paul had been listening to this argument for a week now, in halting installments, as Olivia posed in the dying tech writer's doorway and delivered ultimatums with a sadism barely disguised as professionalism, and the dying tech writer responded in ragged gusts of hard-won air. After a bloodbath of downsizing several years ago, many workers in the General Services Division had been asked to take on extra responsibilities beyond their expertise in purchasing. Olivia had been tasked with the design and implementation of an intranet Web site where TxDoGS offices statewide could order their own office supplies; this site would automatically monitor supply usage and regulate the inventory, even to the extent of automatically generating bids from vendors when necessary. The dying tech writer had been hired as a freelance Web designer to create the page. In other words, on top of keeping the Texas Department of General Services in highlighters, manila folders, and jam-free printer paper, Olivia was also pursuing her own redundancy with kamikaze determination. If the project worked the way it was supposed to, she'd be out of a job.

"As *I* understand it," Olivia continued in her steel magnolia singsong, "you don't receive your final paycheck until I'm satisfied with the work. And I certainly can't call unfinished work *satisfactory.*"

Another desperate, dying wheeze. "It *is* finished," said the tech writer.

"Not until it's tested."

Paul could feel the grinding of Olivia's joined palms like a pressure on his heart.

"You hired me to write it." *Inhale.* "Beta testing is not my job."

"But until it's beta tested, it's not *finished*, and you haven't *done* your job."

They went on, but Paul was already preoccupied with his own racing thoughts. First, Olivia's bound to win, if only because she can breathe. Next, my life could be worse—I could be working for Olivia. Then, if the state legislature has its way, someday we'll all be temps—except for La Cucaracha, who'll always find a way to survive. And, tech writers have agents? Like actors and authors? Even if it does mean working for Olivia Haddock, this guy must make, what, twenty, twenty-five bucks an hour? I have to talk to Rick, Paul decided. Today.

"Do what you have to," Olivia said, "but don't forget? You don't get that last paycheck until *I* sign off on it."

Olivia marched past Paul's door and into her own cube. Paul stared unseeing at his computer screen, trying to gauge if the rhythmic whine of the tech writer's breathing was more agitated than usual. There was no way to tell.

On the dot of noon, Paul took a book out of the cabinet over his desk and went downstairs to the hall outside the lunchroom, where he retrieved his bag lunch and bought a Coke from one of the machines. A line snaked out the door of the cafeteria, and the smell of deep-fried potatoes and grilling hamburgers was almost visible, like a haze. Paul edged past the crowd around the microwaves—men reheating last night's cheese enchiladas, women heating up their lo-cal frozen lunches—and from the archway of the dining room, at the edge of its busy roar, he looked for a small table where he might sit by himself and read. The only empty table was the one next to the Colonel's in the far corner of the room, between two wide expanses of amber-tinted window overlooking the river. The Colonel sat at this same table every day, with his back to the corner, where he could command the widest field of fire. His wife was Japanese, and today, as always, the Colonel used his chopsticks to eat the marvelously compact lunch she'd prepared him—rice, sushi, seaweed—out of a beautiful, enameled black box, his only purchase a steaming Styrofoam cup trailing the string of a tea bag. To the Colonel's left, J. J. glowered over his hamburger, fries, and jumbo soda the way he glowered at his computer screen, while on the Colonel's right, Bob Wier crunched carrot sticks out of a Tupperware tub, his mournful eyes as bright as polished buttons. Across from the Colonel was an empty seat where no one ever sat, and which no one even dared borrow for another table.

Although the three men were Paul's coworkers on the outsourcing project, they had never invited him to lunch with them, and he had never attempted to sit in the empty chair. One time Paul had taken the table next to theirs, reading his book and eating his sandwich and pretending not to listen to their conversation. He hoped to convey that he was ignoring them, rather than being ignored *by* them, but he never really succeeded and ended up instead staring sightlessly at the same page for twenty minutes while the Colonel held forth with the overbearing certainty of the autodidact.

"Certainly the West owes a great deal to the Jews," he had been saying that day. "Take the 'Judeo' out of 'Judeo-Christian,' and you have a mighty thin soup indeed."

"Amen." Bob Wier nodded thoughtfully.

"And there is no gainsaying that they are *mighty* warriors," rasped the Colonel. "The Six Day War. Entebbe. And hell, let's not forget the Masada."

" 'The roar of battle will rise against your people,' " intoned Bob Wier, " 'so that all your fortresses will be devastated.' Hosea ten, verse fourteen."

"But there's no denying," continued the Colonel, "that certain nineteenth-century German Jews have a good deal to answer for. I refer, of course, to that unholy ménage à trois of relativistic values, Marx, Freud, and Einstein."

"Don't forget Darwin," Bob Wier said.

"Ménage à what?" J. J. paused in his Sherman's March across his burger to glare at the Colonel.

"Ménage à trois," said the Colonel, then, to Bob Wier, "Darwin wasn't a Jew, Reverend."

"He wasn't?"

"C of E," said the Colonel. "Bit of a freethinker, actually."

"Ménage à *twat?*" J. J. widened his eyes.

"J. J., c'mon." Bob Wier's cheeks burned bright red.

"*Twa*," enunciated the Colonel. "Ta-*wa.*"

"That's a three-way, innit?" J. J. said.

The Colonel manufactured an avuncular laugh. "Perhaps I should have said 'troika,' my lubricious friend."

"Guys, *please.*" The heat colored Bob Wier's temples and forehead.

By now Paul's ears had been burning. I know what a ménage à trois is, he'd thought. And Darwin was a theist. This daily roundtable of the Colonel's was the closest thing at TxDoGS to intellectual intercourse, and Paul had been a little offended that he hadn't been asked to join in. Of course, if the Colonel had invited him to take the empty chair, he'd have declined—nothing irritated Paul like some blowhard with no trace of irony—but still. The Colonel probably didn't have the nerve to ask a real intellectual to sit at their table.

So today Paul turned on his heel, squeezed past the microwave crowd, edged through the cafeteria line, and went back upstairs to eat his lunch in his cube. Olivia was in the crowd downstairs, and the dying tech writer, thank God, disappeared who knew where during lunch. As he sat at his desk munching a dry cheese sandwich and store-brand chips from a store-brand baggie, he read the last couple of chapters of *The Time Machine* from a fat, battered old Dover book, *Seven Science Fiction Novels of H. G. Wells.* Paul had long since been forced by circumstances to sell off his library, and now he could only afford to buy books at the Friends of the Library shop at the Lamar Public Library, where hardcovers sold for a dollar and paperbacks for fifty cents. But what the hell, he told himself, I'm only reading for diversion these days, like any other working stiff plowing through the latest Grisham or Tom Clancy. H. G. Wells was easy to read, and Paul enjoyed the author's gleeful late-Victorian sense of apocalypse, as Wells eagerly overturned the dominant culture with Martians, invisible men, and beasts surgically altered into consciousness. In *The Time Machine* Wells seemed to imply that the end of the world would come from sheer inanition, with the Eloi as the ne plus ultra of slackers. Fighting to stay awake in his cube every midmorning and midafternoon, Paul understood inanition in his marrow.

Still, even these lurid old potboilers had the power to alarm. Paul had reached the penultimate chapter of *The Time Machine*, where the Time Traveller rockets forward thousands of years into a future of bleak seashores and giant crabs and a waning sun. As Paul sucked down the last warm mouthful of Coke, he was blindsided by a sentence: "I cannot convey the sense of the abominable desolation that hung over the world." This triggered an emotional chain reaction in Paul that left him trembling by the time he reached the end of the next page. The Traveller's every leap forward in time only made Paul's horror worse. "Silent?" he read. "It would be hard to convey the stillness of it. All the sounds of man, the bleating of sheep, the cries of birds, the hum of insects, the stir that makes the background of our lives—all that was over." Paul felt his skin tighten as he sat in the unnatural twilight of his cube; the lunchtime silence all around buzzed in his ears. All the ghostly clattering and clicking and chattering Paul heard when the office was at full throttle was gone, and he half entertained the notion that he was the only one left alive in the building. Then he read Wells's description of the Traveller's furthest south into the future, with its giant, dying sun and its blood-red sea and some hideous, tentacled thing on the beach "hopping fitfully about," and the Traveller himself on the verge of fainting, with his "terrible dread of lying helpless in that remote and awful twilight," and Paul bolted straight up out of his squealing chair, trembling like a child.

"So where is he?" he demanded a moment later in the doorway of Rick's office, his hands in his pockets so no one would see them shake. Rick took his lunch at eleven, which meant that he was often in his office while everyone else was out to lunch. But instead Paul discovered Nolene and a couple of other secretaries, Lorilei and Tracy, seated at the little round table in the corner of Rick's office watching *Days of Our Lives* on the port-

able TV Rick used to review videos from the field. All three
women goggled at the screen, where some sort of fight was
taking place, the salads in plastic shells before them momen-
tarily ignored.

"Excuse me?" Paul said again over the shouting and thumping from the television. He was disturbed to hear the tremor
in his voice.

Nolene sharply raised her index finger and brandished the
underside of a long fingernail at Paul, who knew better than to
speak again. A moment later a gunshot and a final thump
erupted from the TV, and all three women flinched.

"Oh. My. God," breathed Lorilei.

"*Damn,*" said Tracy, clenching her fists. "I *knew* it was him."

"Sumbitch had it coming," said Nolene grimly, and she theatrically twisted her hand in the air and pointed with her long
nail out the window. Paul lifted himself on tiptoe and saw Rick
sitting alone on the bench underneath the live oak in the
courtyard.

"Thank you," he muttered, and he bolted out of the office,
around the corner past Nolene's cube, and through the exit
door. Pushing into the blazing Texas heat was like wading into
molasses, and Paul paused to grip the railing of the little walkway that ran across the entrance to the courtyard. Down below
Rick slouched on the wooden bench with his fingers laced over
his belly and his legs stretched out and his ankles crossed. The
price tag on his shoe was plainly visible; Rick looked as if he
were on sale. Paul let go of the railing and trotted down the
stairs to the courtyard. He was sweating already.

"Rick, could I talk to you for a second?" He kicked through
the brittle leaves on the deck; his feet thumped against the
redwood.

"In't this your lunchtime?" Rick squinted up through the
bare, crooked branches at the sky above the courtyard.

"Yes, but—" Paul's t-shirt was already stuck to his back.

"You're so serious this morning," Rick said, still without
looking at him. "Come take a look at that sky."

"Sorry?"

Rick patted the bench beside him. "Have a seat, Paul. Let's just take a moment."

Paul glanced at the blank amber gaze of the wide windows all around him, then he slowly lowered himself onto the bench next to Rick.

"Now just set and take a look at that sky," said Rick. "In't that a beauty?"

Paul sat stiffly on the bench. The heat was reflected off the windows and the deck; it beat down from the sky. He felt sweat trickling along his sideburns and down the back of his neck. Still, he lifted his eyes up through the dying branches of the oak. Even if Nolene hadn't told him about the oak wilt, Paul would have noticed that something was wrong with the tree; most of its leaves had turned a mottled brown and fallen off. Its branches seemed contorted as if in pain. Every week, a Hispanic guy with a leaf blower strapped to his back came and blasted away the dead leaves; even in the depths of his cube, Paul could hear the whine of the machine. Beyond the tree, beyond the sharp roofline of the building, there was nothing remotely attractive about the sky, which was the whitish glare of high summer in Texas, with a blazing blot of sun. Paul blinked up through the branches painfully, grateful only that the sheer oppressive weight of the heat had stopped his trembling. What the hell am I looking at? he wanted to say.

The moment extended itself almost beyond Paul's endurance. He glanced sidelong at Rick. Not only was his boss looking up at the sky with the wide-eyed wonder of a child at a planetarium—his kinetic eyebrows at rest for once—but there wasn't a drop of sweat on him. He could have been sitting in a snow bank.

I can't stand it, thought Paul. He could feel his hands begin to shake again.

"Welp," barked Rick, slapping his thighs and sitting upright, folding himself nearly in two, "sometimes you gotta stop and smell the roses. Back to work."

He shot to his feet and started across the deck through the litter of dead leaves.

"Um, Rick!" cried Paul, heaving up from the bench through the viscid air. "I need—"

Rick stopped and pivoted on the ball of his foot, grinding that indestructible price tag against the redwood planking. His eyebrows shot up.

"—a raise?" Paul said, sounding much less certain about it than he wanted to.

Rick's eyebrows shot up even higher. It's now or never, Paul thought, I'll never work up the nerve again.

"It's just that the temp agency sent me here as a typist, okay?" He heard his voice rising in pitch the way his students' used to when they were pleading with him about their grades, and it disgusted him. "But you've been working me as a tech writer? And I think . . . well, it's just . . . I was wondering . . ."

That's it, I've blown it again, he thought. I should have kept my big mouth shut. He's going to fire me and get another temp from the agency. Fucked again.

"Way-ul, you're right, goddammit." Rick turned and started up the steps. "Let's go in and work it out with the personnel honchos. But when you're right, you're right."

"I'm sorry?" Paul could scarcely breathe.

"I say, you're *right*, son." Rick looked down from the walkway. "I'll have to clear it with Eli, but that won't be a problem."

"Uh . . . great!" Paul realized he was standing with his palm on top of his head, and he snatched it off.

"Don't look so dang surprised, Paul. You been doing a terrific job, and you know what the man says: Good things come to them that toot their own horn. Now let's go in and get Nolene started on the paperwork."

Suddenly the air seemed cooler, and the tree overhead less decayed. The sun shone with a mellower light. It was as if the Time Traveller had found the saddle again on the Time Machine, and the sky was wheeling backwards, away from the awful silence and the dying sun and the flopping thing on the beach, back towards the good life in his comfortable study centuries before. Paul found his feet at last and dashed up the stairs after Rick, and Rick held the door for him as they went in.

FIVE

ALL OF LAMAR, TEXAS, is divided into three parts. There are
the musicians, slackers, aging hippies, computer entrepreneurs,
and academics in the arboreal old city north of the river; the
Republican, Texas two-stepping, cowboy boot–wearing, SUV-
driving Baptist middle managers in the sun-blasted suburban
prairies south of the river; and the Hispanic and African-
American gardeners, nurses, fast-food workers, and day laborers
crowded into the crumbling streets east of the interstate, among
the taquerias and truck depots and tank farms. The rentier class,
living off the productivity and consumer spending of the low-
landers, have their own enclave in the hill country west of the
river, a separate municipality called Westhill that technically
isn't even part of Lamar. They live along picturesquely winding
roads protected by a savagely enforced sign ordinance, where
only the silhouettes of their houses—vast, gaudy boxes with
giant plate-glass windows and enormous air-conditioning bills—
rise out of groves of fragrant juniper and stands of tough old
live oaks, serrating the ridgelines like teeth.

This, at any rate, was how Paul described Lamar to himself; he called it his Texas Theory of Surplus Value. This reading of the city was a byproduct of his self-laceration. By rights he should have started his residency in Texas in the part of town he called Groovy Lamar, the genteelly shabby neighborhoods of bohemian coffee shops and organic groceries around the university, where he could have walked to work at Longhorn State every day past the pierced and dreadlocked homeless kids on the Strip across from campus. Instead, his academic career in ruins, he had moved into a comfortable, forty-year-old suburban ranch house down among the buffet restaurants and propane dealerships south of the river. Today, as he lurched home through his old neighborhood in his hot, farting little automobile, bumper-to-bumper from stoplight to stoplight on South Austin Avenue, he recalled that his chief consolation when he had lived here, in south Lamar, had been that at least he wasn't living with the no-hopers across the interstate. Which was, of course, where he lived now.

Still, not even the blistering heat and the SUV fumes and the staccato rattling of his car could ruin his good mood. Even TxDoGS could move quickly when it wanted to, and by the end of the day, all the paperwork for Paul's raise had been filed, and all the appropriate signatures—Rick's, Eli's, some woman's in Human Resources—had been obtained. Paul had floated all afternoon. Inspired by Rick's magnanimity to do some actual work, he had photocopied a stack of the latest draft of the RFP for the maintenance managers' meeting tomorrow, and he dove into the deeps of Microsoft Word to see if he could come up with a watermark. He e-mailed Erika, the pert young woman at the temp agency who had placed him at TxDoGS, to ask when he was going to see the raise in his paycheck. Indeed, creeping forward in his car through rush-hour traffic in his t-shirt, smelling his own sweat, he daydreamed about the extra $120 a week he was going to make. That was almost another $500 a month! Almost a rent payment! Even better, Rick, on his own initiative, had asked that the raise be made retroactive for a month. Human Resources had balked at that, but Rick had managed to get Paul at least a retroactive week at the new, $11-an-hour rate. That meant, with his next paycheck, an extra $240 right off the bat! Rick was a saint!

Then Paul found himself idling at the light where he had used to turn off into the leafy neighborhood where he'd lived with Kymberly, and the memory of his fall from grace gathered gloomily on the horizon of his good spirits like a massive Texas thunderstorm. Once upon a time, Paul had been a very promising literary theorist with a very impressive Ph.D. from a very prestigious school, the University of the Midwest in Hamilton Groves, Minnesota. But within a few years of matriculating, he had found himself stuck in the last year of a nonrenewable postdoc at an undistinguished state school in Iowa, cruelly writer's blocked, and up to his neck in a pointless affair with a sleek graduate student in communications, a kinetic California girl named Kymberly. His only hope of professional salvation had been to ride the coattails of his wife, Elizabeth, as she negotiated a tenured position for herself at Chicago University. But riding Elizabeth's coattails depended on Elizabeth not finding out about Kymberly, and that in turn depended on placating Elizabeth's sinister cat, Charlotte, who lived with Paul in Iowa while Elizabeth commuted back and forth to Chicago. What happened next was sort of willfully blurry in Paul's memory, but there had been a titanic battle of wills between Paul and the goddamn cat. Charlotte had hoarded evidence of Paul's infidelity—panties, an earring, wine cooler bottle caps—while Paul had alternated between trying to buy her affection with catnip mousies and fish snacks, and terrorizing her. The battle ended badly for both of them. Call it a draw: Elizabeth found out about Kymberly and cast off Paul like a sack of old clothes, effectively ending his academic career, and Charlotte ended up drowned in Paul's bathtub. Somehow.

An angry honk from the pickup behind him startled Paul; the light had gone green without his noticing. He jerked his foot off the brake and accelerated grumpily through the intersection. Now he had to let the little mental thunderstorm blow itself out. After Iowa, Paul had followed Kymberly to Texas, where she had gotten a job as a junior reporter at a struggling network affiliate in Lamar, KNOW, channel 48. "You're in know *now* with K-Now 48," intoned the announcer, "your home for news and entertainment in central Texas!" while a giant K meant to appear carved out of limestone rotated in a depthless TV null space. But KNOW was fighting for its life in a tough market, and everything was done on the cheap, and Paul came to refer to the station as Know Nothing 48, Home of the Giant Rotating Styrofoam K. The station's threadbare budget worked both to Kym's advantage, allowing a rookie a great deal of airtime on big stories, and against her, allowing her to make all her mistakes live, as she mispronounced names, lost her place in her notes, and asked wildly inappropriate questions of the grieving families of murder victims and death-row inmates.

But then Kymberly toughened up and buckled down. She took a stenography course; she cut her hair into a stylish and professional bob; she bought herself a word-a-day calendar and practiced her pronunciation every morning with steely determination, baring her teeth at herself in the bathroom mirror and carefully working her lips around "eleemosynary" or "prestidigitation." Her performance improved so much that Paul was surprised one evening to realize that the brisk young woman in the trim, lemon yellow suit he was admiring on TV was actually the woman he was living with. This revelation allowed Paul to tap into previously unknown reserves of lust (his desire for her had begun to wane, for all sorts of reasons), and that evening when she came home, he begged her to keep her suit and makeup on, murmuring in her ear, "I've never fucked an anchorwoman before." And Kymberly, even though she was bone tired, allowed him to do it, asking him breathlessly at a crucial moment, "Do you really think I'm anchorwoman material?"

And soon she *was* an anchorwoman, at least on weekends. On Saturday and Sunday evenings she shared the fortresslike anchor desk with an aggressively cheerful fireplug of a guy who doubled as the weekend weatherman, wearing his immense

double-breasted blazer like a cuirass. Paul was bemused to realize that the guy had a crush on Kym; at the end of one of
their first broadcasts together, as he reminded viewers of stormy
weather heading their way, he laid his stubby little hand on
Kym's wrist and said, "You be careful driving home, pumpkin."
" 'Pumpkin?' " said Paul when Kym got home. "I know," she
said, rolling her eyes. "The news director told him not to do it
again. He was *crushed*."
"He looks like a lawn statue," Paul laughed. "The Weather
Gnome."
"Stop!" laughed Kymberly in a two-syllable singsong, bat-
ting his arm, but over time she seemed to find the sobriquet
less funny. Paul was too busy foundering professionally to notice. He taught composition at Lamar Community College for
a couple of semesters, for a thousand dollars per course, but
when the budget was cut they let him go. After that, Kym
agreed to support him for six months while he wrote a book.
He worked fitfully on a memoir of his expulsion from academia,
leaving out the adultery and cat drowning, only to learn from
an acquaintance in publishing that the market was glutted with
memoirs of downsized academics recovering their self-worth,
saving their marriages, and becoming better fathers through
redemptive manual labor. Everybody was looking for a gim-
mick; one guy, Paul was infinitely wearied to discover, was writing horror stories set in academe.

When Kymberly found out that Paul spent more time napping and going to the movies every day than he did writing,
she bullied him into taking a job at a textbook company, the
Harbridge Corporation. For eight months Paul sat in a little
gray cube under harsh fluorescent lighting and composed grammar exercises for grades six through twelve. His job was to up-
date an old workbook by expunging any content that did not
meet the textbook guidelines of Texas and California, the company's two biggest markets. Fundamentalist Texas forbade even
the most benign references to the supernatural (the first step
towards the Satanic sacrifice of newborns), while nutritionally
correct California forbade any references to red meat, white

sugar, or dairy products (the biochemical causes of racism, sexism, and homophobia). Pretty quickly the effort to write exercises that were simultaneously inoffensive to Dallas and San Francisco left Paul struggling to stay awake in front of his computer screen by the middle of every afternoon. In his stupor he began to imagine an actual battle on his desktop, a ragged collision of Lilliputian armies out of *Spartacus:* a well-drilled phalanx of Promise Keepers and West Texas cattlemen on his right versus a scruffy rabble of Berkeley vegans and Earth Firsters on his left.

Paul's supervisor, Bonnie, was an embittered former high school English teacher from Little Rock who had lost her job to budget cuts. He attempted to express solidarity with her as one academically displaced person to another by dropping quotes from Milton and Pound, but this only humiliated her; Bonnie's knowledge of the canon was limited to middlebrow high school "classics" like *Catcher in the Rye* or *To Kill a Mockingbird*, and she didn't get the jokes. In return, she never missed an opportunity to remind him how far he had fallen from his prestigious Yankee university. "Guess they didn't get around to adjective clauses up there in Minnesota," she'd say, handing him back a clumsily executed exercise to do over. Paul retaliated by surfing the Web all day and deliberately missing deadlines. When he was really pissed off, he composed items with inappropriate references that he figured Bonnie wouldn't get—"Mr. Humbert *(brought, brung)* Dolores a banana"—or arranged an exercise so that the first letter of each item spelled out a subliminally subversive message like "MEAT IS GOOD" or "BOW TO SATAN" or (in a twenty-item review exercise he was particularly proud of) "SATAN SEZ EAT MORE CANDY." And when he was feeling unusually ambitious, he combined the two techniques into one exercise:

> In each of the following sentences, underline the *direct object* once and the *indirect object* twice. Not all sentences have an indirect object.

1. I gave Renfield instructions not to wake me until sunset.
2. Lizzie offered her father a close shave that morning.
3. Oliver, have you told Mr. Fagin about the missing wallet?
4. Vita showed Virginia a thing or two.
5. Eagerly, Oscar taught Bosie the backstroke.
6. Sid gave Nancy the surprise of her life.
7. Affectionately, Mrs. Donner gave Jeffrey a second helping.
8. Tara offered Willow a token of her affection.
9. After a delicious Irish stew, Mr. Swift told us his modest proposal.
10. Norman gave his mother a carving knife for her birthday.

Paul complained bitterly about Bonnie at home, especially on those days when she had caught him asleep in front of his monitor in the middle of the afternoon. What he didn't tell Kym was that most of his coworkers were pert and stylish young women ten years younger than him, women just out of college who wore airy sundresses or tight, wraparound skirts to the office all summer long and decorated their cubes semi-ironically with magazine photos of pretty-boy actors. Some of these girls found Paul's wiseass bitterness intriguing, and they slouched fetchingly in his cube doorway and flirted with him about books and movies, grad school life, or last night's episode of *Buffy the Vampire Slayer*. One of them, a dark little Russian emigré named Oksana who worked in the Harbridge science department, took Paul into her bed on the evenings when Kym was working. Oksana had a wry twist to her lips and an adorable accent. "Say 'moose and squirrel,' " he'd murmured to her in the clinch, and she'd slapped him on the backside and whispered salacious Russian in his ear.

On those evenings when Kym was working and moody Oksana did not want to see him, Paul haunted the coffeehouses near the campus, where he could eye bohemian young women or intense graduate students in sleeveless blouses over a copy of the local alternative weekly. He had prepared a story to explain his situation in case he managed to engage one of these thrilling women in conversation; the last thing he wanted them to know was that he was a failed English professor. Instead, he told them that he was a former writer/producer for *The X-Files*, and that he had walked away from his television career and moved to Lamar to write a novel. "I wanted to get out before the show went down the tubes," he was going to tell them, and he had prepared answers to the questions he thought he was likely to get: "He's an asshole." "She's even smarter than she looks." And "I wrote the ones about worms. If it had a worm or worms in it, that one was mine." But in the end, he wasn't able to use the story. In one of the coffeehouses, a renovated old house with creaking floors and mismatched couches and easy chairs, he ran into Virginia Dunning, an old friend of his ex-wife's from graduate school. Paul had always considered Virginia a bit too, well, virginal for his taste, but since he had known her in Hamilton Groves she had picked up a mordant wit that Paul found instantly attractive. To Paul's astonishment and envy, Virginia was not only a tenured full professor before she was thirty, she was already chair of the Longhorn State History Department. To his further surprise she invited him back that first night to her little Texas bungalow, where, as luck would have it, she lived with a cat, whose name was Sam, and who put his ears back and flattened himself to the floorboards at the sight of his mistress and Paul coming through the door. "Don't mind him," said Virginia, "he's an idiot." Paul laughed, but he wasn't quite sure if Virginia was talking to him or to the cat.

Virginia's avidity in bed was yet another surprise. "I've never fucked a department chair before," he murmured in her ear, and Virginia flung him onto his back, straddled him, and said, "Let's see if you're tenure material, Professor." Afterwards she rolled over and went to sleep, and on the drive home, Paul had time to contemplate the three women in his life, none of whom knew about the other two. He'd told Oksana that he lived alone, and he'd told Virginia that he was working as an "independent scholar," a dodge he'd come across during his abortive attempt to write a book. Rattling home through the hot Texas night, Paul thought, my life could be worse.

Shortly thereafter, it was. Oksana discovered Paul and Virginia tête à tête one evening in a coffeehouse near campus, while Kym coincidentally happened to be on the television set in the corner, making vapid small talk with the Weather Gnome. Oksana stalked across the creaking floorboards, screaming abuse in Russian. Then, as Virginia looked on in astonishment, Oksana emptied her double latte into Paul's lap and stalked off, pausing only to add, in her adorably accented English, "Focking esshole!"

Oddly enough, this incident didn't seem to bother Virginia, who simply shrugged it off. But later that same night, as Paul followed Virginia into her bungalow, Sam went into his crouch, hissing and growling before he bolted from sight.

"Idiot," muttered Virginia.

"I don't think he's hissing at you," Paul said, still brushing at the coffee stain on his trousers. "He's hissing at your dog."

"What dog?" Virginia whirled on him.

"That big black dog that came in right behind you," Paul said. "I assumed he was yours." He glanced about Virginia's living room. "I don't see him now."

Virginia stared at him, all the blood draining from her face. "Get out!" she gasped.

"Sorry?"

She drew a shuddering breath, as if gasping for air at high altitude, and shouted, "*Get out!*"

"Is this about the girl at the coffeehouse?" Paul asked, as she slammed the door in his face. "I can explain that!"

The following morning he lost his job at the textbook company. A sharp-eyed copy editor had caught some of Paul's subliminal messages, and that morning the efforts of the entire department had been diverted to reading through every grammar exercise written in the last six months.

" 'EAT ME SATAN'?" said Bonnie, gleeful with schadenfreude. "I suppose you think that's funny?"

In the end Paul was escorted from the building by a beefy

security guard who repeatedly called him "sir" as he yanked Paul's arm up behind his back and marched him to the elevator on his tiptoes.

"I have a real Ph.D. from a real goddamn university, not some peckerwood teacher's college in Arkansas!" Paul shouted. "I graduated summa cum laude! I was a finalist for a Guggenheim!" He glimpsed Bonnie's triumphant gaze one last time, and he shook with rage in the guard's painful grip.

"You fucking cow!" he roared as the elevator doors closed. *"I was almost a Fulbright!"*

By late that evening, Paul was drunk on wine coolers, the only alcohol Kym allowed in the house on the theory that they were less fattening than beer. He lounged in bed watching cable, a clinking heap of empties beneath the bedside table. Hypnotized by the endless whine of some NASCAR race on ESPN, he dimly heard the front door slam and managed to push himself up in bed as Kym posed primly in the doorway in her lime green on-air suit, broad in the shoulders and nipped in at the waist.

"We have to talk," she said, very gravely.

"I can explain," Paul said immediately. In his fruity stupor he tried to cipher out what Kym knew and how she knew it.

"I'm in love with someone else," she announced, luckily before he started to stammer about Oksana, Virginia, and the loss of his job.

Paul stopped trying to stuff the latest empty under the covers. "What did you just say?"

In a matter of moments Paul learned that Kym was carrying the Weather Gnome's child. His immediate reaction, even drunk, was to imagine Kym and the Weather Gnome and their child as a row of lawn statuary.

"This is *outrageous!*" he cried, rising from the bed in manufactured dudgeon. But he bungled the effect by tangling his ankles in the bedclothes and toppling flat on his face.

In the end Kymberly paid him to move out, loaning him enough money for a damage deposit and a couple of months' rent on a new place. He quickly learned that he wasn't able to afford a place in the leafy collegiate neighborhoods he wanted to live in, nor was he able to afford even one bedroom in the nicer apartment complexes in south Lamar. He had to settle for the third part of Lamar, the commercial wasteland past the interstate, which he was now entering on his way home from work. Twenty-five minutes in the car in the heat and traffic had largely cooked away his elation over his raise. Like Dante descending into the lower tiers of seducers, deceivers, and falsifiers, he entered into a curbless region of self-storage units and U-Haul dealers behind cyclone fences and curls of razor wire, interspersed with empty lots of yellowed grass and heat-baked earth. He passed a catfish parlor advertising ALL-U-CAN-EAT in huge block letters on its blank concrete wall; a vast barn of a Texas dance hall with a corrugated tin roof and a neon sign that read RIDE 'EM, COWBOY! in a script of looping lassoes; a ramshackle wooden vegetable stand slung with bunches of desiccated jalapeños; and a windowless cinder-block tavern called This Is It. With a sinking heart he turned down the cracked old two-lane highway to San Antonio, towards his home for the moment, his temporary refuge from the blows and buffets of the world, the small apartment complex he called the Angry Loner Motel.

SIX

IT WAS AN OLD MOTEL from the fifties, two separate oblongs of colorless cinder block, two stories each, facing each other across a wide parking lot of parched asphalt, seamed with cracks and punctured exactly in the middle by the square, rusty, rattling grate of a storm drain. The place's official name was the Grandview Arms, but the only view from Paul's front window was of the apartments across the way, and the only view from his tiny bathroom window in the back was a stretch of Texas savannah littered with rusting pickups and abandoned appliances. Paul's shoulders clenched as he turned off the highway, clanked over the grate at the middle of the lot, and pulled into the space in front of his apartment. He switched off his car, and the engine gasped to a stop. Paul's Colt was the smallest and youngest car in the lot; each of his Angry Loner neighbors drove an enormous, spavined automobile from the seventies and eighties, some extinct Detroit saurian that listed to one side or the other or dragged its rear end as if it had a body in the trunk. Whenever one of these aircraft carriers came to life (which invariably required a two- or three-minute warm-up period of guttural, unmuffled roaring), its engine grumbled, its tailpipe rattled, and its shocks—or what was left of them—groaned and squeaked like old men.

Paul rolled up his windows, snatched his dress shirt off the passenger seat, and hustled out of his car. Two or three of his neighbors always seemed to be lounging in the open doorways of their apartments or slouching over the rail of the second-story balcony, each man dangling a burning cigarette or a can of beer from his big-knuckled hands. He had as much difficulty telling the men apart as he did their cars; they might all have been brothers from some inbred, clannish, conniving family out of Faulkner. The younger Snopes brothers wore scuffed motorcycle boots, tight black jeans, and faded t-shirts, while the older Snopeses wore ancient cowboy boots, blue jeans baggy in the seat, and denim work shirts, untucked over rock-hard beer bellies. Each one, from twenty-five to fifty, had leathery skin and lank black hair and two or three days of thick stubble along his sullen jaw. Some had streaks of dirty gray in their hair; some wore handlebar moustaches, some goatees; but none of these distinguishing marks made them any easier to tell apart. All of them, young and old, had dark, penetrating eyes that seemed to look through Paul to his bones. None of them were bald.

Clutching his limp shirt to his chest, Paul fumbled his key into the lock. The only thing scarier than his neighbors was what waited for him in his apartment. He drew a deep breath. It wouldn't make any difference where he lived, he'd always be coming home to the same thing. He turned the stiff lock and pushed open the door, and the smell of cat pee stung him to the back of his sinuses.

"Oh, Paul! Mr. Trilby!"

Paul paused in his doorway. Mrs. Prettyman, his landlady, was mincing across the parking lot. She lived in what used to be the motel's office, a little brick building at the far end of the lot, and the very instant she stepped out of her door, all the loitering Snopeses along both sides of the motel ducked into their doorways and locked themselves in their rooms. Mrs.

Prettyman curved neatly around the wide indentation of the drainage grate.

"I'm so glad I caught you." Her sharp little heels somehow never caught in the cracks and potholes. "I'd just like a word."

Paul waited in his doorway, his back to the shadowy room behind him. Mrs. Prettyman called herself "the manageress" of the apartments, though Paul was certain she owned the place. This evasion allowed her to deflect any requests for maintenance or extra time in paying the rent. "I'll have to take that up with the owner," she'd say, in her buttery Texas singsong, and then, twenty-four hours later, "The owner says the refrigerator is supposed to make that sound," or, "I'm afraid the owner needs your rent payment this afternoon."

She stopped with one hand on her hip and another, proprietary hand on the doorsill. "Hon, I know you got a cat in there." She gave him a glittering smile, all steel and no magnolia.

"Really." Paul did not invite Mrs. Prettyman in. "Have you ever actually seen a cat come in or out of my apartment?"

"Well now." She waved her hand theatrically in front of her nose. "I don't need to *see* it, darlin', I know it's in there someplace." She replaced her hand on her hip. "It might be you just don't notice it anymore."

Oh, I notice it, Paul thought. That smell had caused him to be evicted from every apartment he'd had since moving out of Kym's house. The Grandview was the last stop on Paul's descent, the one place he was reasonably certain wouldn't evict him. "On my word of honor," Paul said, certain that Texans liked that kind of thing, "there's not another living creature in here but me and the cockroaches."

Which is true, thought Paul. Mrs. Prettyman narrowed her eyes and angled her head, peering past him. On a couple of occasions, Paul had caught her in his apartment when he came home from work, peering under his swaybacked sofa bed on her hands and knees or poking up the stained panels of the ceiling with a broom handle looking for the cat. He bought her off with an extra twenty-five dollars a month; this for a cat that didn't really exist. Now she was obviously trying to shake him down for more, but he was damned if this greedy old harridan was going to get a penny of his raise.

"Come on in and look." He gestured into his hot, malodorous living room. "If you can find the cat, you can have the cat."

"Well now." Her smile tightened, and she stepped back from the door. "If I ever do see a cat around here, I'm going to have to tell the owner."

"Be my guest," Paul said. "Give him my fondest regards."

Mrs. Prettyman scowled at Paul through the crack as he shut the door. He drew a shallow breath and stooped to switch on the air conditioner under his front window; the unit began to chug, pouring a dank mist into the room.

"Hey, kitty," Paul said in a monotone. "I got a raise today. Good news, huh?"

Ever since his final confrontation with the living Charlotte, her ghost had been a continuous presence in Paul's life, waxing and waning like the moon—always there, but not always immediately visible. Paul's memory was deliberately vague about the reasons for his murderous rage at the cat, but he did remember that he was responsible for her death by drowning in his bathtub. During the time he'd lived with Kymberly, Charlotte had been a sly presence, appearing only to Paul, and only fleetingly, tripping him in the middle of the night when he got up to use the bathroom or nipping his toes with her freezing teeth when he went back to bed. When he was trying to write his book, Charlotte got up to her old tricks, unplugging his computer while he was working or weaving between his legs, dank and cold, making him jump right out of his chair. Kym never said a word about Charlotte until the very end of the day Paul moved out, after he had finished loading his few remaining possessions into the back of his Colt. As he lowered himself, exhausted and sweating, onto the sagging springs of his car and pulled the squealing door shut, Kym bolted coltishly out of the house and stooped at his open window. Her hand pressed to her throat, her forehead knotted, she blinked at Paul's lap as she worked up the nerve to speak.

"Well, so long, *pumpkin*," Paul was about to say, when Kym blurted out her last words to him, without meeting his eye.

"Make sure you take *the cat* with you, okay?" Then she dashed back inside the house.

Since then Paul had worked his way down the hierarchy of Lamar's cheapest rentals. As the money Kym loaned him ran out, Paul was forced to sell off his books, his stereo, and his computer. The day after he fetched up at the Angry Loner Motel—the only place that would take him without references or a damage deposit—he found himself at last at a temp agency, being interviewed by Erika, a pert young woman unnecessarily lacquered in makeup. She reminded Paul alternately of Anchorwoman Kym and of a younger Mrs. Prettyman.

"So you were an English professor!" she said, flipping through the ring binder of jobs. "That's *really* good. You must have an *awesome* typing score!"

The next day he was working at TxDoGS and coming home every night to Charlotte, who began to assert her baleful presence more and more strongly. She shut off the air conditioner to leave Paul gasping and drenched with sweat in the middle of the night, then made it roar to life again just as he was getting back to sleep. She switched off the lights when he was trying to read. She extinguished the burners in his kitchenette when he was trying to cook or boosted the flame unexpectedly and burned his food. She turned the water freezing cold or scaldingly hot when he was in the shower. At night, as he tried to settle into his lumpy mattress, he could hear her padding across the carpet or glimpse her slinking silhouette against the piss-yellow glow of the threadbare drapes. On bad nights he felt her walking on the bed, and on the worst ones he felt the sharp pressure of her legs as she stood on his chest and dug her front claws—claws she didn't have when she was alive—into his flesh through his thin blanket, emitting a low hiss that froze the tip of his nose. When this happened, Paul squeezed his eyes shut and whimpered until Charlotte went away.

She was most inventive when it came to Paul's last remaining amenity, an old portable black-and-white TV he had salvaged from someone's curbside trash. Sometimes she allowed Paul to watch what he wanted, limiting herself to a cameo appearance, dozing on the windowsill in the interrogation room in *Law and Order* or trotting along the beach in *Baywatch*. At other times she took over the programming and aired gruesome footage of cheetahs ripping bloody lengths of flesh from quivering wildebeest or particularly savage maulings of zookeepers and lion tamers. She ran Morris the Cat commercials that hadn't been broadcast in years; she resurrected lurid episodes of *When Animals Attack* or *When Good Pets Go Bad;* she kept Paul awake all night with Disney marathons—*That Darn Cat, The Aristocats,* and *The Nine Lives of Thomasina.* One night she sprawled across the top of the set and glowered at him, her tail lashing back and forth across the screen, as she aired an entire eight-episode cable documentary about the cat in history. Paul fell asleep that night to the stentorian narrator repeating for the umpteenth time that "the cat was worshipped as a god in ancient Egypt."

Worst of all was the smell. The apartment and all its fixtures—the bed, the bath mat, the grotty carpet—reeked relentlessly of cat pee. Mrs. Prettyman notwithstanding, Paul never got used to it. One of the few good things about going to work at TxDoGS every day was that for nine hours at least he was free of the ammoniac reek of Charlotte's ghostly urine. As it closed in around him now, Paul dropped onto one end of his foldout sofa and tossed the day's shirt on the other.

"I don't ask for much, Charlotte," he said wearily, "not anymore." He pitched his voice to the middle of the room. Who knew where the cat was? Who knew, indeed, if the concept of "where" even applied to the ghost of a cat? "But I had some good news today, the first good news in a very long time. For the first time since . . . well, since I can remember, Charlotte, somebody was *nice* to me. Somebody did me a kindness, and he didn't have to do it. Somebody treated me like a human being today."

He paused to look cautiously about the room, at the crappy

dresser, at the TV on the shaky little table by the window, at the broken-down armchair by the door. Nothing moved and only the air conditioner spoke, muttering glumly to itself.

"What do you care, right?" he continued. "You're an animal, for chrissake. Hell, you're not even alive." Paul dropped his face into his hands. "I'm going crazy," he moaned. "I'm talking to a dead cat." He glanced up. "Of course, I don't mean any disrespect by that. After all, it's my fault."

Paul flopped back against the cushions and tilted his head back. He felt tears pooling in the corners of his eyes, and he angrily wiped them away. He didn't want to give her the satisfaction.

"All I'm asking," he said, steadying his voice, "is for you to lay off me just this once. Cut me a little slack, okay? Let me sleep. Let me spend a night in peace, and I'll . . . I'll . . ." What? What leverage did he have with a ghost?

He pushed himself up from the couch and addressed the room at large. "You know what? Never mind. Forget I mentioned it. I'm sorry I bothered you."

But strangely enough, Charlotte did not show or manifest herself all night, though he knew she was probably just setting him up for something worse later on. He managed to watch an entire evening of television without a glimpse of her. He rose in the morning almost refreshed, and he showered without any sudden temperature changes and fried his eggs without scorching them. After breakfast he crept towards the door clutching his bag lunch and his shirt for the day, certain that Charlotte was saving up something special for the last moment. But nothing happened as he pulled the door shut and locked it, and he released the doorknob as gingerly as if he were letting go of a hand grenade.

"Thank you," he whispered, still not quite believing it. He dashed to his car, flung his shirt and lunch onto the passenger seat, and roared backward out of his parking spot, banging over the grate. His luck only improved once he hit the main road. Traffic was lighter than usual, the SUVs less overbearing, and Paul made the Travis Street Bridge in record time. The Bank of Texas told him that the time was only 7:54 and the temperature an improbably mild 77 degrees. A surprisingly sweet breeze blew off the river, and there was not a single creepy homeless guy in sight. No early morning guilt trip; no gnomic utterances. Paul felt like singing something cheerful, "Whistle While You Work," say, or something brassy like "Don't Rain on My Parade," or even defiant, like "My Way." By God! he thought. This is what comes of taking charge of your life, this is what comes of asking for what you want.

The light went green, and moments later Paul rolled into the TxDoGS parking lot and found an ideal space—close to the building! Under a tree! He rolled up his windows and sprang out of his car, thrusting his arms through his shirtsleeves in one smooth motion. He sauntered into the building and gave Preston a jaunty salute.

"You look like a man who got a raise in pay," Preston said, an avuncular glitter in his eye. Paul laughed and said, "I'm even thinking of getting me a regular badge, what do you think?"

"Outstanding!" said Preston, offering Paul a visitor's badge and a big martial thumbs-up.

Paul stashed his lunch in the fridge and took the stairs two steps at a time. Good things come in threes, he thought. A raise in pay, a night's reprieve from Charlotte—what's next? He marched through the stairwell door, rounded the corner past the sighing elevator and the recycling box, and walked proudly into cubeland, shoulders squared, back erect. Coming into his aisle, he noted with pleasure that Olivia Haddock had not arrived yet, heard the reassuring wheeze of the dying tech writer, and swung confidently into his cube, two minutes early, on top of his game, ready to take on the day.

Paul pulled up short when he noticed the large Post-it stuck to the middle of his computer screen. He felt a sudden chill, colder than the AC. Even before he read it, he could tell that the Post-it was not from Olivia or Renee; the printing was bolder than either of theirs. And it wasn't from Rick; the printing was too neat. Paul wheeled his chair between himself and the screen and leaned closer, peering at the note, his skin tight-

ening all over his body. It was a larger Post-it than anybody in
the office used, with a smudge in one corner and a little tear
along the side, as if someone had plucked it out of the trash.
The chill raced up his spine and spread to his extremities. In
bold block letters, the Post-it read:

**Are we
not men?**

SEVEN

"DID YOU WRITE THIS?"

Paul had never spoken directly to the dying tech writer before, but now he stood in the doorway of the man's cube holding the Post-it between thumb and forefinger. The tech writer, thin and cadaverous and gray, turned slowly in his chair, away from his monitor and a desktop heaped with toppling stacks of paper. Paul instantly regretted having spoken. The tech writer put his hand to the band of gauze around his throat and inhaled through his tube, a long, plastic wheeze.

"No," said the dying tech writer in his froggy voice.

Leave now, thought Paul. Go back to your own cube. But instead he waggled the Post-it and said, "Did you see who did?"

The tech writer's eyes were surprisingly wide and liquid. He lifted his left hand and pointed upward. Once again he inhaled. "They're up there," he croaked.

Paul resisted the urge to look up at the suspended ceiling; he was afraid he'd hear the creak and slither he'd heard in the men's room yesterday. "Who's up there?"

A high-pitched wheeze. "They're up there."

Paul watched the tech writer warily; he had an unreasonable fear that the man might leap at him. The chill he'd felt when he'd first seen the Post-it was not going away. "Where? On the roof?" *Inhale.* "They're up there." *Wheeze.* "In the ceiling."

Still Paul could not bring himself to look at the ceiling panels. The Post-it trembled in his fingers. "Who's in the ceiling?" he whispered. It's not a cat, is it? he almost said.

"You're late!" boomed Rick, right behind him. Paul whirled, crumpling the Post-it in his fist. Rick rocked on his heels; his eyebrows bounced up and down. How long had he been standing there? "Maintenance managers gonna be here toot sweet, in about"—Rick widened his eyes at the watch on the underside of his wrist—"twenty minutes. We ready to rumble?"

"You bet," Paul managed to say, hoarsely. A corner of the crumpled Post-it was pricking his palm.

" 'Cause I don't see the conference room set up." Rick lifted himself on his toes, peering over Paul's cube at the darkened doorway of the conference room.

"I'm just on my way to pick up the laptop and the projector." Paul gestured over his shoulder. Behind him he heard the steady whine of the dying tech writer and the squeak of his chair as the man turned back to his work.

"Then chop chop, son," said Rick. "Let's get this show off the ground." Rick loped off, chin lifted, eyebrows dancing. Paul slipped into his cube and looked at his calendar. He cursed under his breath: He had forgotten that this morning his team was presenting the draft RFP to the maintenance managers of the districts selected for the outsourcing project. Luckily, he had remembered to book the conference room, the laptop, and the projector, and he still had time to set up the meeting before the managers arrived. He was halfway up the aisle before he realized he still had the Post-it in his fist, and he whirled, nearly blundering into Renee, and dashed back to his cube. He tossed the Post-it in his trash, dashed out past a glowering Renee, stopped short, dashed back again, and retrieved the Post-it. He smoothed the little yellow square against his desktop, then opened his top drawer, dropped it in, and let the drawer slide shut. As Paul passed the dying tech writer's doorway, the little man pointed silently at the ceiling with a bony gray finger.

Paul left the submarine hush of cubeland and hustled down the bright main hallway towards Building Services. Today's meeting was likely to be a tense one. At the suggestion of the free-spending lobbyists of several large multinational corporations, the contribution-hungry Texas state legislature had mandated that TxDoGS outsource, or privatize, the maintenance of its fleet of vehicles—everything from sedans to forklifts to dump trucks—in three of the agency's twenty-five maintenance districts. If private maintenance turned out to be cheaper than using TxDoGS's own mechanics, then the program would be extended to the entire state, and several hundred state employees would be out of work. This morning the maintenance managers in the three districts selected for the pilot program—Odessa, San Antonio, and Nacogdoches—would be introduced to the project. They would be shown the PowerPoint slideshow Paul had concocted, and each man would be given a draft of the project's Request for Proposal, or RFP. The RFP Development Team—Rick, the Colonel, J. J., Bob Wier, and Paul—would explain how it was a good thing that three dozen minimum-wage mechanics in Odessa, San Antonio, and Nacogdoches were about to lose their jobs.

At the end of the hall Paul had a glimpse over the balcony into the lobby below, where Preston rocked on the balls of his feet and smoothed his bushy moustache with two quick strokes, down and across. Then Paul stepped into Building Services, a windowless, two-room suite lined with shelves loaded with slide projectors, video projectors, overhead projectors, tape recorders, and laptops. Nobody sat at the desk in the first room, so Paul went deeper and found Callie the Mail Girl behind the desk in the farther room hunched over something in her lap. She was massaging the back of her long neck with one hand, and as Paul came in, she turned a page with her other hand. Paul cleared his throat, and she whisked her hand away from her neck onto her lap, covering up whatever she was reading.

She blushed a deep red, which made her freckles glow even in the harsh fluorescent light.

"I booked a laptop and a projector for this morning." Paul came up to the desk and tried to see what Callie was reading. She shoved it into the kneehole of the desk.

"Let's go, um, check the sign-out sheet," she said, in her subdued drawl. Under the desk she let go of the volume she was holding, and it made a phonebook-sized thump on the floor. Paul backed up as Callie came around the desk, still blushing. She was easily as tall as Paul, maybe even an inch or two taller. She was also very pale, and Paul swore he could feel the heat from her blazing face as she passed. Standing behind her as she bent over the sign-out book on the desk in the other room, he let his eyes drift down Callie's long waist to her full hips, admiring the tautness of her t-shirt.

Paul backed up as she moved to the shelves. She handed him a laptop without a word, then lifted her long arms and forcefully yanked a bulky video projector off an upper shelf. Paul admired the sudden definition of her upper arm as she lowered the projector onto its little wheels and jerked the towing handle out of its slot. Paul dipped his head and saw a thick volume on the floor under the desk, a computer manual perhaps or an almanac. Callie has aspirations, thought Paul. Don't we all?

"Don't forget to sign it in again," she said, deftly kicking the book under the desk out of sight, "when you bring it back." *Fergit*, she said, and *brang*. Paul smiled at her as he backed out of the office lugging the laptop and dragging the projector on its little wheels, but she had stooped under the desk to retrieve her book and wasn't watching him.

In the conference room, Paul hoisted the projector with a grunt onto the conference table—damn, she must work out, he thought, flashing on Callie's biceps—and plugged both units into the wall and into each other. He started the laptop and dashed back to his cube for the PowerPoint disk as well as the stack of RFPs he'd copied during his fit of conscientiousness yesterday. He placed a copy in front of every chair around the table, then he yanked down the screen at the end of the room and fired up the projector and ran quickly through the slide-show. He clicked on the last slide just as Rick came in the door leading the maintenance managers and the rest of the RFP team. The men distributed themselves around the table in a basso rumble of bonhomie and joshing. Rick edged down the room to sit at the end of the table, with Paul at his right hand.

"This cheer's our *technical* writer," Rick announced, and all eyes turned to Paul. "He used to be an English professor, so make sure you dot your p's and q's."

Paul's face got hot, and he hoped he wasn't blushing as bright as Callie had.

"*Tech* writer?" The Colonel settled into the chair on Paul's right and gave him a long look. "Since when?"

"Since yesterday," mumbled Paul, desperate to change the subject. "The PowerPoint thing is all loaded and ready to go," he said to Rick, pushing over a copy of the slideshow's script.

"Way-ul, let's try this shoe on and see who salutes," said Rick. "Somebody get the lights and shut the door."

"Tech writer," said the Colonel, regarding Paul sidelong. "Huh."

The projector's little fan hummed as the first slide flashed on the screen at the far end of the table. In the pearly reflection of the screen, Paul noted that the visiting managers all sat on one side of the table, the RFP team on the other. To Paul's right sat the Colonel, leaning forward on his elbows with his hands man-fully clasped, as if he were in a briefing room at the Pentagon. On the other side of him, J. J. slumped in his chair, glowering at the screen, while in the chair beyond him Bob Wier nodded sol-emnly as Rick clicked to the next slide, which read:

Districts Selected
1. Odessa
2. San Antonio
3. Nacogdoches

"This is y'all," said Rick, which wasn't in the script. "Your names in lights."

"Ain't we lucky," said the Nacogdoches manager dryly. The other two managers looked on impassively. Odessa was a thin, balding, colorless guy with a turquoise belt buckle who looked like he'd rather be someplace else; San Antonio was a barrel-chested, bullet-headed Mexican American with a canny light in his eye. But the focus of the room, the one man Rick seemed to direct his pitch to, was the Nacogdoches manager, a big, raw-boned, slope-shouldered East Texan, who scowled at the screen. He had found a seat at the corner of the table that allowed him to stretch his long legs, and now he sat with his big hand on the table, drumming his enormous fingers a little more slowly with each successive slide. In the presence of the man's obvious displeasure, Paul was glad he had deleted the obnoxious little animations from the presentation. Rick, however, scarcely seemed to notice the man's disdain, narrating the presentation in his usual clipped singsong. The Colonel kept interrupting, plucking a laser pointer from his breast pocket—"Rick, if I may?"—and directing the managers' attention to a particular bullet point with a wobbly little red dot. He spoke to Nacog-doches directly, man to man.

"Now if you think about it, Mike," he said, in the hearty manner of a general addressing his officers informally, "half the time your boys are sitting on their behinds. They're on the clock whether they have anything to do or not." The laser dot danced across the screen. "Now, with a private vendor, we can work it so we're only paying 'em when they're actually turning wrenches."

"Well hell, how much cheaper you want it done?" Nacog-doches's big paw lay still on the tabletop. "Half my guys're on food stamps, that's how well the state of Texas pays 'em to sit on their behinds."

Before anyone could answer that, San Antonio chimed in. "Your private vendor. He gonna come out in the rain, in the middle of the night, when I got a loader broke down halfway to Uvalde?"

"Now that's a fantastic point," said Bob Wier, self-consciously enthusiastic. "We're real glad you brought that up, Tom."

"The thing is," said Nacogdoches, drumming his fingers again. Everyone else fell silent, leaving only the whirr of the laptop and the hum of the projector's fan. The staticky heat off the projector's bulb was beginning to cancel out the air-conditioning.

"I'm sure y'all put a lot of work on this." He laid his hand on the copy of the RFP on the table before him; like the other managers, he had not touched it yet. "And I appreciate that." He hefted the document and let it drop. "But don't take a dog turd and dress it up like a popsicle and expect us to lick it."

The room erupted in laughter, and Rick took the opportunity to suggest a coffee break. Bob Wier leaped up, switched on the lights, and offered to lead the managers to the coffeepot. Odessa, San Antonio, and J. J. followed him out, while Rick bounded off on his own. The Colonel switched off his laser pointer and clipped it back in his shirt pocket. He edged round the table and paused with his hand on the doorsill, as if he might say something to the Nacogdoches manager, but then he ducked his head and went out. Paul leaned across the table and switched off the hot bulb of the projector, then put the laptop on standby.

"You don't say much."

Paul glanced up. Nacogdoches still leaned back in his chair, his cowboy boot crossed over one knee, his hand still on the conference table. But now he was watching Paul, sizing him up.

"I'm, uh, just a temp." He lowered the laptop's screen and stood. He couldn't think of anything else to say; he felt like a schoolboy waiting to be excused.

Nacogdoches nodded. "Why ain't you teaching English someplace?"

Paul searched for an answer that excluded adultery and a drowned cat, then boiled it down to, "I got downsized."

Nacogdoches jerked his head back and said, "*Down*sized?"

"Last teaching job I had was at the community college, but

they had some budget cuts and I was low man on the totem pole, so . . ."

"Huh." Nacogdoches took another long, appraising look at Paul. "And now you're . . ." He fingered the edge of the RFP, flipping the pages with his broad thumb. Once again, Paul was speechless: No doubt Nacogdoches was thinking about his own guys about to be downsized, with Paul's help. Paul swallowed; he heard a burst of male laughter from the coffee room. Nacogdoches pushed the RFP away from him. He drew a deep breath, drummed his fingers once, twice, three times. Then he let out a sigh and stood, rising to his full height.

"It's a funny ol' world, innit?" he said, and he walked out of the room.

EIGHT

THE MEETING LASTED UNTIL NEARLY LUNCHTIME, which meant Paul had to hustle to return the laptop and the projector to Building Services without losing any of his own lunch hour. Callie was no longer minding the sign-out sheet, so Paul returned the equipment to a large, red-faced gentleman named Ray (according to his ID badge) who was parked immovably behind the desk in the inner room. He blew out a sigh at the sight of the projector.

"Say, do me a favor, bud, and slide that thang up on the shelf, willya?"

"You're kidding, right?" The shelf was shoulder high. Ray only shrugged, so Paul left the projector on the floor, and slid the laptop onto a lower shelf.

"By the way, that girl who was here before," Paul said, signing the book. "She always work in here?"

"Callie?" said Ray from behind his desk.

"Is that her name?" said Paul, though of course he already knew it. "So does she? Work here? Usually?"

Ray pursed his lips and folded his doughy fingers over his spreading belly, a Buddha of bureaucracy, and he looked very significantly from the projector on the floor to the shelf where it belonged. Paul sighed and stooped and, remembering to lift with his legs, hoicked the damned projector up into its berth.

"Callie?" said Ray. "Sometimes she's up here, sometimes she's down in the mail room."

"Okay," said Paul breathlessly, his heart hammering from the effort. Thanks for nothing, he thought.

"Word to the wise, chief." Ray dropped his voice. "She don't like boys." He was trying, at least, to give Paul fair exchange for his effort.

"That so," said Paul.

Ray shrugged. "I'm just saying is all."

After lunch the only landmark on the horizon was an RFP team meeting that Rick had called for four o'clock to evaluate the meeting with the maintenance managers. To make the time go faster, Paul thought of the day as the twentieth century. By ten o'clock of an eight-hour workday (not counting lunch), it was already 1925. World War I was over; the Russian Revolution had already occurred; *The Wasteland* and *Ulysses* had already been published; the *Rite of Spring* had already been performed; modernism was in full spate. By lunchtime, World War II was over; the bomb had been dropped; Milton Berle was already a television star. Sometimes it made the afternoon go faster to glance at the time and think, now the Beatles are on *Ed Sullivan*, now Jimmy Carter is president. But today, by half an hour after lunch, Paul realized that it was only March 1956. The Beatles haven't even met each other yet, he groaned silently. Jesus Christ, I haven't even been *born* yet.

He toughed it out until the Nixon administration and then decided to take his break. As a temp, he was entitled to two fifteen-minute breaks a day, one in the morning and one in the afternoon, which he usually stretched to half an hour each. Since he had missed his break this morning, thanks to the meeting, he figured he was due an hour this afternoon, though he doubted he could get away with it. Still he waited until Olivia was out of her cube so that she couldn't note when he left, then he retrieved *Seven Science Fiction Novels of H. G. Wells* and went downstairs.

The lunchroom was usually empty at this hour of the afternoon. The lights had been dimmed and the sun was on the other side of the building, so Paul was able to read in a pleasant dusk, all alone amid the empty tables and chairs. As he came in, he passed Callie hurrying out, her arms crossed over her t-shirt, her hands rubbing her bare upper arms. She avoided his eye as she passed, hustling around the corner towards the mail room. As he headed towards the Colonel's table in the corner— his usual seat during his breaks—he noticed that someone had left a fat book open on one of the tables against the window. A chair was still pulled out, and a half-empty bottle of Coke stood at a corner of the book. Was this Callie's mystery volume, the one she hadn't wanted him to see?

He weaved between the intervening tables and stood across the table from the pulled-out chair; the book was facing the other way. It was an enormous volume, the pages Bible thin and packed with tiny print. He glanced back at the doorway, then turned the book around. He lifted the cover and saw, to his astonishment, that it was *The Norton Anthology of English Literature*, volume 1. He stooped over the open pages and read a couple of lines of crowded print:

VOLPONE. [*springing up*] Excellent Mosca!
 Come hither, let me kiss thee.
MOSCA.   Keep you still, sir.
 Here is Corbaccio.

"That's mine," said Callie, nearly in his ear. Paul jumped back, and Callie reached past him and snatched the book off the table with both hands, slamming it shut and pressing it to her chest. She was wearing a sweater now over her t-shirt, somebody's huge old cardigan with a little woven belt dangling untied at her hips.

"You just lost your place," Paul said.

"That's okay." Callie clutched the book with one hand and waved her other hand as if to ward him off. She would not meet his eye.

Paul gestured at the table. "I'm sorry. I thought somebody had left it."

"I just went to get a sweater." Callie reached past him again for the bottle of Coke. "They keep the AC so fuckin' high in here." She started to turn away.

"It was open to Ben Jonson," Paul said. "Act one of *Volpone*."

Callie hesitated, not quite looking at Paul. "What did you say?"

"Act one of *Volpone*. Ben Jonson."

"That's not what I . . ." She waved the plastic bottle; flat Coke sloshed within. "I mean, how did you say it, just now? The name."

"Ben Jonson."

She gave a little gasp of exasperation and turned away.

"Vol-*po*-nee," Paul said. "It's Italian. It means—"

" 'Fox.' " She was blushing bright red. "I know what it means. I can read."

"I'm sorry." He shifted his own book under his arm. "I was trying to be cute."

"Didn't work." Her eyes flashed.

Paul shrugged. "Story of my life."

"How'd you know that?" Her eyes burned a little less hot, but there was still a very attractive blush over her cheeks, making her freckles stand out. "How to say 'Vol-*po*-nee' "—she enunciated slowly, as if testing each syllable before she put her full weight on it—"instead of 'Vol-*pone*'?" Here she exaggerated her own accent; Paul wished he could place it.

Paul laughed nervously. How could he tell her without sounding . . . pompous? Arrogant? Bitter? "You wouldn't know it from my present circumstances," he said, "but I have a Ph.D. in literature."

She narrowed her gaze. "What do you mean, your 'present circumstances'?"

He gestured through the ceiling at the weight of the Texas state agency above them. "I never thought Ben Jonson would come up in the dining room of the Texas Department of General Services."

Callie's eyes brightened again, but more with bemusement than anger. "Came up today, didn't it?"

"I guess it did."

"What are *you* reading?" Callie had been balanced on the balls of her feet, ready to flee, but Paul noticed that she had shifted her weight onto one heel. He pulled his book out from under his arm and held the cover out for her to see.

She leveled her gaze at him again. "You need a Ph.D. in English literature to read *that?*"

Paul stuck the book back under his arm. "No. That's why I like it."

Callie nodded. Her cheeks had faded to freckles against pale skin. She started to turn away and hesitated again.

"Vol-*po*-nee," she said again.

"You got it." He smiled—charmingly, he thought. "My head's full of useless crap like that."

Her eyes blazed at him again, but she checked it. He could tell she wanted to say something sharp, but instead she asked him, "What's your name?"

"Paul," he said, then he added, "Trilby." He lifted his eyes to the ceiling again. "I work up in—"

"I know where you work." She was walking away now, the book still clutched to her chest with one hand, the Coke dangling at her hip. Paul watched her go, then he found his seat in the corner and took a moment to settle in—one chair to sit in, another to prop his feet on. He opened his book to the first pages of *The Island of Dr. Moreau*. He sat for half an hour with the volume open on his lap and didn't read a word.

NINE

WHEN PAUL LEFT HIS CUBE FOR THE FOUR O'CLOCK meeting, he passed Rick in the main aisle going the other way. "Head on down and grab a seat," Rick said as he sailed by. "I'm getting our guest a cup of coffee."

What guest? Paul wondered. To his surprise, he saw Olivia Haddock hovering just outside the door of Rick's office, while Nolene typed something and scowled at her computer screen. Through the office door he saw the Colonel and J. J. and Bob Wier seated around the little table in the corner, leaning forward and listening to someone out of sight.

"He's got some nerve showing up here," Nolene muttered, as she hammered at her keyboard, refusing to look at Olivia. "Some people just don't know when they're not wanted."

"Well, he did work here for thirty years, Nolene." Olivia clutched her elbows and lifted herself on tiptoe, craning to see through the door. "When I first got here, he was a *legend*."

"What I'd like to know is, who authorized his visitor's badge?" Nolene lifted her angry gaze and it landed on Paul, who stopped in his tracks. "What part of 'You're fired' dun't he understand?"

Before Paul could think of anything to say, a gust of male laughter erupted through the doorway. Olivia flinched back, as if afraid of being seen.

"Don't you have some work to do, *hon?*" Nolene placed a heavy emphasis on the last word, crushing any endearment out of it. She leveled her gaze at Olivia who, without a word, pushed off from the side of the door and marched away, her arms swinging, her cheerleader's backside twitching.

"Hey, Professor, step on in here," said the Colonel from inside the office. Nolene returned to her computer screen, and Paul moved into the doorway. The faces of the RFP team swung towards him, smiling. A stranger was sitting behind Rick's desk, an older man in a jacket and tie. He had a high, pale forehead and bright eyes, and his sparse white hair was combed straight back in perfect striations. He seemed a little lost in the jacket; the lapels ballooned out from his shirt, and the cuffs came down to his knuckles. The man's shoulders barely rose above the backrest of Rick's chair, but his pale fingers were unusually long, clutching the armrests.

"Professor, meet Stanley Tulendij," said the Colonel, "the man who made the TxDoGS fleet what it is today."

The old man swiveled slowly towards Paul, an unexpectedly chilling sight, since Paul doubted that the man's feet reached the floor. How did he do that? Stanley Tulendij had a prominent jaw and a wide, lipless mouth, and he pointed his chin and his sparkling eyes at Paul and said in a hollow voice, "Is this the young fella?"

"Paul is our tech writer on the outsourcing project," said Bob Wier, his voice trembling. "Paul, Stanley was TxDoGS's fleet manager for twenty-five years."

"The original TexDog," said the Colonel.

"This man's a fucking legend," said J. J., looking uncharacteristically reverent.

"Now son," whispered Stanley Tulendij, "that kinda language—"

"I'm sorry!" gasped J. J. To Paul's astonishment, J. J. actually blushed, and his eyes burned as if he might start to cry. "God, I'm such a fucking idiot."

"No harm done." The man behind the desk made a benedictory gesture, and he swiveled his bright gaze at Paul again. "Come shake my hand, young man." His hand, skeletal and pale, levitated out of his roomy cuff as if on the end of a broomstick. The other men nodded at Paul, urging him on, and he reached across the desk. Who is this guy? he thought. Why is he sitting in Rick's chair?

Stanley Tulendij had a loose grip; his hand was very cool and dry, all papery skin and knobbly knuckles. His fingers reached nearly all the way around Paul's hand. He may be the palest person I've ever seen, thought Paul. In direct sunlight, I'll bet you could see the outline of the old guy's bones. Why, he's as pale as that homeless guy yesterday.

"Stanley Tulendij," said the old man. "A privilege."

"Paul Trilby." He gave a wince of a smile. "All mine."

Paul tried to let go, but the old man leaned forward in the seat and grasped Paul's wrist with his other hand. The light in his eyes brightened, and he looked past Paul to the men around the table. "Oh, he's *good*," said Stanley Tulendij. "I *like* this young fella."

"Might could be he's one of us," said the Colonel, behind Paul. "Don't you think so, boys?"

"Absolutely!" declared Bob Wier. "Praise Jesus!" He smiled broadly, but his eyes were anxious. He looked as if he were about to break into a sweat.

"I suppose," said J. J., glowering at Paul.

Paul tugged his hand free. The old man winked at Paul, and Paul felt the temperature drop in the room, the way it sometimes did when Charlotte was present.

"Hey!" chirped Rick, coming in with a Styrofoam cup of coffee. "I see y'all have made your own introductions." He leaned past Paul and gingerly set the cup in front of Stanley Tulendij. Then he clapped Paul on the shoulder, putting Paul between him and the man behind the desk. "This man is a titan in fleet management, Paul," he said. "I'm honored just to be in his presence."

"Pah!" Stanley Tulendij flapped his pale hand. "Just did my job is all." He put his hands on the armrests and pushed himself up out of the chair in a smooth, swift motion—so swift, in fact, that Paul took a step back, afraid that the old man was going to float right over the desk at him.

"You're not leaving?" said Rick, sounding relieved. "I thought you might sit in." The Colonel, J. J., and Bob Wier all glanced at each other, Paul noted, while Rick maneuvered to keep Paul between himself and the old man. Stanley Tulendij was taller than he'd looked sitting down; he had long legs and a short torso, like a man walking on stilts. This disproportion, and his preternatural paleness, gave him a rather spiderish look as he glided around the end of Rick's desk. As he passed, his jacket gave off a strong whiff of thrift store disinfectant—an odor Paul knew well—and beneath it was something both sharp and sour, like the smell of excrement. Stanley Tulendij paused in the doorway to take his leave. One at a time, Bob Wier, J. J., and the Colonel rose from their seats, shook his hand, and sat down again. Stanley Tulendij gave a puppetish wave, his bony hand wobbling as if on a ball socket.

"I'll be seeing you," he said, looking at Paul, and Paul felt the chill again. He watched the old man's strange, arachnid gait as he walked out the door and down the aisle.

Somebody clapped his hands once, and Paul turned to see the Colonel sitting erect in his chair, grinding his palms together. His eyes were aglow. "Well!" he said. "It seems giants still walk among us."

"Yessir," said Rick, rather distantly. He had moved behind his desk, and he was staring warily down at his chair. He shoved the backrest with the tips of his fingers, setting the chair spinning slowly in place. "I tell you what," he said, "let's put the meeting off till tomorrow. No sense crossing our bridges until they're burned." He looked up. "Y'all check your schedules and let me know what's good for y'all." He waved his hand, dismissing the team. Paul waited for the others to file out ahead of him. Bob Wier's smile was drawn painfully tight, his eyes so sad he looked as though he might cry, and he gave Paul a thumbs-up as he passed. J. J. looked him sourly up and down, and the Colonel winked at him. Paul started after them, but Rick called him back.

"Get rid of this, willya?" Rick held out the still steaming cup of coffee.

Paul hesitated—toss it yourself, Rick, I'm a tech writer, not a busboy—until he saw the look on Rick's face. He held the cup as if it were full of acid about to eat through the Styrofoam.

"Please," said Rick, and Paul leaned across the desk and took the cup. As he left, Rick was still watching his spinning chair, as if counting the revolutions.

Paul ditched the coffee in the trash by the fax machine, then he went around Nolene's cube to the side away from Rick's door and rapped on the metal strip on top of the partition. From Rick's doorway, he heard the tentative creak of a chair.

"So, Nolene," he whispered, when he finally got her attention, "did you ever work with Stanley Tulendij?"

Nolene slowly lifted her gaze to Paul and regarded him coldly. Paul was on the verge of retreating when she lowered her eyes, visibly banked her anger, and looked up at him again. "Hit's no secret. No reason you shouldn't know." She lowered her voice. "Most of the folks here are new in the five years since Stanley . . ." She snapped her fingers. "But I worked under him for six months." She closed her eyes and mastered herself again. "Let's just say that Stanley was *old school* about women in the workplace? 'My wife don't let me tell her how to make biscuits, and I don't let her tell me how to buy parts for a backhoe.' "

"So what does *this* mean?" Paul snapped his fingers. "Did he retire?"

Nolene put her finger to her lips. "They yanked him," she whispered. She glanced around her and syllable by syllable mouthed the words, "*Sex-u-al har-ass-ment.*"

"Really!" Paul lowered his voice further. "Who did he harass?"

She turned abruptly back to her computer screen, and an instant later Rick sailed out of his office and up the aisle. She watched him go, then looked at Paul and slowly shook her head. She wouldn't talk about it.

"At least tell me, did the Colonel and J. J. and Bob work for him?"

"Oh no! That's the funny thing." She glanced up the aisle. "They never did. They all come here since." She kept her voice low, hissing at Paul across the partition. "And yet he comes around to see them every few months or so. In't that the darnedest thing?"

"Huh," said Paul.

"You know what else is funny about those three?" Nolene's voice dropped so low that Paul had to lean over the partition to hear her. "As far as I can tell, they never do . . ."

She broke off and nailed her gaze to the computer screen again. Paul looked up and saw the Colonel loitering by the fax machine, idly fingering the buttons. Nolene slowly shook her head.

"Right," Paul said, raising his voice. "So, uh, when can I expect my first check at the new rate?"

"I dunno, hon." Nolene clattered away at her keyboard. "That's up to your temp agency, not the great state of Texas."

"Okeydoke," Paul said. "Thanks." He started briskly up the aisle. Just ahead of him, the Colonel stepped back into his cube and turned in his doorway. He winked at Paul. "Professor," he said.

"Colonel," replied Paul, hurrying past.

Back in his cube, he almost e-mailed Nolene. They never do what? he wanted to know, his hands hovering over his keyboard. But he doubted that Nolene was so indiscreet as to commit gossip to cyberspace. He'd have to catch her alone again tomorrow.

Meanwhile, it was nearly quitting time, and he began to shut down his computer and tidy his desk. He swept a couple of pencils into his top drawer and let the drawer slide shut. After a moment he opened the drawer again and peered in at the litter of pens, pencils, paper clips, and pushpins. Something's missing, he thought. He bit his lip and stared harder at the clutter in the drawer. Something *was* here that isn't now, he thought. But what? To hell with it, he decided, and he let the drawer slide shut, glimpsing the mild yellow of a Post-it pad.

He jerked the drawer open again. The note he'd found on his monitor this morning was gone, the Post-it that read, "Are we not men?" He pulled the drawer all the way out and peered into the shadows in the back; he ran his fingertips through the litter in the sharp corners of the drawer—gingerly, in case of a stray pushpin—and came up only with a steel letter opener he hadn't known was there and a smudgy three-by-five card. He pushed through the paper clips, the soggy heap of rubber bands, the tangle of clenched binder clips. But the note was gone. With both hands in the drawer, Paul lifted his gaze to the ceiling tiles above him. "They're up there," the dying tech writer had said. He listened for his neighbor's wheeze and heard nothing; he must have left already. He jerked his hands out of the drawer and stood. Go ahead, he thought. Play games with me, asshole, whoever you are.

He heard a sharp hiss and glanced over his shoulder. Maybe the tech writer hadn't left yet. Then he heard it again, a little louder. He caught his breath and thought, I hope that's not coming from the ceiling.

"Ssss! Paul!" Olivia Haddock peered wide-eyed at him around the partition of her cube. "Did you see him?" she whispered.

Paul sighed. "See who?"

Olivia shushed him, then beckoned him sharply, and Paul sighed again and crossed the aisle. Olivia backed into the deepest corner of her cube, glancing past him at her doorway. "Did you meet Stanley Tulendij?" she whispered.

"Yeah." Paul shrugged.

"How was he?" Olivia's eyes shone as though she were a cheerleader asking him if he'd met the star quarterback.

"Well," said Paul, "I hear he was a titan in fleet management."

"What they did to him, you shouldn't do to a *dog.*" Olivia clutched her elbows; her mouth was puckered with distress. "They tossed him away like he was just *trash.*"

"I heard he was fired for . . ."

She shushed him again, sharply. "Listen," she began, and she told him that Stanley Tulendij had been a TxDoGS legend for thirty years, twenty-five of them as fleet manager. He had been personally responsible for the modernization of the state of Texas's fleet of official vehicles in the mid-seventies, skillfully negotiating the prerogatives of the legislature, the bureaucratic inertia of the agency, and the greed of contractors. "That man never, and I mean *never,* put a foot wrong." Olivia shuddered, her hand at her throat. Stanley Tulendij, she continued, had been a shoo-in to be chief of the whole division—"Eli's job," she added, in case Paul was not clear on the hierarchy—and probably the head of the agency, if it hadn't been for . . .

She lifted herself on tiptoe and glanced around again, then lowered her voice a fraction and continued telegraphically. "Five years ago. Budget cuts. Statewide, hundreds, and I mean *hundreds,* of people lost their jobs. Twenty-year veterans. And Stanley? Out of all those managers? The only one who said no. Not *my* people." In the end the man who had accomplished miracles in state government for *years* without ticking off anybody—which was in itself a miracle—managed to tick everybody off all at once. "Suddenly he couldn't do anything right," Olivia said, "and one day he was just *gone.* He was on the job on Tuesday, and on Wednesday it was like he'd *never even existed.*"

All around him, Paul could see the tops of people's heads as they glided up the aisle on their way home. "Nolene told me," he said, "that they fired him for . . ."

"That's a lie!" hissed Olivia. "Don't you believe it! They just *made that up.*" She widened her eyes at Paul. "The next week Rick was in Stanley's old office, and the first thing he did—the *first thing*—was shitcan thirty guys." She only mouthed the word *shitcan.* "And those thirty guys? Most of them had been around for *years.* It was like Rick just pulled a lever and *whoosh!*

They dropped right out of the bottoms of their cubes. Like *trash*. Which only made it worse when . . ."

Olivia shuddered again, and Paul, in spite of himself, felt a little of the chill. She glanced wildly past him, and he turned to glimpse Renee hustling by, clutching her oversized purse. Olivia stooped and snatched her own purse from under her desk and held it before her. She looked like she might flee before she finished the story, so Paul put his arm across the doorway.

"When what?" he whispered.

"The *bus!*" Olivia gasped. "Don't tell me you never heard about the tragedy at Lonesome Knob! That fateful bus ride? The *sinkhole?*"

"Well, no?" said Paul, tentatively.

Olivia dropped her voice even lower so that Paul had to lean in, close enough to smell her shampoo—something fruity—and to see through the tree line of her scalp to the hint of darkness at her roots. Oh, my God, thought Paul, Olivia dyes her hair!

But she was too wrapped up in her story to notice where he was looking. Even in disgrace, she was saying, Stanley Tulendij had refused to let his men lose their jobs without ceremony, so he had chartered a bus—at his own expense! Out of his retirement money!—to treat the thirty cashiered TexDogs to a final, unofficial outing at Lonesome Knob State Park, just outside the Lamar city limits. The signal feature of the park (Paul knew) was Lonesome Knob itself, a great, bald dome of ancient granite, under which ran a warren of caves, largely unexplored; no one knew how far they went. Stanley Tulendij called his outing a "retirement party" and insisted that his men wear their coats and ties. Likewise out of his own pocket, he ponied up for barbecued brisket and hot sausage and a big steel tub full of beer on ice.

"That day there was a terrible storm," whispered Olivia, and for a moment Paul had the same childish thrill he used to get from campfire ghost stories. Olivia clutched her purse and dropped her voice so low that Paul caught only snatches of what she said. He wasn't even sure they were the important snatches:

a sudden Texas thunderstorm—the men took refuge in the bus—a flash flood—the bus carried away—that awful sinkhole—the bus *swept clean*—

"What?" said Paul.

Olivia narrowed her eyes at Paul. "The force of the water busted out the windows of the bus, and just *scoured it out*. All those men . . ." She blinked back tears. All those men, it seemed, had been washed away into the caves without a trace. Only Stanley Tulendij was ever found, clinging to a juniper bush at the lip of the sinkhole, still in his coat and tie, soaked to the skin, nearly drowned.

"And he's never been the same man since," suggested Paul, trying not to smile. He didn't believe a word of this. It had the almost pornographic allure of an urban legend or some mournful, minor-key folk song about a train wreck or a mining disaster. "So now he haunts the halls of TxDoGS, looking in vain for the faces of his missing men . . ."

Olivia's face hardened, and she slung the strap of her purse over her shoulder. "I suppose you think losing your job is funny," she snapped, and Paul was stung to silence.

"Not really," he managed to say.

"You think because you've got a *pee aitch dee*," she spat, "you're too good for this job."

"Not really," Paul said again, hoarsely.

"Ex*cuse* me." Olivia snapped her purse strap between her breasts and pushed past Paul, sailing out the door of her cube and up the aisle.

Paul sighed, then stepped across the aisle into his own cube long enough to switch off his light. He took the rear stairs and passed the mail room, hoping for a glimpse of Callie, but he didn't see her. He signed out and deposited his visitor's pass at the front desk, then threaded his way through the parking lot to his lucky spot under the tree, along the river embankment. He rolled down the windows and opened the creaking hatchback to let out the day's accumulated heat; he took off his dress shirt and tossed it on the passenger seat. Behind him, the departing column of SUVs and pickups rumbled out of the lot; Paul slammed the hatchback shut and lowered himself behind the wheel.

I'm supposed to believe all that? he wondered. A busful of sacked state employees washed into a sinkhole? Stanley Tulendij clinging for dear life to a juniper bush? All of them in business attire?

"They died with their boots on," Paul murmured, and smiled to himself. He started his engine, and the car shook itself like an old dog. Through the windshield glare he squinted over the embankment and across the river. Some of his coworkers' vehicles were already lumbering across the Travis Street Bridge in a haze of heat and exhaust, past insane Texas joggers pounding along the pedestrian walkway during the worst heat of the day. One pedestrian, however, had stopped on the bridge. He was not a stalled jogger: He wore trousers, a shirt and tie, and glasses, and he seemed to be looking this way. His features were hard to make out with the sun behind him, but the shape was unmistakable—a small oval atop a larger oval. It's the homeless guy from yesterday, realized Paul, the egg-shaped man, Señor Huevo, what was his name? Boy G—that was it! Mr. Are We Not Men himself! Paul leaned forward and tilted his hand against the glare. Is he looking at me? he thought, and just then the figure on the bridge lifted his hand and waved.

Paul snapped back in his seat as if he'd been struck across the face. Another movement caught his eye through the driver's side window, and he turned to see Stanley Tulendij step out from behind the tree. Without a glance back, the old man spidered up the embankment on his long legs, and in a moment he had crested the rise and disappeared down the other side.

Paul fumbled at the latch and heaved his door open on its whining hinges. He hesitated, then dashed through the heat up the slope. At the top of the embankment Paul was halted by the sour reek of the river. On the far side of the sluggish water lay the unfashionable end of Lamar's hike-and-bike trail, but on this side, the yellowed grass sloped directly into the weeds at the water's edge, with no interruption but the humped concrete back of a storm drain that emptied into the river. Paul looked both ways; to his left, the embankment curved away around a bend in the river, to his right, it ran unbroken to the bridge. Stanley Tulendij was nowhere to be seen in either direction. Paul turned and looked back down at the nearly empty parking lot. His own car trembled below him, motor running, door open. He turned towards the bridge and shaded his eyes with his palm. The figure at the railing, the oval-on-oval silhouette, was gone. All Paul saw were candy-colored SUVs, nose to tail along the bridge, and the lean silhouettes of joggers, pounding through the Texas glare.

TEN

THE FOLLOWING DAY, surveying the crowded lunchroom for an empty table, Paul was about to turn away and take his sandwich up to his cube again when the Colonel beckoned to him from the far corner. Paul pretended he hadn't noticed and swung his gaze round the room once more—he'd never seen Callie here during lunch, but then he'd never really looked. Then his gaze drifted back to the Colonel, who sat with his chin lifted and his wattles pulled tight, and he lifted his hand over his head, as if signaling a waiter. Before Paul could make up his mind, he was halfway across the room. Bob Wier gave him a sad smile and pushed back the empty chair. Paul took the seat with a shrug.

"Glad you could join us, Professor." The Colonel's eyes twinkled.

"Carrot stick?" said Bob Wier, proffering a Tupperware dish of crudités.

"Thanks, no." Paul emptied his lunch bag one item at a time—cheese sandwich, no-brand chips, pickle.

J. J. worked a burger into his mouth with both hands. "Mmmph," he said.

"We were just discussing the life and work of Marion Morrison." With his chopsticks the Colonel skillfully plucked a crumbling bit of sushi from his beautifully enameled Japanese lunch box.

"The Duke!" said Bob Wier. "The Big Guy!"

"Fuckin' A," said J. J., plucking a soggy bit of lettuce off his lower lip.

"Ah." Paul peeled the baggie off his sandwich. Was he supposed to know who Marion Morrison was? Was he another decrepit, downsized TxDoGS legend like Stanley Tulendij?

The Colonel gave Paul a wry smile across the table. "No doubt you're familiar with Morrison's œuvre." *Oove*, he pronounced it.

"I don't think so," Paul said. "He must have been before my time."

Bob Wier and the Colonel burst out laughing. J. J. gagged on his burger and thumped his fist against his sternum. Through a full mouth, he said, "John Wayne, dickhead."

"Pardon me?" Paul glowered back at J. J.

"Forgive our friend's choler." The Colonel reached around the table and squeezed J. J.'s bicep manfully. "It's his way of showing fellowship. Isn't that right, J. J.?" He squeezed a little harder, and J. J. winced and said, "Sorry."

"Sure." Paul felt his face get hot, and he took a big bite of his sandwich.

Bob Wier said, "I was just saying what a *blessing* the Duke's example was to the American man. A paragon of strength"— Bob Wier balled up his fist—"and tenderness." He opened his hand. It was as if he were gesturing for the benefit of the parishioners in the pews all the way in the back. "Why, even my wife, Barb," Bob went on, "was a fan of the Duke."

The Colonel and J. J. froze and glared at Bob Wier, J. J. crushing his burger, the Colonel squeezing his chopsticks so tightly that a pink fleck of sushi shot across the table. Even Paul froze, involuntarily, his gaze shifting back and forth as he clutched his sandwich halfway to his lips.

"Bob," warned J. J.

"Time to move on, son," intoned the Colonel.

"Right." Bob Wier's face drained of color, and he dropped his gaze to the Tupperware dish before him. He rolled a fat little carrot between thumb and forefinger. "Of course. You're absolutely right."

Still watching Bob Wier, J. J. slowly fed the burger into his mouth. The Colonel dipped his chopsticks into his lunch box. Paul took a cautious bite of his cheese sandwich.

Bob Wier drew a deep, shuddering breath and soldiered on. "It's just that when I think of how John Wayne bore Natalie Wood up in his arms at the end of *The Searchers*—"

"Fuuuuck," said J. J. in a dismissive diminuendo.

Bob Wier widened his eyes. "No?" he said.

"Well, I don't fucking get it!" whined J. J. "Check out her eyebrows, for chrissake! You ever see an Indian with lipstick and blush?"

"The Lord's name, J. J.," said Bob Wier, smiling ferociously.

"Okay, sorry, but Jesus, Bob, what about that other guy, whatshisname, the bad guy, the evil Comanche—"

"Scar," said Paul, without thinking. What am I doing? he thought. He was still wondering what had just happened.

"Yeah, *Scar*." J. J. rolled his eyes. "Fucker had five o'clock shadow, for cry yi. He was sucking in his gut for the whole movie."

"Gentlemen, please." The Colonel laughed, reaching to either side to grasp the wrists of Bob Wier and J. J. "A little decorum, if you please. Our guest here will think we're savages ourselves."

Paul wondered if it was too late to get up and sit somewhere else. Meanwhile, Bob Wier squeezed his eyes shut and moved his lips in silent prayer. Across the table J. J. sighed and dropped his sullen gaze to his paper plate.

"All I was trying to say," Bob Wier said, opening his eyes, "was what a splendid role model the Duke was. Especially as he got older." He poked a celery stick at the tabletop for emphasis. "The very picture of a man aging gracefully." He

crunched off the end of the celery stick. "In great movies like
Big Jake and *Cahill: U.S. Marshall.*"

"*The Sons of Katie Elder*," mumbled J.J. through a mouthful
of french fries.

"Yes! Praise Jesus!" Bob Wier crunched his celery and lifted
his eyes to heaven. "What's that wonderful line from *Chisum?*"

"Jism?" said J.J. with a glint in his eye.

"Knock it off, son," warned the Colonel.

Bob Wier ignored them both. "Somebody asks him . . ."
Crunch, crunch. "Oh yes, somebody says, 'Where are you going,
John?' and he says—" Swallowing his celery, Bob Wier threw
his shoulders back and essayed the lurching rhythms of a pretty
fair John Wayne imitation. " 'Somethin' I shoulda done thirty
years ago.' "

"That's not what he says!" protested J.J., his mouth full.

"So let me get this straight." Paul was astonished to hear
himself weighing in. "We admire John Wayne because he's a
procrastinator?"

Bob Wier broadened his smile at Paul, unsure whether Paul
was joking or not. The Colonel's gaze drilled into him from
across the table. J.J. shot an angry glance at the Colonel, as if
to say, *I told you so.*

This was a mistake, Paul thought, I shouldn't have sat down
here. He was aware of the Colonel's gaze on him.

"Jism," snorted J.J. again, in case no one had heard him the
first time.

"I don't think the professor agrees with you, Bob," said the
Colonel, ignoring him. He had finished his exquisite little lunch
and was closing up the enameled box. He dabbed at the corners
of his lips with a creamy linen napkin.

"Really!" said Bob Wier, a little too enthusiastically. He
folded his hands and peered at Paul earnestly. "It'd be a blessing
to hear your thoughts on the subject."

Paul held up a finger; he was chewing.

"I think what the professor wants to say," said the Colonel,
carefully folding his napkin, "is that in the later movies—pardon me, the later *films*—of Marion Morrison, what we see is

not a role model, not a moral paragon, but an *actor*. And not just an actor, but a vain old movie star in a wig and a corset who let his stuntman do everything but the close-ups." The Colonel smiled across the table. "I think the professor here prefers the dark, neurotic John Wayne of *Red River*, the—how shall I put it?" He placed his hands on either side of his Japanese lunch box. "The Nixonesque John Wayne, John Wayne as King Lear, if you will. And do you know, gentlemen? He's right." He held up his creased palm. Bob Wier nodded earnestly, while J. J. glared at Paul and shoved a limp bundle of fries into his mouth.

"Those earlier films of Mr. Morrison's," the Colonel continued, "are the work of a mature artist, a man at the peak of his powers as a professional *and* as a man. With all due respect to you, Bob, those earlier films convey more of the richness and complexity of *life* than do the more, shall we say, self-indulgent work of his waning years."

"Hm." Bob Wier rubbed his chin.

"A corset," said J. J., chewing slowly. "Fuck."

"Now," The Colonel leveled his gaze at Paul "Is that a fair assessment of your position?"

Paul swallowed his mouthful of cheese sandwich. What he wanted to say was, John *Wayne?* Hell, I don't even like westerns. The only John Wayne movie he remembered really enjoying was a boneheaded epic (he couldn't recall the name) where Wayne, in heavy makeup, played Genghis Khan. But if he had given the Duke's *oove* any thought over the years, then, well yes, he'd have to admit, grudgingly, that he preferred *Red River* to Wayne's later films. But only, he would have hastened to add, because it was the work of a great filmmaker like Howard Hawks, not because of *John Wayne*, for chrissakes.

"Well, okay, yes," he began, but before he could qualify his answer, the Colonel said, "Outstanding. I thought as much. Now, gentlemen." The Colonel emphatically clapped his hands together, once. "Topic B: The welcome, if brief return to our midst of the redoubtable Stanley Tulendij. What are we to make of this unexpected visit?"

Paul took another bite of his sandwich. Bob Wier was snapping the lid of his Tupperware, and J. J. was rubbing his lips with a wad of paper napkin, but both men swiveled their gazes in Paul's direction. Even the Colonel narrowed his eyes from across the table.

His mouth full, his sandwich clutched between his hands, Paul glanced from J. J. to the Colonel to Bob Wier. He forced himself to swallow. "You're asking me?"

The three men watched him intently. They did not say a word.

Paul felt his face get warm again. "I, uh, only just met the guy . . ."

"But you've heard the story," said J. J. "Everybody's heard the story."

"The layoffs," said Bob Wier. "His defiance."

"A man at the peak of his personal and professional powers," said the Colonel, "cut down in his prime."

"Sacrificing himself for his men," said Bob Wier.

"He faced his enemies," said the Colonel, "and drew a line in the sand."

"Cross *that*, motherfucker," said J. J., flinging down his wadded-up napkin.

"The fateful bus trip," said Bob Wier.

"That fucking storm," said J. J.

"The *sinkhole*," intoned the Colonel, leaning across the table and folding his hands while gravely fixing Paul with his gaze.

"I, uh," stammered Paul, "I think somebody might have mentioned it to me . . ."

"The man stood up, Paul." The Colonel's voice was tight with emotion. "He did what a man should."

Paul squeezed his sandwich. They would not stop looking at him. "Well," he said at last, "good for him."

A glance passed between his three companions. They seemed to withdraw the tiniest increment from him, as if he had failed some test.

"Amen," said Bob Wier, burping his Tupperware.

"Yeah, right." J. J. glanced around the room.

The Colonel banked his gaze and silently ground his palms together.

"Nolene told me." Paul was at once foolishly eager not to disappoint these guys and furious at himself for his eagerness. "About Stanley Tulendij." Shut up! he told himself.

"Nolene. Ah, yes." The Colonel frowned at the tabletop.

What's going on here? Paul wondered. What are they trying to get me to say?

" 'I will leave you in the desert,' " Bob Wier said. "Ezekiel twenty-nine, five." He lifted up his hands, playing to the back pews again. " 'Then all who live in Egypt will know that I am the Lord.' Twenty-nine, six."

"There's a Rashomon aspect to the situation, Professor." The Colonel peered significantly at Paul. "You may have heard one version of what happened to Stanley Tulendij, but you have not heard the *truth*."

"Amen," breathed Bob Wier.

You've got it wrong, Paul wanted to say. The point of *Rashomon* is not that one of the stories is true and the others are lies, it's that no one will ever be able to tell. There is no truth, you overbearing son of a bitch. That's what it means to invoke *Rashomon*. And stop calling me professor. . . .

"Paul." Bob Wier clasped his hands together on the tabletop. He almost looked as if he might cry. "It's a real blessing to have you join the team. I just wanted to say that."

"Nuff said." J. J. repressed a belch and pushed himself back from the table. Bob Wier stood also.

"Actually, Bob," Paul said, "I've been—"

"I think what our good friend Paul is trying to say," said the Colonel, "is that he's already been on the team for a good— what is it?—a good six weeks now." He made no move to get up from the table. "Isn't that right, Paul?"

Paul simply stared at the Colonel as J. J. slouched off and Bob Wier swung away. The Colonel leaned back and folded his fingers over his belt buckle.

"I *know* what I wanted to say." Paul kept his voice low. The rumble of the lunchroom was diminishing behind him. He heard the scrape of chairs as other people stood to return to work.

The Colonel lifted his palm. "I should have let you speak for yourself. I know our luncheon conversation is a little overwhelming for a newcomer. The cut and thrust. The attack and parry. I know you want to contribute—I could see it in your eyes, son—but your time will come, don't worry." He watched Paul with a hint of a smile. "I apologize."

Paul smiled tightly and said, "No harm done."

"My two compatriots are both of them fine men," said the Colonel, placing his hands on the table edge. He let his gaze drift past Paul's shoulder to where J. J. and Bob Wier were threading their way out of the room. "Bob's a simple man, but godly. And J. J.'s youthful enthusiasm . . . well, I see myself, thirty years ago." He focused on Paul again. "But there's no culture in them, Professor. Not like there is in you and I." He smiled. "Perhaps even a bit of the *artiste*, no?"

Paul simply stared at him.

"But that's a conversation for another time." The Colonel pushed himself to his feet and slid his chair up to the table. He lifted his glossy lunch box. "You're onto something extraordinary here, son, but you just don't know it yet. In the weeks and months to come, you will look back on yesterday afternoon and say, '*That* was the day I first met Stanley Tulendij.' " He glanced across the lunchroom and lowered his voice. "I think you'll come to find our luncheon repartee the high point of your day. Infinitely more interesting, say, than napping in the toilet."

Paul glanced quickly over his shoulder. The lunchroom was nearly empty; only a few people, one or two to a table, still sat chewing and staring blankly into space. Paul turned back to the Colonel. "I don't know what you're talking about," he said.

"Not to worry, Professor." The Colonel put a finger to his lips. "Our little secret." He winked at Paul. "*A demain, mon frère.*"

Paul, astonished to speechlessness, turned and watched the Colonel stride, stiff-backed, gut first, between the tables of the empty lunchroom towards the door.

ELEVEN

AFTER LUNCH, Paul sulked in his cube for an hour and a half. What was the big deal with Stanley Tulendij? The Colonel and his coterie talked about him like he was . . . what? A general beloved of his troops? A captain who went down with his ship? A titan in fleet management? As far as Paul could tell, the man was not only a disgraced, pensioned-off old buzzard with an unsavory whiff of decay about him, but a man at least indirectly responsible for the disappearance, and possibly death, of a busload of unemployed men. But more importantly, Paul wondered, how did the Colonel find out about my midmorning naps in the men's room? Do they have a camera in there, God forbid? Paul resisted the urge to glance at the ceiling over his head.

How did the Colonel know, Paul fumed, that I prefer *Red River* to *Chisum*? Paul hated it when anybody read him that easily. He further resented the Colonel's presumption of a commonality of taste and interest. Fellow intellectuals, indeed. Back at Midwest, in his grad school days, he'd known undergraduates, for cry yi, who'd have made that pompous autodidact look like . . . look like . . . well, they'd have reduced him to a cinder, that's what. *Artiste*, my ass.

It wasn't long before the soporific effect of the cube smothered Paul's rage. By two-thirty, as his eyelids drooped and his chin dipped towards his chest and watchful Olivia's gaze prickled the back of his neck, he grabbed his volume of H. G. Wells and went down to the midafternoon dusk of the lunchroom. He hadn't planned it, exactly, but this was roughly the same time he'd run into Callie the day before. The lunchroom was empty, so he sat in the Colonel's seat facing the door, with the fat volume open to the beginning (still) of *The Island of Dr. Moreau*. After five minutes of staring at the doorway didn't produce her, Paul lowered his eyes to the book.

CHAPTER THE FIRST
In the Dingey of the "Lady Vain"

I do not propose to add anything to what has already been written concerning the loss of the Lady Vain. As everyone knows, she collided with a derelict when ten days out from Callao. The long-boat with seven of the crew was picked up eighteen days after by H.M. gun-boat Myrtle, and the story of their privations has become almost as well known as the far more terrible Medusa case.

But today Wells read like an instruction manual; Paul's eyes tripped over "Callao" and were completely derailed by "*Medusa.*" His gaze drifted through the yellowish tint of the windows to the parking lot, past the humpbacked ranks of Sports and Trackers and pickups, to the embankment that blocked the view of the river. Where had Stanley Tulendij gone yesterday after he crested the rise? Who was the man on the bridge? Had it really been Boy G? And had Boy G been waving at Paul or signaling Stanley Tulendij? And what was it, Paul wondered, his eyelids pulling down like shades, his chin tugging towards his sternum, what was it that Nolene had been about to tell him yesterday? What was it that the Colonel, Bob Wier, and J. J. never *did?*

Paul jerked his head up, and the narrow print of the book swam before his eyes. His eyes focused and he read, "But I knew now how much hope of help for me lay in the Beast People."

He glanced away from the page and groaned. As he had dozed, the pages had flipped forward on their own to just before Chapter the Thirteenth. How had *that* happened? Dear God, thought Paul, please don't let me sleep on my break. Not on *my own time.* He pushed the book away and pressed his fingers into his eyes, and when he pulled them away he saw a string dangling from the ceiling fifteen feet away. Paul squeezed his eyes shut, then looked again. The string was still there, hanging over a lunchroom table straight as a plumb line, suspended from a little, black, triangular gap where a ceiling panel was askew. At the lower end of the string a little noose was being raised and lowered over a salt shaker in the middle of the table. The noose draped once over the shaker without catching it, then twice, then again, the string above slackening each time. Then, one more try and it caught around the neck of the salt shaker. The string went taut, and the salt shaker swung silently up off the table.

Paul clapped his hands over his eyes and moaned, "Oh, fuck." The room swallowed up the epithet, and in the dark behind his palms he heard only the starship hum of the building's air-conditioning. He thought he heard, just at the edge of audibility, down among the white noise, the surface hiss of his life, the tiniest little *scrape*, as of someone sliding a ceiling panel back into place.

"It's Paul, right?"

He whisked his hands away from his eyes. Callie stood across the table from him, her Norton anthology clutched to her bosom; the book was open and she pressed the wide spine with both hands. She was balanced on the ball of one foot, ready to flee. Oh *fuck*, Paul thought, silently this time, and he glanced past her at the ceiling, where the tiles receded towards the vanishing point in perfect rectilinearity.

"You alright?" It was clear from her intonation that she was asking for her sake, not his.

Paul waved his hands. "I was, uh, resting my eyes." He tried to smile. For the first time in his memory, Callie was wearing a skirt, a shapeless denim skirt that came to her knees but a skirt nonetheless. "I stare at a screen all day," Paul said, "and it makes my eyes . . ."

Callie twisted her mouth, plainly considering a retreat. But then she pushed the fat H. G. Wells volume aside and plunked the Norton onto the table. She was wearing a thin sweater, Paul noted, not very tight, and she bent over the table and turned the massive anthology towards him with both hands. She leaned over the book, one hand splayed against the tabletop, the other hovering over the tissuey page, one long finger extended. Paul stole a glance down the open collar of her sweater and was rewarded with a glimpse of a bra strap. Reading upside down, Callie pressed the nail of her index finger—clear now, but with flakes of red polish in the seam—against a word in one of the tiny footnotes, creasing the page.

"How do you say that word?"

Paul looked up from her collar and met her eyes, which were swimmingly blue. "Sorry?" he said.

"It don't appear in the glossary." Callie squeezed her eyes shut for an instant. "It *doesn't* appear in the glossary."

He waited for her eyes to open again, then he lowered his gaze to the book.

" 'Synecdoche'?" He looked up again. "Is that the word you mean?"

"Say that again," she said, watching his lips. *Agin*, she pronounced it.

"Sit." Paul nodded at the chair across the table, the one he had sat in at lunch, the one she was leaning over now so fetchingly. Callie narrowed her eyes at him, biting her lip, then abruptly pulled the chair out and sat. She crossed her arms and leaned forward on her elbows, her sweater pulled tight across her shoulders.

"Se-*nek*-duh-key," he said, watching her eyes, but she was looking at the book. "Rhymes with Schenectady."

"Rhymes with what?" She looked up at him.

"Never mind. It's from the Greek. It means . . ." She was squinting hard at him, concentrating on what he was saying. "It's when you use the name of *part* of something to refer to the *whole*. Like, uh . . ." The first example that came to his mind was *skirt*, and he shook his head to get rid of it. "Like when you call your car your *wheels*, for example."

To Paul's surprise, Callie gasped. Her whole face relaxed; her eyes widened and her forehead unfurrowed. Her cheekbones lowered, unclenching her freckles. It was beautiful to watch, as if the shadow of a cloud had passed from a mountain lake of deepest blue.

"Synecdoche," she said, and for the skip of a heartbeat, Paul thought she might smile.

"What are they glossing here?" He dipped to the book again, hoping to prolong the moment.

"Glossing?" Her eyebrows drew together, her freckles began to clench again.

"What's the footnote about?" Paul's gaze climbed the page, a long ladder of Elizabethan poesy, either a long poem or a speech from a play. But before he could find the reference, Callie put her long palms over the facing pages.

"That's okay." She pulled the book towards her. "I'm sorry to bother you."

Paul grabbed the outside edges of the book.

"It's no bother." He dipped his head, trying to catch her gaze. "Have dinner with me."

Callie stiffened, half out of her chair, her hands on the book, her elbows locked. Her shoulders were hunched; her lips squeezed tight. She peered at Paul as if through a pair of gun slits.

"You want to have *dinner* with me," she said flatly.

"No," Paul said. His thumbs were a fraction of an inch from her pinky fingers. "I want to *take* you to dinner."

"You want to take me to dinner." Her shoulders did not loosen, but she shifted her weight onto one hip.

"Hello! Hello! Hello . . . !" Paul said in diminishing volume, mimicking an echo.

Callie snorted. She was trying not to laugh. Paul restrained a smile. "Unless you don't go out with guys like me."

She canted her hip a little more sharply and let her elbows relax. "Hon," she said, "I think my history shows I'll go out with prit' near anybody." Then she gasped and clapped her hand over her mouth, her eyes alight. "Oh, shit." She lowered her fingers to her chin. "That's a hell of a thing to say, innit, to some guy who just. . . . You'll think I'm—"

"I think you've got no excuse not to go out with me." Paul leaned back in his chair and gripped the edge of the table, the way the Colonel had a few hours before. "Come on, it'll be fun. I'll tell you all about synecdoche. Or Schenectady, if you prefer." He smiled; she didn't. Keep trying, he told himself. "Or we can branch out into simile. Or sigmatism. Or syllepsis. Or syzygy." Years of graduate training that he thought he'd lost forever came back to him. "Or synaesthesia. I'm real good on synaesthesia."

Callie pursed her lips. "Don't get carried away, cowboy." She crossed her arms, but her shoulders were loose. "It's just dinner."

"Well, when?"

She gave him one last, long, appraising look, then leaned slowly across the table. She took the book with both hands, slammed it shut, and picked it up one-handed, cradling it against her hip. "Tomorrow's Friday, innit?"

"Yes, ma'am." Paul rocked the chair back on its rear legs. "It surely is."

"Well, I can't Friday." She turned and walked away, the book balanced on her hip. *Cain't*, she said. Oh my God, Paul thought, I've just asked out Ado Annie.

"Saturday, then," he called after her.

Callie turned expertly on her heel and kept walking backwards, a sight that startled Paul in his precariously balanced chair. He jerked forward and brought the chair down with a thump, rattling the table. Callie lifted a corner of her lips.

"Alright," she said, and she pivoted again on her heel and swung her hips around a table and out the door.

Paul was still floating later when he went out onto the griddle of the parking lot after work. He rolled down the windows, lifted the hatchback of his car to let out the heat, and tossed his shirt on the passenger seat. The sight of the string dangling from a gap in the ceiling he had consigned to limbo; it was a daydream, a product of subliminal suggestion by the dying tech writer—"*They're up there,*" indeed—and Paul's regular mid-afternoon stupor. H. G. Wells probably didn't help, either. If I want to see weird shit, Paul thought, all I need to do is go home every day and deal with my ghost cat. I don't need any weird shit at work. Get thee behind me, Stanley Tulendij.

But right now, with the prospect of a Saturday night out with an attractive young woman, for all he cared a whole chorus line of Stanley Tulendijs and Boy Gs and dead cats could kick step across the top of the embankment. As he started the stuttering engine and put the car in reverse, he glanced back and noted the trash in his backseat. I ought to clean all that out, he thought. It's bad enough showing up Saturday night in this old heap; what will she think? Paul backed out of the parking spot. Oh hell, he told himself, I'm an office temp going out with a minimum-wage TxDoGS employee. She's not expecting a Lexus.

As he idled noisily in the nose-to-tail line of elephantine SUVs waiting to pull out onto Travis Avenue, Nolene rolled majestically past the nose of his car with her vast bag slung over her shoulder. Paul watched her approach an enormous minivan, and he swung out of line and into the empty spot next to her van. He left his car running, got out, and called to her across the roof of the Colt. She had heaved open the massive sliding rear door and was slinging in her bag; Paul caught a glimpse of not one, not two, but three child car seats in a row along the backseat.

"Hey, Nolene," he said again. She glanced back at him and heaved the other way, leaning into the sliding panel as if she were closing the door of an airplane hangar.

"Hey, Paul." She hooded her eyes and turned to the driver's door with her keys in her hand.

"Yesterday," he said, "when you were telling me about Stanley Tulendij . . . ?"

Nolene let out a long sigh, her hand on the open door and one foot on the little running board.

"You said the Colonel, Bob Wier, and J. J. never did . . . something. You didn't say what."

Nolene lifted one plucked eyebrow and looked warily over her shoulder at the General Services Division Building.

"All I know is," she said, not quite looking at Paul, "everybody in the Purchasing Department brings me stuff to do all day long. But whenever any of *those* three wants me to type something or fax something or process a purchasing order, whatever, the work is waiting on my desk when I get here in the morning." She gave him a significant look and hoisted herself into the driver's seat.

"So?" Paul called out as she shut her door.

Nolene started her van and stared out the windshield. Then she rolled down her window and stuck her elbow out and beckoned Paul. He came around to the side of the minivan, where she looked imperiously down at him.

"So do the math, Paul," she said quietly. "Those boys always leave ever' day a good twenty minutes before I do. And not a one of 'em comes in until eight-thirty, and I'm here, every blessed morning, by seven-fifteen."

"I'm not sure what you mean," Paul said. "What is it they don't do?"

"*Work*, Paul." She widened her eyes at him, as if at a dimwit child. "They don't do a lick of work, *ever.* Not when I can see them, and I sit across from 'em all day long. Colonel's yakkin' to his stockbroker, Bob Wier's speed-reading goldang self-help books, and J.J. surfs the Web all the livelong day." She sighed. "But then, every morning, the work they're not doing shows up on my desk for me to process." She put the van in reverse and gunned the engine. Paul stepped back.

"The only thing I can figure," said Nolene, backing slowly out of her spot, "is that they come in in the middle of the night, and I don't believe *that* for a minute. Not from *them*." She swung the van into the lane and put it in drive. She gave Paul one last, significant look and jerked her thumb over her shoulder towards the building.

"You'd never catch *me* in there after dark." Then Nolene roared away, leaving Paul standing in her empty space, next to his trembling car.

TWELVE

THE FOLLOWING DAY, Friday, Paul avoided luncheon with the Colonel by leaving the building. He ate his sandwich in his car, then spent the rest of his lunch hour at a car wash on the other side of the river. He blasted the outside of his ancient Colt with the high-pressure hose, half afraid that the impact of the spray would loosen his bumper or penetrate the Colt's sun-bleached roof. Still, even the mail girl deserved a clean car on a first date. He forked out fistfuls of trash from the backseat and slotted three quarters, three times, into the roaring industrial vacuum cleaner, sweating right through his t-shirt as he wriggled through the car, pushing the plastic nozzle under the seats and into every cranny of the upholstery. He bought a pine-scented air freshener from the vending machine and hung it from his rearview mirror; the heat inside the car would probably cook it to a nubbin, but at least the car would no longer smell like sweat, old hamburgers, and failure.

After lunch he took his time sheet to Rick, a weekly humiliation, and Rick dashed off his signature without looking up.

Paul hesitated in the doorway and said, "Thanks again for the raise," and Rick glanced up at him sharply, his eyebrows dancing. For an awful moment Paul thought Rick was going to say, "What raise?" But he only said, "You earned it," and waved Paul away.

Then Paul ran the gauntlet of his erstwhile lunch companions. Bob Wier glanced up from his speed-reading and chirped, "Missed you at lunch today!" The Colonel narrowed his eyes as Paul hurried past his doorway. "Don't be a stranger, Paul," he called out. "You're one of us now." J. J. said nothing, slouched in front of his monitor, but a moment later Paul heard footsteps behind him, and he glanced back to see J. J. stumping after him. Paul ignored him, but then J. J. followed him around the corner into his aisle, and as Paul went into his cube and sat, J. J. loomed in the doorway, dangling his wrists over the partition on either side.

"We don't need you," he said, but diffidently, more as if he were stating a fact than making a threat.

Paul swiveled towards J. J. "I beg your pardon?"

"Guys like you." J. J.'s gaze wandered all over, everywhere but towards Paul. "You think you're better than everybody."

Paul sighed. He glanced past J. J. across the aisle, but Olivia, for once, was not in her cube. "No," he said, "I just think I'm better than you."

Paul was surprised at himself, but he was even more surprised at J. J.'s reaction: He laughed, his gaze shooting all over the room. "That's good," he said. "I'm gonna use that one." He nodded and smiled to himself. "It's just . . ."

"What?" snapped Paul. "It's just *what?*"

J. J. slid his wrists off the partition and stepped into the cube. His eyes locked onto Paul's at last.

"Colonel, he thinks you're some kind of genius or something," J. J. said in a low voice. "Whatever. But *I* know you're a fuck up, 'cause I'm a fuck up, too. Okay?"

Paul said nothing. He perched tensely on the edge of his chair and fought to hold J. J.'s glare. From the neighboring cube he heard the hiss of the dying tech writer.

"We got a sweet thing going here," said J. J. "and we don't need you to screw it up."

"What on earth are you talking about?" said Paul. "Lunch?"

"Hey, you wanna call it lunch, whatever." J. J. backed out of the cube, but he pointed at Paul, fixing him in his chair. "Just don't fuck it up." Then J. J. abruptly walked away, leaving Paul turning slowly in his chair.

During his afternoon break in the empty lunchroom he scarcely read a word of H. G. Wells. He was still fuming over his encounter with J. J. Fine, Paul thought, I won't sit at his fucking table during lunch. After a while, though, he realized he was watching the doorway for Callie. They had yet to set a time for Saturday night, and he didn't know where she lived. He let his break drag on an extra ten minutes, turning the page of his book only once, and still she didn't show. I can always look her up in the phone book, he thought as he went back upstairs, but then he realized that he didn't even know her last name. He slouched before his computer screen for the next hour or so, canoodling on the RFP. He wasn't about to track her down. He had already done his bit and asked her out; surely it was up to her to seek him out and tell him where she lived. Christ, Paul thought, I'm going out with a community college student, for all I know; why else would she be lugging around the *Norton Anthology?* Surely she doesn't expect me to trail after her?

Just before quitting time he overheard another hissing exchange between Olivia Haddock and the dying tech writer.

"Today," croaked the tech writer, "is my last day." *Wheeze.* "My contract expires today."

"It's up to you." Olivia's voice ricocheted sharply off the ceiling tiles. "All I know is if the work isn't revised by time I come in on Monday morning, I'm not signing off on your time sheet."

"That's." *Wheeze.* "Blackmail."

"Call it whatever you like. I'm not paying for work that isn't finished."

"It's almost five o'clock." A very long, painful *wheeze.* "On Friday."

"Well, if it were *my* paycheck," Olivia said, mincing away, "I'd make sure the work was done before I went home."

Paul busied himself with shutting down his computer and tidying his desk; he hunched his back against any stray glance from Olivia. He stood, pushed his chair in, and stepped out of his cube just as Olivia stepped out of hers, wearing her purse strap like a bandolier.

"Paul," she said, fixing him with a glare that defied him to bring up her moment of vulnerability the other day after Stanley Tulendij's visit. Paul stepped aside to let her pass. Then he ducked the other way. As Paul passed, the dying tech writer lifted his gaze forlornly to the ceiling. A whine that might have been a sigh issued from his breathing tube.

In the parking lot Paul performed his ritual opening of the hatchback and car windows, catching a whiff of cooking pine as he tossed his shirt on the passenger seat. Well, this is great, he thought as he walked back around the car, slamming the hatchback shut. I drench myself in sweat—on my lunch hour—to clean the car for her, and not a word all afternoon. How am I supposed to find her tomorrow? Follow the bread crumbs? I asked *her* out; the least she could do is give me her number.

"Bitch," Paul muttered, and just then an enormous pickup truck chugged to a stop, its gears grinding, right behind his Colt. The truck had to be at least twenty years old, formerly red, with dimples and dings and a long, rusty scrape along the side panel. The pickup idled unevenly, going *glug glug glug* as Callie draped her elbow out the window and leveled her sunglasses at Paul.

"Are you serious about tomorrow night?" She was wearing a blue tank top, yet somehow, even in the relentless Texas sun, the skin of her long arm was pale, with a sprinkling of freckles across her shoulders.

"Yes," said Paul. "I am." He approached the truck, straightening his spine to suck in his gut. He couldn't read her expression behind the dark glasses, but he liked the quizzical way she pursed her lips.

"What time?" She rocked slightly behind the wheel to the glugging rhythm of her ancient truck.

What's good for you? Paul nearly said, but he imagined Callie was the sort of girl who'd be put off by yuppie indecision, so he said, "Seven."

She looked away, through her cracked windshield. Watching her face in profile, Paul was pierced by the image of him and Callie on a blanket in the bed of her truck in ecstatic carnal congress.

"Fifteen oh eight South Austin Avenue." She worked her right arm on the gear shift, out of sight, her collarbone straining against the strap of her tank top. "Apartment two-thirteen." The gears clashed; the pickup shuddered and went *Glug! Glug! Glug!*

"Got it." Dear God thought Paul, let her work that shift again. *Glug!* went the strings of his heart.

"That your car?" She pursed her lips at the Colt.

"My Jag is in the shop."

"Smartass," she said, and she popped the clutch and chugged away.

THIRTEEN

ON SATURDAY MORNING Paul stuffed his time sheet into the drop box at the temp agency, along with a note to Erika, asking when he'd see his retroactive raise. Then he did his laundry. He used to take his clothes to a coin laundry near campus called Lean'n'Clean, where he could work out on treadmills while his underwear tumbled dry and attempt to strike up conversations with firm, fit, brainy young graduate students in sports bras and swinging ponytails. But he found it too difficult to be simultaneously charming and breathless, and he began to do his laundry closer to home, in a strip mall off South Travis Avenue, at a mercilessly bright Laundromat with an unnecessarily large staff of Latinas who listened to boom box Tejano music at top volume as they folded other people's sheets. The place was always packed on a Saturday morning, and Paul had trained himself in the raptorish watchfulness and hair-trigger reflexes of Laundromat Darwinism, competing for washers, dryers, and folding tables with young mothers dragging huge plastic tubs of laundry and gaunt Snopeses lugging pillowcases full of jeans and t-shirts. Today the wiliest combatant was an elderly white woman who tried to steal Paul's cart and then shouldered him aside at the wall of dryers as forcefully as a linebacker. When he glared at her, she waxed geriatrically coquettish, as fluttery as Blanche DuBois—"Oh darlin', was that *your* dryer?" Paul ended up cramming all his clothes at once into a single dryer with a wonky thermostat.

That afternoon, thinking of his own long-lost *Norton Anthology*, he went to the central branch of the Lamar Public Library, where every Saturday the Friends of the Library sold used books out of cardboard boxes lined up on folding tables. The sale was held in the library's basement in a wide, low-ceilinged meeting room, dankly air-conditioned and harshly overlit. The books were crammed spine up in cardboard boxes with the flaps cut off, divided into the broadest possible categories—hardcover fiction, paperback nonfiction—and people shopped in bulk, the way they might buy surplus cheese, filling up old grocery bags with fistfuls of books. Indeed, the rumbling ventilator and the lack of windows gave the room the Cold War feel of a bunker deep underground and gave the sale's patrons the pasty, troglodytic aspect of survivors of an apocalypse fighting over the last remaining Jackie Collins novel. The struggle for split-spined beach paperbacks was no less Darwinian than the struggle for dryers at the Laundromat. Elderly women nudged past each other scavenging for mysteries with lurid covers, while late-middle-aged men with flinty gazes hunted for Jurassic-era thrillers by Alistair Maclean or Hammond Innes. The table of old vinyl was being strip-mined by a young couple in baggy shorts and flip-flops, she in funky black glasses and he in a faded t-shirt that proclaimed I'VE BEEN TO LUCKENBACH, TEXAS. They were tag teaming the boxes, walking their fingers at a trot through old albums looking for lounge (she) or seventies British rock (he), pausing only to display a find to each other—she showed him Enoch Light, he showed her Mott the Hoople.

Paul fancied himself the most discriminating buyer in the room, looking for just that one book, as if he were in Shakespeare & Company instead of a library basement. Today, however, he wasn't having any luck. Usually abandoned *Norton*s were as common as cast-off *National Geographic*s, but someone, perhaps Callie herself, had cleaned out the library's stock. Most of the old textbooks were heaped on a table in the corner, the elephant's graveyard's elephant's graveyard, but even there Paul could not find a *Norton*. The closest thing to it was a multivolume anthology of English literature, thirty years old, edited and annotated by, of all people, Paul's old nemesis from grad school, a bardolatrous old blowhard named Morton Weissmann. It would serve the same purpose as a *Norton Anthology*, but even at fifty cents a volume, it wasn't worth lugging away ten pounds of obsolescent canon mongering.

He began to trawl the rest of the room, scanning the boxes quickly for a fat Norton binding. After a table or two he became aware that the same guy was always on his left, moving at the same rate, looping around the slower browsers a moment after Paul, following Paul instantly to the next table. Paul glanced at him and his pulse quickened: The man was wearing polyester slacks, a white shirt, a tightly knotted tie, a breast pocket full of pens, and a buzz cut. He wore no name tag, and he was thinner than Boy G, not to mention darker haired and not at all egg shaped. Still, his clothes, Paul noted, were clean but shabby like Boy G's, with threads coming loose around his collar and along the hems of his short shirtsleeves. Paul skipped to the next table, and the man followed right behind him, never taking his eyes off the ranked spines of the books, but not really looking at them. His skin was as pale as Boy G's; his milky scalp gleamed under the lights through the bristles of his thinning hair.

Paul broke away and crossed to the table behind him, and the man crossed with him, appearing on Paul's right, moving ahead of him at a constant rate. Paul got a good look at the pale, creased skin at the back of the man's neck; he smelled disinfectant and the faint tang of excrement. Who *are* these guys? Paul wondered. He kept his eyes on the massed spines before him. He stopped and the other man stopped; he plucked a volume at random out of the box before him—a water-stained paperback of *Worlds in Collision*—and the man next to him did the same. With the paperback in his hand, Paul arched his back and stretched his arms and feigned a yawn, glancing around the room to see how far he was from the door. As he lowered his arms he saw Boy G himself peering through his glasses at him from two tables away.

Paul's pulse began to pound, and his breath came short. Boy G looked the same as he had a few days ago, down to the crumpled name tag. He stared expressionlessly across the intervening tables at Paul, and for an instant Paul thought that the egg-shaped man hadn't seen him. But then Boy G smiled, and Paul caught his breath. Even across the room Paul could see that there was something odd about the homeless man's teeth. They weren't even, but they weren't discolored or gapped like an ordinary homeless person's. Rather, they were dazzlingly bright and serrated like a saw blade, a jagged row of sharp points.

Paul gasped and stepped back from the table, brushing the homeless guy who had been shadowing him. Paul recoiled from the man, and the man smiled at Paul, revealing his own glossy, jagged teeth, each tooth filed down to a sharp point like a New Guinea tribesman's. Both men were smiling ferociously at Paul now, while all around them the other customers shuffled obliviously, their heads lowered, their shoulders hunched, their eyes cast down. Paul felt a scream rising from his solar plexus.

"Al*right!*" someone shouted, and every eye in the place flickered towards the sound. The kid in the Luckenbach t-shirt was flapping an old LP in the air while the girl in the funky glasses smiled up at him.

"Check it out!" cried the kid. "The Strawbs!"

Even the homeless guy next to Paul had turned to watch the commotion. Paul edged away from him, step by step, and then hustled up the aisle. He didn't dare glance back at Boy G, but made a beeline for the door. He swerved around the card table at the entrance, and the old gent manning the cash box reached out and clutched Paul by the wrist. His touch was electric to Paul, and he tried to break away, but the old man held him tight.

"That's fifty cents, son," said the old man.

Paul's rising scream nearly broke loose. He could feel Boy G's jagged teeth nipping at his shoulders and the back of his neck. The old man tightened his grip, and Paul expected to see him bare his own serrated teeth. But the cashier smiled, and his teeth were even and ordinary and yellowed by nicotine. He gestured with his eyes at the book in Paul's white-knuckled grip, the battered old copy of *Worlds in Collision*. Paul released it instantly; the book flopped to the floor. The old man released Paul's wrist, and Paul bolted through the door without looking back and took the steps to the library's main floor two at a time. At the top of the stairs, brilliant Texas sunlight poured through the library's tall front windows. Paul whirled and looked back and saw no pale homeless men coming after him, only a little black girl clutching a copy of *A Spelunker's Guide to Texas*.

Paul groaned and sat heavily on the top step, alarming the little girl. He stayed there until his heart stopped pounding and his knees stopped trembling. Then he rose and trotted back down the stairs into the meeting room. But all he saw was the sale's regular clientele, slowly grazing. Boy G and his sidekick were gone. Paul stepped into the hall and glanced up the stairs to the main floor, then down the basement hallway towards a locked door labeled NO UNAUTHORIZED ACCESS. He stepped inside the meeting room and tapped the shoulder of the old fellow at the cash box.

"You dropped your book," said the old man.

"Is there another way out of here?" Paul murmured.

The old man cocked an eye at Paul. "Somebody after you, chief?" he said.

"Forget it," Paul said, and walked away.

FOURTEEN

AFTER PAUL FINISHED HIS LAUNDRY SATURDAY MORNING, he had left the trousers and the shirt he planned to wear that evening on a hanger in his car beyond the reach of Charlotte. When it was time to get ready for his date, he even considered changing in the car but decided he didn't want to wriggle into his trousers under the eyes of the Snopeses loitering in their doorways. So he retrieved the hanger and hung it behind the bathroom door while he showered, where he could keep an eye on it—even ghost cats don't like water, he had learned—then waited until the last moment before he pulled on the trousers and buttoned his shirt. Then he grabbed his wallet and his keys, stubbed his feet into his sandals, and bolted for the door. He glimpsed Charlotte sprawled across the back of the sofa, and he muttered, "Don't wait up," as he pulled the door shut.

Callie lived in a twenty-year-old apartment complex along one of the down-market reaches of South Austin Avenue; its driveway climbed a short hill between a massage parlor with curtained windows and a head shop emblazoned with a sun-bleached mural of Stevie Ray Vaughn and an armadillo. Paul wound through the dusty parking lot past cars of the same vintage as his own, and he found Callie's building when he recognized her massive pickup parked out front. He pulled in next to the truck and saw Callie herself sitting on the front step of the building, her arms wrapped around her knees. She waved at him to stay in the car, then pushed herself up with a quick brush of her backside. She wore a fitted shirt, faded pink, with the cuffs rolled back once, and a tight black skirt that came to just above her knees. Paul leaned across the passenger seat and opened her door.

"I wasn't sure you were coming," she said as she slid into the seat. *I wun't sure yew were comin'.*

"Am I late?"

"No." Callie tugged at the hem of her skirt. "I just wasn't sure you were coming."

"Well, I wasn't sure you'd go out with me." Paul turned to look between the seats as he backed out. "So it all evens out." He laid his hand on the back of Callie's seat, and she dropped her shoulder a fraction and pulled her arm across her lap. "I heard you didn't like men," he said.

"Who told you that?" She squinted at him. "Ray?"

"Actually, yeah."

"Jackass," Callie intoned. "What Ray means is, I wouldn't go out with *him*." She glanced at Paul. "Not liking Ray ain't the same thing as not liking men."

"Got it." The car idled unevenly under them, and Paul drummed his fingers on the gearshift. "Callie, you look great."

Callie lifted a corner of her mouth and said, "That was smooth."

Paul laughed. "I'm not allowed to give you a compliment?"

She reddened. "I suppose." She pursed her lips. "Thank you."

Back on Lamar Avenue, he headed towards the river, and as they crossed the bridge, she said, "North of the river, huh? Big spender."

Paul had devoted some effort to calibrating exactly where to take Callie. On the one hand, he couldn't afford Lamar's trendier restaurants, and even if he could he wasn't sure Callie would—How should I put it? he wondered—he wasn't sure she'd be *comfortable* in one of them. Hell, he wasn't even sure *he'd* be comfortable in them any longer. The farther up the restaurant food chain he went, the more likely he was to run into Kym and the Weather Gnome, or Virginia Dunning, or even Oksana.

On the other hand, he couldn't exactly take Callie to some south Lamar all-you-can-eat buffet. So with these parameters in mind, he had decided at last on the café at Burnham Market, Lamar's gourmet grocery store, which was owned by the B. B. Burnham Corporation, the parent company of Billy Bob's, the largest grocery chain in Texas. The Market was a showpiece of industrial chic, with bare concrete floors and exposed girders and burnished steel coolers. The place was as notable for what it didn't stock as for what it did: stacks of pricey cola manufactured by anarcho-syndicalists in Colorado, but not a single can of Coke. Tortilla chips hand dipped at a peasant cooperative in Ixtlán del Rio, but not one bag of Doritos. Eighty varieties of imported mustard in tiny, high-priced bottles, but not a single goddamn jar of French's. The place was even a tourist destination of sorts: When Paul had still lived with her, Kymberly proudly took all their out-of-town visitors to the Market to show them the racks of imported bottled water, the vast bins of bulk pasta, the cheeses scrupulously divided by region. Now Paul couldn't even afford to shop at a regular Billy Bob's, and he bought his store-brand cans of chili and no-brand macaroni and cheese at an aging supermarket simply called Food.

But tonight was a special occasion, and Paul thought Callie would be impressed. The Burnham Market Café was attached to a grocery store, yes, but a really nice grocery store. And even though you ordered your food yourself at the counter at the café (which kept the prices down, thank God), the dining room was appropriately dim on a Saturday night, with a pleasant, festive echo to the diners' conversation. As they came in, Callie peered warily up at the tables on the mezzanine level, as if worried about sniper fire.

"You'll like it," Paul said. "The food's very good here."

"Well, if it ain't, we can always run next door and pick up a frozen pizza."

"You want to go someplace else?"

"No, I'm sorry. This is great."

Paul ordered the grilled chicken breast, and Callie ordered pot roast. Paul took the little beeping coaster from the cashier and led Callie upstairs to one of the tables overlooking the main dining room. He fetched both their drinks and returned to find Callie leaning on the table, clutching both her elbows. She frowned over the railing, down at the happy yuppie diners below, the cream of groovy Lamar. The light was dimmer up here, and the brighter light from below sharpened Callie's cheekbones. Her freckles vanished, and her skin took on an almost porcelain sheen. Paul slid her iced tea across the table. "Are you sure you don't want to go someplace else?" he asked.

"I'm sorry." Callie pressed her fingertips against her glass of tea. "It's just that my ex used to love this place."

"Your ex what?" said Paul. "Boyfriend? Husband?"

"Doesn't matter." *Dun't matter.* "Ex sorta covers it." She picked up the tea and swirled it. "He'd say, 'A place like this? This is why we moved to Lamar, baby.' And I'd say, 'It's a *grocery store*, hon. We got grocery stores back in Tulsa.' And he'd say, 'Not like this one.'" She lifted the glass and took a tiny sip. "'Course, he was right. And I do love the pot roast."

"Tulsa, huh?" Paul took a sip of his own tea. He wished he could reach across the table and ease her shoulders back, make her relax a little. She had buttoned her shirt almost to the top.

"Well." She shrugged "That's where I met him. Mr. X. I grew up way out in the panhandle." She watched Paul narrowly across the table. "In Beaver, Oklahoma."

Paul merely blinked, and Callie said, "Don't say it. I heard 'em all already. I've heard every joke there is." He started to laugh, and she pursed her lips. "You don't know what it's like going to Beaver High School in Beaver, Oklahoma, situated on the Beaver River at the heart of Beaver County."

"And the football team was—"

"The Fighting Beavers." Callie covered her eyes.

"I'm not saying a word." Paul laughed. "I wouldn't dare."

"I ain't even told you about the giant beaver at the center of town."

Paul squeezed his lips together to keep from laughing.

"Big statue of a beaver," Callie said, "holding a cow chip."

"A cow chip?"

"Don't ask." Callie shook her head. "Let's just say I got the hell out of there quick as I could."

"Okay," said Paul. "So you went to Tulsa to go to school?"

Callie laughed, a kind of a bark, and leaned back in her chair, still clutching her elbows. "Hell, I didn't even graduate from Beaver High." She glanced down at the diners below. "I followed some college boy to Tulsa. 'Course, he was going to Oral Roberts University, so I didn't exactly, you know, *fit in*." She leveled her gaze at Paul. "So you're going out with a high-school dropout, ex-truck-stop waitress from Tulsa."

Paul lifted his glass to her. "A fighting Beaver."

Callie's eyes blazed. "And don't you forget it."

The electric coaster began to buzz and blink, and Paul excused himself to pick up their order. When he returned with the tray, Callie had already fetched silverware and napkins and set the table. "Waitressing," she said. "It's in the blood."

Paul set her plate of pot roast and mashed potatoes before her, and Callie smiled for the first time that evening. "Girl's gotta eat," she said.

"So," Paul said, "this Oral Roberts student. You followed him to Lamar?"

"Hell no. That didn't last a month once we got to Tulsa. He got himself a fiancée, some beauty queen from Ponca City." She dabbed at her lips with her napkin. "Are we playing twenty questions?"

"I'd have to consult the first date regulations," Paul said, "but that's what you do, isn't it?"

"Okay." Callie made Paul wait while she finished another mouthful. "I met me a, quote, singer/songwriter, unquote, in Tulsa, and I followed *him* to Lamar."

"That's Mr. X?" He took a bite of chicken.

Callie nodded. "Now how'd you get here, hotshot?"

"I followed a TV journalist from Iowa," he said, nearly choking on the word "journalist."

"Is she on TV? I mean, here?"

"Yes," grumbled Paul.

"Really? Which one? Would I recognize her?"

Now it was Paul's turn to divert his gaze over the railing. "Kymberly Mathis. K-Now 48."

"Oh, my God, I know her!" Callie's eyes widened. "She's the one who can't pronounce 'meteorologist.' "

Paul laughed. "Welcome to my nightmare."

"And in't she *married* to one? That little fella, what's his name—"

"The Weather Gnome."

"The *what?*"

Paul drew a breath. "The meteorologist who cuckolded me."

"I'm sorry?" Callie leaned across the table. "What did he do?"

"He made me a cuckold," said Paul, "a man whose partner cheats on him."

"I'm sorry," she said. "I just didn't know the word."

"It's okay," Paul said. "I know it all too well."

"Can a woman be . . . cuckolded?"

"Technically, no."

" 'Cause if they can, then that's what Mr. X done to me. More than once, the son of a bitch."

Paul gave Callie a long look and said, "He's an idiot."

Callie blushed and pushed her potatoes around her plate. "Aw, you're sweet." Then she looked sharply at Paul. "He's a real good singer, though. You should hear him sometime."

Paul smiled. "If you say so."

Callie poked at her pot roast. She glanced at Paul and started to laugh, and she covered her mouth. "Meteo-roll-ologist." She feigned an anchorwoman hair toss. "Meteor-ol-ographer." Paul laughed.

"Course, I should talk," Callie said. "I can't pronounce half the words I come across."

"You did alright on . . . what was it again? The one you asked me about."

"You know."

"Yeah, but I want to hear you say it."

Callie put down her fork and gave Paul a very engaging look. "Synecdoche."

"I love it when a woman talks literary."

"Antagonist." Callie batted her eyelashes at him. "Protagonist."

"Careful, Callie, you're getting me hot."

She dropped her voice and said, in a slow, sultry moan, "Iambic pentameter."

Paul clutched her hand across the table. "Marry me," he said. "Have my children."

Callie stiffened and tugged her hand away. "They got real good desserts here, too." She picked up her fork and worked at her pot roast. They ate in silence for a moment.

"I'm sorry," Paul said. "Did I say something I shouldn't?"

"It's okay." *Hit's okay.* She put down her fork and glanced over the rail. "Mr. X left me when I got pregnant. I got rid of it, thought he might come back." She looked at Paul. "But he didn't."

Paul met her gaze. Don't screw this up, he told himself. "I'm sorry," he said.

Callie sighed. "Is this too much information? Am I breakin' the first date regulations?"

"I'll have to check, but I don't think so."

"Twenty questions, right?" She smiled wryly. "I'm a regular Patsy Cline song."

After dinner, in the car, he asked her if she wanted to get a drink someplace, and she said, "I got some beer back home. If you don't mind sitting on the floor."

He wasn't sure what she meant until she let them into her

apartment. Her air-conditioning was on full blast, thank God, but the living room, a whitewashed box with a glaring overhead light, was empty from wall to wall. Callie steadied herself with one hand against the wall and kicked off her shoes.

"I had to sell the furniture when X moved out." She stooped to pick up her shoes and started barefoot across the carpet. "Sumbitch wouldn't even help pay for, you know, the abortion. So I sold his Fender Stratocaster, too." With this last she gave her hips a fetching little dip. "Serves him right." She tossed the shoes through a dark doorway. "It's easier to keep clean anyhow." She switched on the kitchen light and grinned back at him. "Sit anywhere you like."

Paul kicked off his sandals and sat against the wall under the living room window, the only place in the room where he figured they couldn't be seen from the parking lot. The kitchen light winked out, and Callie came into the living room dangling two bottles of beer. He watched her cross the room to switch off the overhead light. Then she padded across the carpet in the gathering dusk and held out a Cuervo to him by its neck. She knelt beside him, then tucked her legs under her, tugging her skirt towards her knees, and leaned on one long arm.

"Here's to meteorologists." Callie lifted her bottle.

"And singer/songwriters," Paul said, as they clinked bottles. They each took a long pull.

"To anchorwomen," said Callie.

"And beauty queens."

"Here's to Oral Roberts," she said, lifting the bottle to her lips.

They sat silently in the dusk for a moment, watching each other, then Callie lowered her gaze and dug her fingernails into the carpet. Paul set his bottle against the wall and tilted her chin and kissed her. She retreated a fraction of an inch, just for a moment, then kissed him back, curling her hand over his shoulder. Then she lifted her eyes to the window above them and said, "We have to be careful. I sold the drapes, too."

"Well, I won't swing from the ceiling," he said. "Not tonight, anyway."

She hooked her arm around his neck and kissed him again, then she pulled away and held his face between her palms. He could feel the blush of warmth from her face in the dark. "You're not a son of a bitch, are you, Paul?" Her eyes peered into his. "I done had my lifetime quota."

Paul was glad it was dark; who knew what she could see in his face? That question had a lot of possible answers: Yes. Maybe. Used to be. Not so's you'd notice. But she was waiting, and he said, "Are you still in love with Mr. X?"

She gasped, and her eyes widened, but she didn't let him go. Different shades passed quickly over her eyes like cloud shadow. He could feel her trembling. Her palms were hot against his cheeks, and he laid a hand on top of one of hers. "Are you?" he whispered.

"Not anymore," she breathed.

He put his lips to her ear. "That's what I was going to say."

After a while one of them knocked over a beer. Callie tugged him by the wrist and said, "Come on, I'm getting carpet burn anyway." Keeping out of sight of the window, they crawled on all fours, naked and giggling, across the empty expanse of carpet and into the doorway where Callie had tossed her shoes. The swaying moon of her ass vanished into the dark, and Paul rose to his feet and felt along the wall.

"You're headin' for the closet, hon," she said, from the other side of the room, and he stepped towards the sound of her voice, stubbing his toe against something hard and heavy, like a cinder block.

"Ack!" Paul hopped on one foot as Callie laughed in the dark. "The hell was that?"

She turned on a little lamp set on an overturned milk crate, and in the dim yellow light Paul saw a couple of boxes overflowing with clothes, a plastic patio chair against the wall, her shoes in a heap near the closet door. Callie stretched out naked amid the rumpled sheets of a mattress on the floor, as shameless as a cat; she was propped up on her elbow, her other hand stretched along her freckled thigh. Paul looked at his feet and saw that he had stubbed his toe on the *Norton Anthology of English Literature.*

"What is it with you and this book?" He swooped towards the bed, and Callie pivoted suddenly on her hip and stuck out her long leg and kicked the book with her heel, sending it spinning across the carpet. Paul snatched her ankle and tugged her, squealing, halfway off the mattress.

"Stop it!" She pushed against his shoulders, but she wrapped her legs around him. "You'll laugh at me if I tell you."

"I don't think so," said Paul, and he slid inside her, closing his eyes at the exquisite shock of entry. Neither of them moved for a moment, enjoying the sweet tension. Paul opened his eyes and found Callie searching his face.

"I got it at a yard sale." She tightened her calves around the backs of his knees, drawing him deeper. "From a box of free books."

"Did you." Paul dug his toes into the carpet and began to move inside her.

"It was the biggest book." Callie rocked with him on the edge of the mattress. "I figured it'd last the longest."

"You like that?" Paul said, breathing hard. "Things that last a long time?"

"Uh huh." She bit her lip in concentration and fixed him with her blue eyes. "How long you gonna last?"

"Not as long as the *Norton Anthology,*" he gasped.

She hooked her arms around his shoulders and pulled his ear down to her lips. "Try," she whispered.

Much later, long after they had fallen into a tangled sleep, Paul started wide awake in the darkness. He was alone on the mattress, but he knew instantly that someone else was in the room. He heard a sigh and a swallow, then he felt a pressure on the side of the mattress, and he sat up sharply and pushed himself against the wall, his chest heaving. What if it's Boy G and the other homeless guy from the library? he thought. He was afraid he was going to see their ferocious teeth glowing in the dark. Or what if it's worse? What if it's Charlotte? Dear God, Paul thought, don't let that cat follow me here. It's not fair. It's breaking the rules.

Callie switched on the light, and she and Paul squinted at each other in the sudden glare. She was kneeling next to the bed; she had set the *Norton Anthology* on the edge of the mattress. Paul eased down from the wall, but he said nothing.

"I shouldna kicked this," Callie said, and Paul saw she was near tears. "You probably think I'm stupid. You know everything in this book, and it don't mean much to you anymore."

Paul said nothing, but he edged towards her. His heart was still racing, and he was unnerved to see a woman cry, especially one he had been so joyfully fucking only an hour or two before. Callie touched him on the back of his hand, which meant, *Thank you, but don't come closer.*

"Where I come from, nobody's got much, so I didn't know what I was missing." She pressed the book to her breasts. "But when I got to Tulsa?" She drew a deep breath. "I know that must sound stupid to you, Tulsa as . . . as . . ."

"Babylon." He sat very still.

She brushed her cheek with the back of her hand. "Some people got the best of everything. They got the best food, they got the best clothes, they got the best places to live." She gripped the anthology tightly in both hands and held it up; the blue veins stood out between her knuckles. "But this is free. This is the best, too, and I can have as much of it as any rich man. I can know as much about what's in this book as any college girl. *And there's nothing they can do about it.*" She was trembling, and her voice was shaking. Through her tears, her eyes were piercingly blue.

"I can know as much about it as you do!" she nearly shouted, rattling the book at him. Then her face crumpled, and the book drooped in her grasp. Paul got his hands under it and lowered the volume to the carpet, and he tugged Callie onto the bed. He kissed her and wiped her tears with his thumbs, and he lifted her face in his hands and said, "I'm gonna try real hard with you, Callie." To his surprise, he was nearly in tears himself.

Callie sobbed and curled onto her side and pressed her back against him, and he wrapped his arms and legs tightly around her. "I'm really gonna try," he murmured, and at least until he fell asleep again, he believed it.

FIFTEEN

PAUL CAME TO WORK A FEW MINUTES EARLY ON MONDAY.
"There must be a winter carnival in hell this morning."
Preston bounced on the balls of his feet and glanced at his
watch.

"Not only that," Paul said as he took the temporary badge,
"but this is the last time I'll have to sign in."

"You get another job someplace?" Preston lifted his eyebrows hopefully.

"It's not that cold in hell." Paul stepped back from the desk,
swinging his lunch. "I'm getting a permanent badge today."

"How'd you swing that?" Preston said. "I thought you was
only here temporarily."

Paul smiled as he backed away. Yesterday, during a long,
leisurely, postcoital Sunday morning, he had been eating pan-
cakes naked at Callie's kitchen counter when she brushed his
hip with hers and said, "Come see me tomorrow. I'll get you a
permanent ID."

"That answers my question," he had said.

"What question?"

"Who do I have to fuck to get an ID at TxDoGS?"

"Asshole," she'd said, and had flicked her fork at him, spattering him with maple syrup. He'd flicked her back, and she had laughed as he clutched her round the waist and licked the sweet brown specks off her collarbone.

"Let's just say," Paul said now as he backed down the hall from Preston's desk, "I've got a friend in high places."

He put his lunch in one of the refrigerators outside the lunchroom, then took the stairs two at a time and hustled down the hall and around the corner to Building Services. He hadn't seen Callie's truck in the parking lot, but perhaps she'd come in while he was stashing his lunch. He felt jaunty and virile this morning; all his extremities tingled.

"We gotta keep it cool at work, okay?" she'd said to him, when they had finally parted on Sunday. "No PDA at TxDoGS. I mean it, Paul."

He'd agreed, but surely she wouldn't object if he nuzzled her a bit in her inner office, in the deeper recesses of Building Services, the two of them alone among the laptops and the video projectors; but as he rounded the corner and saw Preston at parade rest behind his desk below, he found the Building Services door closed and locked. Not even the florid Ray was in attendance yet. Paul started back down the hall towards his cube, feeling only a tad less jaunty and virile. Things are definitely looking up, he thought, Charlotte and spooky homeless guys notwithstanding. I've got a raise, I've got the respect of my boss, I've got a girl—hell, if my life were a musical, I'd start *singing*.

He swung around the corner of his aisle, trying to decide if he wanted to be Gene Kelly or Fred Astaire, and found his petite, nervous coworker Renee standing in the aisle outside the dying tech writer's cube. Normally he'd have pulled himself up short and gasped an apology for nearly bowling her over, but today even Renee couldn't puncture his good mood. He gave her a jaunty salute, more Astaire than Kelly, and paused in the doorway of his cubicle. Renee turned to him with a ghastly, wide-eyed look, her pale fingers pressed to her mouth.

"You okay?" Paul said. This morning he loved all women, even this one. Renee shook her head and leveled her horrified gaze through the tech writer's doorway, both hands now pressed to her mouth. Paul came into the aisle, and she backed up a step as he edged past her.

The dying tech writer was dead. He lay back in his office chair with his legs splayed and his arms dangling to the sides, his bony wrists and knuckles hanging perfectly motionless. His baggy trousers and oversized sweater seemed to be draped across the chair, empty. His head was tipped back over the backrest, and his gaunt, lifeless eyes stared at the ceiling. The ceiling panel directly over him was askew, leaving a little isosceles triangle of perfect blackness. The yellowed breathing tube poking out of the gauze around the tech writer's neck pointed straight up at the gap in the ceiling.

All the air went out of Paul. His mouth hung open, but he was unable to speak. He looked from the gap in the ceiling panels to the body in the chair and back again. The tech writer's screen saver was running, an endless, slow-motion spray of stars.

"Ohhhh," sighed Renee, and Paul turned to see her swaying, her eyes rolling white. He caught her as she fainted and draped her over the chair of the empty cube across from the tech writer's. She immediately started to slide to the floor, and for a terrible moment Paul was afraid she too had died, that some deadly gas was flowing from the dark triangle in the suspended ceiling. But clutching her under her arms, he felt her rabbitty pulse, and he lifted her onto the desk of the empty cube, pillowing her head with a dusty ring binder. Then he ducked across the aisle to his own cube, avoiding even a glance at the dead man. He picked up the phone to call Preston, realized he didn't know the guard's number, then rooted around in his drawer for the phone list. His hands were trembling so badly he could scarcely punch the buttons, and his voice was equally palsied when he got Preston on the phone.

"It's Puh, Paul," he gulped. "Up in juh, General Services. You better come up. And call an am, am, ambulance."

He hung up before Preston could say anything and collapsed in his chair. He saw specks drifting across his gaze, so he closed his eyes and drew a deep breath. Then he opened them again, and saw a Post-it note stuck to the middle of his computer screen. It said:

A watermark,
with our compliments

Paul blinked numbly at the Post-it. It was blazoned with a smudgy thumbprint, like a seal, and it was creased diagonally, so that it didn't lay flat against the screen. Behind it, his screen saver trailed endlessly and rapidly across a black void, "*I could be bounded in a nutshell . . . I could be bounded in a nutshell . . . I could be bounded in a nutshell . . .* " Paul lifted his trembling hand and nudged his mouse, and the screen saver flickered out, revealing the gray-and-white screen of Microsoft Word. The RFP file was open, the pages displayed two to a screen, the print too tiny to read. Across each page was a large, gray-scale, diagonal watermark that read, DRAFT DOCUMENT. Slowly, fearfully, Paul lifted his gaze to the black gap in the ceiling tiles, certain he was going to see some pale, bespectacled face gazing back at him, grinning at him with sharpened teeth.

He heard the jingle of keys and the rhythmic thump of rapid footfalls, and he stood and saw Preston's buzz cut bobbing above the cube horizon. Paul stepped out of his cubicle as Preston jogged breathlessly into the aisle with the heel of his hand on his holstered sidearm. His keys jangled at his belt; his tight little potbelly bounced against the buttons of his shirt.

"What is it?" Preston gasped, his face the color of baked ham. But Paul only stared numbly at Preston's gun; he hadn't noticed before that the security guard was armed. But why wouldn't he be? Paul thought dully. It's Texas. Everybody carries a gun.

"Son?" said Preston, breathing hard. "What's goin' on?"

Paul stepped back and gestured wordlessly through the tech writer's doorway. With his hand poised over his holster, Preston peered past Paul into the cube, where he noted the dead man's wide-eyed stare, his gaping mouth, the plastic tube pointed at the zenith.

"There's a hole in the ceiling," murmured Paul, and he pointed at the triangular gap overhead with a shaking finger. But Preston didn't even look. Instead he stepped gingerly past the body in the chair and bent over the tech writer's desktop, scanning the shingled papers and notepads. He hooked his finger through the handle of the dead man's coffee cup, lifted it, and sniffed, once, twice. Then he put the cup very carefully back where he'd found it and turned.

"What about her?" He lifted his chin past Paul, towards Renee lying comatose on the desk in the cube across the aisle.

"She fainted," Paul said.

Preston grunted and stepped across the aisle, his palm against the butt of his pistol. He laid two fingers along Renee's throat, grunted again when he detected a pulse, and stepped back into the aisle. He clutched Paul's arm and swung him into the cube with Renee.

"You just set there," he said, "and keep an eye on her." He waved his hand at the tech writer's cube. "And don't touch nothin' in that cube there."

"No chance of that." Paul dropped into the chair across from Renee.

Paul remembered the next half hour in disconnected pieces. At some point, before the EMS guys came, Renee sat straight up off the desk like the Bride of Frankenstein, took one look at the corpse across the aisle, and passed out cold again. Either before or after that, but before the paramedics, Olivia Haddock marched briskly into the aisle, halted, and gave a little, high-pitched gasp. Paul poked his head out of the unassigned cube, and she gasped again, clutching her purse before her with both hands.

"He died," was all Paul could manage to say, and she bolted into her own cube, where he remembered seeing her sometime later, perched on the edge of her chair, her purse toppled over on her knees, both hands pressed to her mouth.

He remembered beefy Hispanic paramedics in white, short-sleeved shirts and black, thick-soled shoes; he remembered a pair of cops with professionally even voices, a man and a woman each with a hissing radio clipped to a shoulder. He remembered the clank of an oxygen bottle and the clatter of a collapsible gurney. He remembered the snap of rubber gloves.

"There's a suspicious white powder in the cup." Preston hovered at the edge of the scene. "Should I notify the Hazmat team? Should I call the FBI?"

A paramedic sniffed the cup. His plastic name tag read P. HERNANDEZ. "That's creamer," he said.

"This fella was in bad shape to begin with," said the other medic, who had plugged his ears with a stethoscope and was placing the metal disc here and there over the dead tech writer's body. His name tag read H. QUIROGA. He glanced across the aisle at Paul. "What was wrong with him?"

"Cancer," said Paul. "I think."

"Well, bag the cup," said H. Quiroga. "But I don't think you can pin this one on Al Qaeda. This ol' boy just up and died."

"There's a hole in the ceiling," murmured Paul.

"Say what?" said H. Quiroga.

Paul swallowed and said louder, "There's a hole in the ceiling. A gap." He pointed, without looking. "In the tiles."

H. Quiroga peered at Paul, and Preston narrowed his eyes. P. Hernandez, who was lifting the coffee cup by one finger into a large Ziploc bag, looked at Paul as well. Then all three men lifted their eyes to the ceiling. Paul drew a breath and lifted his gaze, too. The suspended ceiling was smooth and undisturbed, all the panels firmly settled in place. Preston and the paramedics craned their necks and surveyed the ceiling in all directions, but the panels as far as anyone could see were flawlessly rectilinear, dwindling in perfect perspective.

"That one," Paul insisted, his finger shaking, "that one was crooked when I came in."

The paramedics exchanged a look, but Preston continued to

watch the ceiling, turning slowly in place as if he were surveying the constellations. He stroked his moustache, across and down. H. Quiroga coiled up his stethoscope and lifted an eyebrow at Paul. "Did he say anything before he died?" he asked.

"I wasn't here when he died." Paul's throat was so dry he could scarcely speak.

"Did he cry out, 'The speckled band!' " H. Quiroga suppressed a smile. "Sherlock Holmes joke. Nobody ever gets it."

I get it, you asshole, thought Paul, but he said nothing. P. Hernandez came out of the cube, dangling the cup in the plastic bag, and said to Paul, "Don't mind him, bro. Hector thinks he sees all this weird shit."

"I'm just saying," said H. Quiroga, jerking his thumb over his shoulder at the corpse, "this one looks like he was just plain scared to death." Then he winked at his partner, and both men laughed.

The next thing Paul remembered, the tech writer was zipped up in what looked like a large, plastic garment bag. He remembered P. Hernandez murmuring to H. Quiroga, when he thought Paul couldn't hear, "Don't be scaring the civilians, amigo." He remembered the rattle of wheels as the gurney rolled away, remembered giving his name and phone number to one of the cops, remembered the ring of blank faces gazing in his direction from all around. He remembered the faces of the Colonel, J. J., and Bob Wier lined up like three pale moons rising over the cube horizon. The Colonel was in the middle and his mouth was moving, though he was too far away for Paul to hear what he was saying. On either side of him J. J. and Bob Wier nodded slowly. Just as long as they don't smile, thought Paul.

Nolene arrived, and Paul seemed to remember Preston lifting his gaze silently to the ceiling over the dead man's cube, and Nolene lifting her eyes to the same spot. A glance passed between them, and Nolene nodded. Then she put her massive arm around the trembling Renee and escorted her back to her own cube; from behind, Paul thought numbly, they looked like Pooh and Piglet. He remembered sitting in his own chair in his own cube, drinking a paper cone of water that Preston had brought him. Preston glanced up at the ceiling tiles and lowered his voice. "Are you okay?"

"He must have lain there all weekend." Paul glanced across the aisle at Olivia, but she was gone. When had she left? "He stayed late to work, and he *died*."

"What a way to go, huh?" said Preston.

"Jesus, sometime over the weekend, he did something for me." Paul gestured over his shoulder at his computer. "He got onto my computer and put the watermark Rick wanted in the document I'm working on." He shuddered. "At least, I think it was him." Paul turned suddenly in his chair and looked at his computer screen. The Post-it was gone. He stood abruptly and glanced all over his desk; it must have fallen off. Or maybe one of police officers took it.

"Who else would it be?" Preston said, behind him.

"I don't know," said Paul.

SIXTEEN

THAT MORNING RENEE AND OLIVIA HADDOCK WERE each allowed to take a personal day and go home. Despite his promotion, Paul was still a temp and did not get personal days. Not long after the dead tech writer was wheeled away, Paul's phone rang.

"Paul!" barked Rick. "That watermark I asked you to put in the RFP? How's that goin'?"

Paul was sitting slumped in his office chair, his gaze lost in the tiny print of the two-page spread on his computer screen. The only readable text was the faint, gray-scale watermark on each page, the two of them slanted at an identical angle like a ghostly pair of chevrons: DRAFT DOCUMENT.

"Hey, chief, you there?" said Rick down the phone. "You alive or what?"

"I'm here," breathed Paul.

"Well, I'm relieved. I hear y'all are dropping like flies at that end of the office."

Paul said nothing.

"Now about that watermark," Rick went on.

"I'm looking at it."

"Fan*tas*tic! You figgered it out!"

Somebody did, thought Paul, but all he said was, "Yes."

"Say, print a coupla pages of that bad boy out and let me take a look-see, willya?"

"Okay." As slow as a somnambulist, Paul lifted his hand to his mouse.

"Chop chop, Paul. It's the early bird that gathers no moss."

Paul printed out the two pages on the screen, then levitated numbly from his chair and glided down the aisle towards the printer by Nolene's desk. He had no need to temper his pace this morning—Renee, lucky girl, was home by now, with the covers pulled over her head—but he was afraid to move any faster, afraid of what he might see coming around each corner en route to the printer. The office was sepulchrally silent; the subterranean gloom of cubeland seemed gloomier than ever. The suspended ceiling pressed down from overhead like a bleak, winter overcast, clamping down on the room from horizon to horizon like a lid. What if they're all around me, he thought, right now, in the ceiling, or waiting in the aisle, with their pale faces and rows of sharp teeth? What if—and oh, this was worse—what if one-half of my life has begun to leak into the other half, the nighttime half into the daytime half? What if Charlotte has gotten out of my apartment? What if she's waiting for me in Rick's office *right now*, sprawled across the desk, her tail switching over the edge, watching the door with her fathomless black eyes?

Paul nearly turned around and went back, but his legs carried him onward on shaky knees. He saw no one; he heard no one. He rounded the corner of the main aisle and saw an empty seat at Nolene's desk, the printer heaving out his two lonely pages. Maybe they're all dead! he thought, lurching onward like a zombie. Maybe *I'm* dead! This is the circle of hell reserved for Kitty Drowners and Failed Academics, an eternity of meaningless work in an empty office in an eternal twilight.

Rick's office door was open, and the light from his courtyard window was a painful glare, too bright to look into directly. It shone down the aisle, drawing Paul along on his unsteady feet.

"Hey, pilgrim," said a rasping voice behind Paul, and a firm grip was laid upon his shoulder.

"Jesus!" cried Paul, twisting free.

"Easy, compadre," said the Colonel, his eyes twinkling.

"Don't *do* that!" Paul hated the whine in his voice, and he glanced around him to see if anyone had noticed. J. J. and Bob Wier clutched the tops of their cubes and peered over like a pair of Kilroys, J. J. glowering, Bob Wier's eyes round and shining.

"I think you need a little quality time at lunch," said the Colonel in a gravelly murmur. "Come see us."

Paul waved him away and continued up the aisle towards the printer.

"Don't be afraid, Paul," the Colonel said. "Big changes are coming."

"It's the only way," said Bob Wier.

"The eyes of Texas are upon you," said J. J., "asshole."

The pages from the RFP rattled in Paul's hand as he plucked them from the printer. Nolene had reappeared from nowhere. She beckoned him.

"How you feelin', hon?" she asked, folding her hands on her desktop.

Paul gripped the edge of her cube and struggled to keep his voice low and even. "How would you feel if you found a dead guy in the cube next to yours first thing in the morning?"

Nolene nodded. "Why'n't you take a sick day? I'm sure Rick wouldn't mind."

Just then Rick's voice floated through his door, out of the glare, like the voice of the almighty. " 'Zat Paul out there? You got my watermark, son?"

Nolene sighed silently, with her eyes closed. Then she leveled her gaze, severe and maternal, at Paul. "Or I can *make* it so he don't mind. You just say the word."

Paul waved at her speechlessly and went into Rick's office.

He shut the door behind him and collapsed in one of the chairs across from Rick's desk.

"Here," he said, and he shoved the RFP pages at Rick. They were airborne for a moment, then fluttered to Rick's desktop like a pair of leaves. Rick planted a palm on each one and slid them towards him, lifting his hands to peer at each page in turn.

"Perfect," he breathed, his eyebrows bounding. "Took you long enough, but you got it."

"I didn't do it." Paul dug his fingers into the armrests of the chair to keep them from trembling. His heart was still racing from the fright the Colonel had given him.

"Say what?" Rick's eyebrows bounded to their furthest north.

"I didn't put the watermark in the document."

"Then who did?"

"*He* did!" Paul's voice climbed a couple of octaves. "The tech writer! The guy who died over the weekend!" Paul pointed unsteadily at Rick's door. "He did it for me! And then . . . and then . . . he *died.*" Paul clamped his palm over his mouth to keep from whimpering.

"Ah." Rick flung himself back in his chair so forcefully that he nearly tipped over backwards. Outside the window, the bare limbs of the dying oak seemed to reach towards him out of the glare. Rick clamped his fingers together behind his head and lifted his eyes to the ceiling. "Coupla temps, cubes right next to each other, y'all got to be friends over there." Rick didn't even seem to be addressing Paul but explaining the situation to himself out loud. "I guess that's what y'all call *solidarity.* . . ."

"I didn't even know his name," said Paul.

"Huh." Rick lowered his gaze to Paul and blinked, as if surprised to see him there.

"He died. At work." Paul's mouth was dry. "All because . . . because . . . *she* . . ."

" 'She'?"

"Olivia." Paul's knuckles were white on the armrest. "I heard her tell him he couldn't go home till he finished the job, or she wouldn't pay him. I *heard* her."

Rick lurched forward in his chair. "Way-ul," he said, not looking at Paul. He moved his hands aimlessly among the papers on his desk. "We sent her home."

"What for?" Paul said. "So she can't kill anybody else?"

"Well now," said Rick. "Well now."

Keep your mouth shut, Paul told himself. You need this job. But it was all he could do not to stand and hurl his chair through the glass and into the bony grasp of the oak tree.

"I tell you what." Rick's hands twitched through a pile of folders. "Why don't you take the rest of the day off?"

"Don't you people get it? I'm a *temp*. I live paycheck to paycheck, Rick. I can't afford to lose the hours."

"Yep. Welp." Rick still wouldn't look at Paul. "You won't have to. Just fill in the hours on your time sheet like you always do, and I'll sign it. Go on home."

Paul blinked at Rick. He relaxed his grip on the armrests. "Are you serious?"

"Serious as a heart attack, Paul. Now g'wan, git, before I change my mind."

Paul rose unsteadily to his feet, pulled open the door, and started down the aisle without looking back. He stiffened as he passed the Colonel's cube, but he managed to round the corner without incident. He came around the next corner into his own little side street and stopped short at the sight of florid Ray from Building Services hulking over the desk in the tech writer's cube, clearing the littered desktop into a cardboard box. Paul hurried past him into his own cube, where he dropped in his chair and sat for a moment with his head propped in his hands.

"Jesus H. Christ," he muttered. "They only just wheeled him away." He turned and aimed his voice over the partition into the next cube. "Don't you people have any fucking decency?" He switched off his monitor and his desk lamp and heaved himself out of the chair and into the aisle. Ray stood holding the box with one hand and a fistful of papers in the other.

"Say, bud," he said breathlessly as Paul passed the doorway

of the dead man's cube, "how 'bout you give me a hand here? You could hold the box for me."

Paul shot him an angry glance and stalked away.

In the lobby Preston was on the phone, but he gave Paul a meaningful look and held up his finger for Paul to wait a moment. But Paul just flipped his badge across the counter and kept going. By the time he got to his car and rolled down his windows and opened the hatchback to let the heat out, he was still trembling. He slammed the hatchback and lowered himself behind the wheel, the shocks groaning under him, and he lifted his key to the ignition. But he didn't start the car; he only gripped the steering wheel loosely and stared through his cracked and spotted windshield at the glare of the morning sun off the SUVs and pickups in the parking lot. Little waves of heat trembled off the electric sheen of hoods and bumpers and high roof lines. Beyond the embankment, Paul thought he could actually see the stale odor of the river rising off the water. I left my lunch inside, he thought, but I'm not going back for it. I may never go back into that building again. But where am I going to go? Do I really want to spend the whole day in that grotty apartment with Charlotte? He tightened his fingers around the steering wheel and lowered his head.

"Paul?"

The voice outside his window startled him, and Paul banged the horn with his forehead.

"Aw, Christ!" he moaned. "Are you people *trying* to drive me crazy?"

Callie stooped at his window, her brow furrowed. She wore a man's blue dress shirt and a faded pair of jeans—very nicely, too, Paul thought, even in his distress. She clutched the collar of her shirt together with one hand.

"You okay?" she said.

Paul sighed and sagged back against the headrest of his seat. Callie glanced back at the building, then lifted her other hand and brushed his shoulder with her fingertips. "Ray said you was in kind of a state," she said.

"The guy in the cube next to me . . . ," Paul began. "The tech writer. He—"

"I know," Callie said, crouching closer, rubbing his shoulder. "It's just . . . it could have been me, you know?"

"I don't think so, hon." She brushed his hair with the backs of her fingers. "Poor Dennis, he was real sick."

Dennis. Was that his name? Paul sighed again and said, "Rick said I could go home."

"Good for Rick."

"It's just . . ." He turned to meet her gaze. "The thing is . . ." How could he tell her why he was afraid of his own apartment? Especially now?

Callie bit her lip. She glanced up at the building again, then stepped back and dug in the pocket of her jeans. She pulled out a ring of keys and began to pry one free with her long fingers. "Here," she said, and offered Paul her apartment key.

Paul stared at the key in her palm as if he had never seen anything like it. He looked up and said, "Seriously?" in a little boy's voice.

"Take it." She shoved the key through the window and dropped it in his palm.

"Thank you," Paul breathed. A warm relief spread through him down to his toes.

"I don't have a TV or nothin'. Just, y'know, the anthology." Callie lifted a corner of her lips. "You can brush up on your Shakespeare."

Paul grabbed her by the wrist and tugged her down to the window.

"Don't," she said, glancing at the blank, tinted windows of the building, but he pulled her to him, and she kissed him sweetly. Then she stepped back, blushing. "Just be sure you're there when I get home. I can't get in without that key."

SEVENTEEN

"ARE YOU AWAKE?"

No answer.

"Paul? Are you awake, honey?"

A sigh. "Yeah."

"You okay?"

"Sure."

"You feel tense."

"I guess."

"Anything I can do to help?"

Another sigh.

"Do you like it when I do this?"

"Sure." Pause. "Not right now."

"Well, that's a first." Pause. "What'd you do here all day?"

"Slept. I slept all day."

"I reckon that's why you can't sleep now."

"Sorry."

"It's alright. Means you were real happy to see me when I got home."

"Sorry about that."

"Don't apologize. I was a little surprised when I walked in the door, but *Lord*. Better'n having a cat rub up against you as you walk in the door."

"A cat?"

"Yeah, you know how a cat that's been left alone all day'll rub up against you when you come home? Wind between your legs and such? Well, you were like a big, horny cat—"

"A *cat?*"

" 'Cause you were certainly winding between my legs there for a while—"

"What made you think of a cat?"

"And I made you *purr*, too, didn't I—"

"Why do you say 'a cat'?"

"I know all your favorite places, don't I. You're just a big ol' tomcat."

"Don't."

"Come on, one pussy to another. Who's a good boy?"

"*Stop it!*"

Silence. An angry sigh. "What the hell's wrong with you?"

"Nothing."

"Bullshit." Pause. "You don't have to stay here, pal. You can just find the goddamn door."

"I'm sorry."

" 'Cause I don't need the goddamn aggravation. If I want some sulky, tongue-tied cowboy, I can go down to Sixth Street right now and get me one."

"I said I'm sorry."

" 'Cause I've fucked a lot of cowboys, Paul. I know what I'm talking about, and I'm sick to death of that shit."

"I mean it, I'm sorry."

"Shut up. I ain't done with you." A sigh. "You're my first college professor. I thought you'd be different. But you're just like all the rest. Got plenty to say when you want to get my panties off, but afterwards, it's like lying here with a length of two-by-four. 'Uh huh.' 'Sure.' 'You bet.' " Furious pause. "Well, Fuck. That. Shit."

A long pause.

"Callie—"

"Yeah, go on. Say something smart, Professor."

"Don't call me that."

"Don't call you what?"

" 'Professor.' I hate that."

"Why not? You mean you're not a professor?"

Sigh. "Not anymore I'm not, and I never will be again. I'm a typist, and a temp typist at that. You tell me: Is that a step up or down from a cowboy?"

"Paul—"

"Okay, a *tech writer.* I guess that's better than a typist. By about four dollars an hour. That's what? Another thirty-two dollars a day. Another, let's see, hundred and sixty dollars a week."

"Ooh baby, keep talking. Self-pity gets me hot."

A long pause. "He *died*, Callie! That fucking bitch Olivia worked him to *death!* That poor bastard died *in a cubicle!"*

"Paul . . ."

"He died working overtime! And he wasn't even getting paid for it!"

"Paul, listen to me. He had cancer. He was dead anyway. He just hadn't laid down yet."

"Well, I know just how he feels."

"Jesus Christ on a stick, what planet are you from? You think you're the only person who works a shitty job? 'Cause on the planet *I'm* from, which is planet *Earth*, you son of a bitch, you got it pretty sweet. You get to sit all day in the air-conditioning, and you don't have to deal with the public or take their sass or pick up their trash or scrape the food off their plates or wipe their ass. . . ."

Silence.

"Fuck." A sigh. "First I'm an asshole because I won't tell you what I think. Then when I do, I'm a self-pitying asshole. What do you want from me, Callie? Make up your goddamn mind."

A long silence. "Well." A touch in the dark. "I guess that ain't hardly fair, is it?"

"It doesn't matter."

"Paul . . ."

"Really, it doesn't matter. It's okay. Forget it."

A long silence. Then, in the dark, singing, in a hoarsely sexy voice, an Oklahoma Janis. " 'You haul sixteen tons, what do you get?' " A nudge in the dark. "C'mon, cowboy, you know this."

"You want me to *sing?*"

" 'Sixteen tons, what do you get . . . ?' "

"You're not serious."

Closer, deeper, more sensually. " 'You haul sixteen tons, what do you get . . . ?' "

A laugh, a sigh, then a quavering tenor, a little out of tune. " 'Another day older and deeper in debt . . .' "

Her breath hot on his ear. " 'Saint Peter don't you call me, 'cause I can't go . . .' "

Together, not quite in harmony: " 'I owe my soul to the company store!' " Then, wordlessly, "Do, do, do, do, do do do do."

Laughter. "That's not from the *Norton Anthology.*"

"Not yet."

A pair of sighs. Sheets rustling.

"Okay if I touch you there?"

"Mmm."

"Whoa. Dead man couldn't do *that.*"

"Like you said, I'm dead, but I won't lie down."

"Oh." A gasp. "*Oh.*"

"How's that?"

"That's it."

"Is that good?"

"Oh, that's *it.*" Then, tenderly, "Honey?"

"Yeah."

"Fuck me sweet."

"Like this?"

"Please, yes."

"Right here?"

"Oh, you got it. Yes."

Murmurs. A moan.

Then, louder. "Oh Jesus, I'm close."

Breathlessly. "It's okay, honey, don't wait for me."

"Oh, God, Callie, I don't want to die in Texas!"

Hard breathing. A sniffle.

"There, there, baby, there, there." A kiss. "Me neither."

EIGHTEEN

EARLY THAT TUESDAY a glum Paul stood before a pull-down white screen in Building Services to pose for his permanent TxDoGS badge. This morning Callie displayed all the warmth of a DMV clerk, barking at Paul to look at the red dot on the camera. Still, after the photo, she glanced into the outer office to make sure Ray wasn't lumbering into view, then kissed Paul quickly and pushed him out the door. Forty minutes later, as he stared gloomily at his computer monitor, the laminated badge slid across the desktop at his elbow. Paul gazed without recognition at his own flash-bleached face and zombie gaze. Callie didn't so much as touch his shoulder, and by the time Paul turned slowly in his chair, she was gone. He clipped on his new badge, and then carried the old, temporary one down to the security desk on the first floor. Without meeting Preston's eye, Paul slid the old badge across the counter. "I don't need this anymore."

"How you doin' this morning?" Preston asked, keeping his voice low.

"I'm okay." Paul started to turn away.

" 'Cause if you want to talk about anything," Preston said, lowering his gaze to catch Paul's, "or if you see anything you want to tell me about—"

Paul recognized the look in the security guard's eye. It was Loser's Solidarity, and Paul had seen it before during his long fall from grace in academia. Back then some colleague who was even worse off than Paul would meet his eye in the hallway or across the faculty lounge, with a mournful, liquid gaze that said, *Aren't we a couple of sad bastards?* This look had been worse than being ignored by old friends, worse even than being condescended to by graduate students, because it usually came from some haggard, aging adjunct at the end of his string or, worst of all, from some clapped-out, tenured old hack who, after forty years, had never risen above the rank of assistant professor and hadn't published a book since the Eisenhower administration. It was a look that said, *It's alright. Just lie down and die with the rest of us.*

Paul stepped sharply back as if Preston had tried to touch him. Who the fuck *is* this guy? Paul wondered. Another retired military man padding out his pension. The last thing I need, Paul thought angrily, is sympathy from some ex-master-sergeant. His throat seized up, but he managed to say, "I'm okay," as he moved away across the lobby.

Back in his cube he kept his head down, happy to let the nubbly walls block out the wider horizons of the office. He left only once, to go to the bathroom. At the urinal he found his pulse racing as he strained to pee, and he emptied his bladder at last out of sheer willpower, in squirts and dribbles. The men's room seemed too quiet, as if someone was waiting for him to leave. At first he couldn't bring himself to look up at the ceiling, though he glanced up in the mirror as he washed his hands. The panels were in perfect order. Hurrying back to his cube, he plucked up the nerve to look into the empty cube next to his. The cubicle had been stripped bare. The computer and office chair were gone; not even a stray paper clip remained.

The bare desktop gleamed, and the shampooed nap of the carpet stood in pert swirls.

As he tried to concentrate on the RFP, Paul was aware of Olivia Haddock across the aisle, glaring wide-eyed at her own monitor, her spine rigid, her lumbar pillow jammed tight behind her backside. She battered the keys of her keyboard as if she were trying to drill them through her desktop. What could she be typing with such determination? The poor dead tech writer, the late, unlamented Dennis, had been hired because she couldn't write code, so she certainly wasn't finishing whatever he'd left undone. Indeed, Paul wondered if the tech writer had left her anything to do. No doubt Dennis had hung on, with his death's-head gaze and his whistling breathing tube, until the last keystroke, in mortal hope of a final paycheck. It was as if Olivia had said to him, You can't even *die* until you finish the job, as if Death himself had told him, No, *you* take this job and shove it.

So now Olivia could only be pretending to work, in the grip of desperation about the safety of her job. She knows I'm watching her, Paul thought. She must feel my gaze like needles on the back of her neck. He wanted to rise from his chair and cross the aisle and peer over her shoulder; he wanted to breathe his hot, accusing breath on the livid rim of her ear. She's vamping, he thought. I know the signs. She's trying to look busy, trying to look as if she hasn't *killed a guy*, obsessively filling her screen with nonsense like that poor sap in *The Shining*, "All work and no play make Olivia . . ." Make Olivia *what* exactly? Less guilty? Innocent? Nobody's innocent, thought Paul bitterly, listening to the angry clatter of her keyboard—certainly not Olivia.

The ghostly watermark on his own screen—DRAFT DOCUMENT—swam in and out of focus behind the clotted text of the RFP. When had Dennis had time to add it? Before or after he finished his own work? Was it the last thing he'd done before he staggered, gasping, back to his own cube and keeled over dead? None of the text in the RFP seemed to make any sense to Paul now, or rather, it all seemed to say the same thing, over and over, marching slowly up the screen while the watermark shone through like a phantom:

All work and no play make Dennis dead.
All work and no play make Dennis dead.
All work and no play make Dennis dead. . . .

At lunchtime Paul left his cube in search of Callie, but he couldn't find her. In Building Services, Ray merely shrugged when Paul asked where she was. So to avoid the oppressive bonhomie of another lunch with the Colonel and his sidekicks, Paul left the building and went across the street to a sandwich shop and ate half of a meatball sub that he couldn't really afford. Afterwards he walked once around the GSD Building in the baking heat until he was covered all over in a fine sheen of sweat.

After lunch Paul again sought the comfort of Callie, if only for a moment. He peered through the mail room window on the first floor, where he didn't see her, then he doubled back through the lobby and up the stairs to Building Services, where he didn't see her again. Back at his desk, he bitterly enjoyed the almost unprecedented achievement of seeing Olivia's cube empty while he was settling in to work. After a moment in his chair, in fact, he stood again, furtively surveyed the cube horizon, and then stepped across the aisle to peek at the document on Olivia's computer. Her screen saver was running, a labyrinthine array of self-replicating pipes, and he nudged her mouse with a fingernail. The document popped into view, and Paul's heart stopped: On Olivia's screen, in a two-page display, Paul instantly recognized the numbered paragraphs of the RFP. The print was too fine to read, but the twin chevrons of the watermark bled through the text like a brand.

"Oh fuck," muttered Paul, staggering back and catching himself in Olivia's doorway. Pulse racing, knees trembling, he trotted up the aisle towards Rick's office. "Oh *fuck*," he muttered. "Fuck, fuck, fuck." It was still the tag end of lunch hour, and cubeland was mostly empty. He rattled past Renee's cube without encountering her; the cubes of his three colleagues on the outsourcing project stood empty; not even Nolene was at her desk. Before he could calm himself, Paul erupted through the door of Rick's office, only to be stopped short by the sight of Olivia hovering over Rick like a vampire. Rick's gut was pressed against the edge of his desk; he had spread his elbows, and he drummed his fingers arrhythmically. His eyebrows wobbled as he scowled at a print copy of the RFP, spread across the desk like stunned prey. Olivia bent over his shoulder close enough to bite him, indicating a line of text with one razor-sharp talon. As Paul caught himself in the doorway, Rick continued to frown at the document, but Olivia looked up with the slow, steady, heartless gaze of a raptor.

"*Hel*-lo!" she trilled, in a piercing singsong. "You're back!" She stood erect, away from Rick, and very pointedly glanced at her watch. "Did you get my note?"

Paul clutched the sides of the doorway, rocking on the balls of his feet, ready to flee. "What note?" he breathed.

"I messaged you," she said, "to tell you we had a meeting with Rick"—she glanced at her watch again—"well, *now*."

Paul gripped the metal doorjamb tightly, afraid that if he let go his buckling knees would topple him to the floor. Rick was still pouting at the RFP, and now he lifted his gaze to Paul, his eyebrows bouncing nearly to his hairline.

"You comin' or goin' there, Paul?" he said. "Is you in, or is you ain't?"

Paul pried his fingers off the doorway and slithered into the room. He pressed his back against the wall and crossed his arms awkwardly, then let them drop. Finally he shoved his hands in his pockets. He fixed his eyes on the floor so he wouldn't have to look at Olivia.

"Way-ul." Rick flung himself back in his chair. "Let's get all our ducks in a barrel." He beamed at Paul. "I'm happy to announce a reallocation of manpower—" Rick's state-sponsored sensitivity training pulled him up short like a leash. "Or womanpower. Or whatever. Y'all know what I mean." He dropped his hand on the desk. "Anyhoo, as of today, Olivia is joining the RFP team as a consultant. Seems her other project . . ." Rick sucked his cheeks, gazing at a point in the middle of the room.

"Luckily," Olivia volunteered, rescuing him, "Dennis was able to finish his work before he left us." She pressed her palms together just below her breastbone, as if squeezing some poor, defenseless creature to death.

"That's right!" said Rick, a little too loudly. He drummed his fingers once on his desk.

"Beta testing," muttered Paul, glowering at the floor. He clenched his fists in his pockets.

"Sorry?" said Rick.

Paul swallowed against a dry throat and said, a little louder, "Beta testing. Dennis didn't have a chance to *test* the program before he . . . before he . . ." He felt his face get hot.

"Testing the program wasn't part of his job," Olivia said, widening her eyes in Paul's direction. She spoke as if to a child. "He was only hired to *write* it."

Paul's fists felt like rocks in his pockets. He lifted his hot gaze to Olivia and opened his mouth, but nothing came out.

"I reckon that's all water over the roadway," said Rick, and he hiked himself up to the desk again. "I just wanted you to know that Olivia here is going to be sitting in with us from now on, giving us a new perspective on thangs." Rick glanced at Paul, his eyebrows dancing. "I'm counting on you, Paul, to fill her in on the details, since you're the tech writer and you know the innards of the thing—"

"Rick gave me the password," interrupted Olivia, "so I could print a copy off the server. While I was waiting for you to come back from lunch." She leveled her huntress's gaze at Paul again. "Did you know, Paul, that paragraph 4.3.3 in 'Parts, Supplies, and Fluids' is identical to paragraph 6.2.3 in 'Repair Parts Management'?"

Paul squeezed his fists bloodless and muttered, "There's some redundancy built into the document—"

"Whatever." Olivia squared her shoulders and fixed her gaze on the top of Rick's head. "Is that all for now?"

"What?" Rick was caught off guard, flicking his fingernail at a spot on the fat end of his tie.

"Do you need me anymore right now, Rick?" said Olivia. "I have a *lot* of work to do."

"Git along, then!" cried Rick. "Y'all get back to work and we'll reconvene at a later, uh, a later . . ." He waved his hand vaguely, then gathered up the loose sheets of the RFP in both hands and rapped the edges against his desk. Olivia took the pages from him and maneuvered around the desk towards the door. Paul could feel her force field press up against his; he could almost hear the hum. He pushed himself against the wall as Olivia minced past him, her spine taut, her chin lifted, the RFP pressed to her bosom like a breastplate. When she was out the door, Paul sagged away from the wall and painfully un-clenched his hands; his fingernails had squeezed little, white half-moons into the heels of his palms. Rick cast about his desk and grabbed a folder at random; he spread it wide and dove into it. Paul edged up to the front of the desk, and Rick acted as if he hadn't noticed, lifting a page of the document in the file folder to peer unseeing at the one underneath. Paul knew he was shamming because Rick was reading the file upside down.

"Am I working *for* that woman," Paul asked, his voice low and tight, "or *with* her?"

"Hm?" Rick blinked up at Paul.

"You heard me."

Rick's eyebrows wobbled, and he drew a deep breath. "Well, son, you're working for the Texas Department of General Services at their sole discretion. So just like me, and Olivia, and everybody else in this cheer building, you do whatever's necessary to serve the people of the great state of Texas."

He held Paul's gaze until Paul looked away. The twisted limbs of the dying oak beyond Rick's office window seemed to be reaching for him.

"Is that all?" Rick lowered his eyes to the file folder.

Paul leaned over the desk and, with both hands, turned Rick's file right side up. Then he wheeled out the door. Back in his own cube, Paul could *feel* Olivia across the aisle working her pen like a scalpel through the RFP. He heard the busy tap and scratch of her pen, heard it stop, heard her utter a bone-chilling *"Hm."*

I can't do this, Paul thought. I can't sit here all afternoon while she does *that*. Callie, where the hell are you? He stood and snatched three soda cans from the row of empties against the back of his desk. Squeezing the cans together between his hands, he bolted around the corner into the fluorescent glare of the elevator lobby. He half expected to see Dennis the Dead Tech Writer beyond the tall window, smoking a cigarette and laughing at him, but the landing was empty. On wobbly knees Paul approached the recycling box, a waist-high, square-topped cardboard shaft with a single, can-sized hole in its fitted lid. ALUMINUM ONLY, it read across the front, NO BOTTLES PLEASE. NO TRASH. Paul set the cans on top of the lid, and he violently flattened one of them between his hands, raising sharp angles against his palms. Squeezing his lips bloodlessly together, he jammed the can through the lid, expecting to hear it hit the other cans in the box.

Only he heard nothing. After the *pop* it made going through the hole, the can had made no metallic *clink* of contact with the other cans. It made no sound at all. Paul stood very still for a moment, then leaned over and peered into the hole. All he saw was blackness, so he bent lower and turned his ear to the opening. He still heard nothing, but was that a slight breeze he felt, dank and cold, brushing his earlobe?

He cradled the second can in the curl of his fingers. Without crushing it, he gingerly stuck it through the hole and held it there for a moment. Then, at the instant he released it, he jerked forward over the hole and peered in. Again, nothing, so he turned his ear once more to the hole, listening, listening, until he almost thought he heard, after a long, breathless wait, a tiny, distant, echoing *clink!*

Paul started back from the box. The last can was sitting on

the corner of the cardboard lid. Paul picked up the can and, at arm's length, slowly slid it halfway into the hole. He held his breath, but before he could release it, the can was jerked from his fingers, as if something *inside* the box had grabbed it. Paul leaped back, all the way across the lobby, until he was pressed against the floor-length window. Through the pounding of his pulse in his ears, he swore he could hear, issuing from the infernally black little hole on top of the box, a long, inhuman sigh.

NINETEEN

BUT IT WAS ONLY THE ELEVATOR, making its groan of hydraulic ennui as it reached the second floor. The door rattled
open, and a pert young woman in a trim, green business suit
stepped blinking into the entry. She was clipping a TxDoGS
visitor's badge to her lapel, and as Paul peeled himself off the
window, she turned a blank, overly made-up face to him. Her
eyes lit up and she delivered a megawatt smile.

"Paul?" she chirped, cocking her head. "Paul Trilby?"

"Yes?"

"I was just coming to see you!" She stepped towards him,
beaming. "The security guard sent me up! I almost didn't recognize you!"

"Okay." Paul warily noted the exits—he could bolt around
the corner to the men's room or back through the doorway into
cubeland.

"How you doin'?" The young woman spoke as if she knew
him, canting her head so that her bangs bounced.

"Good." Paul shot a glance at the recycling box, half expecting to see the lid lifted from within by pale fingers.

"I got somethin' for you," said the woman in a kittenish growl, pursing her bright lips. She was clearly a little too much for TxDoGS. The waist of her jacket was nipped in too tight, her skirt was too short, and her legs were too trim. She reminded Paul of a younger, prettier, more fuckable version of his landlady, Mrs. Prettyman.

Erika! he nearly cried aloud. The young woman from the temp agency who had found him the job at TxDoGS! And she's here with my retroactive paycheck!

"Oh, good!" Paul said, with a great deal of relief. After the shock of finding himself yoked to Olivia Haddock, and after his semihallucinatory little encounter just now with the recycling box, fate had wheeled the lovely Erika into view, with her bright mouth and narrow waist and lovely legs, bringing him money.

"I hope you like it," Erika said. She turned up her lovely palm and offered him a little blue cardboard box.

"I beg your pardon?" Paul took the box. TIFFANY & CO., read the lid.

"It's our Outstanding Stand-in award!" squeaked Erika.

Paul lifted the little lid and found a silvery tiepin on a cushion of cotton.

"You've been doing *such* a great job for us here," Erika was saying, "I can't begin to tell you! When Rick called us last week to tell us about your raise—and congratulations, by the way!" she cried, touching him lightly on the wrist. "Well, he just *raved* about you! Said he wished he had a permanent position for you!"

Paul tipped the little box onto his palm. The Outstanding Stand-in tiepin was a reproduction of the agency's logo, a tiny, sexless, stylized figure, arms outstretched, inscribed in a circle.

"It's genuine silver plated!" Erika sounded as happy as if she were receiving the award herself. "It's designed specially for us by Tiffany's of New York City! You can't buy it in stores!"

"I'm not surprised," said Paul. So much for his extra money.

He felt like the little figure trapped in the tiepin—tiny, dickless, crucified.

"Now I made real sure you got the tiepin and not the earrings." Erika sounded a little worried at Paul's lack of enthusiasm. "Unless you *want* the earrings."

"No," said Paul. "This'll do."

"Fantastic!" Erika revved up to full force again. "Keep up the good work!" Her smile dimmed as she turned towards the elevator. The click of her heels into the car was like the last nail being tapped into the coffin of Paul's dignity.

"Erika," Paul said, jumping forward, "about my raise—"

"Sorry?" Erika brightened slightly as the elevator door slid shut, and then she was gone.

Paul fumbled the tiepin back into the little box, then he stuffed the box in his pocket and went back to his desk, his shoulders sagging, his legs like lead. He endured an hour or so in his cube, trying to ignore Olivia's vibe from across the aisle, until finally he snatched up the Wells volume and went down to the corner table in the empty, dusky lunchroom. After only five minutes of pretending to read *The Island of Dr. Moreau*, Paul was in luck; Callie appeared at the far end of the room and weaved between the empty tables towards him, her head down, her arms crossed. Paul closed the book, so relieved he almost teared up.

"You have no idea," he said, before she even sat down, "what a crummy fucking day I've had."

Callie sagged into a seat across the table without looking at him. But Paul scarcely noticed, launching into a recitation of the day's disappointments so far. He didn't tell her about the encounter with the recycling box, but he did tell her about Olivia's reassignment to the outsourcing project and about the Dickless Wonder award, or whatever it was called, that Erika had brought him. He was about to pull the offending tiepin out of his pocket and show her when he noticed how singularly unperturbed Callie seemed by his news. "Did you hear what I said?" He leaned across the table, trying to catch her eye. "I'm working for Olivia now! It's my worst fucking nightmare!" He clenched his fists. "She's already *killed* a guy!"

"Yeah," said Callie, barely stirring. "It's what you were saying last night."

"It's different since last night," Paul protested. "Now we're on the same project."

"Yeah, I got that." Callie scowled at the floor.

"And to top it all off," Paul said, losing steam, "I get this insulting little award from some corporate zombie. . . ."

"Is that what's eatin' you?" Callie looked at him sharply. "Or is it that you're working for one woman, while another woman gets to decide when you get your money?"

Paul sat up in his seat as if he'd been slapped. He hadn't felt this way since the first year of graduate school when Elizabeth, his future wife, had berated him in a crowded seminar for his insufficient appreciation of Jane Eyre's sapphic rage—it was Lizzie's contention that the real love story in *Jane Eyre* was between Jane and the original Mrs. Rochester—and now, as then, Paul was reduced to stammering. "I didn't . . . that's not what . . . is that what you . . . ?"

"Forget it," Callie said. *Fergit it.* She waved her hand as if brushing away cobwebs. "I'm sorry."

Paul stammered on. "What I meant was . . ."

Callie sighed; her face was slowly turning red. "I can't see you tonight." *Cain't,* she said.

"Why not?" Paul suddenly felt even more forlorn. At the very least, this meant a long evening alone with Charlotte.

Callie fiddled with her fingers in her lap; she would not meet his eye. "I gotta do something." She glanced at him sidelong. "I gotta meet somebody."

"Gotta meet who?"

She returned her gaze to her lap. "Mr. X," she murmured.

Paul was speechless for a moment, but finally he said, "The musician?"

"Yeah, the musician," she said wearily. "He wants to talk to me about something."

Paul blinked across the empty lunchroom, seeing nothing. "Okay. Fine." How much disappointment could a man take in one day? He drew his book to him across the table and clutched it with both hands. "Why are you telling me? It's none of my business."

Callie frowned. "Guess it ain't."

Paul stood suddenly so that his chair screeched behind him. "I have to get back to work."

"Me too," mumbled Callie, and she was out of her chair in an instant, swinging between the tables. Paul watched her go, then he dropped back into his seat. He drummed his fingers on the fat book before him. "Mother*fucker*," he said out loud, to no one.

A few minutes later, Paul started up the stairs. As he came around the corner into the elevator lobby, he stopped before the recycling box and its hellish little hole. What a day: a lunch he couldn't afford, after which Olivia had blindsided him, Rick had slapped him in the face, and Erika had humiliated him. And now Callie had just kicked him in the balls. Like a nagging little reminder, the sharp angles of the little jewelry box in his pocket dug into his thigh. In a surge of anger, he yanked the box out of his pocket and shoved it down the hole. To his surprise he heard a *clink!* right away, and he wrenched off the loose lid of the box. It was two-thirds full of crushed and sticky cans.

"Oh, *come on*," cried Paul. He dropped his book to the floor, tossed aside the lid of the box, and yanked the box with both hands away from the wall. The cans rattled and the box nearly toppled, but under where it had been standing against the wall, Paul saw only the scuffed tiles of the floor.

"I don't get it," he said, his anger leaching away. He shook the box again; the Tiffany's box settled a little farther into the rattling cans, until only a corner of it was visible. Then he tilted the recycling box back into place and stooped to retrieve the lid. Without a further glance into the box, he squared the lid over the top and stepped back. He felt drained, bone tired.

I'm losing my mind, he thought, as he picked up his book and went back to his cube.

TWENTY

THE FOLLOWING MORNING, Wednesday, Paul did not see Callie's truck in the TxDoGS parking lot. He circled the lot twice in his rattling little Colt until he was certain it wasn't there. Inside, Preston gave him a look of manly concern, which Paul chose to ignore, and after stashing his wretched lunch in the refrigerator, he stuck his head in Building Services and asked Ray as casually as he could where Callie was. Ray's cheeks bulged with a mouthful of breakfast burrito, and Paul had to wait until Ray swallowed, which was like watching a rat pass through a cobra.

"Out sick," Ray said.

"Ah," said Paul, a little less casually than before.

After an hour in his cube of listening to Olivia across the aisle working on the RFP—she *tsked* and *hmm'd* and sighed—Paul worked up the nerve to cross to her doorway and ask if she had any questions so far about the document or the project. He needed to keep this job, and if keeping the job meant swallowing shit from Olivia Haddock, then, by God, he would close his eyes and open wide. "I'd be happy to hear any suggestions," he said, his jaw clenching involuntarily.

Olivia scarcely lifted her eyes from the page before her, which she was converting into a palimpsest of emendations, marginalia, and the bold lime-green tracks of her highlighter. "When I've finished," was all she said, and Paul retreated to his cube.

The morning crawled by. Paul noodled on the RFP, certain that all the work he had put into it so far was about to be overridden or contradicted in the next day or two by Olivia. He worked himself into a zone of numbness where each passing moment was like a fat drop of water accumulating at the mouth of a leaky faucet, growing and growing and growing until Paul didn't think he could stand it for another instant. Then at last the drop fell in slow motion and plinked into the drain, an utter waste of effort, and another tiny drop began to accumulate, glistening and slow. By the end of the morning he was trying to lose himself in an equally futile sexual daydream about the lovely Erika of his temp agency, in which he never got any further than fumbling at the buttons of her blouse. The fantasy kept stuttering back to the start like a tape loop, and Paul sat gazing sightlessly at his monitor, his head propped in his hand, the side of his face squeezed out of all proportion.

"How are you fixed for lunch, Professor?"

Paul nearly overturned his chair. "What?" he gasped, righting himself.

The Colonel, J. J., and Bob Wier huddled in the doorway to his cube. The Colonel pursed his lips, while Bob Wier beamed at Paul and J. J. glowered into the empty cube next door.

"Pull up your socks and follow me." The Colonel grasped Paul firmly by the biceps and hauled him to his feet. "We're taking you to lunch."

A moment later his three colleagues were marching him in a flying wedge up the hall.

"Where are we going?" said Paul.

"Someplace special." J. J. rubbed his palms together. "Hoo-*wee*."

"Lord forgive us," said Bob Wier.

As they passed through the lobby, Paul twisted around to glance up at the balcony, at the doorway of Building Services, only to see Ray lumbering out of the office. Preston watched the flying wedge pass with a narrow gaze, but before he could say anything, they were out the door. In the heat of the parking lot the four men approached a massive, silvery SUV; the Colonel beeped the enormous vehicle from twenty paces away, and the beast's doors unlocked with a hearty *chunk*.

"Shotgun!" cried J. J., trotting towards the vehicle, but the Colonel brought him up short. "Not today, son." He gave Paul a look of manly approbation. "Mr. Trilby's our guest of honor."

Shotgun? Paul hadn't heard that since high school. He endured a petulant glance from J. J. as he climbed up into the front passenger's seat; J. J. and Bob Wier hoisted themselves into the back. Paul settled into a deep bucket seat and hauled the shoulder strap, as wide as an ammo belt, across his chest. The SUV's leather upholstery and dashboard were a rich winered, like the appointments of a private club. With the push of a button the Colonel locked the doors again, and the solid, metallic *chunk* sounded like a penitentiary lockdown. When he started the engine the whole vehicle purred with power.

The Colonel followed the lunchtime line of vehicles out of the lot, then crossed the bridge. Paul could never see over the parapet from his own low-slung heap, but now he seemed to be looking down at the sluggish green water from an impossible height. Dry, freezing air poured out of the AC vents all along the dashboard, and the Colonel lifted his gaze to the rearview mirror and said, "Cold enough back there for you boys?"

"Mmm," said Bob Wier, and J. J. grunted. In the lunchtime traffic the Colonel's vehicle even towered over other SUVs, and once he revved his engine impatiently at some poor subcompact that had the temerity to pull in front of him. Slowly they entered a street of faux-ethnic chain restaurants with hearty, good-time names along the south bank of the river—Bella Bellisimo, Ay Caramba's, Paddy O'Shaughnessy's—and then the Colonel executed a sweeping left turn into a crowded parking lot. Headlights was a low-slung sports bar with a blue-and-green color scheme and a logo that featured a pair of bright, round headlights, each with a pink aureole right in the center, just faint enough to give a corporate spokesman leeway to say, My goodness, they're just a pair of headlights. I don't see anything else, do you?

The four men swung down out of the vehicle, and the Colonel locked it behind them with his remote, ka-*chunk*. The SUV's own headlights flared once, lasciviously. J. J. and Bob Wier loped across the sun-blasted parking lot. Through the restaurant's wide windows, Paul saw a waitress in a tight, low-cut t-shirt leaning pendulously across a table, delivering a plate of buffalo wings. The Colonel hung back and gave Paul a manly squeeze around the shoulders.

"You a Jew, Paul?"

"Sorry?"

"Are you Jewish, son?"

"Uh, no, actually. I'm not."

"Then you never had a bar mitzvah?"

"My parents were Episcopalians."

"Well, just think of this as your TxDoGS bar mitzvah." He gave Paul one last squeeze. "Today you are a man."

Never had Paul gone so far beyond the pale of his former life. Simply setting foot in a Headlights would have ended his academic career, if he'd still had one. The women he had pursued in the coffeehouses north of the river, close to campus—the earnest graduate students in their sleeveless blouses, or Virginia, the willowy chairperson of the History Department—would at the very least have ostracized him immediately if they'd known. The de facto feminism of his former life made his legs weak as the Colonel ushered him into the restaurant's arctic air-conditioning, but at the same time Paul was breathless with anticipation, like an adolescent discovering a stack of *Playboy*s in the back of his father's closet. At the hostess's podium, J. J. bounced eagerly on his toes, while Bob Wier cast his eyes to the floor. " 'The cravings of sinful man, the lust of the eyes,' " he muttered, " 'comes not from the Father but from the world.' One John, two, sixteen."

The tanned and fantastically fit hostess bounded towards them in a pair of spotlessly white running shoes. She was wearing Headlights colors, a filmy pair of blue running shorts and a cut-off, sleeveless t-shirt in green. The shorts were slashed well up her thigh, and the t-shirt ended just below her breasts. Paul's chief impression was of long, firm, fulsomely healthy arms and legs, and a midriff you could bounce a handball off of. The heat from those arms, those legs, and that tummy was making him sweat in spite of the air-conditioning, and he found his eyes drawn to her breasts like a needle to magnetic north. It was only when the hostess spoke that Paul's eyes staggered from her nipples to her unnaturally bright smile. She plucked four laminated menus from the hostess station and tapped them with her long, red nails.

"Four?" she chirped, cocking her head.

"By the window, if you please," said the Colonel, the only one of the four men to display a modicum of cool. In single file they trailed after the swaying hem of the hostess's shorts. Bob Wier shuffled like a prisoner, his eyes on the floor, his face as red as a homegrown tomato. J. J. swiveled his gaze all around the room, unable to fix on just one waitress; if he could, he would have rotated his head a complete 360. Paul's head withdrew between his shoulders, like a turtle's; he felt as if every woman who had ever been angry at him—his mother, his wry seventh-grade teacher Mrs. Altenburg, his fierce thesis advisor Professor Victorinix, his ex-wife Elizabeth, Kymberly, even Callie—was watching him scornfully. The Colonel, meanwhile, carried himself like the aging, corseted John Wayne crossing the parlor of a whorehouse, shoulders squared, hips loose, confident at every moment that the camera was on him and not on the busty young women all around him.

The restaurant had an automotive theme. Bumpers and mag wheels and gleaming exhaust manifolds were suspended from the lights. Handsomely detailed models of famous stock cars lined a ledge just below the ceiling; half of the fiberglass shell of a Formula One racer, sawn lengthwise, was mounted over the bar. Behind the bar Paul noted a shrine to Dale Earnhardt, framed with little American flags, and on the large TV over the bar a NASCAR race was in progress with the sound off. The tables were already crowded with men, mostly middle aged, mostly middle managers, with here and there a few trim young guys in polo shirts. Just loud enough to make the lunch crowd raise their voices, the sound system played one automotive tune after another. As Paul threaded between the tables after the switching backside of the hostess, he heard "Hot Rod Lincoln" segue into "Pink Cadillac." Then he was settled on a tall stool at a tall table of blonde wood, facing the Colonel, with J. J. and Bob Wier against the window.

"What kind of lubrication can I get you guys?" asked the hostess, and the Colonel ordered a pitcher of Kirin.

"I'll have a Sprite," mumbled Bob Wier, aiming his eyes over the young woman's head.

"They got Kirin on tap here?" J. J. said, twisting on his stool to follow the hostess's rhythmic retreat.

The Colonel followed J. J.'s gaze. "They've got everything on tap here," he said.

"A-*rooo*-ga!" said J. J., miming a cartoon wolf. He curled his fingers before his eyes as if they were popping out of his head like telescopes. He lolled his tongue as if it were unscrolling to the floor.

"First Corinthians, ten, thirteen," Bob Wier said, gazing mournfully out the window into the noonday glare. " 'God will not let you be tempted beyond what you can bear.' "

"Amen." The Colonel laughed.

Bob Wier closed his eyes. " 'But when you are tempted, He will also provide a way out so that you can stand up under it.' "

"Will you relax, Reverend?" J. J. said. "Fuck."

"Bob's afraid one of these girls will recognize him from Sunday school," said the Colonel.

"Lord have mercy." Bob Wier laughed nervously. "Would it have killed you guys to go to Applebee's?"

"I'll bet the professor's never been here before," the Colonel said.

"No," said Paul, barely paying attention. At the moment his cerebellum was at war with his medulla oblongata. His lizard brain was watching a particularly long-limbed young woman with boyishly bobbed hair bouncing towards them on her padded shoes; she was athletically balancing a cork-lined tray with a pitcher and four frosted glasses on it over her head, one-handed, which had the effect of pulling her cut-off tee tighter against her breasts. Meanwhile his cerebellum was trying to pretend that he was in a foreign country where he needed to play along with the local customs so as not to offend anybody.

"Methinks the professor's blood is up," said the Colonel.

Paul glared at him. "Quit calling me that," he was about to say, but he was interrupted by the arrival of the long-limbed waitress. Beaming at them all, she set the brimming pitcher one-handed on the table and lifted one of the frosted glasses from the tray; it was already full, with a wedge of lemon squeezed over the rim.

"Which of y'all had the Sprite?" she sang, and Bob Wier speechlessly waggled his fingers. Extending one long leg behind her, she reached all the way down the length of the table to set the Sprite in front of him. Her tee pulled tight across her supple back, and Paul and J. J. caught each other looking. Only the Colonel maintained any degree of suavity, and even he, Paul noted, cast a discreet glance along the filmy curve of the waitress's shorts. Then she straightened, and all the men at the table breathed out.

"I'm Stony," she said, with a beauty queen's smile, setting out the three empty beer glasses. "Have y'all decided what you want?"

The four men fumbled open their menus.

"Do y'all need a minute yet?"

"No," said the Colonel.

"Yes," said J. J.

"Umm . . . ," said Paul.

"Mmph," said Bob Wier through a mouthful of Sprite.

Stony winked at them and pivoted away. "I'll come back in a sec."

J. J. twisted in his seat to watch her go. Bob Wier gasped and wiped the back of his hand across his lips. Over the edge of his bright menu, Paul caught the Colonel watching him watching Stony's retreat. He dropped his eyes.

"Nobody's putting a gun to her head, Professor," murmured the Colonel.

"What?" muttered Paul.

"Oh, I know what you're thinking." The Colonel smirked at his menu. "You're thinking the lovely Stony does charity work with the homeless in her spare time. It spares you from the guilt over the tingling in your loins."

The Colonel was once again annoyingly close to the truth. Even as his lizard brain throbbed for Stony's world-class midriff, Paul's forebrain was trying to tell him that "Stony" was the waitress's *nom de service*; that her real name was Zoë; that she was only working here until her Fulbright money kicked in and she could leave for Paris to study French women's labor relations at the Sorbonne. Or better still, she already had a NEH grant to work here undercover to study the lives of all the other Fulbright scholars who were working their way through graduate school serving BBQ chicken wings to goggle-eyed middle managers. He felt his face get hot.

"What's the harm in admiring a nubile young woman?" The Colonel closed his menu definitively and slapped it on the table. "After all, it's only natural. It's what she's engineered for. Hell, son, it's what *you're* engineered for." Still looking at Paul, he reached along the table and pressed his finger to J. J.'s jaw, pushing him roughly around to face the others.

J. J. flinched. "What the fuck?"

The Colonel lifted the pitcher one-handed and poured a beer. "The professor here knows exactly what I'm talking about." He pushed the glass in front of J. J. then poured another glass and pushed it towards Paul. "Are you a sporting man, Paul?"

Am I a Jew? wondered Paul. Am I a sporting man? What's he getting at?

"In my experience," said the Colonel, pouring himself a glass, "even your radical Marxist college professor enjoys a bone-crunching gridiron display."

"I'm more of a baseball fan," said Paul, instantly regretting it.

"Of course you are!" cried the Colonel. "It's the national sport of intellectuals. The complexity of it, its fascinating geometry and mathematical precision. Its uncertain pace, its longueurs punctuated by moments of passion and high performance." He took a hearty sip of beer and ran his tongue along his upper lip. "Gives a fellow a lot to think about."

Paul lifted his own beer to avoid having to say anything.

"But consider your *real* sports for a moment, Professor." The Colonel fixed him with his bright gaze. "Your violent sports. What's the point of each and every one of them?"

Paul, swallowing, only lifted his eyebrows.

"I'll tell you," said the Colonel. "It's to get a little pellet of pigskin or cowhide or rubber past *all the other men* on the court or the gridiron, into that *tight, narrow spot* at the end of the field. Which is then the occasion for a moment of pure, blissful, mindless ecstasy. A moment, in other words, of *release.*"

Paul dived into his beer again. It was all he could do to keep from rolling his eyes. Somewhere in officer training school, the Colonel had read a chapter from Freud. If he knew the sort of thing my ex-wife wrote about in her theoretical work, Paul thought, his balls would shrivel and retract into his scrotum like landing gear.

"Football, basketball, hockey, even golf—it's what they're all about," continued the Colonel. "Get that little piece of yourself into the hole. It's what we're all competing for, isn't it?"

"Huh!" gasped J.J., with a puzzled smile. He understood that something lubricious was being talked about, but he wasn't sure what.

"It's about, it's about building *character*," stammered Bob Wier, trying to get in the game.

"Hey, wait a minute!" J.J. sat up straight. "A baseball's a little white pellet—"

"Yes, yes, yes." The Colonel waved his hand dismissively. "Perhaps you weren't listening, son. Baseball's for intel*lec*tuals." He might as well have said, baseball's for *pussies*. "Consider your catcher, squatting with his legs open like a woman, that big, soft mitt between his legs—"

"I was a catcher," said J. J., sounding wounded.

The Colonel sighed and turned his gaze to Paul again. "What do you know about evolution, Paul? The reverend here believes there's no such thing."

"Oh, Lord," said Bob Wier. Paul lifted his beer again to avoid having to answer.

"Every person in this room is engineered for the preservation of the species." The Colonel took another sip and licked his lip again. "Do you know why young J. J. here stares at Stony's breasts? Do you know why *you* do?"

"Because they're fucking amazing?" J. J. glowered over his glass. He was still pissed about the catcher thing. "Fuck, even an intel*lec*tual can see that."

"Guys!" Bob Wier laughed and glanced nervously over his shoulder. "We're in a public place. Do we have to—?"

The Colonel leaned over the table. "It's your genes talking, Paul."

Paul was trying to keep a straight face, but he couldn't help but notice Stony swaying in their direction carrying a tray crowded with plates of food. High over her left breast, over her collarbone, she had pinned a bright yellow button, but at this distance Paul couldn't read it. She stopped at a tableful of guys and distributed the plates, while the men's faces swiveled towards her like sunflowers towards the morning sun.

"You know what I mean, Professor," the Colonel was saying. "Deep in your mitochondrial DNA, you see a perfect mother for your offspring: a young, healthy, strapping woman with a strong, shapely pelvis for giving birth, and firm, full breasts for giving suck."

J. J. smirked. "Giving what?"

"Oh, God." Bob Wier put his face in his hands.

"Did you say *suck?*" said J. J.

"Young J. J.'s mind is in the gutter, Professor, but then his mind is *supposed* to be in the gutter. He's *supposed* to be thinking about spreading his genes to every young woman in this room, thus maximizing his genetic legacy. It's certainly not love. It's not even lust. It's the selfish gene guaranteeing its own survival, like salmon swimming upstream to spawn, mindless and shrewd, all at once."

"You know," said Paul at last, lowering his beer, "a little Discovery channel is a dangerous thing." It was like being trapped in hell with E. O. Wilson.

The Colonel manufactured a hearty laugh and rocked back from the table. "Very droll," he said.

Stony arrived and squared her shoulders. "How 'bout it, guys? What's your pleasure?"

The men fell silent in the presence of tawny Stony. Paul found himself wondering what to do with his eyes and his hands, and at last he folded his fingers together on the cool tabletop and glanced sidelong at the fulsome curve of her breasts. Then he lifted his eyes to the yellow button at her shoulder, which read ASK ME ABOUT OUR TENDER CHICKEN STRIPS!

"I'll have the chicken strips," said Paul.

"I believe I'll have them, too," said the Colonel.

"So," said J. J., leaning in, "is that breast meat?"

"It's not just breast meat, hon," said Stony, a little more cannily than was attractive. "It's tender, *juicy* breast meat."

"Sounds fingers-lickin' good," said J. J., leaning closer.

"Oh, they are! Especially if you dip them in our own special dippin' sauce!"

"Wow, dippin' sauce." J. J. was hanging off his stool. "What's in that?"

Bob Wier hyperventilated speechlessly, his eyes wide as coffee cups.

"He'll have the same, my dear," said the Colonel. "Chicken strips all round."

"Outstanding!" Stony reached along the table again to collect their menus; J. J. settled back on his stool and theatrically fanned himself. She swung away, and all four men sagged a little in their seats, unaware until that moment that they'd all been sitting a little straighter.

"No doubt you've noted Stony's professional detachment," the Colonel said, watching Paul. "She smiles and thrusts her bosom at us, but she keeps that certain distance."

"Fucking cocktease," muttered J. J., half turned around on his stool.

"A professional necessity," Paul heard himself say, "in a place like this." Paul knew he shouldn't argue with this blowhard, but it was such a relief to be asked his opinion on something and to have his opinion listened to. After all, didn't he have eight years of graduate school training in talking about gender? "It's what this place is *engineered* for, isn't it?" Paul went on. "The tease. The slap and tickle."

"No fucking shit. They're all fucking teases." J. J.'s restless gaze bounced from one waitress to another. "None of these bitches would give a guy like me the time of day."

"That's one way to put it, my hormonal young friend," said the Colonel over his beer. "But look at it from her point of view. Hers is a finely calibrated performance, and I don't just mean her professional restauranteur's hospitality. It's *her* genes speaking." He sipped and smacked his lips. "Young Stony wants to attract a robust fellow like you, or the professor here or even an old buck like myself, but she's prepared to make us *work* for it. While it's in the male's interest to spread his seed as widely as possible, it's in Stony's interest to find a potent, yet reliable fellow who will participate in the raising of her offspring. Given the investment of time involved, Stony can only yield to a man who she can be certain will feed and protect her offspring. To oversimplify, young J. J. here is interested in the *quantity* of partners, while the discriminating Stony is interested in the *quality* of *one* partner."

"What's he saying?" J. J. narrowed his gaze at Paul.

"That you'd like to fuck them all," Paul said.

"Fucking A." J. J. sat up straight and took a manful drink of beer. "Fucking bitches."

Propped against the window, desperately watching the traffic outside, miserable Bob Wier was repeating scripture to himself under his breath.

"Do you think I'm wrong, Professor?" said the Colonel.

Paul hesitated. Did he really want to argue the construction of gender with this jerk? His ex-wife Elizabeth, the theorist of gender, would have handed this loser his genitalia about twenty minutes ago. But then Lizzie wouldn't have been sitting in a Headlights to begin with, would she? She wouldn't know what it was like to be a man surrounded by other men, waited upon by half-dressed young women, sitting here half aroused, with his hormones singing in his blood. She couldn't possibly get what it was like to stew in your own humidity, heat prickling the backs of your eyeballs, sweat coming out on the palms of your hands. Dear God, he thought, what if the Colonel is *right?*

"Do you know what 'essentialism' means?" Paul heard the condescension in his own voice.

"No," laughed the Colonel, "but I can guess. All your fancy literary jargon doesn't hold any water any longer, Professor. I'm talking science, son, *science.* Philosophy is over. There is no more philosophy."

"Well, that's a relief," said Paul.

"The world's turned upside down, Paul," said the Colonel fiercely, leaning across the table. "Suddenly they don't *need* men any more. Single mothers. *Lesbian* mothers. Or they forgo motherhood altogether and compete directly with us in the marketplace. Why maximize their genetic legacy, why pick a mate, why have children at all, when they can *take our jobs.* Look at all the childless women in our office: Olivia, Renee, Nolene."

Paul remembered the three child-safety seats in the back of Nolene's van. "I think Nolene has kids," he said.

"She might as well not have them," spat the Colonel. "Is she home with them? Ensuring their safety and survival? Hell no, she's at work, raising them by proxy. It's not *natural,* Paul. Don't you get it?" He clasped Paul's forearm in a painful grip.

"Easy," Paul said, but he couldn't pull free.

"Look across the length and breadth of our office, Paul. What do you see? Cube after cube of women working at jobs that men used to have. Cube after cube of *women not raising children.*"

There was a breathless silence at the table. Even Bob Wier stopped praying and turned away from the window. J. J. gripped his beer with both hands and shifted his gaze from the Colonel to Paul and back again. Paul tensed his arm under the Colonel's grip. The Colonel fixed Paul with a furious, penetrating gaze.

"Here we go, fellas, get 'em while they're hot." Stony swung her tray close to the end of the table, extending her long arm to place a large plate in front of each man. On each plate was a heap of chicken strips on one side and a heap of seasoned fries on the other, surrounding a little dish of pinkish dippin' sauce. "Can I get you boys anything else?"

The Colonel released Paul and sat back; he drew a deep breath and let it out slowly. Paul leaned back, too, and rubbed his arm where the Colonel had grasped him.

"I think we're fine," said J. J., and Stony winked at them and went away.

"I got a little heated there, son," said the Colonel. "I apologize."

"No harm done," said Paul. In the silence that followed, he lifted a chicken strip and dangled it over the pink sauce. J. J. picked one up, too, and plunged it into the sauce.

"It's just," the Colonel went on, "we used to be competing *for* women. Now we're competing *with* women." They all watched the Colonel as his forehead knotted and unknotted. He gazed at his plate of chicken strips as if he'd never seen anything like it before in his entire life.

"What does a man do to ensure his survival now?" He looked up at Paul meaningfully. "What do men do, gentlemen, working together, as *men*, to ensure *our* survival?"

Before anyone else could answer, Bob Wier groaned, and the other three men looked down the table at him.

"Not here okay?" he said. "Not now. Can we just eat?"

TWENTY-ONE

AFTER LUNCH, in the skin-loosening heat of the parking lot, the Colonel clapped J.J. on the shoulder and said, "You got shotgun on the way back, son." He turned to Paul and raised his eyebrows over the lenses of his sunglasses. "You don't mind sitting in the back on the way home, do you, Professor?"

Squinting against the glare off the pickups and SUVs all around, his gullet burning from the unsubtle spicing of Headlights's dippin' sauce, Paul shrugged. J.J. beamed victoriously and hoisted himself up into the front passenger seat of the SUV. At the rear of the vehicle, out of sight of the Colonel as he heaved himself up into the driver's seat, Bob Wier touched Paul on the elbow.

"It's not too late for you," Bob whispered tremulously. His eyes were wide and beyond mournful.

"What?" said Paul.

Bob Wier glanced forward, through the dusky tinting of the SUV's rear window. "You can still walk away," he whispered.

This was different from Preston's offer of sympathy and self-pity earlier that morning; Bob Wier looked desperate, as if he were pleading with Paul for something. But before Bob or Paul could speak again, the basso beep of the SUV's horn made them both jump. "C'mon, girls," shouted the Colonel out his window, "let's shake a tail feather."

By the time Paul climbed into the backseat next to Bob Wier, Bob was smiling. After forty minutes in the unshaded parking lot, the enormous vehicle was full of a baking heat, but as soon as the Colonel started the engine, frigid air began to pour from the AC vents.

"If you want to make your pitch, Reverend," said the Colonel over his shoulder, "now's the time. You got a captive audience for five minutes. The professor here is full of beer and chicken strips."

"*Tender* chicken strips," said J. J.

The SUV lumbered out of the parking lot and into the lunchtime traffic. Next to Paul in the backseat, Bob Wier adjusted himself sideways, pulling a knee up on the seat. He broadened his smile, but his eyes still pleaded silently with Paul. "Tell me, Paul," Bob Wier said, "what do you know about distributed sales?"

Up front the Colonel and J. J were snorting with repressed mirth.

"Sorry?" Paul said. "What are 'distributed sales'?"

"I'm glad you asked!" chorused the Colonel and J. J. and they burst out laughing.

"Guys, come on," said Bob Wier, with manly cheerfulness. In the back he gave Paul a meaningful look. "Maybe Paul's not as cynical as you two reprobates." He licked his lips and said, "I'm glad you asked, Paul. Distributed sales are—"

"The opportunity of a lifetime!" cried the two men in the front.

"Come on, now!" protested Bob Wier. "I put up with y'all during lunch."

The Colonel, still chortling, lifted a conciliatory hand from the wheel. "Let him talk." J. J. continued to hiss with laughter.

"These fellas can joke all they want," Bob Wier said, "but

I'll tell you, Paul, this really is the opportunity of a lifetime."
He glanced nervously up front, then slowly shook his head.
"You've heard of Amway, right?"

What on earth are you getting at? Paul wanted to say, but
he simply turned away and stared out the window. Bob Wier's
pitch was for something called TexGro, a world-class line of
lawn care products developed by an internationally recognized
team of agricultural research scientists at Texas A&M, right
here in Texas! Paul tuned him out. They were rolling across
the Travis Street Bridge already, and Paul gazed down from the
SUV's improbable height at the river below and wondered what
it would be like to plunge from the bridge into the sluggish
water. Would it be thrillingly cold, like the bracing midwestern
streams of his youth? Or would it be tepid, like the tap water
here in Texas? He felt a touch on the back of his hand, and he
turned to Bob Wier.

"And here's the great thing, Paul," Bob Wier said, "this re-
quires only a *small initial investment* on your part." He shook
his head even more vehemently.

"I don't think the professor's buying it, Bob," said the Colonel. He was watching them in the rearview mirror. Bob Wier's
face folded shut, and he retreated to the corner of the seat.

Paul glanced past J. J. and out the windshield at the General
Services Division Building at the far end of the bridge. His
cube, nestled in the building like the cell of a worker bee, had
never seemed so inviting. He was about to turn to his own
window again when J. J. pointed across the dashboard towards
the left side of the bridge. The Colonel turned to look, and
Paul idly followed his gaze.

He caught his breath. Standing against the parapet of the
bridge, each with his shoes together and his hands hanging
straight at his sides, were three pale men. Boy G stood in the
middle, the man from the library stood to his right, and a man
Paul had never seen before stood to his left. All three wore
white, short-sleeved shirts, thin neckties, and buzz cuts. They
stood preternaturally still in the noonday heat and the reek off
the river, and all three watched the Colonel's SUV across five

empty lanes, their heads swiveling to follow its progress. At the
SUV's closest approach, the Colonel gave the men by the parapet a quick thumbs-up. Paul twisted in his seat, and even from
a distance, as the homeless men glided by, he thought he saw
all three men smile jaggedly. Paul tried to twist around the
other way to look out the rear window of the SUV, but Bob
Wier grabbed his arm.

"Wouldn't you like to be *your own boss?*" Bob Wier was
nearly in tears. "No one to tell you what to do?" Bob shot a
glance at the Colonel and smiled. "You sell these products at
your own pace, out of your own home!"

Paul pulled his arm free. He leaned forward between the
two front seats and said, "Can you stop the car?" But the Colonel was already guiding his vehicle into the TxDoGS parking
lot, spinning the steering wheel one-handed. As soon as the
SUV was berthed against the building, Paul jumped out, leaving
Bob Wier smiling speechlessly in the backseat. Paul jogged
quickly between the gleaming vehicles in the parking lot and
up the embankment alongside the river. At the top, panting and
sweaty in the heat, he shaded his eyes with his palm and peered
through the glare off the river, trying to make out the silhouettes of the three homeless guys on the bridge. But all he saw
were the boxy outlines of vehicles gliding above the parapet.

"Do you want to be a galley slave all your life, Paul," asked
the Colonel, behind him, "sweating in an airless hold, chained
to your bench?"

Paul turned, breathing hard. "What?"

"You heard me, son." The Colonel pushed heavily up the
embankment and stopped a few feet from the top. He glanced
along the river at the bridge, then pulled off his sunglasses and
squinted at Paul. "Do you want to end up like poor ol' Dennis,
all alone in your cube, pulling on your oar until you keel over
dead?"

Paul looked away at the General Services Division Building,
then back at the bridge, then down the slope at the Colonel.
"Who are those guys on the bridge?"

The Colonel stood with one foot higher than the other,

and he rested his big-knuckled hand on his flexed knee and dangled his sunglasses. Beyond him, across the parking lot, J. J. had thrown his arm around Bob Wier's shoulders and was leading him into the building.

The Colonel drew a deep breath and let it out slowly. He peered into the distance, then looked up at Paul again with a knowing glint in his eye. "What are you doing Saturday night?"

"Why don't you answer my question?" Paul insisted. He hated the high pitch of his voice. "Who are those guys?"

"Do you like to sing, Paul?"

"Do I like to *what?*"

The Colonel stood up straight, swinging his sunglasses from his index finger. "Friday night, Professor. Karaoke night at Casa Pentoon." He started down the embankment and called back, "And bring that lil' Oklahoma gal, if you want." He gestured over his shoulder. "We'll talk then."

"What's Friday night?" Paul called after him from the top of the embankment. "What are we going to talk about?"

The Colonel paused and looked back up the slope. He gave Paul a smile that creased the corners of his eyes.

"The opportunity of a lifetime," he said.

TWENTY-TWO

THAT NIGHT, after a dinner Charlotte couldn't ruin—no-brand hot dogs on no-brand buns, with no-brand chips and cola—Paul unfolded his creaking sofa bed and turned on his little black-and-white TV. As the air-conditioning unit rattled under the window, Paul sat on the end of the lumpy mattress in his t-shirt and shorts and clicked round the dial in the jittery light from the screen. After fifteen minutes of fidgeting with the rabbit ears, the local PBS station came in the clearest, showing an aggressively vulgar old Britcom from the seventies called *'Ow's Yer Knickers?* about three women in a lingerie shop. The youngest was a scrawny, hawk-nosed punk with piercings and jagged hair; the next oldest was a sour, middle-aged divorcée; and the oldest was a zaftig, sixty-something widow with blue hair like a helmet, named Mrs. Prestoil. Their antagonists were assorted customers—usually stammering, red-faced, clueless men—and Mr. Lancet, who owned the butcher's shop next door, and his shop assistant Stig, a buck-toothed, pasty-faced lad with a yen for the young punk. Mrs. Prestoil's shtick was lead-footed double entendre, accompanied by raucous laughter from a studio audience of lubricious Londoners.

"I couldn't find my pussy last night," trilled Mrs. Prestoil. Big laughs.

"She couldn't find her pussy with both 'ands," said the punk, in a snarling sotto voce. Bigger laughs.

"What's happened, dearie?" drawled the divorcée, examining her nails.

"I'm afraid someone's *snatched* her," wailed Mrs. Prestoil.

"Someone say 'snatch'?" said Stig, sticking his head in from next door.

"Crikey," said Paul as he sprawled across his rumpled sheets. He concentrated harder on the program than it probably deserved because he was trying not to brood about recent events. Who was Boy G, and what did he want with Paul? And who were the men with him? Surely their saw-blade dentition was the product of Paul's imagination. And why, thought Paul, shifting restlessly on his groaning bed, why were the Colonel and his dopey little lunch group showing so much interest in him all of a sudden? Had the Colonel really given the three men on the bridge a thumbs-up, or had he imagined that, too? And how on earth did the Colonel know about Paul's "lil' Oklahoma gal"?

On the television, smirking Stig slouched into the lingerie shop.

"Someone's snatched her pussy," explained the divorcée on the television.

"Is that even *possible?*" said Stig, goggle-eyed.

Where *was* Callie? Paul wondered. What was she doing? And who was she doing it with? Even the Britcom wasn't loud and vulgar enough to divert his inflamed imagination from constructing a detailed picture of Mr. X. In Paul's head the singer/songwriter from Tulsa was tall and lanky, with sleepy eyes and a sensual mouth and a ponytail, and he looked good in faded jeans and a denim shirt open to the third button, and he stretched out on Callie's narrow mattress while Callie's fingers popped buttons four, five, and six, on her way to Mr. X's big silver belt buckle in the shape of the state of Texas. . . .

Charlotte interrupted his bitter reverie by prancing along the end of the bed, her spiky silhouette strobing before the TV screen. She gave Paul a chilling look, then curled over herself on a corner of the mattress and began to lick her ectoplasmic privates.

"Subtle," said Paul, edging away from that corner of the bed.

Someone on the TV was banging on something, but no one in the lingerie shop seemed to notice. The banging continued, and Paul groaned, "Somebody answer the fucking door." Charlotte lifted her head and perked up her ears. The banging got louder, and a woman's voice said, "Paul? I hear your TV."

Paul scuttled to the end of the bed and turned down the television. No one apart from his landlady had ever knocked on his door here, and it wasn't Mrs. Prettyman's voice. Kymberly didn't even know where he lived, and neither Virginia nor Oksana would have bothered to look him up. He lifted his trousers off the chair at his little dining table.

"Coming," he shouted, hopping into one leg and then the other. He glanced back at the bed. Charlotte's eyes were round and fathomless and fixed on the door. Paul unkinked the chain and slid back the deadbolt.

"Hey." Callie hunched in the doorway in sandals and jeans and a tank top. In the long, summer twilight, she was still wearing her sunglasses. "You gonna invite me in, or do I have to stand out here with all these cowboys staring at me?"

Paul looked past her to see more than the usual assortment of Snopeses silhouetted in the yellow light of their doorways or dangling beers off the balcony across the way. The appearance at the Angry Loner Motel of a woman who wasn't Mrs. Prettyman was something of an occasion. Paul glanced back into his apartment. The dead gray glare of the TV played across the folds of his rumpled sheets, but Charlotte had vanished, so he stepped aside. Callie tilted her sunglasses onto her hair as she entered, and Paul winced at the way she wrinkled her nose at the smell.

"You have a cat?" Callie glanced round.

"Not really," said Paul. "How do you know where I live?"

"Saw your address when I made your badge yesterday." She peered into his kitchenette and through the door of his little motel bathroom. "Did the guy *before* you have a cat?"

"Have a seat." Paul swung the chair away from his table. He sat on the edge of his bed, tugging on the hem of his t-shirt so that his gut didn't bulge so noticeably.

Callie swung the chair around and straddled it backwards, leaning her elbows on the back and dangling her sunglasses.

"So," she said, "how was your day?" She wouldn't look at him for some reason, gazing at her hands instead, or at the silent television, or over Paul's head. After a moment Paul said, "My day was peculiar. How was *your* day?"

"Peculiar, huh?" Still she wouldn't look at him. "What was peculiar about it?"

Paul hesitated before answering. "My three colleagues on the RFP project took me out to lunch."

"They take you someplace good?" Callie scowled at the glasses in her hands. "Or they take you to Sonic?"

"Headlights," he sighed. "They took me to Headlights."

Callie looked at him at last. "No shit!" She laughed harshly. "Hellfire, son, that means they *like* you!"

"That piss you off?" he said.

"Hell no," she said, a little too heartily. "Just because you went to a titty bar for lunch?"

"Whoa!" said Paul. "It's not that kind of place."

" 'Course it's not!" Callie waggled her fingers, as if copping a feel. "It's a *gentlemen's* club. Bring the goddamn family."

"A little slack, Callie, okay?" Paul said. "It wasn't my idea."

"*Course* not. I bet if you was to ask half the guys in Headlights, it was the *other* guy's idea to go."

Paul folded his hands in his lap. "You asked me," he said. "I told you."

"Yeah." She dropped her gaze to the floor. "Yeah, I reckon I did."

She twirled her glasses and tensed her legs, and Paul was certain she was going to get up and walk out, and he'd never see her again. Fuck it, he thought. Let her go.

Callie drew a deep breath and sighed. "Saw Mr. X yesterday," she said.

"Ah."

"Didn't go so well."

"I'm sorry to hear it."

Callie grimaced, as if to say, What are you gonna do?

"Why are you telling me?" Paul said.

She sighed again. "Well, that's the question, ain't it?"

"It's not like you owe me an explanation."

"I know that. I just needed to tell somebody, and I figured I might as well tell you."

"Okay." Paul was pretty sure he didn't want to hear this.

"Basically," Callie said, swinging her sunglasses and glancing round the room again. "Basically . . ."

Paul crossed his arms. *'Ow's Yer Knickers* flickered at the corner of his eye.

"The sumbitch wanted me to loan him some money." She looked at Paul, and even in the dim light her eyes looked red from crying. "And he wanted to fuck me."

Paul felt his face get hot. "Did you?" he said.

Callie's face flushed and her eyes burned, but she said nothing. She did, Paul thought. She fucked him. Son of a *bitch!*

"You got no right to ask me that," she said in a low voice.

"No? You can give me a hard time for going to a 'titty bar' "—he made quotation marks with his fingers—"that isn't really a titty bar, but I can't ask an obvious question."

"Paul—"

"You tell me your boyfriend's back, you call in sick—"

"Paul, shut up." Callie gave him a look that drilled right through him. Paul glared back, but his mind was racing. If Callie had fucked Mr. X, then why would she come all the way out here, to the wilder fringes of Lamar, just to tell me about it?

"Nothing happened." Callie kept Paul steadily in her sights. "With Mr. X. I didn't do it."

Paul said nothing. He was astonished at himself, at how badly he wanted Callie to be telling the truth.

"I gave the sumbitch the money he wanted," she said, "and then I told him to get lost. I figured that was stupid enough. I didn't have to fuck him on top of it."

Paul noticed Charlotte crouching in the shadows under the table, gazing wide-eyed at Callie, her tail switching back and forth.

"Callie," he said, but she cut him off with a gesture.

"You want to know where I was all day?" Her voice trembled. "I was curled up on my bed bawling like a little girl." Callie stood and pushed the chair away. She fumbled with her glasses. "And then I came out here, like an idiot, thinking that you could . . . that you might . . ."

Under the table Charlotte watched Callie with her furious, hollow-eyed gaze. Callie started for the door, and Paul jumped up. "I'm sorry," he said. "You said you were going to see this guy, and I just didn't know . . ."

He gingerly laid his hand on her warm shoulder, and when she didn't pull away, he turned her and draped both arms around her. Over her shoulder he kept an eye on Charlotte.

Callie hunched tensely in his arms. "Ain't your fault," she said at last. She relaxed and tilted her forehead against Paul's. "Ain't his either, really. I should know by now."

"Callie." Paul folded his arms around her neck, and Callie wrapped her arms around his waist. Over her shoulder, Paul saw that Charlotte had disappeared. As best he could with Callie's warm cheek pressed into his neck, he scanned the apartment for the ghostly cat.

"It's okay," said Paul, not certain that it was. "It's okay." He wondered what Charlotte would do if Callie stayed the night.

Callie unwrapped her arms from around his waist and fixed Paul with a narrow, meaningful look.

"What?" he said. The hair went up on the back of his neck, and he wondered if Charlotte was doing something behind him.

"Put your shoes on, stud," said Callie. "Let's go for a ride."

TWENTY-THREE

CALLIE DROVE. She didn't say much as they left town, but Paul was satisfied to watch her long fingers grasp the big black knob of the gearshift and ram it from first to second to third. Her whole arm tensed when she shifted, and the strap of her tank top pulled away from her shoulder. Paul wanted to lean across the long, bench seat and lick her collarbone from one end to the other.

Well past Lamar city limits, out beyond the new strip malls and the enormous limestone grocery stores and the new subdivisions of vast, square, luxury homes on little plots of mesquite and juniper, the truck roared and rattled towards the salmon strip of sky where the sun had just set. The big, four-lane state highway swooped around and under the hills, and the wind rushed through the windows, thumping in Paul's ears and rippling his t-shirt. Even this late in the evening, the air was still hot. "The AC don't work," was all Callie had said since they'd left his apartment. "Never did." But Paul didn't mind. The hot wind felt good to him, polishing his skin and loosening his joints.

Farther from Lamar the hills turned black against the turquoise sky. The traffic thinned out. Here and there a faint light shone out of the darkness on one side of the road or the other, but mostly the view was of the pavement bleached by the headlights, the humpbacks of the hills, and the stars starting out of a rich black sky. About twenty minutes beyond the last sign of civilization, a little green sign—LONESOME KNOB STATE PARK— pointed to the right, and Callie downshifted just enough to make the turn onto the ranch road in an unholy clashing of gears and a rattle of spraying gravel. This two-lane road dipped and rolled through the dark even more like a roller-coaster than the big four laner, and Paul caught glimpses of bare rock along the shoulder, and stubby cactus, and gnarled live oaks, and, once, down a sudden, precipitous drop, a ranch house lit like a miniature railroad model by its own yard light at the bottom of a steep valley.

"Where we going?" Paul shouted over the roar of the wind and the growling of the truck.

"Place I know," Callie shouted back, shooting him a grin in the greenish light of the dashboard.

A few minutes later Callie downshifted again and crept along the road, watching the brush beyond the narrow shoulder on the right. The truck chugged along, going *glug glug glug*, until at last a long, steel gate rolled into the headlights. Callie pulled into the sunbaked ruts of the turnoff, jammed the gears into park, and jumped out of the truck. Paul leaned out the window and read a gunshot TRESPASSERS WILL BE PROSECUTED sign, while Callie stepped up on the lowest rung of the gate, leaned fetchingly over one end, and did something to the latch that made the whole long gate swing slowly inward. *Glug glug glug glug glug*, went the truck, rocking Paul and sending a thrill through his loins. Then Callie trotted back through the headlights to the truck, jammed the gears into first, and chugged over the thrumming cattle grate. When she stopped again, Paul said, "I'll get it," and he jumped down out of the truck into the hot shriek of crickets and pushed the gate shut; the metal was still warm from the day's heat.

Beyond the gate the truck climbed a rutted two track through the bony grasp of live oaks. At last the gnarled fingers of the oaks began to recede, and the truck rumbled through the dark, groaning and jouncing, into a wide meadow of tall grass. The field was open to an enormous sky on top of a round hill, surrounded like a bald man's fringe on all sides by silhouettes of low brush. The dry grass hissed under the front bumper, bleached white in the headlights, and just before Callie switched them off Paul saw the shuddering haunches of a deer as it leaped into the junipers at the edge of the field.

Callie cut the engine and heaved open her door and said, "I'm really angry, Paul, so I reckon it's your lucky night." She slammed her door, and Paul scuttled out of his side of the cab. He was wearing sandals, and even in his febrile excitement, he worried about scorpions in the grass. The crickets shrilled all around, and the stars blazed overhead.

"Are you serious?" Paul said across the bed of the truck. He could scarcely believe his good luck.

Callie had already hoisted herself up the side of the pickup, throwing one long leg over and then the other. She stood in the rocking truck bed, the shocks groaning beneath her, and she grabbed the hem of her tank top and stripped it off one-handed, leaning over the cab to toss it through her window. Her breasts gleamed in the starlight.

"Git yer britches off, cowboy," she said, kicking off her sandals and popping the button on her jeans. "This is my favorite way to go."

And—oh, what bliss it was to be alive on that evening!—they fucked a couple of times on an old army blanket in the bed of her truck, under an endlessly black sky full of hot stars. Crickets screamed all around them in the heat as they rocked together on the blanket, and Paul thought he might die from happiness—at the sweaty clutch of her thighs around his waist, at the hot, slippery grip of her cunt, at the rhythmic *slap slap*

slap of their flesh. Paul's usual repertoire of transgressive endearments escaped him, and he gasped wordlessly, driving single-mindedly towards the goal while Callie clawed at his ass and shoulders and grunted encouragement. But what he liked best, what he planned to remember fondly behind his eyeballs and in the tips of his fingers for the rest of his days, was when he lay flat on his back and she straddled him, her brow knotted, the veins standing out in her neck, her mouth a perfect, bloodless *O* of concentration. The cold metal ridges of the truck bed cut into his shoulders and backside through the itchy blanket, but he didn't care. The sight of her swaying above him, hot and pale in the starlight, her freckles like flecks of ash in the sheen of sweat on her shoulders and breasts, only sweetened the pain. They were ecstatically noisy; the truck creaked merrily under them like an old brass bed. At one point Callie leaned over the side and yelled, "Shut up!" at the screaming crickets. "Y'all are *distracting* me!" she hollered, grinding against Paul until he groaned like a man in agony.

Afterwards, they lay slick with sweat side by side, watching the twinkling stars in the electric black above the truck, listening to each other pant in the heat. There wasn't a breath of a breeze.

"I don't want to spoil the buzz," Paul gasped, "but this isn't about me, is it?"

"It's *mostly* about you," Callie panted.

"You used to come here with Mr. X, didn't you?"

She laced her fingers through his and squeezed. "Yeah, but you were better."

The squeeze shot straight down his spine and nearly made him hard again. "Thanks for the endorsement, but that's not what I meant."

"It *is* what you meant," laughed Callie. "It's what y'all always mean." She let go of his hand and raised herself on her elbow, looming over him against the stars. He could smell her in the heat; right now, he'd have happily licked her clean.

"I needed to take this place back," she said, "with a *nice* guy."

"Again, I don't want to kill the buzz, but I'm not that nice."

"Nice enough." She flopped back down on the blanket. "Seriously. I'm not."

"Well, at least you're not the motherfucker who knocked me up and then ran off with a sorority girl." She snorted. "Plus we ain't even drunk."

"Really? A sorority girl?" Silently Paul thanked Mr. X for driving Callie to this pitch of anger. For once it was a pleasure to reap the rewards of some other guy's boorishness. "Did he bring her out here?"

"Change the subject," said Callie.

"Come on, did he? Is that why you brought me?"

"Change the subject!" shouted Callie.

"Um . . ." Paul couldn't think of a thing, but suddenly Callie rolled against him, scratching lightly at his chest with her bitten nails.

"So why ain't you teaching someplace?" She winced and said, "*Aren't.*"

"Callie, it's okay," he laughed. "It's not like there's going to be a quiz later."

Callie sighed. "So how come?"

Paul was glad that the dark hid his irritation. "Same reason you aren't waiting tables. I wanted something with a little more self-respect."

She slapped his chest lightly. "Well, if you don't want to talk about it, just say so."

"There's nothing to talk about. Some things just don't work out."

"Don't I know it." She rolled onto her back again.

They were quiet for a moment, listening to the crickets, watching the sky, smelling their own juices rising off them in the dark.

"Does it bother you I got an abortion?" She laid the back of her hand on his chest.

Oh, Christ, thought Paul. "I thought we were done with twenty questions."

"Does it?"

"I honestly haven't given it a moment's thought."

Callie slowly rolled her knuckles up and down his chest. Paul thought it was the finest sensation of his life. His cock began to stir happily.

"You tell some boys something like that, they think you're easy," she said. "You tell some others, they think you're a heartless bitch." She swiveled her head against the blanket to look at him. "Some boys, they don't mind so much that you did it, they just don't want to hear about it."

"Honestly, Callie," Paul said, "it doesn't bother me."

"What's the worst thing *you* ever done?" She scrunched her eyes. "I mean, *did*."

Paul groaned, and Callie rolled over onto her stomach and pressed her palm against his shoulder. "I mean it. What's the worst thing you ever did? I told you mine."

Paul shifted under Callie's weight and wished she'd just throw her leg over and ride him again. "Change the subject," he said.

"It's my truck." She slapped his shoulder. "Only I can change the subject."

What can I say? thought Paul. That I cheated on my wife? That I cheated on the woman I cheated on my wife with, and then cheated on *that* woman, too? No doubt Callie would believe him. His sexual history would only reinforce her embittered waitress view of the world.

"I was divorced." Paul could scarcely believe he'd said it.

"Divorced!" cried Callie gleefully. *Dee-vorced*, she said it, like a country singer. "From the meteorologist?"

"Before her." The stars above trembled in the humidity.

"How come?"

Paul shrugged. "I said tomato, she said tomahto."

"Come on." Callie was wheedling him now, squeezing his love handles. "You're a college professor, for cri yi. What'd you do, sleep with a student?"

I should have kept my mouth shut, Paul thought.

"How bad can it be?" Now Callie was practically on top of him. She tugged his chin between her thumb and forefinger and forced him to look at her. "I murdered a fetus," she said, her face ghostly in the starlight, her eyes unfathomable. "Whatever you did can't be as bad as that."

"Depends," Paul said, without meaning to. "How do you feel about cats?"

"Cats?" She let go of his chin, but she didn't pull away. Paul slid out from under her and doubled over, reaching for his trousers.

"We ought to head back," he said. "We both have to work tomorrow."

She laid a hand on his shoulder, but more tentatively than before. "I'm just funnin' with you, Paul. I don't mean nothin' by it."

"Anything." Paul stood in the rocking truck bed with his back to her and yanked his trousers up. "You don't mean *anything* by it."

"Yes, *sir*." Callie jerked her jeans into the air, slapping them against the side of the truck. "Will *that* be on the exam, Professor?"

They bounced back down the two track to the gate without speaking, the truck glugging angrily. At the road, before the truck even stopped, Paul heaved open his door and jumped out to get the gate, half afraid as the truck rumbled over the cattle grate that Callie might just keep going and leave him there. But she waited as he shut the gate, her elbow hanging out the window, her eyes dark hollows in the dashboard light. Paul climbed into the cab and slammed the door, and she jammed the truck into gear. They roller-coastered back up the two-lane road towards the main highway. With each free-fall dive down a hill, Paul was lifted slightly off the seat, and he felt a regretful little tingle in his balls. The truck banged around a rocky curve and then rattled over a low water crossing. FLASH FLOOD AREA, read a sign over the culvert, DO NOT DRIVE INTO RUNNING WATER. A-fucking-men, thought Paul, sneaking a glance at Callie's angry cheekbone in the dashboard light. It seemed to Paul that she was taking the road faster than she had coming the other way. She's in a hurry to get back to Lamar, he thought. She's in a hurry to be rid of me.

At the junction with the highway, she skidded to a gravel-slinging stop. Dust churned through the headlights. Then she gunned the truck out onto the road and started to coax it gear by gear up to the speed limit.

"I killed a cat." Paul lifted his voice over the rising whine of the truck. "I drowned it in a bathtub." He looked at her and found her gazing back at him along the seat. "I guess that's the worst thing I ever did."

She didn't say anything for a long time, working the stick shift up through second and third. Paul's stomach tightened the longer the silence went on, and he began to regret having said anything. He was certain this was his last evening with Callie, and the sad thing was, he actually sort of liked her. As the hill ahead was silhouetted in the orangey glow of Lamar, she said, "Why'd you do that?"

"Kill the cat?"

"Yeah."

Paul swallowed. Did he really want to tell her this? "It's a long story," he said.

"It's a long way back to town," she said. "Radio don't work neither."

So all the way back, rolling through the dark over and under the hills, past the spreading subdivisions and the late-night supermarkets with their empty parking lots in the harsh fluorescent glare, and finally along a gaudy strip past the drooping pennants of car dealerships and the red glare of fast-food joints and the forlorn glow of check-cashing emporia, Paul told Callie the story of Charlotte. To his own astonishment, he told her the truth: about his failing academic career, about his bloodless marriage with Elizabeth, about his giddy affair with Kymberly, about his war with the cat to keep the affair secret. Callie said nothing all the way into Lamar, but now and then she looked at him, as the light from a streetlamp or the glare of a neon sign glided over her through the windshield. Paul, meanwhile, gazed out the windshield without really seeing anything. He felt numb by the end, and when he reached the part about drowning Charlotte, he didn't relate all the awful details: how he'd torn his apartment apart in a rage looking for her; how he'd grasped her, yowling and flailing, by the scruff of her neck; how he'd put her in her cat carrier in the bathtub and turned on both taps. His right forearm began to sting where, in the right light, he could still see the faint traces of the scratches Charlotte had given him that night.

All he could do now was rub his arm and say, "So I drowned her in the bathtub." Bless me, Callie, for I have sinned.

"You mean, like kittens in a sack?"

Paul stomach twisted. "Yeah, like that."

"Whew," was all Callie said.

Paul fell silent and gazed into his lap. He decided there was no point in telling Callie about the aftermath—she already knew that he'd lost his academic career, and she wouldn't believe that he was still haunted by the ghost of a cat. He scarcely believed it himself.

When he looked up again, the truck had stopped; through the windshield he saw his own apartment door in the glare of the headlights. Callie's truck was chugging in place, and Callie was watching him down the length of the seat.

"Why'd you want to know that?" Paul met her gaze. "What the worst thing I ever did was?"

Callie shifted her gaze out the windshield, as if she were looking at a distant horizon instead of the brick wall of the apartment five feet beyond the hood of the truck. She drew a breath to speak, caught herself, then drew another breath.

" 'Cause with every guy I ever been with, sooner or later I find out what the worst thing they ever done is. And usually it's what they done to me." She turned to him. "I figured this time I'd get it out of the way first thing. Then maybe we could work our way up from there."

"Well, now you know." Paul yanked on the door latch, but Callie leaned down the seat and caught his arm.

"I'm glad you told me," she said. "Now we know the worst about each other."

Not quite, Paul thought. He still hadn't told her about Charlotte's ghost.

"Now I know two things about you," Callie said. "One is, I got to watch you like a hawk around other women, but what else is new?"

"What's the other thing?"

"That there's at least one way I don't have to worry about you hurtin' me."

"What's that?" His arm was still burning.

"I don't have a cat," Callie said, and she kissed him.

Paul's head was spinning as he fumbled for his keys at the door of his apartment. Behind him Callie's truck banged over the loose grate at the center of the parking lot, then grumbled out onto the road. As he fitted his key into the lock and opened the door, he heard her roaring away, heard the stuttering whine of each gearshift—first, second, third—and he imagined the marvelous flexion of her gear-shifting arm. Then he sort of floated into his apartment, amazed to think that at the end of this long, impossible, humiliating day, he had had ecstatic, sweaty sex under the stars in the bed of a pickup truck with a passionate girl; that he'd told her the worst thing he'd ever done (more or less); and that, miraculously, the girl was still speaking to him afterwards. He felt more relief than joy, it was true, but as he felt for the light switch inside the door, he was certain that nothing could make this day any stranger.

Certain, that was, until he turned on the light. Someone had been in his apartment and tidied it up. Paul was not the most fastidious person in the world, and it was instantly obvious that the small-scale chaos of his little flat had been put in some sort of order. The chair from his dining table, which he had set in the middle of the floor for Callie, had been returned to the table. The table itself was clean and uncluttered, the thrift shop salt-and-pepper shakers set to the side, the little stack of paper napkins wedged between them. His secondhand dishes—the battered pot he'd boiled the hot dogs in, and his purple plastic plate—had been washed and set to dry in his dish drainer. Paul saw all this instantly, and as he closed the door behind him and edged warily into the apartment, he saw that the floor of his kitchenette had been swept, that his little counter was clean of

crumbs and stains, and that the enameled top of his dinky little
three-burner stove had been scrubbed spotless.

"Who's here?" Paul whispered, afraid to move any deeper
into his own room. "Mrs. Prettyman, are you in here?"

But the apartment was too small for anyone to hide in. He
peered through his bathroom door and saw that the tub
gleamed a little brighter, and his towel hung a little straighter.

"Charlotte?" he said, his voice beginning to tremble. "Did
you do this?"

But Charlotte was nowhere to be seen, having vanished into
the ether, or wherever ghost cats went. He turned slowly away
from the kitchenette, as if afraid to turn his back on his newly
gleaming stove and countertop, and saw that his bed was still
pulled out but that someone had tucked the sheets and blanket
in all around, military style, tight enough to bounce a quarter.
The pillow had been smoothed flat and centered at the head of
the bed.

And then, as Paul's pulse pounded in his ears, he saw, neatly
centered on the bed, resting lightly on the taut drumhead of
his blanket, the little blue Tiffany's box that he had discarded
that afternoon at work, the Outstanding Stand-in award that he
had jammed in among the crushed and sticky cans in the recycling box. It sat on the middle of his bed, almost glowing, as
if at the center of a little spotlight.

"Oh boy," Paul said, to no one in particular.

TWENTY-FOUR

AFTER A FITFUL NIGHT, miraculously uninterrupted by Charlotte, Paul gave up trying to sleep and got out of bed at 6:30. As a result of last night's energetic lovemaking, he ached in muscles he hadn't known he had, so he showered longer than usual, letting the hot water soak into his thighs and his shoulders. As he shaved he was pleased to find a bright purple hickey just above his left nipple, and he took a moment in the glare of the overhead light to twist this way and that in the mirror, looking for another. But his anxiety crept up on him again as he dressed, so, as he prepared his breakfast, he made some executive decisions about the carnival ride of the previous day. His graduate training in literary theory had taught him that there was no one, indisputable interpretation of any situation. There is no truth; all reality—Paul reminded himself as he poked at his scrambled eggs with his plastic spatula—is linguistic. So there was no reason to accept the hegemonic construction of yesterday's events.

In other words, Paul decided, I do not work for Olivia Haddock, and this morning I'm going to make that fact clear to that spineless little milquetoast Rick. That's number one. Next, Paul decided, the recycling box is a recycling box, not the portal to some bottomless, infernal pit. I was upset, he thought, my mind was playing tricks on me. Just as it was—decision number three—when I thought I saw the Colonel give a thumbs-up to Boy G and the others on the bridge. For obvious reasons— thank you, Charlotte—I am prone to seeing the bizarre around every corner.

Paul sloshed the eggs, still runny, onto his purple plate, and retrieved the salsa from the dank recesses of his fridge. Number four: no more lunches with the Colonel and his stooges. I don't know what they want from me, and I certainly don't want anything from them. He doused the eggs liberally with salsa, then hesitated with a forkful halfway to his lips. What number am I up to? he wondered, then decided, I tidied up my own apartment last night, before Callie showed up. I just don't remember doing it. And finally, I stuck the Tiffany's box in my pocket without thinking about it, brought it home myself, and left it on the bed. 'Nuff said. The end.

After breakfast, Paul put the Tiffany's box into his lunch bag with his cheese sandwich and his little baggie of pickles. As he carried it out to his car in the early morning heat, he was intercepted by Mrs. Prettyman, who came teetering down the parking lot in her high heels as if walking on tiptoe. "Oh, Mr. Trilby!" she sang.

Paul didn't care if she saw him roll his eyes. "Good morning, Mrs. Prettyman." He opened his creaking door and slung his lunch onto the passenger seat.

"The owner would like to know," said Mrs. Prettyman as she clicked around the rear of Paul's car, "if you have a room-mate."

Paul slouched in the open door of his car with his hand on the roof, a very Snopesish pose.

"Because the terms of the lease explicitly state," she went on, with her hand at her throat, "that each extra occupant costs an extra one hundred dollars a month."

Paul had never signed a lease; he had never ever seen one. "I don't have a roommate," he said. Mrs. Prettyman must have seen Callie last night, but he didn't know what to call her in front of his prying landlady. Yes, she was his squeeze, his inamorata, but she certainly wasn't his roommate. "A friend of mine came by last night," he said, "but she doesn't live with me."

"I don't mean the young lady in the pickup truck," Mrs. Prettyman said with an insinuating intonation. Did this woman do nothing but peer through her curtains? "I meant the pale gentleman."

"The pale gentleman?" Even in the morning heat, Paul felt a chill.

"Well, I don't know his *name*." Mrs. Prettyman rubbed her clavicle with her long, nicotine-stained middle finger. "I just noticed him fiddling with the grate."

"The grate? What grate?"

"The storm sewer?" chirped Mrs. Prettyman helpfully. "In the middle of the parking lot?" She half turned, and Paul lifted himself on his toes to peer at the square, rusty grate behind her.

"What do you mean, fiddling with it?"

"Well, truly, *I* don't know," his landlady said, leveling her gaze at him. "But he was fiddling with it, then he stood up and went into your apartment. So I figured *surely* he must be a friend of yours."

"How did he get in?" Paul felt chilled all over. What did she mean by "pale gentleman"?

"Honey, you must have given him a key because I surely did not."

Paul glanced back at his door. He was positive he had locked it when he left with Callie.

"Then I happened to look up from my program about, oh, twenty minutes later?" sang Mrs. Prettyman. "And out he come and commenced to fiddling with the grate again."

Paul swallowed. "Where did he go?" He wasn't sure he wanted to hear the answer.

"Well." Mrs. Prettyman canted her hip. "I got up to come out and have a word with him—I figured the owner would like to know?—but by time I got to the door, he was gone."

Paul glanced along the balcony across the parking lot. "Did anybody else see him?" He wondered if he could pluck up the nerve to question his hard-bitten neighbors.

Mrs. Prettyman narrowed her gaze. "So I can tell the owner that you do not know this man?"

"No, I don't know him."

Mrs. Prettyman edged closer to Paul, and for the first and last time, she seemed to take pity on him. "Are you missing anything? Did he take anything?"

Paul warded her off with a gesture. This was not what he wanted to hear; this was not the construction he wanted to impose on the events of the previous evening. He had intervened against the hegemonic discourse—there had been no pale gentleman in my apartment bearing Tiffany's boxes, tidying up. Because if there *had* been, then Paul's own construction of the day before, his brave little house of cards, would come tumbling down, and he would have to reckon with the Colonel signaling the men on the bridge, with the groaning void below the recycling box, with the froggish croak of Dennis the Dying Tech Writer whispering, *"They're up there. . . ."*

"Nothing was taken," Paul insisted.

Mrs. Prettyman dropped her voice to a whisper. "Because I *do not* want to have the police out here. Not if I don't have to." The moment of pity was over; this sounded like a warning.

Paul stepped around her and walked back to his apartment door and gave the knob a good, hard twist. "See?" he said. "Locked up tight." Maybe she hadn't seen anything, he wanted to tell her. Maybe she ought to lay off the gin and tonics after dinner, or whatever it was that floated Mrs. Prettyman's boat. Maybe, for some reason he couldn't fathom, she'd tidied up his apartment herself and was concocting a story to cover her behavior. But if that was the case, why did she have to mention that the gentleman she saw was *pale?* It certainly hadn't been

Mrs. Prettyman who had left the Tiffany's box glowing balefully in the middle of his bed.

He edged past her again and got into his car. "I have to go to work," he said, starting the car.

Mrs. Prettyman stepped back and raised her voice over the tin can rattle of the Colt. "Is there something the owner needs to know?" she said as Paul backed out. "You don't want to be keeping anything from the owner."

Paul threw her a nervous little wave and pulled away. Fifteen minutes later he was waiting in traffic in the middle of the Travis Street Bridge, peering anxiously between the looming SUVs and back through his rearview and side mirrors looking for Boy G. His pulse fluttered; his mouth was dry. But the pale, homeless man was nowhere to be seen, nor were any of his pale compatriots, and Paul rattled across the bridge and into the TxDoGS lot. He found a space against the river embankment and rolled up his windows and locked the car. Then he climbed the embankment and descended the other side nearly to the river. The sky was still a delicate blue—the sun had not yet bleached it white—and the slanting light picked out the bright yellow jerseys of a pair of rowers on the river, sculling in rhythm across the water like a pair of long-legged insects. Paul dug in his lunch bag and brought out the sharp-edged square of the Tiffany's box. He hefted it for a moment. Then, as the rowers passed under the bridge, he hurled it as hard as he could out over the river. It sailed, tumbling, over the humped back of the storm drain culvert and landed far enough out in the water that Paul could not hear a splash. The morning light caught a little sparkling crown of water, but to Paul's dismay, the box did not sink. Instead it wobbled slowly away on the greenish current, bobbing in the rounded swell thrown up by the two rowers. He watched it for a moment, hoping it would go under, but finally he furled his lunch bag shut and went inside.

TWENTY-FIVE

As PAUL PASSED THROUGH THE MAIN LOBBY, Preston beckoned him. "You got a minute?" he said.

"I have a badge, remember?" Paul plucked the new ID out of his pocket. "I don't have to sign in anymore."

"Just take a second," Preston said, beckoning again.

Paul stopped but kept his distance. "I'm kinda late . . ."

Preston glanced to either side. "I'm sort of conducting my own investigation of "—he lowered his voice—"recent events." He beckoned Paul one more time and leaned over the desk. "You ever see anything weird, you'd tell me, right?"

Paul started to edge away again. He really did not want to talk about this. "Preston," he said, gesturing over his shoulder, "I really have to get to work."

Preston started to say something else, but suddenly he stood back from the counter and stiffened.

"Gentlemen," boomed the Colonel. He sailed gut first, spine erect, across the lobby between Preston and Paul. Preston's leathery face turned red, and he picked up a clipboard and studied it hard. Paul caught the Colonel's slipstream but not too close. He stashed his lunch and took the stairs to the second floor. His stomach knotted as he passed the elevator and the recycling box and came into the subterranean light of cubeland. Who knew what horrors awaited him? Dennis the Dying Tech Writer sprawled in Paul's chair, gray skinned and grinning like a skull? Boy G crouched in a corner of Paul's cube, his eyes glowing green like Gollum's out of the shadows? Or Charlotte herself, sprawled like the Cheshire cat across the top of Paul's monitor, her switching tail strobing across Paul's screen? Or perhaps all three—Paul's skin tightened at the thought—hunched around his monitor and turning slowly, in eerie unison, to grin at him as he came through the door. . . .

But as he swung into his cube, what Paul saw was worse: a new Post-it from Olivia pasted against his streaming screen saver. It read, in her razor-sharp print:

RFP TEAM MEETING
RICK'S OFFICE
8:00 AM.
SHARP.
—O. H.

Paul whirled. Olivia was not in her cube, so he jerked the Post-it off his screen and ripped it in half, then ripped it in half again and stuffed it into his wastebasket. He jiggled his mouse to get rid of the screen saver—the motto was beginning to annoy him—and marched out the door, around the corner, and up the aisle towards Rick's office to announce his decision not to work for Olivia. He blundered straight into Renee and caught her by the shoulders. "I'm, I'm, I'm *sorry*," he stammered, the two of them wheeling round each other like square dancers. Renee stamped her foot against the carpet, instantly red faced and speechless, and Paul let her go—

gingerly, so that she wouldn't fall—and rounded the corner. Ahead, all three of his luncheon companions were gliding out of their cube doorways like wooden soldiers on an antique clock. The Colonel cocked his eye at Paul and waved him alongside, putting his arm around Paul's shoulders. "What's going on here, Professor?" he murmured in Paul's ear. "What's Olivia up to?"

"How should I know?" Paul said.

"You sit across from the little bitch." The Colonel's blunt fingers dug into Paul's arm. "If there's something we need to know, you might give us a heads-up."

As they approached Rick's office, Nolene looked up at them from her monitor and rolled her eyes. Inside, Olivia had pulled a chair up to the front of Rick's desk, her knees together, her heels lifted, the balls of her feet pressed to the carpet. She clutched a notepad on her lap, her hands neatly folded over the pad, her pen clutched between them. She nodded as each man came into the room. Bob Wier cowered in the corner, putting a chair between himself and the rest of the room, and J. J. tried to prop himself casually on the lip of the little round table across from Rick's desk. The Colonel maneuvered Paul into the office ahead of him, then set his feet at parade rest, crossed his arms, and lifted his chin. Paul hunched near the door with his hands in his pockets. Behind the desk Rick lifted his eyebrows at the little crowd. A copy of the RFP, heavily emended, was spread before him.

"Looks like we counted our chickens before the barn door was shut." Rick's eyebrows danced. "I've asked Olivia to join the team, and she's hit the ground flying." Olivia dipped her head.

J. J. edged off the table, and after a glance at the Colonel, crossed his arms and affected a pout. Bob Wier looked wildly about like a trapped animal. The Colonel sniffed and said, "Welcome to the team, Olivia."

"*Thank* you," chirped Olivia, without looking at him.

Rick waved his hand vaguely. "Olivia, why don't you, uh . . . ?"

"I've taken the liberty of making copies of the RFP with my

edits." Olivia half rose from her chair and lifted a stack of fresh copies, collated and stapled, off the corner of Rick's desk. She thrust them towards Paul who, after a sullen pause, heaved himself out of the doorway and took the stack. He handed a copy each to J. J. and the Colonel. Bob Wier reached gingerly out from behind his chair and snatched a copy from Paul's grasp.

"I'm not suggesting that we go through it now." Olivia perched again on the edge of her chair. "I'm sure we all have too much work to do."

Paul flipped through the pages of Olivia's edit. The original, on Rick's desk, was as bright as an illuminated manuscript, with lime-green highlights and Olivia's sharp marginalia in red pen; in the photocopy in his hands, the red commentary was black, and the highlighter came through as long, gray blots swallowing line after line. Paul tried to read what Olivia had done, but his rage and terror turned the letters to cuneiform.

"So what I'm suggesting, with Rick's approval," she continued, and Rick flipped his hand in the air, *okay, whatever,* "is that the team take some time to digest my suggestions, and that we reconvene on Friday morning—"

"Tomorrow?" gulped J. J.

"—and take the whole day to go over the document, line by line, in light of my suggestions." She swiveled her gaze round the office. "If that's okay with you all."

"Tomorrow?" whimpered Bob Wier.

"Well, you have all day today," said Olivia. "And if we each take it home with us tonight—"

"Tomorrow's good," barked the Colonel. He had not budged from his stance; his arms were still crossed, biceps bulging. His copy of the RFP was rolled up and squeezed nearly in two in one tight fist. "We'll all make it a priority."

"That's good enough for government work," announced Rick, pressing his palms against the pages of the RFP. "Paul," he said, darting a glance in Paul's direction, "whyn't you book the conference room and the laptop and projector for tomorrow, all day?"

Paul's throat seized up, but at last he managed to croak, "It's kinda short notice—"

He was interrupted by a loud harrumph from the Colonel. "The professor's holding out on us," he said. "I hear tell he's got some *pull* in Building Services."

All eyes turned to Paul, who wanted to shrink against the wall. He glared at the Colonel.

"Sure," he rasped. "No problem."

"Well then!" Olivia widened her eyes and stood up. "Let's all get to work."

"Yep, you betcha, let's do that." Rick waved at them all as if from the deck of a departing cruise ship. Paul and the Colonel stood aside, and Olivia minced out the door and up the aisle. Then J. J. slouched after her, and Bob Wier disentangled himself from his chair and slipped quickly away. The Colonel ostentatiously waved Paul ahead, and then fell in step beside him. He put his arm around Paul again and directed him up the aisle into his own cube, settling Paul into a chair in the narrow space across from his desk. J. J. and Bob Wier crowded in after them. The Colonel flung his rolled-up RFP onto his desk and sat. He folded his hands and glowered at Paul. J. J. glowered at him, too, from the cube doorway, his copy of the RFP crushed under his arm, while Bob Wier clutched the document with both hands and nervously surveyed the cube horizon.

"Professor," the Colonel said in a low voice, "you might have warned us."

"About what?" Paul shifted uneasily in the chair. His copy of the RFP was coiled loosely in his hand.

"About Olivia joining the outsourcing project," the Colonel said.

"I only found out yesterday." Paul hated the way his voice shot up in pitch.

"You coulda said something at lunch, dickhead," hissed J. J.

"She's going to ruin it for all of us," whispered Bob Wier, his eyes wide and white.

"You've been sitting across from her." Behind the desk the Colonel crossed his arms and stared hard at Paul. "Whatever you've been doing over there, she's been keeping an eye on you, and now she thinks she can muscle in and take over the whole goddamn project."

Paul nearly erupted out of his chair. "What I've been *doing* over there," he said, struggling to keep his voice down, "is writing the goddamn RFP." He shook the document at the Colonel. "I do all the research, I do all the writing, I do *all the fucking work!*" He stopped and drew a breath. Bob Wier shot a nervous glance at the Colonel, as did J.J., and the Colonel lowered his gaze to his desk.

"Jesus Christ," Paul said, dropping his voice an octave, "did you think I wouldn't *notice?*"

"The professor has kind of a faggy intonation sometimes." J.J. looked to the Colonel. "Have you noticed that?"

"J.J.," warned the Colonel.

"You've been a real blessing to the team," Bob Wier said to Paul, in a quavering voice. "Which is why we'd like to invite you to—"

"Reverend!" barked the Colonel. "Shut. Up."

Bob Wier shrank lower, his shoulders rising up around his ears.

"Invite me to what?" Paul glanced from Bob Wier to the Colonel to J.J., who glared angrily at the floor. "Invite me to *what?* What the fuck is going on with you guys?"

"Karaoke night." The Colonel uncrossed his arms and touched the top of his desk with the tips of his fingers. "Friday night. The whole team's invited."

"Even Olivia?" J.J. glanced up.

"Especially Olivia," said the Colonel.

The three men exchanged a look while Paul watched from his chair. But before he could say anything, the Colonel stood up and said, "Dismissed. We'll reconvene at lunch."

Bob Wier hurried out the door, while J.J. fixed Paul with one last angry glance before he left. Paul stood.

"You have a choice to make, Professor." The Colonel smoothed out the RFP with the edge of his palm. "You can be a slave for Olivia Haddock, or you can be a man."

Paul waved his copy of the RFP dismissively and moved out the door.

"We keep you alive to serve this ship," the Colonel called after him. "Row well and live."

TWENTY-SIX

PAUL AVOIDED LUNCH WITH THE COLONEL BY PERSUADING
Callie to take him to Sonic, and they sat in the hot cab of her
truck with the windows rolled down, in a hot breeze redolent
of hot fried foods, and ate cheeseburgers and fries. Paul couldn't
remember the last time he'd shared a meal with a woman at a
drive-in. His ex-wife wouldn't have been caught dead in one—
like most postmodern theorists, she was a frightful snob—and
Kymberly would have quizzed the plump waitress with the paper hat and the coin changer on her belt about the fat content
of every goddamn thing on the menu. It was different with
Callie. As hormonal as a fifteen year old, still thinking of the
night before, Paul got a teenaged thrill from the way their fingers brushed when they reached into the bag of fries at the
same time. They slouched across the big bench seat, their
shoulders touching, and traded commentary about the patrons
in the vehicles on the far side of the awning.

"See that slick sonuvabitch in the Jeep Cherokee?" Callie
asked, with her mouth full.

"The one on his cell phone?" Paul wiped his fingers on a paper napkin. "He's in real estate."

"Worse than that," said Callie. "He's the kind of snake who buys people's houses in foreclosure and then leases their own house back to 'em—at twice the interest."

"Weasel."

"Plus he's cheatin' on his wife."

"C'mon," Paul said, "how can you tell that?"

"Look at the way he's smilin' and laughin' on the phone. A guy don't smile like that when he's talking to his wife."

"How do you know he's married? Maybe he's single, and he's talking to his hot new girlfriend." Paul waggled his eyebrows lubriciously.

"You can see his ring, where his hand rests on the steering wheel. God," she laughed, waving her burger, "look how he's curling his fingers around the wheel. Look how he's *rubbing* it! He ain't thinkin' of the little woman." Callie took an enormous bite of the cheeseburger and a pickle oozed out the other side and landed *plop!* on her darling clavicle.

"I'll get that," Paul said. He wanted to pluck the pickle off her warm skin with his teeth.

"Easy there," she said. She sat up straight and pinched it off herself between two fingernails. Then she rewarded him anyway with a greasy kiss.

On their way back to work, Callie manhandled the stick shift and maneuvered the big, rattling truck through lunchtime traffic, and Paul almost felt he should confide in her. He was beginning to think she might have some rough, sensible, working-class way of looking at his predicament, some Oklahoma gal's prairie insight into how to deal with a cheerleading queen like Olivia Haddock or with the oppressive military bonhomie of the Colonel. But at the moment he was happily drowsy, with a bellyful of ground beef, a hot breeze rippling his shirt, and a warm, diffuse, noonday lust for the woman at the other end of the seat.

"How 'bout I come to your place tonight?" Callie said as they pulled into a spot in the TxDoGS lot.

"My place?" Paul said, stirring out of his stupor of beef and desire.

"You've been to my place twice. I thought I'd come over to yours this time."

"You, uh, you were there last night."

"Unless you don't want me come over." She gave him a canny look. "Maybe your *other* girlfriend is coming over tonight."

"Other girlfriend?" Paul laughed nervously. "I should be so lucky."

"Ha. Ha." Callie tugged at the door latch. "I'm not kiddin', cowboy. I'm coming over." She heaved the door open on its whining hinges. "I want to see that cat you say you don't have."

Paul reached along the seat and clutched Callie's arm, keeping her in the truck. He had thought that last night's moment of more or less sincere vulnerability had bought him all the credit he needed for the time being, and now he found himself calculating the likelihood of an appearance by Charlotte if Callie came over. The ghostly cat had been fairly discreet when Paul had lived with Kymberly, but then, it had been Kymberly's house. Now that Charlotte had Paul all to herself, he wasn't sure she'd be willing to share him. And there was still Mrs. Prettyman to reckon with, not to mention the beetling stares of all those horny Snopeses.

"You know what?" Paul said abruptly. "Come on over. We'll get a pizza. We'll watch a little TV, make a little love. We'll read to each other from the *Norton Anthology*." Back off, you freaking dead pussycat, he thought, I have a *girl*, goddammit. And I'm going to have noisy, athletic sex in my own apartment tonight, and you're going to vanish in a fucking puff of smoke.

"Okay, now you're foolin' with me," Callie said.

"No, I'm not." He took her hand in both of his and kissed her. She tasted deliciously of mustard and onions and pickle. "Really, truly I'm not," he murmured, and kissed her again.

Callie was blushing when he pulled away, and he heaved open his door and got out of the truck. He heard Callie's door bang shut, and then she was alongside him, looking at him quizzically. "What ain't you telling me?" She gave him a playful rap with the back of her hand.

He walked backwards before her. "You kind of have to see it to believe it."

Inside the lobby, Callie stiffened her spine and marched across the lobby, trying to make it look as though she and Paul had not come in together. For his part, Paul pretended that he didn't see Preston beckoning him, and he followed Callie up the stairs and into Building Services. "What are you doing?" she hissed just inside the door.

"I need to book the laptop and projector for tomorrow," he said, and then, in a loud voice, "How you doing, Ray?"

In the inner office Ray sat massively behind the desk; a row of tacos leaned together before him in a little cardboard tray. He lifted a taco carefully, so as not to spill any of the filling, opened his mouth, and bit the entire thing in two. His cheeks bulged, his lips tightened, but he didn't lose a speck. "Mmmph," he said.

"Tomorrow?" Callie said loudly, glaring at Paul. "I'll have to check the book." She slapped the schedule book open, and Paul leaned over her shoulder as she filled in his name. Then, with another glance back at Ray—the other half of the taco had just disappeared—she bit Paul quickly on the neck and shoved him out the door. As Paul came out of the office, Preston was hauling himself up the last couple of steps onto the balcony. He pivoted heavily round the railing and called out, "Paul! Hold up!"

"I'm late back from lunch," Paul said, but Preston caught him by the elbow and dragged him around the corner up the hall towards cubeland.

"How you doin'?" Preston said breathlessly, backing Paul up against the wall with his belly.

"You keep asking me that." Paul tugged his elbow free. "I'm fine."

"Good. That's good." Preston wheeled around his belly so that he stood next to Paul with his back against the wall. He glanced both ways up the hallway, then he held Paul with a solemn gaze. "You remember what I asked you this morning?"

"About seeing anything?"

"You know," Preston sniffed. "Anything weird."

"Weirder than a guy dying in the cube next to me?"

"All due respect?" Preston glanced past Paul down the hall. "That was unfortunate, okay, but it wudn't *weird*, per se. You understand the difference?"

Paul said nothing. What did Preston want from him?

"What I mean is," Preston said, "have you seen anything . . . different? Really out of the ordinary?" He fixed Paul with his gaze again. "Something, you know, you're not really sure you saw it."

Preston fingered the strap that held his pistol in its holster. Why should I trust this guy? Paul wondered. Would he believe me if I told him what I've seen? And anyway, Paul reminded himself, he'd decided over breakfast that morning that nothing out of the ordinary had happened, that it was all a product of his imagination. Still, Paul heard himself say, "Well, actually, since you asked—"

"Good afternoon, ladies," boomed a voice, and Paul flattened himself against the wall. Preston stepped into the hallway and reflexively popped the snap on the holster, pressing the heel of his hand against the pistol grip. The Colonel swung gut first down the hallway, working a toothpick between his molars.

"*Mister* Pentoon," said Preston, narrowing his eyes.

For Paul, stationed between them, it was like watching two bull walruses squaring off. The Colonel rocked back on his heels and lifted his chin and gazed down his nose at Preston, even though Preston was a half a head taller. The security guard squared his shoulders and smoothed his thick moustache with thumb and forefinger, across and down. Then he looked rather ostentatiously at his wristwatch, still keeping his other hand on the butt of his gun.

"Twelve-fifteen," he said to the Colonel, every inch the officer-on-parade. "A little late back from lunch, ain't you?"

The Colonel gazed over his head, as if he were considering something. "I don't believe," he said, "that I've ever heard that question before from your pay grade."

Preston narrowed his eyes into a steely Eastwood squint.

The Colonel worked his toothpick. "Shouldn't you be watching the front desk?"

Preston shifted his hand on his gun. "You never know where they're gonna get in, do ya?"

"Paul," barked the Colonel, shifting his gaze. "We missed you at lunch today."

"Yes," Paul gasped. There was such a powerful military vibe in the air, he nearly said, "Yes, *sir*."

"You know," the Colonel continued, with an insinuating air, "I don't mind you abandoning us at lunch, especially if you have a better offer," and he carved the curve of a woman in the air with the edge of his hand, "but I don't think Preston here's your type."

"By your leave, *Colonel*," said Preston, "Mr. Trilby and I have a security matter to discuss."

The two old soldiers fixed each other with a deadly glare. The Colonel's toothpick quivered erect out of the side of his mouth, while Preston's chest rose and fell slowly. Paul wondered if he was going to have to dive for cover. Finally the Colonel lifted the toothpick out of his mouth and said, "Carry on, then." He brushed by Preston, missing him by inches. Preston didn't budge.

"Just don't stand there all day, girls." The Colonel flicked the crushed toothpick at Preston's feet. "Someone might mistake y'all for a couple of old hens."

As the Colonel's heels clacked down the hall, Preston let out a long, slow sigh and dropped his hand away from the holstered gun. "God*damn*," he breathed.

Paul waited until the Colonel had disappeared around the corner at the far end of the hall, then he whispered, "What was that all about?"

Preston shook his head. "Dun't matter," he said, and he took a step back towards his post. He stopped abreast of Paul and said, "Just . . . if you *see* anything you think I ought to know about, you be sure to *tell* me, alright?"

"Alright," Paul said.

"He wasn't a colonel." Preston's voice was tight with emotion. "He wun't *never* a colonel."

"What?" said Paul.

"Colonel Travis," said the security guard bitterly. "That's his *name*, not his rank. His daddy named him after the commander of the Alamo."

Paul glanced down the hall to make sure the Colonel had gone.

"Highest rank he ever made was sergeant," Preston said. "He was a pastry chef in an officer's club in South Korea."

"Seriously?" Paul whispered.

"You ask him." Preston lifted his chin. "While I was catching hell in the Lebanon and the Gulf, that sumbitch was decorating Christmas cookies in fucking Seoul."

"I didn't know," Paul said. "I just assumed—"

"Yeah." Preston thumped down the hall on the heels of his boots, and just before he turned the corner he said, just loud enough for Paul to hear, "*I* was a colonel." Then he was gone.

TWENTY-SEVEN

"SO LEMME GET THIS STRAIGHT." Callie sat up and swung her legs over the edge of Paul's bed. "This cat you say you drowned." She glanced over her shoulder, the heels of her hands pressed to the mattress, her toes pinching the dingy carpet.

"Charlotte." He lazily stroked the sweaty bumps of Callie's spine.

"Right, Charlotte." Callie frowned. "You say she's still here."

A long sigh. "Yes." I should have kept my mouth shut, Paul thought.

"In this apartment." Callie's face was half turned toward him, without looking at him. "Like, haunting you or something."

"Yes." He rolled his knuckles against the warm, tight muscles of her back.

"And you can see her and stuff." She had the tiniest bulge of a belly, which Paul found fetching. It was creased in little folds.

"Yes."

"Can you see her right now?"

Just to be sure, Paul glanced round the room. "No," he said. Callie had showed up at his door after dinner with a change of clothes and the *Norton Anthology* in a little nylon gym bag. "You said we could read to each other," she had said.

At the moment, though, the English canon was the farthest thing from her mind. "But you *do* see her," she was saying. "Sometimes."

"Yes." He let his hand drop.

"And she's dead."

Another sigh. "*Yes.*" In his postcoital stupor, when he loved the whole world, Paul had mistakenly believed that he could build on his moment of vulnerability from the night before in Callie's pickup truck. He'd thought that if he began with his ghost cat, he could work up to telling her about Boy G and the pale homeless guys he'd seen at the library and on the bridge. Now he wasn't so sure. He reached for Callie, but she pushed herself up from the squeaking bed—a wonderfully rhythmic squeak just a few minutes ago—and stooped to pick up Paul's shirt from the floor.

"And that's why it smells like . . . like *cat* in here." She shrugged the shirt on, both arms at once, like James Dean. Paul couldn't decide if this was a good sign or a bad sign. She was getting dressed, sort of, but she was putting on *his* shirt after all, and she canted her weight on one marvelous hip as she slowly buttoned it from the bottom. Paul propped himself up on one elbow. She knows what she's doing, he thought.

"It stands to reason," he said, crossing his legs at the ankle.

She only did the bottom three buttons, leaving the shirt open to the matched curves of her lovely breasts. "So even though she's a ghost, she can still, you know, pee and stuff." She began to pace before the end of Paul's bed in a long, swinging gait. Oh yes, thought Paul, she *knows* what she's doing.

He smiled at her. "Let's just drop it."

Callie pivoted on the ball of her foot and paced back the other way. "So does she have little ghostly fleas?"

"Seriously." Paul was beginning to get aroused again. "Forget I said anything."

"You brought it up."

"The hell I did!" he laughed. "You *asked* me, this afternoon, after lunch!" A naked girl in my shirt, Paul thought. I can't believe I fall for it every time.

"Okay," she said, "but you reckoned right *now* was a good time to tell me about your dead cat?" She put her hands on her hips, widening the gap in the shirtfront, and in the yellow glow of his bedside lamp, Paul caught a glimpse of one perfect, adorable nipple.

"Come back to bed," Paul said.

"I swear, you got the damnedest idea of pillow talk."

"Can we drop it now?" What would she do, he wondered, if he lunged for her? Kymberly used to love that when she was in the right mood.

"Didn't you say I'd have to see it to believe it?" She stopped pacing.

"Yes." He pushed himself up and tucked his knees under him.

She spread her hands and looked wide-eyed round the apartment. "Okay, then, where is she?"

"What if I said that she's right behind you." It wasn't true. Paul began to crawl slowly down the mattress towards Callie.

"Okay, now you're creeping me out." She warned him off with a gesture.

"Aha! So you do believe me!" He coiled himself to pounce.

"See, now, I didn't say that." She pushed in his direction with the palm of her hand. "It's just . . . well, either I'm in bed with a guy who's haunted by a cat, or I'm in bed with a guy who *thinks* he's haunted by a cat, or I'm in bed with a guy who wants *me* to think he's haunted by a cat."

"There's one more possibility." He let himself sink back on his heels.

"What's that?"

"You're in bed with a guy who wants *you* to think that he thinks he's haunted by a cat."

"Whoa, Professor, now you *are* creeping me out." Callie waved both palms in his direction.

"Here, kitty kitty kitty." Paul crept across the lumpy mattress.

"Stop it!" she laughed, backing away.

"And don't call me professor." Paul lunged, and Callie shrieked. But he only reached around her legs and snatched her beat-up old gym bag off the floor. He dived into it and came up with the *Norton Anthology*. As Callie danced back, catching herself against the wall, Paul tossed the bag aside and flopped back on the bed with the fat volume on his lap. He propped himself up with a couple of pillows, making the bedsprings squeal. He heaved the book open and flipped through the tissuey pages.

"Be careful!" Callie said. "You'll mess up my book."

Paul stretched himself out and lifted the book in both hands like a massive hymnal. "Here we go," he announced. "'My Cat Jeoffry,' by Christopher Smart." He propped the book against his chest. "'For I will consider my cat Jeoffry,'" he intoned. "'For he is the servant of the Living God duly and daily serving him. . . .'"

"Not that." Callie inched towards the bed. "That fella was half crazy."

"'For first he looks upon his fore-paws to see if they are clean,'" Paul continued. "'For secondly he kicks up behind to clear away there. . . .'"

Callie stepped up onto the bed, making the springs twang, and Paul caught his breath—first at the sight of her long legs descending from the tails of his shirt, but then at the sight of Charlotte sprawled across the top of the TV, her tail switching back and forth across the blank, gray screen. Paul dropped his eyes to the book and caught his breath again, for the next line read, "For when he takes his prey he plays with it to give it a chance."

Callie straddled him on her long legs and then dropped to her knees, rattling the whole bed, nearly shaking the book from Paul's grasp. Her warm weight against his loins made him hard again. She placed her hands across the page he was reading from and looked at him gravely. "Don't read that," she breathed.

He peered around her. Charlotte watched them both from the top of the TV, her eyes wide and fathomless.

"What are you looking at?" Callie said.

"Nothing," said Paul. His mouth was very dry all of a sudden.

Callie half turned her head as if to look at Charlotte, but not quite far enough. She sat thoughtfully for a moment. Then she faced Paul again and pressed her fingertips along his jaw so that he looked at her. He hoped she couldn't see the fear in his eyes.

"Let's read something else," she murmured, and she took the book from his hands. They shifted slowly together, Paul slipping farther down the bed, Callie settling more tightly against him. His shirt billowed out from her, and he caught her warm, salty scent. She turned the book over and laid it flat against his chest, flipping slowly through the pages.

"Callie," he said, but she put a finger to his lips and said, "Shh." She found the page she wanted and pressed her palm against the open pages, flattening the binding against his sternum. "Just listen," she said, and she began to rock slowly against him.

" 'In this strange labyrinth how shall I turn?
Ways are on all sides, while the way I miss:
If to the right hand, there in love I burn;
Let me go forward, therein danger is.' "

Her accent was as strong as ever, but she read as if she were making the words up as she went along. As she read, Paul slowly slid his palms up her taut thighs.

"Who wrote this?" he said, watching her.

"Mary Worth," Callie said.

"Mary *Worth?*" The way she moved against him was exquisite.

"Hush up," she said, and she continued:

> " 'If to the left, suspicion hinders bliss,
> Let me turn back, Shame cries I ought return.
> Nor faint though crosses with my fortunes kiss;
> Stand still is harder, although sure to mourn.' "

He slid his thumbs under the tails of the shirt and slipped his cock inside her. Callie inhaled sharply, but she kept reading.

> " 'Then let me take the right or left-hand way;
> Go forward, or stand still, or back retire.
> I must these doubts endure without allay
> Or help, but travail find for my best hire.' "

The springs of the creaky old sofa bed sang sweetly. Paul knew that Charlotte was still there, somewhere, watching—angrily? enviously?—or with some feline diffidence he'd never understand. Whatever it was, he couldn't take his eyes off the tremors of pleasure crossing Callie's face. The heavy anthology rose and fell on his breastbone, and Callie pressed the pages flat with her thumbs, the tips of her fingers brushing his chest. She squeezed him with her thighs, and Paul moaned and closed his eyes and felt her hot breath on his cheek as she breathed the last lines into his ear.

" 'Yet that which most my troubled sense doth move,' " she whispered, " 'Is to leave all, and take the thread of love.' "

TWENTY-EIGHT

IN THE MORNING, just before he was pinched awake, shaking and sweating, by the icy little needles of Charlotte's teeth, Paul dreamed of a vast cubescape that ran endlessly into a dim twilight, an infinity of cubicles grown over with gray fabric. At the center of each cube stood a pale, buzz-cut man in a shirt and tie, his breast pocket full of pens and mechanical pencils, his eyes wide behind a thick-lensed pair of glasses. Each man wore a smudgy HELLO! MY NAME IS name tag, each with a different unreadable name. Above the cubescape the knotty ceiling was hung with gray stalactites, and fat, gray droplets fell slowly but steadily, each with an echoing bathhouse *plink!* streaking the gray fabric of the cube partitions and splashing the milky foreheads of the pale men, who seemed not to notice. Apart from the steady chorus of droplets, the only other sound was an arrhythmic murmuring, indecipherable at first, until one by one the men smiled, each one pulling his cracked lips away from a row of sharpened teeth. Like a rising tide it came to Paul what they were saying, not in unison, not a chant, but each man whispering individually, in a feverish monotone, "Are we not men? Are we not men?"

Then they opened their jaws wide and all rushed at him at once, pouring up the aisles between their cubes, and Paul fled from them up a series of long, clammy tunnels, each tunnel narrower than the last. Behind him he heard the whispery patter of many feet and the frenzied mumbling of the pale men. Then the mumbling swelled up behind him, and Paul was in his bed, looking up at the grotty ceiling tile of his apartment, listening to the geriatric chug of his air-conditioner. Down the length of his naked body—his skin as pale as the faces of the men in the cubicles—he saw Boy G at the end of his bed, watching him through his thick lenses.

"Boy G," whispered the homeless man, his lips barely moving, "conquers by gentleness."

Am I still dreaming? wondered Paul, and then Charlotte was crouching on the mattress, her tail coiled round her, her ears flattened. She hissed at Boy G, and the homeless man recoiled, his eyes widening behind his glasses. Charlotte turned, opened her jaws as wide as they would go, and drove her teeth into Paul's big toe.

Paul screamed and sat bolt upright in bed. There was Charlotte for real, crouching next to his bare ankle and growling at him. Paul flung a pillow at her, and the cat vanished as the pillow swished through the space where she had just been.

"Ah, Christ." Paul rubbed his toe and swung out of bed. "Callie?" he called out, limping through the tiny apartment, but she had already left. The shower stall was wet, a damp towel draped over the curtain rod. In his eagerness to follow her, Paul skipped breakfast; he wanted to get to work early so that he could set up the conference room for the meeting today. On the Travis Street Bridge, waiting for the light in his rattling car, he kept his eyes fixed on the traffic light at the far end, without so much as a glance to the right or left. His dream had shaken him, and he hoped to avoid even a glimpse of any pale figure wandering among the SUVs. A few moments later he swung into the GSD lot and, because he was still a few minutes early, found a spot close to the building. In the first-floor lobby, Preston nodded to him but said nothing. Paul climbed the stairs to Building Services, but the door was closed. With a glance over the balcony railing at Preston, who was still watching him, Paul headed down the long, second-floor aisle towards his cube. Despite his dream, what he feared most was another Post-it this morning from Olivia, some vicious message pressed to his computer screen that would jangle his nerves and unsettle him all day long. He nearly passed the men's room, then realized that he might not get a chance for a break later in the morning—especially if Olivia was running the meeting—so he went back and pushed through the door. Rick was at the sink already, leaning towards the mirror and tending to the part in his hair with infinite patience, both hands poised over his head. Paul passed behind him to the urinal, unsure if Rick had even seen him.

"Hey, Paul!" Rick called out from the other side of the modesty barrier.

"Yeah," said Paul from the urinal. From habit, he kept an eye on the ceiling panel over his head.

"Y'all took a look at Olivia's edits, right?"

"Sure." Paul zipped up and flushed the urinal with his elbow.

In front of the mirror Rick was still carefully trawling his comb through his hair. "We all set for the big pow-wow this morning?"

"Yes," said Paul, washing his hands.

Rick stepped back from the mirror, turned his head and smiled, turned his head the other way and smiled. "Faaaan-*tas*tic!" he said, and he slipped the comb into his back pocket and swung out the door, letting it bang behind him.

"Fantastic," murmured Paul. He leaned heavily on the counter and surveyed his face in the mirror for a moment. Then he straightened, wiped his hands, and banged out the door. Rounding the corner into the elevator lobby, he ran straight into Boy G.

"Jesus Christ!" cried Paul, jumping back.

The homeless man stood at the recycling box, his fat, bloodless fingers curled under the lid. He was wearing the same clothes he always wore—trousers, baggy in the seat, a thread-bare white shirt with a breast pocket full of mismatched pens, his astronomical tie, wire rims with bulbous lenses. He still sported his smudgy name badge with its bold block printing. His milky scalp gleamed under the fluorescent lights. For the first time Paul noticed his shoes, lace-up black Oxfords scuffed along the sides and gleaming with wet.

"Am I still dreaming?" Paul said out loud. He glanced over his shoulder and then through the door into the twilight of cubeland. "Are you real?" he gasped.

Boy G slowly turned his bug-eyed stare in Paul's direction. "Boy G's no fool," he said, in his whispery undertone.

Paul felt a clammy chill that had nothing to do with the air-conditioning, and he edged slowly around the homeless man. Boy G rotated slowly in place to follow him.

"Who are you?" Paul said.

"Myself," breathed Boy G.

Paul edged closer to the door. "*What* are you?" he said.

"Myself," said Boy G. "Can you say the same?"

There was a long, mournful, hydraulic groan as the elevator arrived at the second floor. Boy G hissed and flashed his savage teeth, then dashed round the corner. Paul was afraid to move until he heard the thump of the men's room door, and then he leaped forward himself, nearly bowling over Renee as she stepped out of the elevator. She shrieked and leaped back, but by then Paul had rounded the corner. He stiff-armed the men's room door and held it open, his muscles trembling. In the glare of the lights Paul saw no one, only his own reflection in the mirror, wild-eyed and panting, but in the far corner, over the farthest stall, the one where Paul occasionally caught a nap in the morning, he saw something black—the scuffed heel, per-haps, of a lace-up black Oxford—rising into a gap in the ceiling, and then the ceiling tile scraping back into its frame. Then he heard a long, slow creaking as something large moved above the ceiling towards the door.

Paul jumped back into the hall and let the door thump shut. He hustled round the corner into cubeland and into his own aisle. His heart pounded, and his hands shook. Please be at your desk, Preston, he prayed, please please *please* be at your desk. He halted for a moment just outside the doorway of his cube and lifted his eyes to the ceiling, making an anxious circuit of the ceiling tiles around his cube. Nothing moved or bulged or creaked. He held his breath and listened. Nothing.

He exhaled and stepped into his cube and froze. On the desk next to the keyboard, squarely at the center of the pool of light from his desk lamp, sat the Tiffany's box, wilted and warped and stained with river water.

TWENTY-NINE

"WHY ISN'T HE WRITING ALL THIS DOWN?" said Olivia, who was seated to the left of Rick.

"Why isn't who writing what down?" said Rick, from the head of the table.

"Why isn't Paul writing down what everyone is saying?" Olivia twirled a pencil between her fingers as skillfully as a majorette.

To the right of Rick, Paul kept his gaze on the glowing screen of the laptop. "I'm waiting for the consensus," he muttered.

"For the what?" said J. J., out of the twilight somewhere to Paul's right. Colonel, J. J., and Bob Wier all sat on Paul's side of the table, while Olivia sat all by herself on the other side.

"What the professor's trying to say," said Colonel, "is that he's waiting for us'n's to come to an agreement on how the paragraph should read."

"It's not for him to decide how the paragraph should read,"

said Olivia. In the glow from the screen at the far end of the room, her face floated as pale as ectoplasm.

"That's not what I'm saying," muttered Paul.

"That's not what he's saying, Olivia," said Colonel. He balanced his laser pointer between his fingers, itching for a chance to switch it on.

"I think there should be a record of everyone's ideas as we go along," said Olivia. "Of who proposed what."

There was a general sigh from the men down the length of the table, and Colonel said, "With all due respect, Olivia, what we need is a firm consensus on the finished document, not a record of the *process*. Who cares who says what?" He glanced either way down the table. "Am I right, gentlemen?"

"Fuckin' A," mumbled J. J.

"Amen," breathed Bob Wier.

"Hm," said Rick, gazing at the backs of his hands.

"The professor here," said Colonel, "is a tech writer, not a stenographer."

Paul hunched his shoulders and avoided meeting Olivia's eyes, but even so her gaze drilled through Paul's forehead and out the back of his skull.

"And anyway," Colonel continued, "I don't think he can type that fast."

The men laughed, and Olivia sighed. Once again she beat a tactical retreat on this subject. It was not the first time she had brought it up, but it was the first time since lunch. She laid her pencil against the tabletop with a distinct *click* and folded her hands over it, as if sheathing her weapon. Across the table J. J. slumped in his seat, his head propped in one hand, and Bob Wier shifted restlessly, both of them silvered by the glow from paragraph 4.3.3 of section 4.3, "Parts, Supplies, and Fluids":

> 4.3.3 The Vendor shall be responsible for damage and costs caused by the use of substandard or non-OEM parts, supplies, or fluids.

"I thought . . . ," Bob began, stabbing the air meekly with his hand.

"Yessir!" barked Rick. A vent in the rear of the projector threw a hot sliver of glare back across the tip of Rick's nose and the bulge of his cheekbones. "Speak up there, Bob!"

"I mean," Bob Wier went on, jerking his hand back, "what was wrong with the RFP the way it was?"

"Yeah," said J. J.

Olivia gasped in exasperation and looked beseechingly at Rick. Rick, however, merely puffed out his cheeks and made popping noises with his lips. All day Rick had been spiritually hors de combat, staring into space or fussing with his tie while Olivia and Colonel conducted a light-saber duel in the dark over the conference table. Olivia gestured with her pencil, and Colonel parried with his laser pointer, bouncing the little red dot all over the screen. Olivia pushed to tear out every paragraph and start over, and Colonel dug in his heels as if each passage were scripture. Rick had stepped in to adjudicate only two or three times during the morning, and since lunch he had been mostly silent, letting the battle wash back and forth across the table before him.

Now Olivia plucked her pencil off the table again and poked it at the screen. "We *require* the vendor to buy OEM parts in the first place," she said. "So how can we make him responsible if the parts fail? It's not his fault."

"Parts is parts," drawled J. J., his voice slurred by boredom.

"Whose side are you on, Olivia?" Colonel rolled the laser pointer between his thumb and forefinger. "Ours or the vendor's?"

"Plus," Olivia continued, ignoring him, "isn't there a hyphen in 'substandard'?"

Before he could stop himself, Paul said, "No!" rather hotly.

"Whoa!" chorused the men along Paul's side of the table.

"The professor speaks!" Rick said merrily.

"Well, there isn't," muttered Paul. It was nearly quitting time, and they had been sitting in the overheated semidark, blinking at the screen and listening to the buzz of the projector's fan, since eight-fifteen that morning. The meeting was supposed to have started at eight, but Paul had been so rattled by the discovery of the Tiffany's box—the rest had never happened, he was sure of it—that he had taken longer than expected to set up. And, quite apart from the stress of sitting for hours in the same room with Olivia, he had kept an eye cocked all day at the ceiling, watching for bulges or sudden gaps or the heel of a black Oxford.

"Way-ul," Rick was saying now, "I don't think we're gonna get to the end of this today."

"I can stay late," Olivia said.

J. J. groaned, and there was a sharp intake of breath from Bob Wier's direction.

"Yeah, well." Rick raised his eyebrows at his wristwatch. "I can't. We'll reconvene on Monday."

"Yesssss," breathed J. J., and there was a long, slow *creeeeak* as he shifted in his chair. Paul's gaze shot to the ceiling again. He'd spent hours listening to every squeak and groan of every chair in the room, and yet each little noise still took him by surprise, stretching his nerves a little tighter. "What's that?" he gasped.

Rick stretched in his own chair, making it creak as well. "What's eating you, son?"

"You been acting hinky all day," said Colonel. "You see a ghost or something?"

Across the table Olivia rapped on the tabletop with the sharp end of her pencil. "Could we at least finish this paragraph before we leave?" she said.

All the men groaned except for Paul, who didn't make a sound.

"At least," insisted Olivia, raising her voice, "at least let's have Paul enter the revisions so far before he goes home tonight. . . ."

"I don't believe Paul has the level of badge," said Colonel, "that allows him to remain in the building after business hours."

"I have a pretty low-level badge," Paul said.

"One of us could stay with him," Olivia said. "As I said before, I can stay late."

Paul's hands began to tremble over the laptop, making the keys rattle. This was even worse than he'd imagined: Not only would he have to be here on his own time, after hours—"You'd never catch me in there after dark," Nolene had said—but he'd be alone *with Olivia*. On Monday morning his coworkers would find him dead in his chair, a gray, desiccated, bloodless husk.

"Not tonight you can't," said Colonel heartily. "Have you forgotten already?"

"I beg your pardon?" said Olivia.

"Karaoke night, my good woman," boomed Colonel. "My house, tonight, seven P.M. sharp. I believe I announced it when we convened this morning?"

He glanced round the table, and J. J. and Bob Wier nodded eagerly. Olivia glanced wildly at Paul, as if afraid he might get away.

"I, uh, can't make it tonight." Rick tapped his own wrist-watch, and he put his palms on the table, preparing to heave himself up. "I have other, uh . . . I won't be able to . . ."

"How about tomorrow morning?" snapped Olivia, restraining Rick with a hand. "Saturday morning, Paul?" she said, fixing Paul with her gaze. "Can you meet me here tomorrow?"

Before Paul could say a word, Colonel grasped his wrist and said, "Yes he can, on one condition."

Olivia glanced furiously from Colonel to Paul and back again. Rick subsided into his seat. "What condition?" she said.

"Well, it seems we can't prevail upon our redoubtable leader here to favor us with a tune this evening." Colonel glanced at Rick, who looked like a whipped dog. "But surely Olivia will grace us with her presence," Colonel continued. "Perhaps the SMU fight song. Or even a cheer or two."

Olivia scowled. She was clearly calculating just how much face she could afford to lose.

"Because if you put in an appearance," Colonel went on, "I

can guarantee the professor here will be at your beck and call tomorrow morning, bright and early."

"Wait a minute . . . ," Paul began, and Colonel silenced him with a really brutal squeeze of his wrist.

"Go Ponies," said Colonel, crinkling his eyes at Olivia.

Olivia lifted her eyebrows at Paul.

"Professor?" said Colonel. "Tomorrow morning? Eight A.M.?"

"Sure," said Paul, miserably. He and Olivia would be alone, but at least it would be daylight.

"That's settled, then." Colonel popped his laser pointer into his breast pocket and placed his palms on the tabletop. "I believe y'all will find an e-mail in your inbox with directions to Casa Pentoon." He stood, and J. J. and Bob Wier stood as well. The meeting was over.

"And remember!" cried Colonel, as Olivia minced out the door. "Everybody sings!"

THIRTY

"I CAN'T DO IT," Paul said.

"Can't do what?" Callie's passenger door was open, and she already had one foot on the curb.

"I can't go in there." Paul had stopped his noisy little car in front of Colonel Travis Pentoon's house in Westhill, the well-to-do community across the river from Lamar. The sun had still been up when he and Callie had entered the labyrinth of winding, leafy streets, and even though Colonel lived in the flatter, more down-market region of the neighborhood—the really expensive homes were higher up, along private drives or behind security gates—Paul had gotten lost. As the rat-a-tat of his decrepit old Colt reverberated off the creamy walls of $200,000 ranch houses, twilight had slowly gathered under the carefully tended stands of live oak. Callie hadn't been any help; instead of navigating, she had frankly rubbernecked, bending towards Paul to peer out his window or hanging halfway out her own to get a good look at someone's cavernous two-car garage or expensively landscaped lawn.

"Dang," she breathed. "Ain't we in a drought? How do they keep the grass so green?"

Paul had said nothing. He was searching among the looming hedges and ornamental shrubbery for the sign to Wicker Way, Colonel's street.

"They must spend more on water," Callie said, "than I do on rent."

At last Paul had found the street, and they had crept through the twilight until they found the address stenciled on the curb. Colonel's long, redbrick ranch house sat a little lower than the street, under the canopy of a huge, old live oak that filled the front lawn like a banyan tree. One massive branch stretched out and up from the broad-chested trunk, like a bodybuilder flexing his biceps. A couple of Japanese lanterns hung motionlessly from the branch in the breathless heat, casting a mellow glow over a limestone-bordered Japanese garden and a little flagstone walk. Another red lantern hung over the imposing front door instead of a porch light. Colonel's enormous SUV was berthed out of sight somewhere, but three other cars—a family minivan that must have been Bob Wier's and a couple of newish subcompacts—were parked in his wide driveway. Paul couldn't even bring himself to switch off the engine, and his car rattled angrily in place. The last thing he wanted to do tonight was spend more time with these people.

"What's the problem?" Callie said. She was wearing the same skirt she had worn on their first date and a tight tee that bared her upper arms and displayed an inch and a half of belly button. "Is it the singing?

"No," Paul said. Having to sing was only a fraction of what made him anxious. What did his three lunch companions want from him? What was Colonel going to reveal to him this evening? And who knew what bourgeois horrors awaited him in Colonel's suburban castle? And (he wondered, way at the back of his brain), how could Colonel afford a house like this on a TxDoGS salary? Worst of all, Olivia was going to be here. Even if he managed to relax in front of the men, how could he possibly relax in front of her? How could he enjoy an evening with Olivia when the next day, Saturday morning, he was going to be alone with her in the darkened cubescape at work? And did he really want to hear her *sing?*

Callie got out and slammed her door, and she came around the front of the car and bent at Paul's window like a traffic cop.

"Step out of the car, mister."

"Callie, let's just go."

"No way, cowboy." She lifted the handle on Paul's door and hauled it open on its groaning hinges. She leaned past him and switched off the engine, and the car coughed into silence, leaving the enthusiastic suburban crickets to fill the swelling darkness. Then she squeezed onto his lap, careful not to bang the horn, crooked her arm around his neck, and faced him nose to nose.

"So fess up," she said. "How long have you known about this evening, and when were you planning to tell me?"

"I only found out about it today," Paul lied. The pressure of Callie's backside on his lap, the steady throb of her pulse in the long curve of her throat, the mild heat of her breath on his cheek—all were making it hard for Paul to maintain his stubbornness. He nuzzled her neck, but she tipped his head back with her finger.

"You know what I think?" *Thunk,* she said. "I think you didn't want your coworkers to see you with your little trailer trash girlfriend."

Paul groaned, aroused and annoyed all at once. He locked his gaze with Callie's and said, "That's not true." And, mirabile dictu, it wasn't. It was the other way around—Paul didn't want his lively new lover to see what a bunch of losers he worked with.

"They already know about us," Paul said, "or at least Colonel does. He told me to bring you."

"Whatever." Callie pressed her cheek to his and whispered in his ear. "You promised me a night out." She bit his earlobe. "If you were planning to get lucky tonight, you better deliver." Then she was off his lap and out of the car, her heels clicking up Colonel's twee little flagstone walk.

Paul caught up to her breathlessly at the door. In the glow of the paper lantern, Callie straightened her shoulders and gave the hem of her top a pert tug. Then she pressed the bell, and inside the house they heard a recording of a gong, a long, muffled clang. Paul started to laugh and Callie slapped his arm, but before either could say a word, the door swung open and a tiny Japanese woman in an orange track suit lined with racing stripes beckoned them in.

"Welcome!" she said, with an aggressive smile. Her hair was loose and attractively streaked with gray. "You must be Paul!"

"And this is Callie," Paul said.

"Hey." Callie stuck out her hand.

"I am Yasumi, Colonel's wife." She took Callie's hand and then Paul's, giving each a brisk, efficient shake. "Or, as we sometime say, I am Mrs. Colonel, ha ha. Mind your step."

She led them at a trot down through a sunken living room, lit only by a single, dim lamp, and Paul glimpsed paper scrolls and a Japanese screen and a sixties-vintage fireplace with a low mantle. The room smelled of air freshener.

"You find us easy?" asked Yasumi without looking back.

"Yes," said Paul, hurrying to keep up as the orange track suit retreated into the gloom.

"We got lost," said Callie.

"It's not so hard," said Yasumi. "Down the steps. Low clearance. Mind how you go."

Because it was built on a slope, Colonel's house had that rarest of domestic amenities in central Texas—a basement. Paul and Callie followed Yasumi single file down a narrow, carpeted stairway, paneled in plywood and hung with framed photographs of Colonel in uniform. Paul held back to look at the pictures, but at the bottom of the stairs Yasumi ushered Callie past her and then gestured briskly for Paul.

"No time!" she said, smiling ferociously. "You look at pictures later. We almost start without you!"

Paul reluctantly turned away from a photo of a younger, thinner Colonel at attention in a dress uniform, behind an enormous cake that read DUTY, FREEDOM, HONOR in red, white, and blue frosting. At the bottom of the stairs, Paul stepped into the brighter light of a long, paneled basement. To the right of the stairs a plywood partition with a plain wooden door in the middle cut across the room, but to the left the room ran all the way to the end of the house. The long walls of the basement were hung with movie posters—*The Great Escape, Bullitt, Seven Samurai*, but also *Gigi, My Fair Lady*, and *The Umbrellas of Cherbourg*. Immediately to the left of the stairs, in an alcove in the inside wall, a bar with two padded stools was backed with a mirror and an impressive array of bottles; on the wide bar top were platters of cold cuts, crackers, cheese, and crudités, and a stack of plastic plates and cutlery. Across from the bar, the outside wall was interrupted by a wide, glass sliding door. Beyond the glass, and through his own reflection and the glare of the room, Paul saw a couple more paper lanterns shining from the branches of a live oak, and a lawn sloping away into the dark.

"Professor!" cried Colonel from the far end of the room. He stood on a small, raised platform behind an array of electronic equipment upholstered in black and hung with a tangle of wires. A wide projection TV screen hung on the wall, and two black speakers as tall as Colonel's wife flanked the little stage. Colonel picked up his drink and stepped down from the platform. He was out of uniform this evening, in an immense Hawaiian shirt splashed with giant red-and-orange flowers, a pair of loose cotton trousers, and big plastic sandals. Paul had never seen Colonel in a short-sleeved shirt before, but he was not surprised to see that the man had arms like a stevedore's.

"You found us!" Colonel swung gut first round a couch and an assortment of comfortable chairs—an old, overstuffed armchair, a plush loveseat, a La-Z-Boy—arranged in a semicircle facing the platform. "We were about to send out a search party."

Despite its tidiness, the basement had a musty smell, as if the carpet had been soaked and improperly dried. Paul worried it might squish under his feet and fill his sandals with brackish water.

Colonel swung his hand in a wide circle and met Paul's in a crushing grip; his bulging forearm was thickly carpeted with steel-gray hair. "She's a firecracker." He winked towards Callie, his breath a haze of Rémy Martin. "I can see already that she's going to be the life of the party. Drink?"

Behind the bar, Colonel made up a scotch and water for Paul, while Paul worked his fingers to restore his circulation and watched Callie introducing herself at the far end of the room. As Yasumi chaperoned, Callie shook hands all around, even with Olivia. She was glowing from within, like one of the paper lanterns outside, and Paul could tell, with a mixture of embarrassment and tenderness, that Callie was prepared to enjoy herself, that she meant to be a little loud and flirty this evening. She was swinging her shoulders and shaking hands vigorously with a flushed Bob Wier, who looked like Pat Boone in a pullover, slacks, and penny loafers without socks.

"What can I fix your lady?" asked Colonel. "She looks like a Wild Turkey gal to me."

"Sure," said Paul. J. J. eyed Callie hungrily from the La-Z-Boy, where he reclined in a pair of sharply pressed trousers, a blue, double-breasted blazer, and a fiery red ascot. A pair of narrow Italian-style loafers were propped on the chair's footrest, and he held a martini at a dangerous angle, the skewered olive threatening to pitch over the lip of the glass. He looked like a surly adolescent masquerading as Dean Martin. Olivia sat by herself at the corner of the couch, perched right on the edge, her legs tightly crossed, improbably attractive in a tight pink top and a pair of capri pants that showed off her firm cheerleader calves. She cradled a drink in both hands and directed her sour expression particularly at Callie. She looked like a prom queen in mufti, forced to socialize below her station.

Colonel gestured at the food and said, "Fix yourself a plate." Then he handed Paul his scotch and a tall whisky for Callie, and he came around the bar and gave Paul a manly squeeze around the shoulders. "Better fix her one, too, huh?" he added, in a lubricious murmur. "Bet she has an appetite, am I right?"

He sailed off, carrying his own drink, and Paul crept after him, trying to look invisible.

"Gang's all here!" announced Colonel. "It's showtime!"

"Oh, goody!" said Yasumi, clapping her hands.

"Everybody topped up?" asked Colonel.

J. J. blearily waved his glass in the air.

"Outstanding!" said Colonel, hopping up onto the platform. Callie took her drink from Paul, and she smoothed her skirt and sat on the loveseat, tugging Paul down next to her. Immediately Yasumi bent to whisper something in her ear, and Callie blushed and stammered, "Oh gosh, sure. I didn't know." She stood and pulled Paul up with her, leading him to the couch.

"The loveseat's reserved," she murmured to Paul, who was alarmed to find himself in the middle of the couch, with Callie hotly clutching his hand on the left and Olivia stiffly ignoring him on his right. Callie sniffed her drink, then squeezed his hand and leaned against him.

"Wild Turkey," she whispered happily. "How did you know?"

Yasumi kicked off her track shoes and curled up on the loveseat with her feet under her. Bob Wier settled into the overstuffed armchair, holding a can of Sprite with the tips of his fingers. His wide, fixed smile was belied by his eyes, which looked as if he expected someone to sneak up behind him.

On the platform, Colonel moved to center stage and cleared his throat into a hand microphone, and out of the speakers came a seismic rumble that resonated in Paul's chest and rattled the bottles behind the bar. Yasumi theatrically clapped her hands over her ears and shouted, "Too damn loud!" Colonel adjusted a knob on a console to his right and cleared his throat again; the rumble wound down to a tremor. Yasumi gave him two thumbs-up. Colonel sipped his drink and lifted the microphone.

"Good evening, colleagues," he said, his voice bounding off the plywood all around. "Good evening, ladies. Welcome to Casa Pentoon. For those of you who've never joined us before," Colonel intoned, "what we're working with here is the Murakami MeisterSinger 9.1, a professional, Japanese karaoke machine." He placed a paternal hand on the matte black console to his right. "You can't get them here in the States. Hell, even in Japan you can't even get one for home use. This mean, song-slinging son of a bitch comes with six thousand songs already stored up." He tightened his grip on the corner of the console, as if he were ruffling its hair. "You heard me right, compadres. Six *thousand* songs. If it's got lyrics and a melody, it's in here."

From the depths of his chair, J. J. shakily saluted the mighty MeisterSinger with his glass. Yasumi clasped her hands tightly before her, her eyes wide with devotion. Even Callie, pressed to Paul's side, looked flushed and happy.

"Of course, this puppy's got a few custom *modifications* of my own design." Colonel paused to sip his drink. "Some of y'all know what I'm talking about," he added, to knowing laughter from J. J., Bob Wier, and Yasumi, "while the rest of you have some surprises in store."

"Patton!" shouted J. J.

"Shh!" hissed Yasumi, with a sharp glance at the La-Z-Boy.

Colonel dipped his head modestly and lifted his drink. "I'm not promising anything," he said. "We'll see how it goes."

Yasumi cupped her mouth as if she were shouting across a stadium and said loudly, "Sit down!"

Colonel raised his glass. "We who are about to sing, salute you," he said. "Let the games begin." He stepped to the controls and flicked some switches; a row of little red lights on the console streaked to its fullest extent, then subsided. The projection screen behind him flickered to life, showing a soft-focus view of a garden, a slow-motion shower of cherry petals. As "Sukiyaki" oozed through the speakers and the row of red lights pulsed, Colonel worked a dimmer switch that lowered the lights in the basement. He bent to a little microphone in the console.

"Who'd like to go first?" he breathed, his jowls devilishly limned by the red lights.

To Paul's horror, Callie shifted eagerly on the couch next to him, unlocking her grip on his fingers to slowly raise her hand. But before Paul could snatch her arm down, Yasumi had shot to her feet.

"I go first," she said. "Break the ice." She leaped barefoot onto the platform and seized the microphone. "You know what

I want to hear," she said, and Colonel gazed into a little monitor next to the console and worked a touch pad. Then he gave his wife a kiss, stepped down off the platform, and settled heavily on the loveseat, spreading his orangutan arms wide. A throbbing eighties beat pounded from the speakers, and on screen appeared a twenty-year-old work-out video, showing ripe young women in tights and leg warmers and headbands, swinging their asses and pumping their arms. The words to the song crawled across the bottom of the screen in purple letters.

" 'Let's get *phys-i-cal, phys-i-cal,*' " sang Yasumi, only half an octave below a tuneless Yoko Ono screech, " 'I wanna get *phys-i-cal, phys-i-cal.*' " She bounced up and down on her toes, punching the air for emphasis. " 'Let me hear your body *talk,* body *talk.*' "

Paul tried to catch Callie's eye, but she was rapt, her eyes alight, her lips mouthing the words. She drank deep from her Wild Turkey, then she saluted Yasumi with her glass and gave a hearty Oklahoma yell. Paul caught Olivia watching Callie, and he glared at her to make her look away. A moment later he glanced at her again, and Olivia sat forward with her legs tightly crossed. Her lips were pursed and she had a bemused light in her eye, but her toe was swinging to the beat.

Paul sagged back against the couch and downed half his scotch. Somebody please, he thought, kill me now.

THIRTY-ONE

FORTY-FIVE MINUTES LATER Paul was drunk and singing his second song. This one he got to pick himself, and he was trying to keep up with a syncopated arrangement of "I'm Beginning to See the Light." His first song, half an hour earlier, had been selected by Colonel, and Paul had hunched over the microphone and mumbled the theme song from *Branded*, while on the screen behind him the words crawled below the craggy, bleached-out visage of Chuck Connors.

" 'What do you do when you're branded,' " he had droned tunelessly, " 'and you know you're a man?' "

Now, however, he managed a rhythmic little sway that had more to do with Glenlivet than with the song. He tried to hang back from the beat for a more sexy delivery, but he lost the thread of the crawl and tried to catch up, stumbling over the words.

" 'I never cared much for moonlit skies,' " he crooned, " 'I never cared much for . . .' No, wait. 'I never winked back at . . .' Oh shit. Can we back this thing up?"

From the loveseat, with his wife wrapped around him like a squid, Colonel roared with laughter. Bob Wier nodded encouragingly from the chair where he perched with the same can of Sprite he'd had all evening. He'd sung only once, clutching the microphone and lifting his watery eyes to the suspended ceiling and singing, " 'If I give my soul to Jesus, will she take me back again?' " in an unsteady tenor. "I'd like to dedicate this song to my wife, and to my kids, Brian, Bitsy, and Bob, Jr.," he'd said during the intro, with a catch in his throat.

"Where's his wife?" Callie had asked, already half drunk. "Why ain't she here?" Paul pulled her close and whispered in her ear, "I'll tell you later."

After Bob Wier, J. J. had charged the stage, stumbling over the edge of the platform. He'd moved his martini glass in a circle and slurred into the microphone, "How'd all you people get in my room?" Then he hogged the machine for three songs in a row—"Summer Wind," "Ain't That a Kick in the Head," and "Mack the Knife," which he performed complete with finger snaps and Bobby Darin ejaculations—"Hut! Hut! Hut!" When it was Olivia's turn, she had whispered her request to Colonel, who mounted the platform to work the console. As three Gilbert and Sullivan geishas appeared on the screen behind her, Olivia stiffened her backbone, put one foot forward, and, holding the mike with both hands, warbled a well-drilled rendition of "Three Little Maids from School Are We," hitting each word with sharpshooter precision.

After that, Colonel had chugged through "The Gambler" in a growly baritone, but the star of the evening so far had been Callie. Colonel had insisted on picking Callie's song, but she rose to the challenge, planting her bare feet wide on the stage, gripping the mike as if her life depended on it, and belting out "Me and Bobby Mcgee" in a smoky, sultry alt-country drawl. Well into his second scotch—or was it his third?—Paul got a little aroused watching her. She shook her head and cocked her hip and balled up her fist for emphasis, and during the end of the song, during all the "na-na-na-na"s, she did a sexy little dance in place with her eyes closed, and Paul's heart lifted like a party balloon. Afterwards she blushed bright red and peeked through her hands as J.J. hooted and Colonel slammed his hands together and Yasumi jumped up and gave her a hug. Bob Wier clapped politely, while Olivia didn't clap at all, watching evenly from her end of the couch with her chin propped between thumb and forefinger.

After that, Colonel had suggested a break, but Paul had lurched onto the platform and insisted on doing another song, partly to out–Bobby Darin J.J. and partly to catch up to Callie. He slurred his words and giggled and lost track of the lyric, but towards the end he finally got the hang of it—" 'Now that your lips are burning mine, I-I-I-I-I'm beginnin', dah dah dah dah *dah*, to *see* the light' "—and Callie bit her lip and leaned towards him, her eyes alight. Then the song ended, and Paul bent at the waist in a floppy bow. The room erupted in applause; even Olivia clapped. Callie gave another Oklahoma holler, and J.J., who had passed out in the recliner—head tipped back, mouth wide open—lurched awake in the La-Z-Boy, crying, "Patton?" Paul staggered from the platform, and Callie wrapped her arms around him and kissed him on the ear.

"Take five, folks!" Colonel announced, pushing himself up from the loveseat. "Smoke 'em if you got 'em."

Paul had no memory of disentangling from Callie, but he found himself being escorted down the carpet by Colonel towards the door in the partition at the far end of the room. Behind him he heard Yasumi saying something, though he couldn't tell what, and he heard Callie laughing loudly. Colonel clutched him round the shoulders, half leading Paul, half holding him up, and he let go when they got to the door so he could dig in his pocket for the key. The next thing Paul knew he was sitting in a stiff, straight-backed chair in a cramped little office, still clutching his glass, and Colonel was closing the door. The office was windowless and dank, lined with gray metal shelves full of books and papers and videocassettes; the only light came from a humming fluorescent desk lamp on the rigorously ordered blacktop of a huge old Steelcase desk. Colonel placed his hand, one, two, three, on three tall, neatly stacked piles of manuscript on the desk.

"The others don't even know I'm working on this," Colonel said, settling into a creaking wooden office chair. "They wouldn't understand."

Paul craned his neck from his seat and saw that each stack had a title page, "Volume I," "Volume II," and "Volume III."

"It takes a person of some sophistication and erudition," Colonel went on, "to appreciate what I'm doing here. Not everybody would see the point of an epic poem about my Vietnam service."

Each stack was at least a foot high. There must be thousands of pages, Paul thought in his Glenlivet haze. Oh dear God, what if he asks me to read it?

"You were in Vietnam?" Paul felt the blood draining from his face.

"No," Colonel said, narrowing his eyes, "but I served *during* Vietnam."

"As a pastry chef?" I'd be handling this better, Paul thought, if I were sober.

"An army travels on its stomach, Paul." Colonel didn't seem fazed in the slightest. "It's an underrepresented topic in the canon of military literature."

"You're not a real colonel, are you?" Paul heard himself ask.

Colonel dipped his head and smiled grimly at the floor. "I was—I am—Master Sergeant Colonel Travis Pentoon, United States Army, retired." He lifted his gaze to Paul. "I say that with real pride, Professor. The heart of any army is its noncommissioned officers. It was the color sergeant who built the British Empire, not Lord Kitchener. The Roman Empire stood on the back of the centurion."

"I didn't mean to imply—"

"No apology necessary!" Colonel lifted his palm. "It's an obvious question. But they also serve who only stand and bake." He laid his hand gently on the middle stack of the three. "That's what this is all about."

Paul sagged back in his seat. Seriously, he prayed, to Whoever might be listening, kill me now. Please.

"Now I can see by your eyes, Paul, that you're eager to dive into this manuscript." Colonel leaned forward in his creaking chair and folded his hands between his knees, his Hawaiian shirt billowing over his thighs. "But you're not ready for what's in here yet. There'll come a time when you are, but not yet, son, not yet. And anyway," Colonel continued, "I mention my magnum opus only as a means to an end."

"Sorry?" said Paul.

"Now Bob and J. J., they're good old boys, and I absolutely trust them with my life. As they do me." Colonel looked up at Paul from under his bushy eyebrows. "But I think of myself not just as a proud master sergeant, not just as the best goddamn baker on the Pacific Rim, but as a warrior-philosopher, Paul, in the great tradition of the samurai, or the magnificent Prussian soldiers of Bismarck's army." He leaned a little closer. "And what I'm hoping to bring into our brave little company is someone who is closer to my intellectual equal, my *peer*, as it were. Someone with a sophisticated appreciation of the higher things in life."

Don't say it, thought Paul.

"We're exactly the same, you and I," said Colonel.

Oh boy, thought Paul.

Colonel lifted a finger. "Don't say anything. Just listen." He lowered his voice. "I know you're not where you want to be. You didn't set out all those years ago in graduate school to be writing technical documents for the Texas Department of General Services. But what if I told you, Paul," he continued, inching his chair closer, "what if I told you I could guarantee you lifetime employment? And not just lifetime employment, Paul, but a job that left you free to pursue almost anything you wanted to do?"

The room was very quiet, though Paul heard laughter and music from the other side of the door. He lifted his drink, but the glass was dry.

Colonel waved his hand over the three heaps of epic poem.

"When do you think I wrote this, Paul? In my free time?" He grunted with laughter, his eyes bright. "Not bloody likely."

Paul could scarcely breathe. Colonel had literally backed him into a corner of his cramped little office. Paul couldn't stand without pushing Colonel out of the way, and he couldn't even lean back any farther in the chair.

"You gonna let life, that bitch, grind you down, Paul? You gonna stay whipped for the rest of your days?" Colonel's eyes burned. "Are we not men?"

Someone rapped loudly on the door of the office, and Paul hiccuped in surprise. Colonel rolled back in his chair. He closed his eyes, drew a breath, and mastered himself. Then he laid his arm casually along the desk, lifted his chin, and raised his voice. "Come in."

The door swung open, letting in a puff of air-conditioning from the rec room. Bob Wier stood in the doorway, silhouetted against the light from the far end of the room. He glanced from Paul to Colonel.

"He's here," Bob Wier said.

THIRTY-TWO

WITH HIS ARM AROUND PAUL, Colonel guided him back
through the rec room and through the sliding-glass door, into
the sticky Texas night. Without releasing Paul, Colonel paused
and sent Bob Wier back inside.

"Wake him up." Colonel nodded in the direction of J. J.,
comatose in the La-Z-Boy. As Bob Wier slid the door shut,
Paul saw, as if through the bright gate of suburban Valhalla,
Yasumi and Callie behind the karaoke console on the platform
selecting songs from the computer monitor; they had put their
arms around each other's shoulders and were giggling like sorority sisters. A bored Olivia inched along the wall, surveying
the movie posters. Bob Wier tugged at J. J.'s wrist, trying to
pull him up out of the recliner. Then Paul was wheeled away
in Colonel's iron grasp.

"This way, Professor," said Colonel. "Come meet our special
guest."

Paul, still clutching his empty glass, stumbled down the
slope, ducking at the last instant the glowing ball of a paper

lantern. For a moment he couldn't see in the dark beyond the lantern, and he was dizzied by the screech of the crickets and the doppler whine of mosquitoes. Colonel released him, and Paul wobbled on his heels.

"Mighty good to see you again, Professor," said a hollow voice out of the humid, high-pitched gloom. Colonel nudged Paul farther down the lawn, where it descended into a dry creek bed thickly bordered by juniper and bristling mesquite. Stanley Tulendij glided out of the dark, his pale face appearing at the farthest reach of the lantern light. He was wearing the same slacks and sport coat Paul had seen him in last week in Rick's office, and he spidered up the slope on his long legs. "I hear you're ready to join our merry crew." He offered his bony hand to Paul. His eyes sparkled in the dark.

"What merry crew?" asked Paul warily.

Stanley Tulendij took Paul's hand in his loose, cool grip. "I think we have some friends in common." He tugged Paul by the hand down the slope. Paul staggered, and Colonel took the glass out of his hand and hauled him upright by the elbow.

"This is an important moment in your life, Paul," he growled. "Pay attention."

With Colonel on his left and Stanley Tulendij on his right, Paul peered into the gloom at the foot of the slope. At first he saw only the spiky silhouette of the mesquite against the pale limestone of the creek bed, but after a moment he became aware of a pair of pale eyes peering at him over the top of a bush. Then he saw another pair, peering through the thorny branches, and another, then four, five, as many as six pale faces with buzz cuts peering over or through the bushes from the dry creek bed. They shifted as Paul watched, moving around and behind each other, floating like balloons or dropping out of sight to reappear a few feet farther along or out of the shadow under a bush down near the ground.

Oh brother, thought Paul. I'm so fucking drunk.

Each pale face watched Paul with eyes that did not catch the light of the lanterns but seemed to glow from within like an animal's eyes. The figures weren't speaking in unison, but each murmured to himself, like the pale men in his dream that very morning. Paul could not quite make out the words, but he didn't need to. He knew what they were saying.

Please tell me I'm drunk, he thought. Please tell me I'm not really seeing this. He staggered back from the faces, digging at the grass with his heels, trying to push himself up the slope. But Stanley Tulendij and Colonel each tightened his grip on Paul, holding him in place.

"No no no no no," breathed Stanley Tulendij. "There's no need to be afraid. These benighted souls are my brothers, Paul."

"Your brothers," said Colonel in Paul's ear.

"*Our* brothers," said the two men together.

There's no one there, Paul told himself. I'm not really here.

"Sacked by the state of Texas, forgotten by their families." Stanley Tulendij's breath on Paul's cheek smelled faintly of rot. "And cursed, Paul, yea, *cursed*, even unto darkness by the Almighty God himself." His long, bony fingers seemed to curl all the way around Paul's arm. "Who tried to drown them all at once, like a sack of puppies, washing them away into the long, cold darkness under Lonesome Knob, where they tumbled and rolled, and they rolled and tumbled—"

"Is he here?" said J. J. loudly, thumping down the slope from the house.

"Shh!" hissed Colonel.

"He's getting the story," whispered Bob Wier, padding silently behind J. J.

"—until they washed up deep, deep in the caves under the streets of Lamar," continued Stanley Tulendij, "where I found them at last, after long tribulation, huddled together, in their final extremity, living off the very vermin of the caves."

"Eating rats," said Colonel.

"Spiders," said Bob Wier.

"Centipedes," said J. J.

Why can't I see pink elephants, thought Paul, like everybody else?

"Lost men," continued Stanley Tulendij in Paul's ear, "broken men, shattered men, *hopeless* men. Drooling, gibbering, bloodless wraiths, reduced to the state of animals. They were beyond reason when I found them, Paul, driven mad by their humiliation and their nearly deadly ordeal. I offered to lead them back up into the light again, but they wouldn't come. They wouldn't come."

The pale, shifting faces in the creek bed seemed to have multiplied by mitosis, doubling every few seconds, jostling each other behind the mesquite. "Are we not men?" they muttered, though Paul told himself he wasn't *hearing* them; it was the whisky talking, chanting inside his head, "*Are we not men? Are we not men?*"

"I could not lead them home," said Stanley Tulendij, trembling with emotion, "but I could not abandon them."

"Why not?" chorused Colonel, J. J., and Bob Wier.

"Because they were men!" exclaimed Stanley Tulendij.

Honest to God, Paul thought, I'm never drinking Glenlivet again.

"But what could I bring them from the world above that had thrown them away and forgotten them?" Stanley Tulendij went on. "What does a lost man want more than he wants food or shelter or woman?"

Dream or not, Paul thought, here's hoping the answer isn't "tech writers" or "failed English professors."

"Work," said Stanley Tulendij tremulously. "A place in the world. A reason to live." He squeezed Paul's hand to the point of pain. "And what do they offer their comrades in the world above?"

"Freedom," breathed Colonel.

"Amen," said Bob Wier.

"Fuckin' A," said J. J.

The other men were all crowded around Paul now, looming at him in the lantern light. Okay, Paul told himself, if I'm dreaming the figures in the creek bed, then I'm dreaming these guys, too.

"Have you ever read the story," asked Bob Wier urgently, "of the shoemaker and the elves?"

"It's a pretty sweet deal," said J. J.

"It's a dialectic, Paul," said Colonel, the warrior-philosopher. "They do all the work, and we get all the credit."

"I'm dreaming, right?" said Paul aloud. He looked at his feet, hoping to see himself floating half a foot off the ground.

"It's a kind of a dream," said Colonel, "a dream come true."

"Okay." Paul sagged a bit in the grip of Colonel and Stanley Tulendij. "I'll play along. For the sake of argument, let's say this is really happening."

The other men laughed. "Really happening," said Colonel. "That's rich."

"Typical," said J. J. bitterly.

"They do your work for you," Paul said, nodding down the slope into the dark. He thought of what Nolene had told him last week about Colonel, J. J., and Bob Wier—"They don't do a lick of work, *ever*," she'd said, "but every morning the work they're not doing shows up on my desk." The pale faces below seemed to bubble a little higher; the murmur rose to a rumble. "But what do *they* get out of it?" Paul said.

The four men crowded around Paul exchanged a glance.

"We offer them something from time to time," said Colonel.

"Like a sacrifice," said J. J. "Kind of."

" 'The fire and wood are here,' " Bob Wier said with a catch in his throat, " 'but where is the lamb for the burnt offering?' Genesis twenty-two, seven."

Colonel shouldered Bob Wier aside. "Don't listen to him," he murmured, his breath hot in Paul's ear.

"Okay," said J. J., " 'sacrifice' is maybe too strong a word."

"It's something you'll never miss," said Stanley Tulendij, and he swung Paul around and started to walk him back up the slope towards the bright rectangle of the sliding door. "Not really."

Paul surprised himself by resisting a bit; he tried to twist out of the grasp of the men on either side, tried to crane over his shoulder to see into the creek bed at the bottom of the slope. All he saw was Bob Wier gnawing on his knuckle, his eyes brimming with tears in the lantern light. Then the grip on each of Paul's arms tightened, and they marched him towards the house.

"So are you in, Professor?" said Colonel, digging his blunt fingers into Paul's elbow.

"You're either with us or agin' us, Paul," said Stanley Tulendij, tightening his grip.

"The line forms on the right, babe," J. J. said.

Paul gave up struggling and let them carry him back towards the house. Fuck it, he thought, it's all a dream anyway. Behind him, the murmur of the pale figures in the creek bed faded into the electric burr of the crickets. From the house came the jolly thump of a galloping bass line, and through the door they could see Callie and Yasumi dancing together on the platform, swinging their hips and singing along with the Bananarama version of "Venus," more or less in harmony.

" 'She's got it," they sang, *swing, swing, swing,* " 'yeah, baby, she's got it . . .' "

The giant TV screen pulsed with parti-colored light like a sixties discotheque, and vivid greens and blues and reds washed over the faces of the five men just beyond the glass.

" 'I'm your Venus,' " sang Callie, " 'I'm your fi-yuh, at your de-zi-yuh.' "

Stanley Tulendij's eyes widened, and he relaxed his grip on Paul's hand.

"Who's that splendid little filly?" he said.

"That's no filly," Paul said, yanking his other arm free of Colonel's grip. "That's my . . . that's my . . ." My what? he thought.

"Not her," said Stanley Tulendij. "The little lady at the bar."

The four other men swiveled their gaze to the bar, where Olivia perched on one of the stools with her cheerleader legs crossed. She leaned one elbow on the bar top and picked absently at the plate of crudités. She bit a celery stick in half as if she were crunching on a human bone.

Paul started to laugh. That proves it, he thought. I am dreaming. "Olivia?" he said aloud, before he could stop himself.

The other men shifted in the dark, exchanging glances and saying nothing.

"Seriously," said Paul. "*Olivia?*"

Stanley Tulendij's eyes shone with the same animal glow as the eyes in the creek bed. "That's a fine figure of a woman," he said.

"Take her," Paul laughed, "she's yours. You'd be doing everybody a favor."

The song pounding through the glass seemed to fade, and even the cricket shriek and the dive bomb whine of mosquitoes went away. The other men seemed to recede into the dark, and Paul found himself alone in a little bubble of silence with Stanley Tulendij. The old man turned slowly to him, the Day-Glo colors of the karaoke screen washing rhythmically across his face. His eyes were wide and bright, and his lips drew back in a skull-like grin. He took Paul's hand and shook it gravely.

"Done," he said, and a moment later he was gone, gliding on his long, crooked legs down the slope, under the tree, and into the dark, beyond the glow of the paper lanterns.

THIRTY-THREE

PAUL STARTED AWAKE IN A HEART-HAMMERING PANIC, sprawled nude along the edge of a narrow mattress. In the crepuscular light he saw a clumsily plastered ceiling, a scruffy carpet littered with discarded clothes, a half-open doorway into an empty room. He sat up and nearly swooned from the pain in his head, as if two great hands were squeezing his temples together, trying to crack his skull like a coconut. He groaned and put his head between his knees, and tried to remember where he was and how he'd gotten there.

He heard a noise behind him, and he turned to see Callie wedged against the wall on the other side of the mattress, snoring face down into her pillow, her back bare to the waist. Paul sighed and tugged the crumpled sheet up to her shoulder blades. Bits and pieces of the end of karaoke night were coming back to Paul. J. J. had bellowed "Patton!" from the La-Z-Boy until Colonel had mounted the stage and worked the touch pad. A giant American flag had filled the TV screen, and as Colonel stepped before it and squared his shoulders, Bob Wier rose to his feet and cried, "Tennn-*hut!*" J. J. struggled to rise from the recliner and gave up, but Yasumi sat up straight on the loveseat. Paul was slumped on the couch as if he'd been poured there, with Callie propped against him. Olivia was nowhere to be seen. During a long trumpet fanfare, Colonel sucked in his gut and saluted. Callie started to laugh, but Yasumi glared at her and Callie clapped her hand over her mouth. At last the fanfare faded, and Colonel stood at ease. The "Patton March" played quietly through the speakers.

"Now I want you to remember," growled Colonel, without the microphone, "that no bastard ever won a war by dying for his country." He began to pace, pumping his fist. "He won it by making the other poor dumb bastard die for *his* country."

Shortly after that, Paul began to pass out in a slow fade, interrupted by exclamations from Colonel—"*Wade* into them! Spill *their* blood!"—and repressed hilarity from Callie. The next thing he remembered clearly was staggering up the basement stairs, propped up by Callie; with his shoulder he knocked every photograph on the staircase wall askew. When he tried to go back to straighten them, Callie hauled at him from above and a pair of small hands, probably Yasumi's, pushed at him from below.

Then they were tottering across Colonel's front lawn, in the dark under the tree, where the paper lanterns had gone out. Callie took Paul's keys from his pocket and leaned him up against the passenger door of his car. It seemed to take her forever to make her way around the car and let herself in and unlock the passenger door, and in that eternity Paul remembered Olivia stalking towards him across the lawn, out of the dark, dangling her own car keys, scarier and more determined even than George Patton.

"So," she'd said, "will I see you tomorrow morning?"

Thank God! Paul remembered thinking. She's still here; she hasn't been spirited off into the dark by Stanley Tulendij like some maiden carried off by the Erlkönig.

"You bet!" Paul had declared happily, with no idea what she was talking about. "I'll be there."

Now, as he struggled with his hangover on the edge of Callie's mattress, he wasn't sure how much of the night before had actually happened—Olivia approaching him in the dark like a marauding angel; Colonel channeling George C. Scott; the creepy confab in Colonel's backyard, with the pale faces floating in the creek bed—and how much of it he had simply dreamed after tumbling drunkenly into bed at Callie's apartment.

"You bet," he said now, squatting naked on the edge of the mattress, mimicking his own drunken chipperness. "I'll be there." Then suddenly he remembered where he was supposed to be this morning—assuming it *was* Saturday morning—and he lurched to his knees on the carpet and pawed through the litter of clothes by the side of the bed. After a frantic search he found his watch and squinted at it in the dim light of the windowless bedroom. Quarter after two, it said, and the two palms against his temples pressed harder until he groaned. "Oh *fuck*," he said, over and over, until it occurred to him to turn the watch right side up. Now it read quarter to eight, which wasn't much better. He wasn't *entirely* certain, but he was pretty sure he was due to meet Olivia at TxDoGS at eight. He found his shorts and rolled onto his back to pull them on.

"Callie," he whispered. "*Callie.*" Pulling on his shirt, he knelt by the mattress and gently shook Callie's arm.

"Unh," said Callie, into her pillow.

"Where are my keys?" he said, still whispering.

Callie lifted her face a millimeter from the pillow and painfully cracked a crusty eye. "There's no need for you to shout," she rasped.

"Forget it, I found them," said Paul, treading on the keys as he hopped one leg at a time into his trousers.

The traffic between Callie's apartment and TxDoGS wasn't too bad on a Saturday morning, and he even rolled into the empty parking lot a minute or two early. Olivia was just locking up her trim little Corolla as his Colt clattered alongside at the main entrance. She had exchanged her capri pants for sensible shoes, slacks, and a cotton sweater for the air-conditioning. As Paul hauled himself out of his car, his head throbbing, she glanced at her watch and then looked him up and down. She didn't say a word, but he could tell she had noted that he was wearing the same clothes he'd had on last night. Fuck her, Paul thought, wishing he'd had time to shower and brush his teeth.

"Good morning," he managed to say, squinting against the pain in his temples.

"Good morning," sang Olivia, and she marched towards the door, digging in her purse for her badge. She swiped it through the card reader, and as the lock clicked open, Paul scooted forward to hold the door for her. She minced ahead of him without a word, and he followed her out of the heat and into the darkened lobby.

The door clicked shut behind him, and the emptiness of the building on a Saturday morning closed around them both, swelling out of the hallways and down from the balcony. Paul shivered, feeling a chill. Olivia didn't seem to notice, sailing past Preston's empty security desk and up the stairs. Paul tiptoed after her, along the balcony past the locked door of Building Services and around the corner into the main hallway, where only every third or fourth light was on. The rumble of the ventilators seemed louder in the gloom, and Paul shot nervous glances into the shadows of the door wells and at the corners of the ceiling. Olivia marched heedlessly up the hall, illuminated only when she passed under one of the infrequent lights, and fading again in the dark between, a busy silhouette against the glare from the tall windows at the far end of the hall. Paul trotted to keep up with her, not wanting to go any deeper into the empty building but not wanting to be left behind.

The lights were out in the elevator lobby, and the sunlight through the glass wall seemed to taunt Paul with its inaccessibility. He edged round the recycling box as Olivia's switching backside retreated into the deeper gloom of cubeland, where all the lights were out. Paul hesitated in the doorway, peering at the dim, labyrinthine outline of the cube horizon. Objects that rose innocently above the horizon in the light—the top of a filing cabinet, a hard hat, someone's ficus plant—looked menacing in the gloom; Paul expected the round outline of the hard hat, halfway across the room, to lift slowly and reveal a pair of eyes watching from below the brim.

Olivia turned on her desk lamp, filling her cube with yellow light. The light struck across her cheekbones and nose, turning her eyes into hollows, and she lifted her purse off her shoulder and glanced back at the doorway.

"Paul?" she said. "Are you coming?"

"Sure." Paul edged past the darkened conference room and then rounded the corner and went into his cube, keeping close to the fabric wall. He fumbled for the switch to his own desk lamp, nearly panicking when he couldn't find it. At last it clicked on, and the yellow glow that filled his cube only made the gloom all around seem darker. Across the aisle, Olivia perched on the edge of her chair, switching on her monitor and moving her mouse to deactivate the screen saver. Paul winced as his own chair squeaked under him, as if worried that it might give him away. With an unsteady hand he turned on his own monitor.

"Would you like some coffee?"

Paul jumped in his seat; he hadn't heard Olivia get up and cross the aisle. She watched him wide-eyed, her palms pressed together just below her breastbone. His head began to pound again, as if she were squeezing it between her hands.

"Yeah," he said hoarsely. "Sure."

Olivia held out her hand. "Twenty-five cents, please."

Paul, speechless, only blinked at her.

"For the coffee fund." She sighed and rolled her eyes. "You're supposed to put a quarter in the cup for every cup you drink."

Paul stood to dig in his pocket, his shoulders hunched against the dark. He handed her a quarter, then glanced around him, over the cube horizon.

"Why don't you call up the RFP from the server?" she said. "It will take me a few minutes to make the coffee."

She turned and disappeared silently up the aisle, and Paul watched anxiously over the top of his cube until the doorway of the coffee room filled with bright, fluorescent light.

"Olivia?" he called out weakly. When she didn't answer, he raised his voice. "Olivia!"

Olivia stepped into the bright doorway with the coffeepot in one hand and a paper filter in the other. She lifted her eyebrows at him.

"I'm, uh, I'm just going to splash a little water on my face." Paul gestured over his shoulder. Olivia said nothing, but simply stepped out of the doorway.

The men's room was pitch-black when Paul gingerly pushed open the door, so he stood in the hall, snaked his arm inside, and groped for the light switch. Through the crack in the door he watched the fluorescents flicker on, filling the room with a bluish glare. Then he pushed the door wide and surveyed the room, squatting down in the doorway to check under the sides of the stalls. At the sink he ran the water full blast, for the sound of it, and in the mirror he kept an eye on the ceiling as he bent over the sink and splashed two handfuls of water on his face. He pumped a little liquid soap into his palms, then, glancing once more at the ceiling in the mirror, closed his eyes and quickly scrubbed his face. He opened his eyes again, blinking against the water dripping off his eyebrows, and fumbled a handful of towels out of the dispenser. He mopped his face and turned off the water, pausing with his hand on the tap to listen hard. With the crumpled paper towels in his fist, he surveyed the ceiling tiles above him. But he saw nothing and heard only the water gulping down the drain.

"Suck it up," he told himself, but not too loud. "Grow up."

He turned off the men's room light as he left, though he did it from the hall, reaching back through the door for the switch. His face tingling, his head throbbing less painfully, his nerves buzzing less anxiously, he walked through the bright sunlight of the elevator lobby, passing the recycling box without even a glance. As he came into cubeland he noted immediately the twin, square pools of light in his and Olivia's cubes, printed against the gloom, and the bright rectangular glare of the coffee room doorway. Over the rumble of the AC he could even hear the busy little trickle of the coffeemaker. He successfully resisted the urge to scan the cube horizon again, and he allowed himself to fall heavily into his squealing chair. His screen saver streaked slowly across his monitor, so he bumped the mouse, and then called up the RFP from the server. The trickle stopped, and a moment later Olivia arrived. "I noticed you don't have your own cup," she said, and he took a Styrofoam cup from her, secretly pleased that she hadn't startled him.

"I forgot to ask if you wanted sugar or creamer," Olivia said as she carried her own cup—FOLLOW YOUR BLISS, it said—into her cube.

"Black's fine." Paul turned away, blowing across the coffee as he lowered it to his desktop. "So, Olivia," he said, lifting his voice as he faced the glow of his monitor, "how do you want to work this?"

He heard a bump and scrape from across the aisle, as if she were moving a ring binder along her desktop. "Do you want to look over my shoulder," he said, "or shall we work together from our own separate monitors?"

He heard her chair creak, heard it roll against the carpet.

"What do you think?" Paul said. "Olivia?"

He picked up his coffee and, slouching in his chair, turned slowly to look across the aisle. Olivia's chair was spinning slowly in place, empty. Then, as he watched, her shoe dropped onto her desk from above with a soft slap, and Paul lifted his eyes to see Olivia's wriggling legs, one foot bare, rising into a gap in the suspended ceiling. Several pairs of pale hands were grappling with her, hauling her from above into a black square where a ceiling tile had been a moment before. Olivia's sweater was rucked up, baring her doughy midriff; her legs kicked and pedaled at nothing. Paul heard a muffled cry, and the groan and squeak of the ceiling tiles all around the gap. The tiles bulged and sagged, and out of the dark Paul heard thumps and grunts. Suddenly Olivia's legs jerked a little higher into the ceiling, and Paul felt a searing heat on the back of his hand.

"Agh!" he cried, instinctively dropping his cup from his violently trembling hand. Hot coffee splashed across the carpet, soaking immediately into a dark stain. An unusually loud thump made him look up again; only Olivia's flailing calves hung from the hole in the ceiling.

"Oh, God," breathed Paul, and a moment later, to his astonishment, he had crossed the aisle, jumped up on Olivia's desk, and leaped to grab her ankles. He caught one and held on, his feet crashing against her desktop, making her cup jump and slosh coffee all over her computer. Smoke and sparks began to sputter out of the unit, filling the air instantly with an acrid chemical reek, but Paul hung doggedly onto Olivia's ankle, stretching himself to his full length like a cat reaching for a treat. With a grunt he lunged for her other ankle and caught it, and he managed to haul her slightly down out of the gap, as far as her thighs.

The computer on the desk was popping and sizzling, and a gray thread of smoke stung Paul to the back of his nostrils. "Olivia, knock it off!" Paul cried as she began to kick harder. "Quit kicking!"

Then one of the pale arms reached out of the ceiling and, with a cold, clammy grip, peeled the fingers of Paul's right hand off Olivia's ankle, bending his fingers back so painfully that he let go with a cry. He leaped again, trying to regain her foot, and another pale hand descended out of the dark and gave Paul's left hand a vicious slap.

"Goddammit!" cried Paul, smoke rising all around his waist, sparks flying round his ankles, but before he could leap again, a pair of arms grasped him round the knees and hauled him violently off the desk. Olivia's ankles were wrenched from his grasp, and he crashed painfully against Olivia's clattering chair. The chair heeled over, and Paul landed in a heap on the floor, the wind knocked out of him.

"Ahhhhhh," Paul groaned, twisting off his bruised hip onto his back, and the last two things he saw were Olivia's twitching heels—one shod, the other bare—vanish into the dark above him, and the round, bleached face of Boy G—his glasses awry, but as expressionless as ever—looming over Paul with his clenched fist cocked over his shoulder.

"Boy G," said Boy G in his breathless monotone, "the one and only." Then his fist fell, and Paul was out cold.

THIRTY-FOUR

PAUL CAME TO IN HIS OWN BED, alone, with the covers tucked up to his chin. Charlotte crouched weightlessly on his chest, watching him from inches away with her fathomless black eyes. Paul felt no pressure from her—what does a ghost cat weigh?—but he felt a freezing cold seeping through the blanket over his heart and something else, an electric buzzing in his chest. Paul realized to his horror that Charlotte was *purring*.

"Nice kitty," Paul whimpered, feeling the cold all the way down to his toes.

Charlotte thrummed like a little Harley through the blanket. It was a strange, weightless, icy buzzing, but she was purring nonetheless. Nose to nose with Paul, she opened her wide, black mouth and made a tiny, mewling cry. Then she vanished.

It took Paul a minute or two to catch his breath, but at last he flung back the covers and jumped out of bed, chilled with sweat, his heart pounding. His brave little air-conditioner was chugging under the window, and for a moment Paul cowered in the corner of the room in his underwear, rubbing his arms against the chill. Sunlight glared through the gaps in his front curtain, and he glanced at his bedside clock, which read 7:00 A.M.

What day is it? Paul wondered, and he tiptoed to the end of his bed and turned on the TV. After a moment of static, he pulled in a network morning show, where the ferociously pert hostess was grilling the author of a new book about cat behavior.

"It's my firm belief," said the author, a hearty, gray-haired lady in a bush jacket, speaking in a ringing English accent, "that to keep a cat perpetually indoors is a kind of abuse."

"Like I can get her to go outside," Paul muttered.

Then he noted the date and temperature in the corner of the screen. It was 80 degrees already, and Monday morning. "Where did Sunday go?" Paul groaned aloud. "Where have I been?"

Still shivering, he tugged the blanket around his shoulders. What's the last thing I remember? he thought, and as the image of Olivia's wriggling legs came back to him, he pulled the blanket tighter and glanced nervously around the room. Well, *that* certainly didn't happen, he told himself, not *really*. If it had happened, why am I waking up here instead of on the floor of Olivia's cube? And where did Sunday go? And where's Callie?

Paul stood up and let the blanket slip to the floor. I've been here all weekend, he decided. I must've gotten really drunk on Friday night, and Callie brought me home and poured me into bed, and everything since then, up to and including Charlotte purring on my chest, has been one long, bad dream. I'm letting my imagination get the better of me, he decided. I haven't been myself all week. Ever since Dennis the Tech Writer died in his cube, it's all been one long, emotional hangover, and it's all been messing with my head. Suck it up, Paul told himself. Quit screwing around and go to work.

"She quit," Rick said, an hour later in his office. He sounded a little stunned. "Vamoosed. Took her ball and went fishing." He looked up at Paul from behind his desk, his eyebrows wobbling independently of each other. "You have any idea why?"

Paul shrugged. He tried not to show it, but he was as stunned as Rick. He had come warily into cubeland a few minutes before, having convinced himself that Olivia would be at her keyboard, angrily typing away, ready to whirl on him as he slunk into his cube.

"Where the hell were you on Saturday morning?" she'd snap. "I made all the changes myself."

But her cube was empty—her chair neatly pushed in, her desk lamp dark, her computer purring to itself on standby with the monitor off. He lifted his eyes to the ceiling where the tiles ran towards the vanishing point without interruption. He stooped to her computer and sniffed for the residual reek of burnt plastic but smelled nothing. He even peeked into her coffee cup, but it was bone dry.

In his own cube there was no coffee stain on the carpet, not even a damp spot. On his desk he found the revised RFP, neatly stacked next to his keyboard. Without sitting down, he thumbed through the first few pages, noting that all of Olivia's changes had been seamlessly incorporated into the text. Abruptly he turned and carried it quickly past the empty cubes of Colonel, J. J., and Bob Wier, past the appraising gaze of Nolene, and into Rick's office, where Rick sat paging through a copy of the same document.

"What'd you boys do to her Friday night?" Rick said now, scowling up at Paul.

"Nothing," Paul protested, annoyed at the rising pitch of his voice. "What did she say we did?"

"She didn't say nothin'," said Rick. "She didn't come in this morning."

"Really?" Behind his eyeballs Paul saw Olivia's legs paddling in the air. "Then how do you know she quit?"

Rick stabbed a loose piece of paper with his thumb and spun it around for Paul to read. It was a sheet of TxDoGS letterhead with Saturday's date, Rick's name and title, and a salutation. Paul leaned over the desk and read it, afraid to pick it up. The body of the letter was one sentence:

I hereby resign from the Texas Department of General Services, effective immediately.

Paul recognized Olivia's precise signature. The sheet of letterhead itself was a little frayed around the edges, and near the bottom was a broad smudge, like a smeared thumbprint.

"She say anything to you?" asked Rick. His eyebrows wouldn't stop bounding.

"No!" Paul snapped upright and backed away from the desk, twisting the RFP between his hands. "I haven't seen her since . . . since . . ."

"Saturday morning?" Rick gestured at the revised RFP, spread across his desk. "Did she let you in?"

"I wasn't here Saturday morning," Paul heard himself say, and he desperately wanted to believe that he hadn't been. I was out cold, he wanted to say, I was sleeping it off, I was dead to the world. . . .

"Hoo doggie." Rick shook his head. "Then when the hell did you do this?" He thrust a large, smudgy Post-it over the desk at Paul.

HERE'S THE REVISED RFP.

PAUL

"Ain't that your handwriting?" Rick said.

"Yes," gulped Paul. "Yes, it is. But I didn't—"

Someone clapped Paul on the shoulder, and he jumped three inches straight off the ground and nearly sent the pages of the RFP flying.

"The professor didn't come in on Saturday," said Colonel, digging his blunt fingers into Paul's shoulder. "He was much too hungover. I dragged my own sorry ass out of bed Sunday morning and let him in the building."

"Yesterday?" asked Rick, skeptically.

"Yessir," said Colonel. He released his raptor grip and rubbed Paul's shoulder. "In't that right, Professor?"

"I guess." Paul felt breathless and dizzy. He was afraid that if Colonel let go of him, he'd pass out and topple over.

Rick settled back in his chair and lightly hammered the armrests with the heels of his hands. He blinked across the desk at Colonel. "Olivia say anything to you about quitting?"

"She didn't say anything about quitting, *as such*," said Colonel. He let go of Paul, and he crossed his arms and rocked back on his heels. Paul felt behind him for the little round conference table and propped himself against it.

"Olivia got a little loose on Friday night, if you know what I mean," Colonel said. "I had a long chat with her, and she mentioned something about making a change."

"Huh," said Rick.

"Talked about looking for greener pastures, searching for herself, following her bliss, that sort of thing."

"Dang," said Rick.

"It was all highly metaphorical."

"She say why?"

"A gentleman never betrays a lady's confidence," Colonel said with a smirk. "But have you ever seen that old movie *Summertime*?" He winked over his shoulder at Paul. "Or *The Roman Spring of Mrs. Stone*?"

Rick looked utterly confused.

"A middle-aged passion!" laughed Colonel. "A little autumnal hanky-panky." He lifted a hand to ward off the question Rick had no intention of asking. "Further than that, sir, I am not prepared to go. Let's just say," he continued, "that our Olivia was giddy as a schoolgirl."

Paul's jaw dropped at the enormity of this lie, not to mention at the image of a giddy Olivia. Rick merely looked miserable. This was way more than he wanted to know.

"Way-ul." He slapped the armrests and heaved himself forward. "She left us in the friggin' lurch."

"Just like a woman," said Colonel. "Good thing Paul here stepped up to the plate, isn't it?"

"Hm?" Rick was trying to lose himself in the text of the RFP. Colonel planted his palms on Rick's desk, leaned across, and caught his eye.

"Paul's saved our bacon," he said, lowering his voice and holding Rick in his bright gaze. "He's saved all that hard work we did last week and incorporated all the changes in the RFP. And on his weekend, no less."

"Well, I guess he has," said Rick. He leaned around Colonel and caught Paul's eye. "Good work, Paul."

"Huh," Paul said weakly, waving a finger.

"In fact," Colonel insisted, "now that we got a gap in the ranks, as it were, we ought to think about calling in the reserves and plugging them into the front lines."

"Calling who?" said Rick. "Plugging what?"

"We have a permanent position open," Colonel said, pushing back from the desk, "now that Ms. Haddock has swanned off to 'find herself,' or whatever the hell." He made a pair of quotes in the air. "And we got a first-rate man right here, ready, willing, and able." He hooked his thumb over his shoulder at Paul.

Rick worked his tongue around the inside of his cheek.

"Seems to me," Colonel continued, "a smart manager would take this here lemon"—Colonel flicked Olivia's resignation letter with a finger, sending it airborne a few inches—"and make lemonade." He stepped back. Paul shifted restlessly against the table.

Rick ground his palms together. "When you're right, you're right," he said, as if to himself. "No use crying over burnt bridges." He lifted his eyebrows unsteadily in Paul's direction. "You interested in a permanent job with us, Paul?"

Before Paul could answer, Colonel said, "Of course he is."

"I'll get the personnel honchos on it." Rick's hands fluttered over his desktop. "Paul, you come see me this afternoon."

Colonel nodded at Paul, and Paul said, "Sure."

"Back to work," said Rick, and Colonel grabbed Paul by the elbow and marched him out the door.

"Not a word," Colonel hissed in Paul's ear, as Nolene watched them retreat up the aisle. Colonel steered Paul into his own cube and planted Paul firmly in the chair in front of his desk. Colonel took his own chair and leaned towards Paul with his hands tightly folded.

"Where is she?" Paul whispered. He clutched the rolled-up RFP on his knees. "What did you did to her?"

"*I* didn't do a goddamn thing to her." Colonel's eyes blazed across the desk. "And I don't know where she is. What's more, *you* don't know where she is."

"No, I don't," murmured Paul. "But I know what I saw."

"Paul," said Colonel, "when you left my house Friday night, you were drunker than a whole boatload of sailors on a three-day liberty. If I told you that you saw Elvis, Jimmy Hoffa, and baby Jesus step out of the mothership on South Austin Avenue and sing the 'Hallelujah Chorus,' could you tell me I was wrong?"

"No," said Paul miserably.

"Goddamn right you couldn't." Colonel caught himself and glanced to either side. Paul followed his gaze and saw just the eyes and forehead of J. J. over one wall of the cube, and the eyes and forehead of Bob Wier over the other.

"*Git,*" snapped the Colonel, and J. J. and Bob Wier dropped out of sight. Paul twisted the RFP between his hands.

"Now there's only one question you should be asking yourself, Paul." Colonel pinched his thumb and forefinger so tightly together that they turned white and pointed them across the desk at Paul. "Is your life better this morning than it was last week?"

Paul could scarcely bear Colonel's burning gaze, but he couldn't look away. In spite of himself he thought back to a week ago, when, just about this time of the morning, he was gazing down at the gray, sunken features of Dennis, the Dead Tech Writer.

"Tell me true, Professor," breathed Colonel. "You get points for honesty."

"Yeah," gasped Paul finally. It felt like his last breath. "It is better."

" 'Nuff said." Colonel unpinched his fingers. Without taking his eyes off Paul, he heaved a sigh and settled back in his chair. Then he stood, gestured for Paul to stand, and met him in the doorway. He put his arm around Paul and gave him a manly squeeze.

"Relax, Professor," he said, as he gently shoved Paul up the aisle. "You just got tenure."

THIRTY-FIVE

"WHERE'D SHE GO?" Preston asked Paul a few minutes later. He slid Olivia's ID badge across Paul's desktop and then stepped back, filling the doorway of the cube. Behind him Ray, from Building Services, was cleaning out Olivia's cube, collecting her personal effects—her FOLLOW YOUR BLISS coffee cup, her lumbar pillow, a little bouquet of imitation daisies—in a cardboard box. Preston draped a large hand over the partition on either side of Paul's door.

"What's this?" Paul glanced at the badge.

"Found it on the security desk this morning," said Preston, watching Paul.

"Didn't you hear?" Paul returned his gaze to his monitor, where he was paging through the revised RFP. "She quit."

"That's what I heard."

"She must have left it on her way out the door."

"On a Saturday?"

Paul glanced at the badge again, noting its little, square picture of an unsmiling Olivia Haddock. "Maybe she didn't like long good-byes."

"Maybe." Preston shifted in the doorway, blocking Paul's view of Ray in the cube across the aisle. "You know why she quit?"

Paul stared hard at the text on the screen, every word gone blurry. "Check with Rick."

"I did," Preston said. "He says you saw her after he did. Says you was supposed to meet her here Saturday morning."

Paul paged down to the next section. He was slouching in his seat, but it was getting harder to feign boredom with Preston looming over him.

"Look, Paul." Preston lifted one of his hands. "I ain't accusing you of anything. It's just, we need to know where to send her stuff." He stepped aside just enough to give Paul a glimpse across the aisle. Ray stood with the box curled under one arm, his other hand digging through the shadows at the back of Olivia's desk.

"She's got a home phone, right?" Paul lifted his gaze to Preston. "Call her up."

"She ain't there neither," Preston said. "Phone's been disconnected."

Paul pushed himself up in his seat. "I give up," he said. "Where is she?"

"So you wasn't here Saturday," Preston said, "when she resigned."

Paul swiveled in his chair, hunched forward, and clasped his hands between his knees. He was aiming for a look of exasperated sincerity. "No, I wasn't here Saturday," he said. "I was home, in bed, sleeping off Friday night, if you really want to know." He looked up at Preston with wide eyes. "I didn't come in until Sunday. Colonel let me in."

Preston scowled. "Colonel."

"Yeah."

"*He* let you in."

"Yep."

"On Sunday?"

Paul gave Preston a look of sincere exasperation.

"Be real easy for me to check if Colonel's badge was used yesterday," Preston said.

Paul hadn't thought of that. It was getting difficult to hold Preston's gaze, and he began to wonder if there might not be a surveillance camera in the lobby and a tape somewhere showing a pixilated image of him and Olivia crossing the lobby on Saturday morning. But then, plucking up the courage of his conviction that this was all a dream, he reminded himself that none of what he remembered from Saturday morning had really happened. For all he knew, Colonel was telling the truth, and all the tape showed—assuming there was a tape—was Colonel and Paul scooting across the lobby on Sunday. Or, for that matter, Elvis, Jimmy Hoffa, and baby Jesus.

"I thought you weren't accusing me of anything," Paul said.

"No, I ain't." Preston sighed heavily. "I'm sorry." Preston glanced over his shoulder. "It's just . . . remember what we talked about t'other day?"

"About . . . ?"

Preston dropped his voice. "About you tell me if you see anything. You know, out of the ordinary."

"That's funny," said Ray, out of sight behind Preston.

"You remember that?" Preston said, narrowing his eyes.

"This ain't her computer," Ray said. "Number don't match."

With some reluctance, Preston turned slowly away from Paul. "What?" he said.

Paul glimpsed Ray around Preston's belly. Ray had set the box down and was cataloguing the contents of Olivia's cube against a checklist on a clipboard.

"This ain't her computer," Ray said. "Serial number don't match up with the number she was assigned."

"Then whose computer is it?" said Preston.

Ray licked his fat thumb and paged through the papers on the clipboard. The mild exertion of cleaning out the cube was making him sweat, and his broad forehead glistened in the fluorescent light.

"Huh," said Ray. Paul could hear him breathing all the way across the aisle.

"What?" said Preston and Paul, simultaneously.

"That's funny," said Ray.

"*What?*" chorused Preston and Paul.

"Used to belong to what's his name." Ray rotated slowly on his own axis, and with his blunt chin indicated the empty cube next to Paul's. "Fella who sat over there."

"Dennis?" gulped Paul.

"You mean the fella who—?" Preston began.

"Whatever," said Ray. "It's his computer. Or was his, before he—"

"Don't say it," Paul groaned.

"What's it doing in *her* cube?" Preston moved across the aisle.

"Good question," said Ray. "I thought it was down in storage."

"Then where's *her* computer?" Preston stooped past Ray, peering past the computer at the cabinet over the desk. He felt under the cabinet and stood again, rubbing his fingers together. His fingertips were smudged with black. He looked across the aisle. "Paul?" he said. "You know anything about this?"

Paul pushed himself unsteadily to his feet. "No," he whispered.

Preston sniffed his fingers and wrinkled his nose, then he stepped across the aisle and snatched Olivia's ID off Paul's desk. "Excuse me," he said, marching up the aisle with the heel of his hand on his sidearm.

"Twitchy son of a bitch, ain't he?" said Ray.

"I guess," Paul said, watching Preston's head and shoulders glide away through the labyrinth of cubes.

"Say listen," Ray said, "I don't suppose you'd give me a hand getting this computer out of here. She's got to go all the way back down to storage. . . ."

"Excuse me," Paul muttered, and he glided up the aisle, in the opposite direction from Preston. A minute or two later, he was in Building Services, where he found Callie bent over the sign-up book in the outer room.

"Hey," she said, giving him an equivocal look, but he caught her by the elbow and tugged her into the inner office. She brightened a little, misunderstanding his intent, and as soon as they were out of sight of the hallway, she wrapped her arms around his neck and kissed him. "Apology accepted," she said.

"Apology?" Paul said. They stood with their foreheads touching.

She widened her eyes at him. "No?" she said. "Where the hell were you all weekend? I figured you'd be out of it all day Saturday—God knows I felt like shit—but when I come over Sunday morning, I hammered on your door for prit' near fifteen minutes."

"Was my car there?" Paul searched her face.

Callie stared at him. She loosened her grip, but kept her hands draped over his shoulders. "Don't you know?" she said.

"Callie." Paul curled his hands around her long wrists. "Where was I Saturday morning?"

Callie blew out a sigh. "Um, well, *Saturday*." She let go of him and stepped past him into the doorway where she could watch both him and the outer office. "Last I remember is driving your car back to my apartment—you got short legs, by the way." She glanced into the outer office and lowered her voice. "Then I remember dragging your sorry ass up the stairs to bed."

"Was I there when you woke up?"

"No. You wasn..." She winced. "You weren't. But then I didn't wake up till noon. I figured you went to meet Olivia at work."

Paul sighed and turned away, pacing a nervous little circle in the inner office. "Olivia's gone," he said.

Callie looked puzzled. "What do you mean, she's gone?"

Paul's mouth was very dry. With Callie looking at him so intently, it was hard to think straight. He heard a voice that sounded just like his in his head, saying, don't tell her anything, just take her by the hand and lead her out into the parking lot, and get in her pickup truck and drive away and don't look back.

Don't be stupid, he heard another voice say, sounding much like the first one, you can't run forever. You lost your career and your wife and everything you ever worked for. You have to hit bottom sometime. Colonel's right, the voice went on, you've got it good, finally, after much too long. You've got a permanent job, a sweet deal, a safe harbor. Okay, so it's not exactly what you planned on, not tenure at a research university—no book-lined office overlooking the leafy quad, no slim, influential volumes from major university presses, no fetching graduate students hanging on your every word. It's just a job in state government, life in a cube, but it's also a steady income and benefits and job security like nobody else has except maybe the pope and federal judges.

"Olivia quit," Paul heard himself say.

"Quit?" Callie looked even more puzzled. "How come?"

He couldn't bring himself to meet her gaze. The voices in his head were still contending with each other. Think what you're doing, said the first voice, while the second one said, for chrissakes, what you're being offered here is *better* than tenure. Yes, Colonel's magnum opus is probably unreadable, but at least he's writing a book. Think what *you* could do with access to a computer and all that time in a cube with *nothing else to do*. . . .

"I don't know," Paul said. "She just did."

"When?" Callie put her hand to her throat. "We just saw her on Friday night."

"She came in on Saturday morning and left a letter for Rick." Paul drew a breath and continued. "Then she left her badge at the security desk and took off."

"Did you see her?" Callie glanced once more towards the hallway, then stepped towards Paul. "I mean, was she here when you got here?"

Tell her what happened! said the first voice. This girl's the best thing you've got going right now. Be a man for once in your life and tell her the truth!

Don't be an idiot, said the second voice, you saw nothing on Saturday, you heard nothing. Olivia's gone, and everybody's better off. Hell, maybe even *Olivia* is better off wherever she is. Callie doesn't need to know.

Callie's the one untainted thing in your life! said the first voice.

Why not keep it that way? said the second. What she doesn't know can't hurt her.

"I don't remember what happened." Paul's throat clenched, and he could barely get the words out. "I don't remember anything until I woke up this morning."

Callie peered at him. "Really?"

He looked away from her. "Really," he said hoarsely. The voices in his head had gone silent.

"Jesus," breathed Callie, and she brushed his shoulder with her fingertips. "Aw, honey, you really can't hold your liquor, can you?"

Paul was on the verge of tears, and he didn't know why. "That's not all." He drew a deep breath. "They're giving me her job."

Callie's hand rested on his shoulder. "Really," she said.

"Yes." Paul met her eye as best he could. "Probably. Rick's looking into it."

"That's quick," she said. "I mean, her chair's still warm, idnit?" A slow smile spread across Callie's face.

"What?" he said. He felt his face get hot.

"You're gonna be a lifer," she said, with an ironic twist to her lips. "A TexDog."

Paul laughed bitterly and said, "Fuck you."

She let her hand trail off his shoulder. "Pretty soon," she said, "you're gonna be too good for the mail girl."

What happened next astonished them both. He seized her tightly around the waist and kissed her hard. She put her palms against his shoulders, but she didn't push him away, and after a moment, she folded her arms around him and pressed herself as tightly against him as he was pressing himself against her. He could feel her heart pounding, could feel the blood rushing through her arms, could feel the warm slide of muscles in her back. The heat rising off them was more than the sum of their two bodies, and Paul, his eyes squeezed shut, thought he might happily die in this hot darkness, that he might spin away with her into the void and never come back.

They parted, gasping for breath, both of them wide-eyed and flushed.

"Callie," he said, and his eyes filled with tears.

She put her fingers to his lips. "You're having a good day," she said. "Don't push your luck."

"Callie," he insisted, trying to pull her close again.

"Shh." She cupped his face in her palms and wiped his tears with her thumbs. "You got the job. Olivia's gone." She smiled. "That means you win, right?"

"Right." Paul sniffled. "I win."

THIRTY-SIX

LATE FRIDAY NIGHT, Callie roused Paul from a doze as they lay postcoitally entangled by the flickering light of the TV.

"So what's eatin' you?" she said. Paul blinked up at the TV light on the ceiling and stirred, Callie's arm across his chest, her warm thigh across his lap.

"What makes you think anything's eating me?" He massaged the sleep from his eyes with the heels of hands.

"Something is," Callie said. "I can feel it."

"Nothing," insisted Paul.

"Bullshit," Callie said, and under the sheet she twisted a handful of love handle.

"Ow!" cried Paul.

"I ain't fixin' to play this game with you every goddamn night." She vigorously propped herself on an elbow, making the mattress bounce. "I asked you a question, mister."

Paul sighed. It was true, he had passed the last four days numbly. He felt as if he had retreated to the center of his own head: He could see out of his eyes, he could hear through his

ears, but he reached and touched and moved things just with
the tips of his fingers. Smells seemed to come to him distantly;
food had no taste. When he got up from his desk and walked
the aisles of TxDoGS, or down the hall and out the lobby and
across the parking lot to his car, he felt like he was in one of
the Martian tripods in *The War of the Worlds*, as if he was some
sort of slithery, boneless, alien polyp sitting in the control room
of a giant machine, working the blinking controls with big,
spatular flippers as the machine strode, whirring and clanking,
across a miniature landscape. When he turned his head, he
seemed to be looking down on the world from a height, dis-
passionately scanning the villages and roadways below for a
house or a hay wagon or a frantic, antlike refugee he could fry
with his heat ray.

"I'm waitin'," said Callie, who got folksier as she got more
demanding. She rapped his sternum with her forefinger.

The only emotions that penetrated the rind of Paul's numbness were fear and lust. What he feared mainly was that everyone around him—Colonel, J. J., Bob Wier, and Rick and
Preston and Nolene, even Callie—would learn his secret, that
at the top of the striding, insect-jointed legs and under the
gleaming metal carapace of the machine, he was a Martian, a
soft, palpitating, defenseless thing, vulnerable to the tiniest ter-
restrial virus. Charlotte, of course, already knew how vulnerable he was, but she had been strangely dormant all week,
limiting herself to fleeting appearances in the shadowy corners
of his apartment, dashing along the edges of his peripheral
vision.

Callie tilted Paul's face towards hers with the tips of her
fingers. "I'll count to three if I have to," she said.

Her unblinking blue eyes seemed both remote and bright to
him, as if he were looking up at her from the bottom of a well.
Apart from his fear of being found out, the only other emotion
that reached Martian Paul in his dark little control room was
his piercing desire for Callie, who somehow transmuted his fear
and rage—magically, alchemically—to tenderness.

"You're the only . . . ," he began, and Callie sighed ostentatiously and looked away, down the length of their twined legs to the television, which they had been running with the sound off as a love light. Tonight Charlotte was treating them to *Born Free*.

"Does your TV ever show anything without lions in it?" She drummed her fingers lightly on his chest.

"Sometimes I get tigers," Paul said, relieved that she'd changed the subject. "Or cheetahs. The odd panther, now and then."

"And's that all because of . . . what's her name?"

"Charlotte."

"Charlotte. Huh." Callie lowered her head to his shoulder and curled against him. She reached for his wrist and pulled his arm around her. "What do you boys talk about at lunch?" she said, her jaw working against his shoulder. "You and Colonel and them others."

Paul wondered why Callie wanted to know. In his numbness he remembered the past five days as a blur. Only Monday was still clear to him, when a bored, heavy-set woman in Human Resources had conducted a pro forma interview with him in an empty conference room, asking him questions off a checklist without really listening to the answers. Then she had handed him a paper cup with a plastic lid and sent him to the men's room, where he squeezed out six ounces of warm pee for the state of Texas. By Tuesday morning, barring a bad result from the drug test, he was a Tech Writer II for the Texas Department of General Services, with a salary of nearly $27,000 a year— the largest sum, Paul was alarmed to realize, he'd ever earned in his life. That same day a gum-smacking techie in a Hawaiian shirt spent two minutes at Paul's keyboard and gave him access to the World Wide Web, and Callie herself photographed him again for a new badge, one with an electronic stripe, like Olivia's.

After that, the blur set in. At the moment, as Callie breathed against him, he couldn't remember whole blocks of the week— what he'd had for breakfast on Tuesday, say, or whether he'd spent Wednesday night at his place or hers.

"It's up to Colonel," Paul said. "He decides what we talk about."

"And the rest of you just sorta sit there and nod?" She shifted her head against his chest.

Paul wasn't sure what to say about that either. He now permanently occupied the fourth chair at Colonel's table in the corner of the TxDoGS lunchroom. Indeed, Colonel had started to call Paul's seat the Paul Trilby Chair in Literary Studies, or, worse, the Olivia Haddock Memorial Chair; Paul was still working up the nerve to tell him to knock it off. The last of his bag lunches—one final sandwich of nameless cheese on no-brand bread—slowly desiccated in one of the office fridges, until (unbeknownst to Paul) someone swiped it. Paul could now afford to buy hot lunches from the cafeteria, and he remembered eating a burger and fries, and a slab of meatloaf with mashed potatoes, and chicken fried steak with cream gravy, and a surprisingly good platter of cheese enchiladas with refried beans and rice. He couldn't remember which day had been enchiladas and which had been meatloaf, but he did remember Colonel's greeting the first day he had arrived at the table bearing a tray.

"Welcome to the good life, Professor," Colonel had said.

"I don't think Colonel likes me," Callie said, hugging Paul a little more tightly. "I run into him in the hall the other day, and I told him I had a good time at his party last week, and he just looked at me like . . ."

"Like what?" Paul said, but he already knew the answer. In his general emotional torpor, he only remembered pieces of Colonel's lunchtime performance, such as a lecture on the decline of the American presidency. "The last twenty years . . . hell, the last *forty* years of presidents have been whiners and perverts and headcases," Colonel had declared. "Degenerates, like the later Roman emperors." And a disquisition on the superiority of the American Browning automatic rifle to the British Lewis gun. "Not to take away from our brothers across the Pond," Colonel had said, "but give me an American weapon any time." And a history of the British Empire on film, from

The Four Feathers to *The Man Who Would Be King.* "The sequel to *Zulu*, the egregious *Zulu Dawn*? A slander on the English fighting man."

But the lunchtime conversation Paul remembered best had taken place on the embankment along the river, where Colonel had invited him, without J. J. and Bob Wier, for a postprandial stroll. Had it been Wednesday? Paul wondered. Thursday? Today? He couldn't remember, but he did remember vividly what Colonel had said as they paced up and down the yellowed grass alongside the sluggish glide of the river.

"Now that you've ascended to the middle class, Professor," Colonel said, his arm around Paul's shoulders, "you need to get yourself a quality woman."

"I beg your pardon?" Paul said.

"I understand what you see in Miss Oklahoma." Colonel squeezed Paul. "We all like a ride on a frisky young colt now and then. But she's wild, Paul, an untamable mustang, and you deserve a thoroughbred, something with breeding and dignity—"

"Whoa!" Paul cried, twisting free of Colonel's grip. "You seriously need to back off."

Colonel shook his head ruefully at the hormonal folly of younger men. "The girl is trash, Paul. You want a solid woman who knows her place, not some lippy bitch who'll lead you around by your cojones." Colonel narrowed his gaze. "I think you know what I'm talking about. Sooner or later, you're going to have to give her up."

"What do you mean, give her up?" Walk away, Paul told himself, but there he stood, waiting.

"Do you love her?" Colonel had said with a wicked smile, and Paul had stalked away at last, with a dismissive gesture.

"You just answered my question," Colonel had called after him.

"Oh, you know," Callie was saying now. "Like I was the mail girl or something."

"Want me to beat him up for you?" *Do you love her?* Colonel had said. Paul tightened his arms around Callie.

"Wouldja?" She tilted her face so that he could see her eyes. "You never answered my question."

"What question?"

"Why do you sit with them? Are you part of the club now or what?"

Christ, thought Paul. Was he part of the club? He was still convinced that nothing unusual had happened on Friday night or Saturday morning, that he had been drunk and insensible for much of those twenty-four hours. And yet, when he had arrived at work every morning these past few days, the RFP had been waiting for him on his desktop, each of Rick's changes from the previous day already entered into the document. All Paul had to do was . . . nothing. Paul had nothing to do. Colonel had winked at him at lunch one day—which day?—and said, "What are you going to do with all that free time, Professor?" He had a dim, drunken memory of someone—J. J. or Bob Wier or Colonel himself—asking him, "Do you know the story of the shoemaker and the elves?" Or, Paul wondered during his break, as he turned the pages of *Seven Science Fiction Novels of H. G. Wells* without reading them, was it more like the Eloi and the Morlocks? And if we are Eloi—Colonel and J. J. and Bob Wier and me—then what do the Morlocks want from us? They do our work, but what do they want in return?

"Paul? You fadin' on me again?"

Paul sighed. "The first day I sat with him this week," he said, to the crown of Callie's head, "Colonel said to me, 'Welcome to the good life, Professor.' "

Callie looked up at him again. "What's that supposed to mean?"

"The obvious, I guess," Paul said. "I've got a permanent job and a salary and a dental plan. A better ID badge. Web access. The American Dream."

"It's more than a lot of people got," Callie said. He could feel her tense up against him.

"I'm not complaining, Callie, truly I'm not." And why should I? he thought. It's better than what I had before.

"It's not like you're better than anybody else," she said.

She might as well have slipped a shiv between his ribs. He lifted his arm away from her. "Olivia Haddock told me the same thing," he said.

Callie sat up with her back to Paul, her cheekbone and breast limned by the silvery light from the TV. "Sorry." She glanced back at him. "It's just . . ."

"It's just what?" Paul said icily.

Callie spoke to the TV screen, hunched over in bed. "Well, ever since I met you, all you done is . . . *complain* about how far you've fallen, and now when things are looking up, when you're making a little progress, you seem . . ."

"You were going to say 'whine' just now, weren't you?" Paul's fear and anger were contending in equal measure just now; the returning memory of Saturday morning was scaring the bejesus out of him. The image of Olivia Haddock's last stand had popped up uncomfortably a number of times during the week: while he was drowsing before his monitor, surfing the Web, or in between forkfuls of enchilada at lunch with Colonel, or even when he was tumbling happily in bed with Callie. No matter what he was doing, he could see behind his eyeballs Olivia's legs flailing in the air; the pale hand descending from the gap in the ceiling to slap him; the fish-eyed gaze of Boy G.

"Look, I'm sorry, I didn't mean to sound like the Red Queen," Callie said, chopping the air with her hand, "but why *can't* you be happy with what you got? Why can't you be happy with . . ."

"The Red Queen?" Paul laughed. "Jesus, where'd you come up with that?"

"It's from—"

"I know what it's from," he said. "How do *you* know what it's from?"

Callie whirled on him in bed, looming over him with her finger inches from his nose. "Don't you dare condescend to me," she said. "Don't you *dare*."

Paul started to get aroused. "We all like a ride on a frisky young colt," Colonel had said. "Do you love her?" He smiled and slid his hand around her hip to the small of her back, and he tried to work his thigh between her legs, but Callie pushed herself away from him. She bounded awkwardly off the bed and stumbled through the clothes on the floor. She crossed her arm over her breasts and clutched her shoulder, and she stooped to pick through the limp jeans and underwear.

"Oh, c'mon," said Paul, pulling the sheet over his tumescent lap. "Aren't we going to work this out?"

"I ain't in the mood for 'working it out.' " Callie gestured a pair of quotation marks in the air, without looking at Paul.

"Callie, I'm sorry." Paul scootched to the edge of the bed and tried to catch her eye. "I'm being a jerk."

Callie tugged on her panties and then her jeans. All Paul heard from her was the angry hiss of her breath. She stooped again for her shirt.

Paul mouthed a silent *fuck* and flopped back on the bed. On the TV screen the *Born Free* lions sprawled across a rock in the African sun, their fat tongues lolling between their enormous canines. On top of the TV Charlotte sprawled in exactly the same attitude, her front paws pushed forward, her head sunk between them, eyes half open. Her back legs were splayed off the edge of the set, and her tail strobed slowly back and forth across the screen. Paul glanced at Callie to see if she had noticed, but she was buttoning her shirt with her back to him. Paul let his head drop onto the pillow, and he watched the TV's light flicker across the ceiling.

"Callie," he said, "without you . . ."

She looked at him over her shoulder. "Without me, what?" she said.

"Without you . . . ," Paul began. He had no idea how to finish the sentence.

Callie turned and stooped for her sandals, dangling them by their straps, and to Paul's surprise she dropped to her knees next to the bed. She set the sandals neatly to one side, and she leaned over Paul, her hand lightly on the sheet over his chest.

"Let's go," she said.

"Okay," murmured Paul, and he pushed himself up to kiss her. But she pushed him back.

"That's not what I mean." Her eyes were clear, and she watched him calmly. "I mean, let's *go*. Let's git. Let's get out of this town and not come back."

"What?" Paul said.

She met his gaze with her own; wherever he tried to look, she was looking back at him. "You hate Texas, you hate the heat, you hate your job, you hate the folks you work with."

"Yeah, but . . . ," breathed Paul. All his muscles were pulling tight under the sheet. His stomach was clenching.

"Well, me too, cowboy." Her hand was warm and firm against his chest. "Don't let it go to your head, 'cause it ain't saying much, but you're the best thing to happen to me in this whole goddamn state."

"Really?" said Paul.

"There's nothing in this shitty little apartment that's yours, 'cept your clothes, right? So let's toss 'em in my truck and take off. We could be in Mexico by sunup."

"Mexico?" He felt his stomach clench.

"Or wherever. We could be in California the day after tomorrow."

Finally Paul managed to lift himself on his elbows. Her hand pressed lightly on his chest. "Are you serious?" he said.

"Serious as a heart attack, lover." She slid her hand over his shoulder and curled her fingers around the back of his neck. "I followed one boy to Tulsa, and another boy here, but I never asked a boy to follow *me* before."

"Wow," said Paul.

Callie moved her face close to his, her eyes half shut. "C'mon, Paul," she breathed. "Let's. Just. *Go*."

She kissed him very tenderly, and Paul stopped breathing. He could feel his blood pulsing in his lips. Callie pulled away, and he couldn't help himself: He turned his gaze away from hers and looked down the bed at black-eyed Charlotte on top of the TV, her tail swishing metronomically across the screen. Callie half turned to see what he was looking at, but caught herself. She pushed back from the bed and stood; she stubbed her feet into her sandals.

"She ain't there, Paul," she said quietly, as if to a sleepless child.

"Yes she is," said Paul, unable to take his eyes off the cat. "Turn around and look."

"I don't have to. She ain't there." Callie bent over the bed and kissed Paul on the forehead. "She's in here." Then she turned and crossed to the door, swinging her hips.

"Callie," Paul said.

She hesitated with the door half open, but she didn't look back.

"See ya," she said, and then she was gone.

Paul lay on his elbows, gasping. He could still feel the imprint of her kiss on his forehead and on his lips. On top of the TV Charlotte split her flat head in a vast, black, jagged yawn.

"Fucking bitch!" Paul shouted, and he flung his pillow at her. She vanished and the pillow swept the jerry-rigged rabbit ears off the set and onto the floor; *Born Free* vanished in a blizzard of static. Outside, Paul heard the starting grumble of Callie's truck, heard the whine of reverse gear, heard the rattle of the drainage grate in the middle of the parking lot as Callie backed over it. Paul propelled himself from the bed towards the door, tangled his legs in the sheets, and fell to his knees. Snarling in frustration he stripped the sheet away and lunged for the door. He wrenched it open and stood there, breathless and naked and semi-aroused, and saw only his battered Colt and the dusty wrecks of his neighbors' ancient automobiles and, printed in silhouette against a yellow doorway, a single, slouching Snopes dangling a beer at his hip. Callie was gone, and Paul could only hear the rising gulp of her truck, climbing through its gears, away from him. Paul looked down at himself, and he stepped back and slammed his door.

"Paul?" said a voice behind him, and Paul started violently. He whirled and flattened his back against the inside of his apartment door.

Bob Wier stood rubbing his hands in the middle of Paul's room, while behind him a couple of pale homeless guys in white shirts and ties were peeking out of Paul's bathroom. The lower half of another guy hung from a gap in the suspended ceiling over Paul's bed, his shirt pulled tight over his soft torso. He dropped to the bed, landing on his feet and making the springs twang, and as he bounced he adjusted his glasses. The glare in his lenses from the TV obscured his eyes.

Bob Wier inclined his head solicitously towards Paul. "Is this a bad time?" he said.

THIRTY-SEVEN

THIS ISN'T HAPPENING, Paul told himself. This is a dream.

"We have to hurry," said Bob Wier nervously, as the pale men hovered around Paul, handing him his shorts, his trousers, his shirt. "You don't want to be late."

One bloodless pair of hands lifted his shirt from behind so that Paul could slip his arms through the sleeves, while another pair of hands worked the buttons. "Late for what?" said Paul.

But Bob Wier wasn't listening. He had cracked Paul's front door and was peering watchfully into the parking lot. Through the door Paul heard the distant rumble of late-night traffic on the interstate.

"What's going on?" asked Paul numbly. He felt sapped, drained, which only served to convince him further that this wasn't really happening, that someone hadn't just tugged up his trousers and zipped his fly and buckled his belt, that someone else hadn't just lifted his right foot, and then the left, to put on his sandals.

"Let's go," Bob Wier said, and he slipped out the door. Paul felt the soft grip of several pairs of hands urging him out into the hot night.

The parking lot of the Angry Loner Motel was as still as Paul had ever seen it. No one stood along the balconies; no open doorway threw a wedge of yellow light onto the pavement; not one shabby curtain twitched. Even Mrs. Prettyman's windows were dark. Apart from the distant roar of the highway, the only sound was the soft scrape of feet against the asphalt and Paul's own shallow breathing. Bob Wier wrung his hands again near the storm drain at the center of the lot, while another pair of pale men in shirt and tie and glasses hovered near him. How many of these guys are there? Paul wondered, and he tried to glance over his shoulder at the ghostly men hustling him across the asphalt, but they only pushed harder, making him dash along on his toes.

"Hurry," whispered Bob Wier, nervously scanning the balconies on either side, and the two pale men next to him stooped and hauled up the drainage grate without a sound.

"Wait a minute," said Paul, and he locked his knees, scrabbling at the asphalt with the heels of his sandals. "What the—"

But the hands lifted him bodily into the air and lowered him into the wide drain, where another pair of hands reached up for Paul's ankles. He pedaled his legs madly, for all the world like Olivia Haddock being lifted into the ceiling, but the hands grasped him firmly and tugged him down into the drain. As he descended Paul glanced up and saw the anxious face of Bob Wier surrounded by the moon faces of several pale men, all of them printed against the black sky.

"Don't fight it," whispered Bob Wier.

The hands beneath him placed Paul's toes on a narrow rung, while hands from above did the same with his fingers. Paul found himself descending under his own power. The rungs were chill and damp, and a similarly chill, damp breeze blew from below, tickling Paul's ears and wafting up his pant legs. Looking up again he saw Bob Wier's backside and the scuffed soles of his penny loafers as he lowered himself into the drain, while below, when Paul dared to look, he saw a pale scalp descending into the dark and even farther below, little flashes of light gliding to and fro at the bottom of the shaft.

Not happening, Paul chanted silently, not happening. I'm fast asleep and Callie's fast asleep next to me. I'm wrapped in my baby's arms, and this is a dream.

Still, it was an unusually vivid dream. They descended far enough that Paul's arms and legs started to tremble from the exertion, but just when he needed to stop and catch his breath, the hands below grasped his ankles, then his calves, and then his waist, steadying him as he stepped off the ladder onto a gritty floor. The flashes he had seen from above turned out to be pale men wielding flashlights, and as the beams glided all around him, a dizzy Paul noted roughly carven walls of rock, streaked with damp. The beams caught glittering drops of water along the low ceiling, and Paul felt the humidity of the tunnel close around him like wet gauze. Sweat started out of his hairline and under his arms.

Bob Wier came down out of the drain a little out of breath, and his footsteps scraped along the gritty floor of the tunnel towards Paul. Pale men dropped silently out of the drain like large, plump spiders, mingling among the ones waiting at the bottom. In the jittery glare of the flashlights, Paul tried to count them, but their faces shifted and faded too quickly. He couldn't even hear them breathe, which, he scolded his dreaming subconscious, was an unnecessarily creepy detail.

"I'm dreaming," Paul said earnestly to Bob Wier.

"Sure," said Bob Wier, catching him by the arm and tugging him down the tunnel. "Whatever you say."

As they marched downward into a dank breeze, Paul managed to smile. I might as well enjoy this, he decided. The ol' lizard brain is working overtime tonight. The beam of the lead man's flashlight bored down the tunnel ahead of them; against the glare Paul saw the silhouettes of several heads, each eggshaped outline furred by a buzz cut. He glanced back and was blinded by the beams of a couple more flashlights. The tunnel was full of the reverberating tramp of feet. Just relax, he told himself, and have fun with it.

"Hi ho!" he sang. "Hi ho! It's off to work we go!"

Somebody cuffed his ear from behind, and Paul cried, "Ow!" Ahead, he glimpsed Bob Wier's profile in silhouette, looking back over his shoulder. "Try to take this seriously, Paul," he said.

Up ahead he saw the flashlight glow reflected off a bend in the tunnel, and then the walls of the tunnel swung away and the ceiling lifted, and the air became less close and a little less humid. In the play of flashlight beams Paul saw a wide, natural cavity of creamy yellow stone, the walls and ceiling etched smoothly into sharp peaks and shallow scallops, like meringue. The floor here was smoother and firmer, with less grit, and the farthest beam showed a broad track winding away into the dark.

"Okay," Paul said, beginning to feel pleased at the DVD quality of his subconscious, "this is pretty good."

Silhouetted against the beam ahead was a low, squarish outline, and then the flashlights from behind illuminated a scruffy little golf cart, a two seater without an awning, its white side panels dinged and smudged. Out of the dark the hands of pale men guided Paul up onto the passenger seat. Bob Wier squeezed next to him, his knees spread wide around the little steering wheel. He turned the ignition, and the little cart vibrated to life. He switched on the cart's headlights and stepped on the accelerator, and the cart whirred forward, its fat little tires crunching against the track. Paul looked back to see the pale men standing in a bunch, all of them watching him go, their flashlight beams lancing in every direction. On a sudden whim he stood up in the cart and waved to them with the back of his hand, like departing royalty.

"My good and faithful subjects," he trilled, in a queenly falsetto. "God bless you all."

Bob Wier grabbed him by the belt and hauled him back into his seat, just before Paul could be brained by a low hanging rock.

"I just want to say," said Paul, "that this is the *best* dream I've ever had."

"Listen, Paul." Bob Wier's face was in the dark, while ahead of them the creamy peaks and scallops of the cavern walls glided through the headlamps. "You need to prepare yourself for what's about to happen."

"Oh, alright." Paul settled back in the narrow little seat, feeling more effervescent by the minute. "I'll play along."

"They're going to demand a sacrifice from you tonight." Bob Wier grimly maneuvered through the dark with both hands on the wheel.

"It's a kind of hazing, right?" said Paul, blithely. "You guys are going to paddle me or something."

"It's the hardest thing you'll ever do." Bob Wier's expression was unreadable in the dark. "Take your wife, your only wife, whom you love, and offer her as a burnt offering."

"What?" said Paul. "What'd you say?" The buzz of the golf cart reverberated off the cave walls. "What book of the Bible is *that*?"

"The Book of Bob," said Bob Wier.

"Well, it's not funny," said Paul. "I don't want it in my dream."

"I offered her up, thinking, you know, at the last minute the angel of the Lord would intervene." Bob's voice was barely audible over the whirr of the motor and the crunch of the tires. "But He didn't come. God let me down, Paul." Bob Wier choked and looked away. Paul glanced at him, but all he saw was Bob's silhouette against the glow of the headlights.

"But then, to be fair," Bob Wier said, "I'm no Abraham."

After that they rode in silence, and Paul crossed his arms and sulked. The cart passed several turnoffs and branchings of the cavern, and Bob Wier always took the widest path. The damp breeze blew stronger in their faces, and the walls moved farther back from the pathway, so that much of the time the dim little headlamps illuminated only the pebbled surface of the wide path, with nothing but darkness beyond. This is getting boring, Paul thought, and after a glance at Bob Wier to make sure he wasn't watching, Paul surreptitiously pinched himself in the thigh, trying to wake himself up. I'd rather be watching *Born Free*, Paul thought, than riding a golf cart into hell with Bob Wier.

But then he saw a glow up ahead, an illuminated patch of rock beyond the headlights, and Bob lifted his foot from the accelerator and let the cart's motor grind down to a stop just before a curve. A steady light shone from around the bend, and Bob switched off the ignition and stepped out of the cart, gesturing in the dim light for Paul to follow. Around the curve Paul found himself in the upper reaches of an enormous natural amphitheater, where a rubbled floor descended to meet the sloping ceiling at a narrow point far below. The room was thickly forested with dripping stalactites hung from above and soapy bulges of flowstone below. Some of these formations had joined in the middle, forming slender, gray-green columns, smooth and knotted like long strands of nerve tissue. A mellow light came from all around, from bulbs set in nooks and crannies and linked by loops of fat cable.

Bob Wier led Paul down a narrow path that wound between the columns and the stalactites, and Paul had the feeling that he was walking through the strings and lumps and tissues of somebody's brain. *My* brain, he decided. That's where I am. I'm dreaming of a journey to the center of my own head. He laughed aloud with delight. This dream was turning out to be a concatenation of every subterranean narrative he'd ever read or seen, from highbrow to lowbrow and every brow in between, a Mixmastering of Dante and Jules Verne, of *Tom Sawyer* and *Buffy the Vampire Slayer*, of the Mines of Moria and the Hall of the Mountain King. He looked up and was well pleased with the fecundity of his subconscious. The ceiling was forested with pale, almost translucent soda straws, and seamed with small stalactites like jagged mountain ranges seen from above. To either side, in niches like private boxes at the farther reaches of the amphitheater, the formations were growing together like connective tissue, and out of these crannies the pale faces of homeless guys watched Paul. He thought he heard a steady murmuring; it wasn't the usual—"Are we not men?"—but something else that he couldn't make out.

The air was cooler as they descended but more humid, and Paul thought he smelled something other than the dank air of the cave, something that reached to the back of his nostrils. But he couldn't place it, and he mopped his forehead and flung the sweat away from his fingertips. Bob Wier had sweated a wide streak down the back of his polo shirt, and he seemed to be gasping even more than the exertion demanded. They had reached the lowest circle of the amphitheater, where a passage led to an even brighter chamber beyond. The wind was coming from that narrow gap, and Paul thought gleefully, what next? Trolls? Dinosaurs? A Balrog? The circle of panders, seducers, and flatterers?

"Hey, Bob," said Paul. "Mind if I call you Virgil?"

Bob Wier stopped and glanced with wide-eyed anxiety back up the slope. Paul turned too, to see several pale men with flashlights trooping down the path from above—How'd they get here so fast? Paul wondered, then thought, fuck it, don't ask, it's a dream—while others filtered out of the crannies, stepping carefully down the slope around the soapy bulges of stalagmites. Their murmuring was getting louder, but Paul still couldn't make out what they were saying. He turned to go forward again, but Bob Wier held him back with a hand on his shoulder and fixed him with an intent gaze. He lifted his hand from Paul's shoulder and turned it palm up, offering Paul the ignition key of the golf cart.

"Take it," he said in a low, urgent voice. "Take it and go back the way we came. It's not too late for you."

"Maybe Virgil's too formal," Paul said, still determined to get into the spirit of things. "How 'bout just 'Virge'?"

"I beg you," breathed Bob Wier, his eyes filling with tears, "in the name of Christ Jesus, go back now. I'm going to hell, but you still have a choice." He essayed a trembling smile. " 'Work out your salvation with fear and trembling, for it is God who works in you.' " He swallowed hard and said, "Philippians, chapter two, verses twelve and thirteen."

Paul's smile faded, and his next remark—"Don't be a buzz-kill, Bob"—faded on his lips. He glanced down at the key in Bob Wier's trembling palm, but then it was too late, as the gathering tide of pale men reached the bottom of the path.

"What is the law?" they were murmuring. "What is the law?"

They flowed around Paul and Bob Wier, and with the mild pressure of their hands swept both men through the passage into the next room.

THIRTY-EIGHT

THE PASSAGE WAS LOW AND NARROW AND S-SHAPED, and Paul could not see what was ahead, only the glow of electric lights. Having decided that all this—the caverns, the pale men, the torment of Bob Wier—were features of a dream, still Paul was surprised and a little alarmed to follow Bob Wier around the final curve of the passage into an aisle running between the gray upholstered walls of cubicles on either side, under bright, fluorescent fixtures. At first he assumed that, following the peculiar logic of a dream, he was now wandering the aisles of the General Services Division of TxDoGS. But the lights were much brighter, and as he squinted against the glare he noted that the fabric of the cubes was mottled and streaked with damp; that the thin carpet under foot was lumpy and uneven, a thin padding over hard rock; and that the faces of the men rising from their desks all around him were not the faces of his co-workers in the world above but those of pale, homeless men, their glasses glaring in the light, their milky skin gleaming through their buzz cuts. The cube walls came up to Paul's cheekbones, as they did at TxDoGS, and he saw the bulbous heads rising from the centers of cubes all around him, some taller than others, some broader in the forehead, but all with the same blank gaze. Because of the glare of the lights, Paul could not tell how far the cubes receded into the distance. Straight ahead, past the cringing shoulders of Bob Wier, he saw that the aisle ended in a T, and that at the intersection of the two aisles an iron pole crusted with reddish rust rose straight up into the air. Next to the pole waited Boy G, his arms hanging straight at his sides, his glasses pushed all the way up his nose, his pens lined up, his name tag neatly centered over his breast pocket.

The faces peering over the cube horizon on either side all turned to follow Paul's progress up the aisle, and he glanced back to see the men who had followed him down the amphitheater crowding up the aisle behind him. The murmuring grew louder as the men in the cubes joined in.

"What is the law?" they muttered. "What is the law?"

As he got closer to the intersection, Paul noticed that the iron pole was a sort of ladder, with L-shaped iron rungs protruding at right angles, at alternate heights on either side; unlike the rusty central pole, the rungs were worn smooth to a dull gray sheen. Paul glanced up, but the top of the pole was lost in the glare of the lights. The tang he'd detected in the air in the amphitheater was sharper here, like the smell of burning oak.

As they reached the junction of the aisles, Bob Wier stepped to one side, and Boy G's gaze fell on Paul, who felt a tremor of cold up his spine.

"Who are you?" whispered Boy G in his toneless voice.

Paul sweated under the lights, in the clammy humidity of the cavern. He felt the pale men crowding behind him.

"Myself?" he said, uncertain what else to say.

Boy G turned his magnified eyes to Bob Wier, who licked his lips and glanced from Boy G to Paul. "He's a man," Bob Wier said.

"A man! A man! Like us!" murmured the pale men behind
him. Out of the corner of his eye, Paul saw the pale faces above
the cube horizon nodding in agreement.

"He's a man," Bob Wier said again. "He must learn the law."

"Say the words," murmured the men all around. "Say the
words."

Paul felt the chill tightening his skin. I wonder if it's too
late, he thought, to get that key from Bob.

Boy G turned and walked up the perpendicular aisle to the
right, and Bob Wier followed, gesturing curtly for Paul to follow. Paul turned to see if he could go back, but the pale men
in the aisle were pressing forward, murmuring, "Say the words,
say the words," while the other pale men began to filter out of
their cubes into the aisle, murmuring, "A man like us, a man
like us."

"Um, Bob?" said Paul, edging up the aisle. "Could I talk to
you for a second?"

But Bob Wier ignored him, and Paul had no choice but to
follow. Suddenly the cubicles ended on either side, and Paul
found himself walking on the cave floor again. Beyond the glare
of the fluorescent lights he saw ahead of him a vast, oval cavern
of creamy yellow rock, like custard, its ceiling dripping with
stalactites and soda straws and other, more delicate formations
like hanging draperies. Water dripped in an irregular rhythm
from above; Paul felt the tap of droplets on his scalp and his
wrist. Along the left side of the cavern, across a wide, shallow
pool of clear water, were three huge formations in a row. The
one closest to Paul was a creamy hillock like a huge lump of
melting vanilla ice cream. As from a leaky tap, water dripped
from a cluster of thin, bladelike projections above, then pulsed
in shallow waves down the broad, soapy slopes of the hillock
into the pool. The formation farthest from Paul, at the end of
the cave, was like an eroding sand castle, a clotted cluster of
blunted stalagmites that rose nearly to the dripping roof. And,
in the middle, was the tallest and most striking formation, a
long, curved, blunt-ended column that stuck out of a wide, conical base of flowstone and rose in layers of long, saber-fanged

stalactites nearly to the ceiling. It looked, depending on your point of view, like an enormous stack of decaying wedding cake, or a giant, sagging candle, or—as Paul, the ex-husband of a gender theorist, couldn't help noting—a giant, erect, rotting phallus. The column's reflection in the clear water of the pool trembled with each drop of water from above.

"Professor!" cried a voice, and Paul turned to see Colonel approaching him from the right side of the cave. "You've joined us at last!" Colonel was wearing his office kit—dress shirt with sleeves rolled down and cuffs buttoned, tie knotted firmly up under his dewlaps—and he joined the procession and pumped Paul's hand firmly and warmly.

"A big night, son!" His face was flushed, whether with whisky or excitement, Paul couldn't tell. "We've been preparing for your feast."

He threw his arm around Paul's shoulders, squeezing him tight and gesturing towards several rows of long, folding tables along the right side of the cavern. Each table was covered with a long, checkered tablecloth and lined with mismatched chairs. At regular intervals along each table stood a little skyline of salt-and-pepper shakers; rolls of brown paper towels upright on spindles; and bottles of hot sauce, jalapeños, and barbecue sauce. At the far end another table was set crosswise, where Paul recognized the landscape of classic Texas barbecue: stacks of paper plates and plastic utensils; potato salad and coleslaw in big plastic bowls; a metal bowl heaped with pickles; wedges of cheese, tomato, onion, and avocado on wide platters; loaves of white bread still in their plastic wrappers; a pair of sweating aluminum urns of iced tea; and a big Crock-Pot of beans, plugged into a fat, orange extension cord that snaked away into the recesses of the cave. At one end of the table stood a squat plastic barrel full of Dr. Pepper, Big Red, and Shiner Bock on ice.

"Yo!" cried J. J., who stood behind the farthest table in jeans and t-shirt and a baseball cap, tending to two large barbecue smokers, each an enormous black metal drum on four legs with a firebox like a low, square snout at one end. The floor of the cave was on a slight incline, tilted to the left, and the front wheels of each smoker were chocked with wedges of wood to keep them from rolling across the cave into the pool. J. J. wore an apron, not like some suburban backyard chef, but like a pro, the string wrapped around his waist and tied at the front. Black smoke puffed from the little chimney at the end of each smoker, staining the stalactites above with soot, and as Paul watched, J. J. lifted a short length of oak from a neat stack of logs.

"Hope you brought your appetite, dude!" J. J. said, and he opened the front door of the firebox of one of the smokers with a rag and fed the oak into the hot, hellish glare of the fire, shoving the log deeper with a long, iron poker. This isn't so bad for a dream, Paul thought. As a Yankee, he wasn't as enthusiastic about barbecue as some, but he didn't mind a plate of smoked brisket and hot sausage now and then. The only odd thing was, all Paul detected from the smokers was the burning wood, not the warm, fatty aroma of slow-roasting meat. J. J. kicked the firebox shut and set the poker to one side with a bright clang. Whatever they were having, J. J. hadn't even started cooking it yet.

"Now it's time to do your bit," said Colonel, bracing Paul around the shoulders and walking him slowly up the cave at the head of the procession. "There's a little bit of, well, ritual involved, but nothing you can't handle." Bob Wier and Boy G fell in a step or two back. "It's kind of an initiation rite." Colonel's avuncular tone had an edge of mischief in it, like a winking frat boy leading a pledge into a darkened room. "And, of course, it's also our way of thanking these boys for everything they do for us."

Colonel guided Paul towards the central, phallic formation, while from behind came the shuffle and scrape of many feet, and the steady susurrus of murmuring, all of it punctuated with the plink of water in the pool and reinforced by the swelling echo of the cave.

"It's the price we pay, Paul," murmured Colonel. "Mind you, it's not their steady diet, but let's just say they've developed a taste for what we can provide them." At the edge of the pool Colonel stopped and gently but firmly propelled Paul forward.

Reluctantly, Paul stepped onto the first of a series of stepping stones in the water, each a big, thick, fried egg slice of stalagmite. The water trembled with each step, and at last Paul stepped gingerly onto the slick, creamy surface at the conical base of the giant column.

"My boy!" cried a voice, and he looked up to see Stanley Tulendij stepping out from behind the column. He was wearing a frayed, faded, powder blue tuxedo with wide lapels and bell-bottom trousers. It was the sort of thing a teenaged boy might have worn to the prom twenty-five years ago, which made it simultaneously antique looking and much too young for Stanley Tulendij. Even in the garish tux he kept his spidery aspect—the trousers were too short for his long, peculiarly jointed legs, while the jacket was too big. His head wobbled on top of his long, thin neck, which didn't even come close to filling the voluminous collar of his frilly shirt. He came to the middle of a wide ledge at the base of the column, and his flat jaw split in a wide smile. He spread his arms, his bony hands sticking out of the wide, empty cuffs of his jacket.

"We've been waiting for you!" he said. "You've been the apple of our eye."

The murmuring of the pale men rose to a rumble, and Stanley Tulendij lifted his voice. "And now, gentlemen! Colleagues! Fellow Texans! Our lovely new queen!"

The murmuring diminished almost to silence, and just as Paul was thinking nothing else could surprise him, Olivia Haddock stepped out from behind the phallic column, wearing a faded, red velvet prom gown, with red satin gloves that ran over her elbows and a little, clear plastic tiara. The velvet was worn away in long creases down the folds of the skirt, while the bodice was a little tight on Olivia, squeezing her bosom bloodless. She wore a fraying, yellowed sash across her shoulder that read VIKING QUEEN CWNHS HOMECOMING 197—" The rest of the date was lost around the curve of her hip. She stood next to Stanley Tulendij on the ledge, one foot placed before the other, her red satin palms pressed together before her sash. In the breathless silence she scowled down the slope at Paul.

"You're late," she said.

With one foot on the slope of the cone, Paul goggled at the sight before him. This dream was turning uncomfortably strange. Indeed, with the unexpected appearance of Olivia, the dream seemed to be turning into a nightmare. She had disappeared only a week ago, and now she was not only alive and well, but somehow, in the foreshortened time of Paul's dream, she had become queen of the underworld. Paul glanced back, chilled to his spine, and immediately behind him he saw bright-eyed Colonel urging him forward with a nod, while a stricken Bob Wier wrung his hands. Behind them clustered a frighteningly large crowd of pale, homeless men in white shirts, ties, and glasses, their pale scalps gleaming through their stubbled hair, their lips pulled back from their sharpened teeth as they began to murmur again, "A man like us. Say the words."

"Come," said Stanley Tulendij, and the old man beckoned him up the slope, slowly curling his hand. Paul could almost hear the bones clattering in those long, pale fingers. Olivia glowered at him, and Paul nearly said something inappropriate, like, "I thought you were dead." But he didn't, and despite the chill he felt, he started climbing the slick slope, up a series of narrow steps cut into the living rock. Near the top he looked back once more, and beyond the crowd of homeless men he saw the two smokers radiating trembling waves of heat and breathing black smoke like a pair of idling locomotives, the door of each firebox outlined by a seam of red flame. To the right he saw the cubescape under the fluorescent lights, which were suspended by a tangled web of wires from the ceiling of the cave. Under the lights Paul saw one pale man walking through the labyrinth of cubicles, and while he couldn't be sure from this distance, Paul thought it was Boy G. Nearly lost in the glare, the figure came to a cube at the center of the labyrinth and stooped out of sight.

At the top of the slope Stanley Tulendij hooked his fingers through Paul's elbow and settled the younger man on the ledge between himself and Olivia Haddock. Olivia gave him a cold, sidelong glance, looking him up and down.

"You're alright then?" Paul murmured.

"No thanks to you," said Olivia.

"I tried," protested Paul, struggling to keep his voice down. "Didn't you feel me grab your ankles?"

Olivia shushed him with a red satin finger to her lips. Stanley Tulendij was stepping to the front of the ledge. He threw his arms wide. "What is the law?" he cried, his hollow voice reverberating the length and breadth of the cavern.

Next to Paul, Olivia clasped her hands before her and blew out a sigh, but below them, the crowd of homeless men swelled forward to the edge of the water, Colonel and Bob Wier at the front. The mouths of the pale men opened wide like hymn singers, their pointed teeth gleaming.

"When the going gets tough," they chanted, "the tough get going. *That* is the law. Are we not men?"

"A quitter never wins, and a winner never quits. *That* is the law. Are we not men?"

"Winning isn't everything, it's the only thing. *That* is the law. Are we not men?"

"Don't mess with Texas. *That* is the law. Are we not men?"

The men below swayed from side to side, clapping once when they came to "*That* is the law," and the resounding slap of their hands rang around the cavern like feedback. Colonel and Bob Wier swayed right along with the others, though Bob Wier was now openly crying. Beyond the fringes of the crowd, J. J. swayed and dipped his shoulders in place, while to Paul's right, Stanley Tulendij waved his bony hands in the air like a conductor. To Paul's left, Olivia blew out another sigh and rolled her eyes. Paul wasn't sure what to do, so he just swayed feebly, pretending to clap, but not bringing his palms together.

"It ain't over till it's over," chanted the men. "*That* is the law. Are we not men?"

"Never let the bastards grind you down. *That* is the law. Are we not men?"

"Remember the Alamo! *That* is the law. Are we not men?"

"Let a smile be your umbrella. *That* is the law. Are we not men?"

"And this above all!" cried Stanley Tulendij, lifting his arms higher. Under the momentum of their chant, the men continued to sway for a moment longer, but then steadied themselves at the cry of Stanley Tulendij. As the reverberation of their clapping and chanting died away in the recesses of the cavern, Paul saw Boy G returning from the cubicles bearing a large, blue sack over his shoulder.

"In the daylight world," Stanley Tulendij called out, his voice ringing round the rocks of the cave, "the rule is, 'To thine own self be true.' But here," he cried, the men below moaning in expectation, "the rule is, 'To thine own self be . . .' "

There was a long, breathless pause, during which Paul heard only the *plink! ploink!* of dripping water. Boy G advanced on the crowd with a noiseless tread, bearing his burden closer. Olivia Haddock rolled her tongue around in her cheek.

"Enough!" roared the crowd of pale men. "To thine own self, be *enough! That* is the law. Are we not men?"

Stanley Tulendij threw his arms in the air, and the men cheered and whistled. They stamped their feet and shook their fists in the air.

"Finally," breathed Olivia Haddock, restlessly tapping her foot.

As Boy G reached the back of the crowd with his burden, they parted to let him through. The closer ones reached out to stroke or caress the bundle over his shoulder as he passed. The ones at the rear of the crowd lifted themselves on tiptoe and ran their tongues over their jagged teeth. Only now, as Boy G came closer, did Paul realize that his burden wasn't a sack, but the backside of someone's pair of jeans. Boy G was carrying a person, doubled over at the waist, with her head and shoulders dangling behind him and Boy G clutching her legs in front. Stanley Tulendij caught Paul's eye and winked.

"Enough, my boy! It's a word of shattering power!" He clapped Paul on the shoulder. "Make it your battle cry!" He glanced past Paul, his eyes brightening at Olivia. "Isn't that right, my lovely queen?"

"Whatever," said Olivia.

Now Boy G was stepping across the pool on the flattened stalagmites, his tread making a moiré of intersecting waves on the surface of the water. He bent slightly under the weight of the woman as he started up the steps carved into the rock. Suddenly Paul realized that he knew that backside, and all the breath was sucked out of him. At the same moment he heard the brisk, rhythmic scrape of metal against metal, and he looked over the heads of the crowd to see J. J. stroking a long-bladed knife against a sharpening steel. The murmur of the men below grew louder, saying a single word, and it wasn't until Boy G had reached the ledge at the base of the column that Paul realized what they were saying.

"Meat!" they murmured. "Meat! Meat! Meat!"

Boy G stooped to one knee and tipped the woman off his shoulder onto the rock, where she stood unsteadily for a moment before sagging to her knees, her hands bound before her and her chin drooping to her breastbone. Her mouth was gagged by a handkerchief tied behind her head. Boy G backed away from her, swiveling his wide, cannibal smile past Stanley Tulendij and Paul and Olivia, and then he turned to descend the rock. Olivia glanced sidelong at the bound woman, then at Paul. Her lips were pursed, and Paul realized that she was trying hard not to smile.

"Think you're better than us," Olivia said, sotto voce. "We'll just see about that."

"Behold!" cried Stanley Tulendij, startling Paul, who turned to see the old man grasp the top of the kneeling woman's head and tilt her face up for all to see. "See what Paul has brought us!"

At the base of the formation, the men were chanting louder, "Meat! Meat! Meat!" Colonel was chanting along with them, his eyes shining with an unholy light. Next to him Bob Wier didn't chant but only stared into the clear cave water at his feet, lifting his hand to wipe the tears from his eyes with thumb and forefinger. Across the cave J. J. stropped his knife with a brisk, professional rhythm, faster even than the beating of Paul's heart. Only when he had no place else to look did Paul lower his eyes to the face of the woman at his feet. Her eyes were wide and frantic, her skin very pale. Her freckles were like flecks of ash across her cheeks; the gag cut into the corners of her mouth. Paul's heart stuttered and he nearly fell to his knees himself, for he was looking at the face of his Oklahoma lover, Callie.

THIRTY-NINE

"OKAY, I'VE HAD ENOUGH," said Paul in a loud voice, to no one in particular. "I want to wake up now." This only provoked a grumble of laughter from the crowd of men below and even a hollow chuckle from Stanley Tulendij. Olivia issued an exasperated gasp. "Very droll, Professor," called out Colonel from the edge of the pool. "No, seriously," said Paul. Callie looked up at him beseechingly, and Paul looked away, unable to bear it. "This isn't funny anymore. I'm not enjoying this."

Stanley Tulendij, his lipless mouth fixed in a cadaverous grin, bent close to Paul. "She won't feel a thing," he said with an avuncular wink. "Not for long, anyway."

The murmuring from below—"Meat! Meat! Meat!"—grew even louder, and Paul looked down to see the crowd parting for J.J., who approached the pool ceremoniously bearing the big knife across his upturned palms. At the edge of the pool, he handed it off to Bob Wier, who grimaced and handled the blade as if it were red hot, immediately passing it off to Colonel, who took it solemnly. He held the handle with one hand and laid the gleaming blade lightly across his other palm. He stepped across the trembling pool on the stepping stones and started up the slope, his shining eyes fixed on Paul.

"Wait a minute." Paul backed up against the base of the big, sagging pillar behind him. "Let's just stop for a second." Callie was trembling. The soles of her sandals were bent back as she knelt on the sweating stone. She wore the same clothes she'd had on when she'd left his apartment—jeans, a man's old Oxford shirt—and she'd left his apartment, Paul thought, before he had started dreaming. Maybe, he thought frantically, her presence in his apartment had been part of the dream as well, and he began desperately to wonder just how far back it went. Had his affair with Callie been a dream all along? Had his wooing by Colonel and his cronies been a dream? Maybe all of it had been a dream, he thought, feeling the sweat pouring down his temples: his job at TxDoGS, his life with Kymberly in the suburban ranch house, maybe even his whole experience in Texas. None of this ever happened, he thought. *I never lost my teaching job, I never got divorced. I never drowned a cat in a bathtub. This is a fantasy, a cautionary tale, and I'm fast asleep in Iowa, with Lizzie snoring beside me and Charlotte, dear, sweet Charlotte, purring happily at my feet.* He glanced all around him for some definitive sign of unreality, but all he saw were the wide eyes of the pale men watching him from below and the dripping stalactites above, pointing at him like spears.

By now Colonel had reached the ledge, and he knelt on the top step and fixed Paul with his gaze and lifted the knife towards him.

"What about her?" cried Paul, pointing at Olivia. "I mean, I gave you her already, right?"

The crowd of murmuring men gasped as one, and Olivia dropped her jaw and goggled at Paul. Colonel sighed and looked exasperated, but before he could speak, Olivia had placed her clenched fists on her hips.

"Outrageous!" she cried. "*Outrageous!*" She swung her ferocious gaze from Paul to Stanley Tulendij, who grinned weakly.

"Now, dearest," he said, waving his wobbly palms at her.

"Stanley," said Olivia, her lower lip trembling, "are you going to let this, this *person* speak about me in that manner?"

"Now, sweetness," said Stanley Tulendij, and he crossed in front of Paul to comfort Olivia. His arms curled around her; his pale fingers twitched on her bare shoulders. Olivia pressed herself against the wide, blue lapels of his garish tux. "Outrageous," she sniffled.

Below, the pale men shuffled in place and mumbled to themselves. At the front of the crowd J. J. bobbed anxiously from foot to foot, while Bob Wier clutched his own elbows, looking nearly as pale as the cave dwellers pressed around him. Colonel hissed at Paul to get his attention, and Paul came warily forward, crouching next to Callie, whose eyes darted frantically in every direction.

"Suck it up, Professor," Colonel whispered. The knife quivered in his hands, casting its gleam across Paul and Callie's faces. "We've all done this. J. J. gave them his girlfriend, and believe me, J. J. doesn't come across a girlfriend very often. Hell, Bob here gave up his *wife.*"

Callie groaned. At the foot of the slope, Bob Wier looked up as if he'd heard his name. His eyes widened, and his face paled even more. Suddenly he turned away from the pool. J. J. grabbed at him, but Bob twisted free and pushed back through the crowd towards the rear. J. J. shrugged and faced front again.

"But *you* didn't," whispered Paul, "give up your wife."

Colonel's bright eyes narrowed. "You ain't the only one, Professor, who's ever had a wild little mustang. Yasumi never knew about her." He lifted the corner of his lips in a lubricious grin. "You know how it is."

Callie was watching Paul now, sidelong.

"About cheating on my wife?" said Paul, struggling to control his voice. "Or human sacrifice?"

Colonel shrugged and said, "Call it whatever you want, Paul. We all do it." He grinned again. "Are we not men?"

"Alright, that's it!" barked Olivia, and everyone turned to see her push out of Stanley Tulendij's embrace. She loomed over Paul with one fist balled against her hip, while Stanley Tulendij dithered behind her.

"Are you going to let this *slacker*, this *Yankee* get away with this?" she declared, sweeping the crowd below with her furious gaze. "Because correct me if I'm wrong, but these other three losers have already done it." She gestured with her free hand, her red glove taking in Colonel and J. J. Bob Wier was across the room, doggedly stuffing more wood into the firebox of one of the smokers.

"So what makes Paul so special? Is it because he has a *pee aitch dee?*" She waved her long, red, satin finger in the air, sistah style. "Puh-*leeze*. He's here, he's accepted the benefits y'all have offered him, and now it's time for him to *do his duty.*"

The crowd below was rapt. Their mouths hung open, their teeth glistened, their eyes shone with something like adoration. Even J. J.'s eyes were twinkling. Olivia drew a breath, then she stooped and hooked the satiny fingers of one hand through the collar of Callie's shirt, and the fingers of her other hand through Paul's collar, and hauled them both to their feet. Colonel stood, too, under his own steam. Paul felt something smooth and cool and hard against his right palm, and Colonel closed Paul's fingers around the handle of the knife. Olivia lifted Paul's left hand around Callie's shoulders and placed his palm under her chin. Callie flinched at the touch. She had squeezed her eyes shut, and Paul could feel her shuddering.

Olivia stepped back and put her hands on her hips. "So get with the program, mister," she declared, "and cut her throat."

Paul's hand trembled under Callie's chin, so he dropped it to her shoulder. She flinched again; her breath hissed in hot bursts through her nose.

"It's okay," Paul whispered. "This isn't really happening. This is a dream. You're not even here."

"Mmm mmm mmm!" Callie said through the gag.

"I'm *waiting*," said Olivia.

"Now, Paul," said Colonel, holding up his palms and rocking on the balls of his feet, "each of these gentlemen behind me is crazier than a jaybird and hungrier than a coyote. They're fixed to eat something tonight, and if it's not her, well, then, we go to Plan B." He glanced back at the crowd. They were pressing forward, licking their lips, gnashing their teeth, drooling. "Let's just say," Colonel said in a low voice, "we're having you for dinner, Professor, one way or the other."

Paul could scarcely see six inches beyond his nose; everything else was washed out of all recognition. His mind raced as if he were a dying man reliving his life in an instant. Behind his eyeballs he saw an almost comically speeded-up highlight reel of every bad decision he'd ever made, in glorious, unfaded, mid-fifties Technicolor: himself at his computer, not finishing his book; himself and Kymberly, cheating on Lizzie in his marriage bed; himself cheating on Kymberly with Oksana, et al.; himself lowering the howling Charlotte in her cat carrier into the bathtub and turning the taps on full blast; himself sprawled uselessly on the bed, listening to Callie drive away. . . .

His heart twisted with regret, and his vision was further blurred with tears. The humid, smoky air around him seemed to cool for a moment, as if he stood in the doorway of a freezer, and for one, delirious instant he swore he felt the smooth, sidelong brush of a cat winding a figure eight between his legs. Then the silky pressure faded and the cave's dankness once again clung to his skin. His vision cleared as if someone had wiped his eyes, and one thought somehow rang as clear as a chime at the center of his head: If this is a dream, if none of this really matters, then why not be a hero?

"I won't do it," he breathed, and he tightened his arm around Callie's shoulders, pulling her closer. She tensed under his grip, but he held on tightly. Colonel edged towards him, reaching for the knife. Olivia vibrated with fury a few feet away, while Stanley Tulendij, his eyes alight, twitched behind her. The crowd below strained forward, nearly pushing J. J. into the water. Across the cave Paul saw Bob Wier pushing one more log into the blazing firebox with the iron poker. The smoker was overheating; smoke gushed from the chimney and puffed from the seams of the doors.

"No," Paul said louder, "I won't do it." The knife trembled so violently in his hand that Paul was afraid he was going to drop it, but he waved it unsteadily at the Colonel.

"Mm mm!" said Callie through the gag. *"Mm mm!"*

"Oh, for God's sake, we'll be here all night," said Olivia. "I'll do it."

Paul turned to fend her off, but Colonel grabbed his wrist in a crushing grip. Callie struggled in Paul's grasp; Paul tottered at the edge of the stony ledge; Colonel squeezed his wrist ferociously, and the knife loosened in Paul's grip.

"Ahhhhhhhhhhhhhh!" bellowed Bob Wier from across the cave. Reflexively everyone turned to see him heaving on the wooden handle at one end of the smoker. He had kicked the chocks away from the front wheels, and slowly the smoker started to roll forward down the incline. Grimacing and white-faced, Bob dug in with his loafers and pushed the handle from behind, and the smoker picked up speed across the cave, its wheels squealing, its metal panels rattling. Bob had opened the door of the firebox at the front end, and as the smoker rolled faster, flames streamed backwards out of the box, scorching the sides of the drum and sending hot sparks and glowing embers bounding along the cave floor. "'I will pour out my wrath upon you,'" cried Bob Wier, banging the long iron poker on the drum of the smoker, " 'and breathe out my fiery anger against you!' "

"What the hell?" said Colonel, loosening his grip on Paul's wrist for an instant. Paul tightened his grasp on the knife and, still clutching Callie, yanked his hand free, slashing Colonel deep across his forearm.

"Son of a bitch!" cried Colonel, jerking his arm into the air. He nearly toppled backwards down the slope. The gash in his sleeve flapped, blood soaking into the fabric.

"Ezekiel!" panted Bob Wier, "twenty-one . . . thirty-one," and with a final, mighty effort, he heaved the smoker, jouncing and rattling and flaming, into the crowd. It rocketed down the incline towards the pool like a runaway little locomotive, the blunt snout of its firebox breathing flame and streaming black smoke. The pale, homeless men tumbled away from the blazing firebox in every direction, squealing as the sparks shot among them. Bob Wier charged right behind the smoker, swinging the poker with both hands like a club, sending some pale men flying while others scrabbled away spiderwise on their hands and knees. J. J. scrambled backwards on his ass, like a crab.

"Run, Paul!" cried Bob Wier breathlessly over the tremendous clatter of the runaway smoker. "Take her and run!"

The smoker thundered to the edge of the pool and tumbled in, roaring firebox first. A great wave of cave water heaved over the lip of the pool and washed squealing pale men across the floor, and an immense eruption of steam boiled out of the water, a roiling, hissing cloud that shot to the ceiling and gusted to either side, obscuring the flailing Bob Wier and the sliding homeless men. The wave of cave water sloshed high up the slope out of the cloud, and Colonel, still cursing, pedaled wildly on the slick rock, then toppled backwards, sliding on his back through the water into the steam. Callie broke away from Paul, only to be confronted by a wild-eyed Stanley Tulendij, who hunkered down on his long legs and spread his hands wide like a knife fighter. Callie hollered something through her gag and planted her foot in the old man's groin, and he gasped long and loud and crumpled in his tux like a bag of bones. Steely-eyed Olivia tried to do the same to Paul, but he staggered backwards, waving the knife, and Olivia lost her balance in her long skirt, landing hard on her hip and sliding down the slick rock into the water, vanishing into the steam.

"Callie," gasped Paul. Gusts of hot steam wafted past him, and he lost her. But before he could call out again, she shouldered past him like a running back, leaping in long strides down the slope towards the cubescape, losing her footing at last and sliding on her backside into the water.

"I'm coming!" cried Paul, and he dropped to his ass with spine-crushing force and tobogganed after her down the rock. Because of its clarity, the water had looked only a few inches deep, but it turned out to be waist high and, despite the steam, piercingly cold. The shock of it made Paul gasp, and he stumbled, dunking himself, and came up sputtering and waving the knife.

"I'm coming!" he gasped again, but Callie was charging through water up to her waist, swinging her shoulders. She reached the edge and without looking back gripped a stalagmite with her bound hands and hoisted herself, streaming with water, out of the pool. Paul struggled after her through the freezing water, and he glanced back and saw that the steam was slowly dissipating. The spot where the smoker had gone into the pool was still bubbling like a hot spring, and one end of the drum was heeling over like a sinking oil tanker. Somewhere in the mist both Olivia and Colonel were shouting, and through the fading cloud of steam Paul saw the dim silhouette of Bob Wier still laying about him like Beowulf with the poker. "Praise . . . Jesus . . .. ," he gasped, connecting with a solid thud, but he was slowly being pulled down by the swarming heap of pale men.

At the edge of the pool Paul hauled himself out, his clothes clinging and heavy with water. Kneeling on the cold, gritty stone, panting for breath, he saw a few of the nearer figures in the cloud of steam glancing back at him, and he heaved himself to his feet and started after Callie, towards the cubes. He'd lost his sandals in the water, and his feet slapped painfully against the hard surface of the floor, leaving muddy prints in the grit. He still had the knife, though, and he held it before him as he entered the main aisle of the cubicles, the threadbare carpet feeling grainy and rough under his feet. At the junction of the two main aisles, he found Callie crouched with her back to the cube wall, out of sight of the far end of the cave. She had lifted her bound hands to her face and was trying to pry off the gag with her thumbs. Her shirt was plastered to her skin, and she was trembling.

"Wait," said Paul, and he crouched before her and tried to take her wrist. She jerked her hands away at first, her eyes angry and wild, but Paul showed her the trembling knife, and she nodded curtly, offering her bound wrists. Paul steadied the knife with both hands and sawed through the cords, and Callie flung the scraps away and reached behind her head and tore off the gag. Rubbing her wrists, she opened her mouth wide and drew a long, wheezing breath.

"Callie," Paul said, glancing round the corner down the aisle into the far end of the cave. The steam had mushroomed to a haze up under the roof, and Paul saw a wriggling heap of men. Bob Wier was nowhere to be seen. Some of the men in the heap were raising their fists and hammering something out of sight, but others were reaching into the heap and coming out again with ragged scraps of something in their fists. One pale face lifted above the scrum, its teeth smeared with blood. Paul looked away.

"We have to . . . ," he began, but Callie braced her back against the cube wall and kicked him in the chest. She had lost her sandals, too, but the solid blow of her bare heel knocked Paul on his ass and sent the knife skittering across the carpet.

"Motherfucker!" she said, careful to keep her voice low. "What have you done?"

"Callie!" Paul gasped. "It's okay! This is a dream. This isn't happening."

"Then *wake up!*" she snapped, crouching forward, getting her feet under her. "It may not be happening to you, but it's sure as hell happening to me!" She glanced around the corner, and Paul followed her gaze. The heap of wriggling men had collapsed in on itself. J. J. was off to one side, stomping angrily in a circle. Colonel was standing, but bent nearly double, gasping and clutching his arm. Olivia Haddock had pulled her gown up to her knees and stripped off her gloves and her homecoming sash, and she was crawling up the slope towards Stanley Tulendij, who lay in the fetal position at the base of the big phallic rock.

"Listen," said Paul, but Callie whirled on him and said, "The only thing I want to hear from you is how I get out of here."

Paul met her eyes and nearly burst into hysterical laughter. But he mastered himself and glanced up the aisle, towards the passage where he and Bob Wier and the procession of pale men had entered. Callie started convulsively in that direction, but Paul grabbed her arm. "Not that way," Paul hissed. "It's too far, and we'll get lost." He glanced up the other aisle, towards the ravenous heap of pale men ripping Bob Wier to shreds. "They'll know a way to get ahead of us."

The light in Callie's eyes nearly flared into panic, but then she looked past him and her eyes focused on the pole ladder at the junction of the aisles. She pulled free of Paul and dashed, crouching, to the ladder. She lifted her head warily over the cube horizon and then started to climb, lifting her knees and placing her feet without looking, her gaze fixed on the pole above her.

"I don't know where this goes," Paul hissed, but he had already scrambled after her to the foot of the ladder. Above him Callie's backside disappeared into the glare of the lights. "Oh boy," breathed Paul, and he grasped one rung and stepped up onto another and started to climb.

Before he knew it, Paul had risen past the fluorescent fixtures, up into the coils and loops of black wiring. Above him he saw Callie climbing as energetically as a monkey, while below he saw the dusty metal cowls of the lights and, below that, the cubescape laid out like a map, each cubicle fitted with a battered little computer, each desktop covered with neat stacks of paperwork and littered with pens and highlighters and coffee cups. Paul struggled upward, his arms and legs beginning to tremble, and he glanced down the length of the cave and saw the pale men still swarming over the livid scraps of Bob on the floor. Colonel was sitting at one of the folding tables while J. J. bound his arm with a dishtowel; Olivia had propped Stanley Tulendij up into a sitting position and was stroking his large, white forehead with one of her limp, sodden gloves. The pool was still sloshing from side to side; tendrils of steam still wafted from the surface of the water; and in the rippling refractions Paul saw the wreck of the smoker with its legs up like a drowned black dragon.

He looked away, suddenly afraid that his mere gaze would draw other gazes in return. Above him the pole ladder rose into a perfectly round hole drilled into the ceiling, wide enough for a person, the edge of the hole rimmed already with the stumpy beginnings of dripping stalactites. Callie was already ascending into the hole, and Paul's heart lifted. We're almost there, he thought, a few more seconds and we're out of sight. He pulled harder; above him only the dirty soles of Callie's feet were visible in the hole.

"Callie!" Paul whispered eagerly. "Wait for me!"

Some trick of the cave, some subterranean acoustical freak, caught his whisper and magnified it, and it echoed round the walls of the cavern like a pinball, bounding off the ceiling, ricocheting off the stalactites, reverberating against the walls. All the faces of the homeless men turned as one, like sea anemones, away from the shredded form that had held their attention, and looked up towards the source of the echo. Colonel and J. J. glanced up angrily through the glare of the fluorescent lights. At the base of the pillar, Olivia Haddock leaped to her feet, letting Stanley Tulendij fall over like a sack of meal.

"There they go!" she shrieked. "Bite them! Kill them! Off with their heads!"

With an awful, yearning groan, the pale men leaped up and swarmed down the cave towards the cubicles and the ladder. Colonel jumped up, shoved J. J. aside, and started after them. Paul looked away and climbed frantically towards the hole. Suddenly, Callie's face loomed out of the darkness. She reached down and grabbed Paul's arm and hauled him up into the gloom.

"Nice work, jackass," she said. "Come on."

FORTY

PAUL TRIED NOT TO LOOK BACK, and soon they were
climbing in near darkness. He glanced down once and saw the
distant, dwindling circle of light obscured by wriggling shapes
and pale faces looking up at him, so he lifted his gaze to the
blackness above and hauled harder. Above him he heard Callie
grunting with exertion, and the slap of her feet on the rungs,
and the slight *ping* each rung made when she let go of it. Paul
felt warm droplets against his face, and he wasn't sure if they
were the condensation of the tunnel or drops of Callie's sweat.

"You still there?" she asked once, panting, and Paul could
only grunt in return. He had no way of telling how much time
had passed or how far they'd climbed; for all he knew they could
have been climbing for hours or for five minutes. His cerebellum told him, we can't be that deep, but his lizard brain told
him he would be climbing in the dark for the rest of his life.
The thought that the ladder might not go anywhere was too
much to bear, so he concentrated on his hands and feet.

"I feel a breeze," said Callie, and a moment later, his arms and legs shaking with exhaustion, Paul felt it too, first from one direction, then from the other. They were passing side passages in the tunnel, but they both kept climbing. Under his palms and the soles of his feet, Paul thought the ladder vibrated to a more complicated rhythm than that of his and Callie's ascent, and he thought, too, that he heard sounds from below—the faint ringing of the ladder's rungs and a steady, bubbling murmur. He didn't stop to listen.

A moment later the tunnel ended, but the ladder continued. They still climbed in pitch darkness, but the sweating rock walls fell away, and they found themselves climbing through a narrow space that extended into the distance on either side. The reverberation of their efforts—their harsh breathing, the ring of the ladder—made a duller and flatter sound. The air was drier and dustier. Paul felt cobwebs brush his face, and his back scraped against a metal beam and a bristling wad of insulation.

"We're in a building," panted Callie. "I think we're in the wall."

The soft clang of her feet on the rungs stopped, and Paul stopped when he touched her foot with his trembling, sweaty hand. She caught her breath in the darkness above him. "That better be you," she said.

"Why are you stopping?" He tightened his hand on her foot.

"We're at the top." She fumbled at something in the dark. "There's a latch, I think."

Paul looked down; the light at the bottom of the tunnel was a twinkling pinprick now, and the ringing and murmuring he wasn't certain he'd heard before was perfectly clear now. "For chrissake, just yank it," he said.

She grunted above him; something rattled violently. "Got it!" she cried, and at the same instant an avalanche of crushed and empty soda cans cascaded down the ladder, rattling off Paul's head and fingers, and clanging against the ladder. Sticky little droplets of warm soda pattered against his forehead. Paul hunched his shoulders and ducked his head until the cans clattered down the ladder, then he looked up into a dim light to see Callie hoisting herself through a little square hole. He glanced down one last time to see the fading flash of crumpled aluminum as the cans tumbled into darkness, then he raced up the last few rungs. There was a hollow thud as Callie knocked away the cardboard box over the trapdoor, and Paul put his palms on the cold tile on either side of the trapdoor and levered himself out. Callie reached into the hole and tried to pull the door shut, but there was no handle on the upward side.

Paul sat panting on the floor. They were in the second-floor elevator lobby of TxDoGS. The only light came from a street-lamp in the empty parking lot, through the tall windows of the stairwell. "Oh, God," Paul said. "We're at work."

Callie jumped to her feet. Her clothes were still wet, her shirt still plastered to her skin. Sweat and condensation from the tunnel dripped off her face, and her palms and feet were coated with grime. She lunged suddenly, startling Paul, crossing the lobby to an office chair tilted to one side against the window. One of its wheels was broken, and someone had left it with a note taped to the back that read TRASH. Callie swung it into the air by its arms and jammed its broken undercarriage into the open trapdoor. It was too big to go down, but Callie stamped on the seat with her bare foot until the chair was tightly wedged in the hole.

Paul pushed himself to his feet against the wall, trying to catch his breath. "Callie, let's just get out of here," he said, but she continued to stomp on the chair, gritting her teeth and grunting with each blow. Finally he caught her by the arm and dragged her around the corner into the hall.

"Paul!" someone called from the far end, and Paul and Callie stopped short and clutched each other. The hall was full of shadow, and a tall silhouette was running heavily to-wards them in the dim light from the main lobby. Paul and Callie yelped simultaneously and ran back the other way. They hit the crash bar of the door to the outside landing, but it wouldn't open, and Callie, howling wordlessly, began to pound on the glass with her fists. Up the hallway behind them the footfalls came closer, so Paul grabbed Callie by the wrist and pulled her away from the door and through the doorway into cubeland. He whirled her in front of him, then reached back and tugged at the door, which was usually propped open against the wall. It wouldn't budge, so Paul kicked at the little hinged doorstop, painfully stubbing his bare toes, until it popped up and he was able to slam the door shut. He fumbled over the surface of the door until he found the deadbolt and locked it. Instantly a huge silhouette filled the narrow window down the center of the door, and the door shook violently under a series of blows.

"Paul!" cried a muffled voice, and Paul blundered backwards into Callie.

"C'mon." She pointed across the dim cubescape. "We can use the exit by Rick's office."

Paul let himself be dragged for a few steps, but then he dug his heels into the carpet. "Wait wait wait," he said, in an urgent whisper. "Listen."

The hammering on the door had stopped; the figure in the window had gone away.

"Paul, goddammit, let's *go*," Callie said, but Paul clutched her tightly and said, "Shh!"

It was sometime in the middle of Friday night, possibly even early Saturday morning, and the office was lit only by two or three widely spaced fluorescent fixtures. A little more light leaked through the outside windows from the building's bright security lights, but for the most part the empty cubescape before them was in twilight, obscured as if by a mist. All around them, filling the midnight silence of the cubicles, Paul and Callie heard a steady creaking and the muffled murmur of voices. Both of them lifted their eyes to the suspended ceiling. The panels seemed to be bulging and shifting the entire length and breadth of the room.

"They're up there," breathed Paul. "They're in the ceiling."

Simultaneously they broke into a run, down the aisle past Paul's cube, then right into the main aisle toward the copy machine, booking as hard as they could go for the exit at the other end. Callie ran in long strides, knees up, fists clenched, pumping her arms like a sprinter. Paul hammered after her, each impact

of his bare heels jarring him all the way up his spine. Callie
disappeared round the next turn, and Paul raced around the
corner and blundered straight into her, nearly bringing them
both to the floor. Callie had braced her heels, her hands pressed
against the cube walls on either side of the aisle. Ahead of them,
just outside the door of Rick's office, the lower half of a pale
man swung from a square gap where a ceiling panel had been
shifted aside. His legs wriggled and he slipped lower, dangling
by his fingertips, the ceiling creaking painfully above him. Then
he dropped silently to the floor, crouching nearly on all fours,
his fingertips brushing the carpet. It was Boy G. He lifted his
pale moon face to Paul and Callie; his eyes gleamed through
the lenses of his glasses. He smiled, baring his serrated teeth.

"Are we not men?" he whispered.

Behind him, over Nolene's low-sided cube, another ceiling
panel was already opening up, and Paul clutched Callie around
her waist and heaved her up the aisle back the way they had
come. They stopped again when they saw the blur of another
pale man dropping out of the ceiling near the door where they
had come in. Closer still they saw yet another pale man ooze
head first out of a black hole in the ceiling; he curled around
the lip of the hole like a fat spider until he dangled by his
fingertips and dropped out of sight. Along the far side of the
room Paul saw a pair of round, buzz-cut heads bobbing rapidly
along the cube horizon, scurrying up the aisle.

"In here," whispered Callie, and she dragged Paul into the
large cubicle called "the library," because of the tall metal bookcase full of TxDoGS regulations in ring binders just inside the
door. It was where Paul had first gotten a good look at Callie,
as she slouched against the wide worktable and sorted the mail
amid the litter of pens, pencils, staple removers, and scissors.
Just inside the door Callie started to heave on the metal bookcase, and Paul helped her pull it over onto its side across the
doorway with an almighty clang. Ring binders cascaded to the
floor about their feet and flopped open. Callie crouched and
started snatching items off the work surface, but Paul stayed on
his feet, glancing wildly about them. All around the room now

panels were opening up in the ceiling—some pulled back, some twisted askew, some tumbling out of the hole into the cube beneath—an irregular checkerboard of black squares out of which descended feet, hands, moon faces. Murmuring filled the room like surf as pale men in white shirts and ties dropped onto desktops, chairs, and the tops of filing cabinets, punctuating the darkness with soft thumps and bangs. As the men sank below the cube horizon, Paul could feel each thump in the floor through the bare soles of his feet. He heard desk drawers opening and closing, and scampering in the aisles. The murmuring began to swell up the aisles and over the edges of the cubicle where he was trapped with Callie, a clackety-clack rhythm like a train, over and over again in an awful, whispering chant, "Are we not men? Are we not men? Are we not men?"

A sharp, electric whine startled him, and he looked down to see Callie crouched just under the edge of the work surface, an array of office supplies clustered around her on the carpet—a heap of pencils like pick up sticks, a steel letter opener, an enormous stapler. She was feeding one pencil after another into an electric pencil sharpener, but she did not take her eyes off the ceiling. Paul glanced up at it himself. The panels over the cube were rippling, and Paul heard creaking and the thrum of some metallic strut or support. At an especially loud creak, he ducked under the work surface, squeezing in next to Callie. The pencil sharpener ground away. Neither one of them looked at the other.

"You're a son of a bitch," muttered Callie.

"What?" said Paul.

"You heard me." She laid the sharpened pencils in a fan at her feet. "When Olivia bared my throat and Colonel handed you the knife," Callie hissed, still watching the ceiling, "what took you so long to do something?"

"Callie, I don't think this is the time." The creaking in the ceiling shifted, and Paul saw one panel bulge and then another.

Callie turned on him, her eyes blazing with rage and hurt. "You had to *think* about it!" she shouted—so loudly, in fact, that all the other sounds around them—the patter of feet, the murmuring chant, even the creaking of the ceiling above—went completely silent. She wouldn't take her eyes off him, and in the electric stillness, Paul touched her with a trembling hand.

"Aw, honey," he said, "I'm an intellectual. I have to think about everything."

The ceiling above the cube gave way, several panels all at once, and in a cascade of dust and shards of tile, J. J. fell cursing into the cube, landing hard on the little heap of tumbled ring binders.

"Fuuuuck!" he shouted, throwing his arms over his face as fragments of ceiling panel pelted him. Coated in white dust and still wearing his barbecue apron, he tried to stand, but his feet kept slipping on the loose binders. Paul jumped up from under the work surface and cast about for something to defend himself with. He snatched up a big three-hole punch with a weighted base, and cocked it over his shoulder like a club.

"You faggot," panted J. J., trying to haul himself up by the toppled bookcase. "I knew you'd be trouble the moment I saw you."

"Stay back!" cried Paul, his voice shooting up an octave. The three-hole punch rattled in his grip.

"You're a fuckin' dead man," laughed J. J., finally pushing himself erect.

"He's not the only one," said Callie, and she launched herself from under the desk and past Paul, a sharpened pencil protruding between the fingers of each fist, an eraser braced against each palm. She swung both fists at the same time, one high and one low, then danced back, slipping on a ring binder and landing on her ass. J. J. wobbled on his feet, one pencil stuck in his right cheek, the other in his waist, just above the apron. He looked down at his punctured gut, then gingerly felt the pencil in his face. His eyes were wide, and his mouth worked soundlessly for a moment. "Aw, *heck*," he said.

"Dear God!" gasped Paul, turning to gape at Callie, and at that moment the bookcase toppled over with a loud clang on top of J. J., crushing him against the scattered binders. The two pale men who had pushed it over leaped onto the flattened bookcase as the metal boomed under them. At the same instant, two more pale men came shrieking through the air from opposite directions, soaring headfirst out of the darkness as if they'd been catapulted, their arms and legs wriggling. They tumbled into the cube; one landed on the worktable, the other crashed into the cube wall on the opposite side. The wall groaned under him and then rebounded, flinging him back into the cube on top of Callie.

Everything happened very quickly. The pale man on top of Callie leaped up immediately, shrieking and pawing at the letter opener jammed into his ear; he clawed his way up the cube wall and toppled over it into the next cubicle. Hissing and baring their teeth, the two pale men on the bookcase scuttled forward, one towards Callie, the other towards Paul. At the same moment Paul felt the blunt, cold fingers of the man on the desk behind him pawing at his head and shoulders. Callie came up from the floor with the massive stapler in her hands, and she expertly popped a lever at the hinge and cast aside the stapler's base, swinging the upper half one-handed at the pale man approaching her. Paul twisted away from the fumblings of the man behind him, squeezed his eyes shut, and swung the three-hole punch blindly in a two-handed grip at the man before him. The punch connected with a loud *thump!* and Paul felt the shock of the impact all the way up both arms.

"I got him!" he cried, opening his eyes to see the pale man topple over the bookcase. But just then the man behind him wrapped a spiral phone cord around Paul's neck and yanked it tight, pulling Paul right off his feet. Paul dropped the punch and scrabbled at the cord with his fingers, trying to pry it away from his windpipe.

"Callie!" he gasped, and even as his eyes bulged from his head, he saw Callie strike again and again at her adversary with the stapler, shouting with each swing. The pale man dodged, baring his jagged teeth and swinging at her with his open hands. Paul's toes barely brushed the carpet as the cord cut deeper into his throat. Black spots spun before his eyes. Blood pounded in his ears.

Then, just as he was about to lose consciousness, he heard—
one, two, three times—the very satisfying *ka-chunk* of the stapler, and the accompanying squeal of the pale man, and the
thump of his body hitting the floor. Down the darkening cone
of his vision, Paul saw Callie reach towards him, snatch something off the desktop, and then brandish a pair of scissors. She
snipped the phone cord around his neck, and it whipped away.
She jammed the scissors upward, and as Paul landed gasping on
the floor, he heard the squeal and crash of the pale man on the
desktop.

"C'mon!" cried Callie, and she dragged the gagging Paul to
his feet. She pressed the bloodied scissors into his hand and
snatched up the stapler again for herself, and she tugged him
by his shirt over the rattling bookcase and into the aisle. In the
intersection of the aisles they glanced either way to see little
knots of crouching pale men, clustered together, swinging their
arms and chanting. Flecks of spittle flew from their gaping
mouths. Callie started up the aisle towards Rick's office, and
Paul walked backwards behind her, waving the scissors in his
trembling hand as the two knots of pale men came together in
the intersection and crept after them. In the open space by the
fax machine, Callie stopped and Paul backed into her. The men
behind them paused just out of reach. Paul glanced over his
shoulder to see another knot of men between them and the exit,
crouching low, their teeth gnashing, their fingers brushing the
carpet, murmuring, *"Are we not men? Are we not men? Are we
not men?"*

"Paul! Callie!" someone shouted in a muffled voice, and
through the window of the door Paul saw the bushy eyebrows
and thick moustache of Preston. He pounded on the door and
gestured over his head, pointing to his right. "Rick's office!" he
shouted. "Get inside Rick's office!"

The pounding stopped and Preston disappeared from the
window. The pale men on either side crept closer, swaying and
muttering, *"Are we not men? Are we not men?"* Boy G loomed
out of the middle of the group by the exit, spreading his arms

wide like a revivalist preacher. He spread his jaws wide and snarled like a beast.

"If we go into Rick's office," Callie said, her voice shaking, "we'll never get out again."

The two of them wheeled slowly, back to back, brandishing the stapler and the scissors. "Maybe we could smash the window," Paul said, but before Callie could answer, something crashed loudly into the fax machine and tumbled into the aisle. A computer monitor rocked onto its side at Paul's feet, its screen shattered. A moment later a metal filing cabinet drawer, full of files, crashed into the wall of Colonel's cube and rebounded into the aisle, making the clutch of pale men fall back. Paul and Callie looked up. The narrow, twilight space between the cube horizon and the ceiling was filled with flying objects, all headed in their direction: another drawer, an office chair with its wheels spinning, a keyboard trailing its creamy cord. A water cooler bottle tumbled end over end, spilling water in a wide arc. At the same time a hail of smaller objects began to pelt Paul and Callie: staplers, tape dispensers, a Rolodex, computer mice, cell phones. Callie crouched as low as she could; a coffee mug half full of cold coffee hit Paul between his shoulder blades.

"Goddammit!" shouted Callie, and she ran through the barrage of ring binders and pen cups and hard hats into Rick's office; Paul was a half step behind her. The pale men on either side rushed after them, and Paul slammed the door in their faces. But it didn't have a lock, so he dropped his scissors and planted his back against the door, digging his heels into the carpet. The bright security lights in the corners of the courtyard filled Rick's office with a harsh, bleaching light, throwing the stark shadows of the dying oak's branches across the walls and desk and carpet. Paul saw Preston in the courtyard below, prowling the deck on the balls of his feet, holding his semiautomatic pistol at his shoulder in a two-handed grip. When he saw Callie and Paul through the window, he waved them towards the courtyard and shouted something. Callie dropped her stapler, snatched up the chair next to the little table, and slung it as hard as she could against the window. But the window didn't break, it only thrummed, making the office hum with a deep bass note like the inside of a bell. At the same moment Paul felt a steady, almost irresistible pressure against the door at his back.

"Hurry!" he cried, and Callie shouted wordlessly and whanged the chair against the window again. Still nothing happened; the bass thrumming only deepened. Callie hadn't even chipped the glass. She roared in frustration, hurling the chair over her head at the glass. It bounded back at her, and she batted it aside, then she slid over Rick's desktop on her hip. She tried to lift his high-backed office chair, but it twisted from her grasp and crashed to the floor.

The soles of Paul's feet burned across the carpet. Over his shoulder he saw pale fingers curled around the edge of the door, and the chant came through, *"Are we not men? Are we not men?"*

"Callie!" cried Paul, and Callie cast about frantically and grabbed Rick's computer monitor with both hands, yanking it out to the limit of its connecting cords, then with a mighty effort wrenching it free, the cords flailing wildly like snakes. Paul whined with exertion and dug his toes into the carpet, and Callie hoisted the monitor over her head with both hands like a caveman flinging a boulder and heaved it at the doorway. But the shot went wild, and Paul ducked as the monitor crashed against the edge of the door and then landed with a crunch in the middle of the floor. He was propelled forward onto his knees, and the door slammed open against the wall.

"Are we not men?" chanted the mob of pale faces in the harsh light, but right in front, wedged together in the doorway, were Colonel and Olivia Haddock. Colonel's tie was loose, his shirt front streaked with grime and damp, his forearm wrapped in a towel that was soaked with blood. His eyes were wild and his chest heaved; one shoulder was crushed against the doorjamb, the other arm propped across the door, blocking Olivia. Her eyes were cold and furious; the tiara was gone and her hair awry. Her red velvet homecoming gown was ruined, soaked and

stained, clinging to her like wet terry cloth. She clawed at Colonel's arm, trying to get into the room, while behind them the faces of the pale men bobbed and swayed.

"You got one last chance, Professor," gasped Colonel. He stared at Paul almost as if he couldn't see him, and Paul scrambled to his feet, dancing around the shattered monitor in the center of the office. Callie snatched Rick's desk lamp off the desk, yanked its plug out of the power strip, and began to hammer at the glass behind the desk with the weighted base of the lamp, grunting with each blow. Paul glanced back and saw Preston below in the courtyard pointing his pistol at the window with one hand, and waving Paul and Callie away with the other.

"Get back!" Paul heard him shout, but then Preston glanced up and leaped aside at the last minute as a pale man landed *plop* on the deck from above. From opposite sides of the glass, Paul, Callie, and Preston saw pale men scuttling along the roofline of the courtyard, beyond the glare of the security lights. Several had already made the leap down to the deck, and Preston grasped his weapon with both hands, jerking it from side to side as he was backed up against the trunk of the dying oak by three crouching pale men. Another pale man had leaped into the upper branches of the tree, and he swung like a spider downward, limb by limb, hand over hand, towards Preston.

"Paul, you got . . . ten seconds . . . to kill her," panted Colonel, his arm trembling under the pressure of Olivia and the pale homeless men behind him. "I can't . . . hold them . . . any longer."

Olivia's mouth was cursing silently, spittle flying from her lips. Some of the homeless men were already reaching over Colonel's head or trying to crawl between his legs. Over his own head Paul heard the sickening creak of the ceiling, and he saw bulges moving from panel to panel. One of the panels over the desk started to slide away.

Paul snatched Rick's phone off the desk and yanked the cord free in one go. He twirled the handset at the end of its cord like a bola, glancing from the door to the ceiling. Callie put her back into the corner of the two windows and squeezed the neck of the lamp. Paul met her gaze for an instant. "I love you," he almost said, but he didn't think she'd want to hear it just at the moment. Instead, he turned towards the door, swinging the handset faster. "Come and get me," he said.

Colonel shook his head. "You're a fool," he said, and slowly relaxed his arm. Olivia crouched, gathering her sodden skirt in one hand. Pale hands reached above and around Colonel and Olivia. Boy G's savagely smiling face appeared in the gap over the desk.

Then everyone—Colonel, Olivia, the pale men in the doorway, Boy G, even Callie and Paul—was frozen in place by a long, murderous hiss. The temperature in the room dropped drastically, as if an arctic wind had blown through, and the skin of Paul's arm started out in goose pimples. Standing on the corner of Rick's desk, hissing evilly at the doorway, was Charlotte, her black jaws wide, her ears back. Her fur bristled, and her tail stood erect. Her back arched like a cardboard Halloween cutout.

Colonel and Olivia recoiled in the doorway, and the pale men behind them shrank back, moaning in unison, a long, diminuendo "Ohhhhhhhhhhh!" Charlotte lifted her black gaze to the ceiling and hissed again, and Boy G's face retreated into the darkness.

"What the hell is that?" gasped Callie.

Paul stared at Charlotte in wonderment. He'd never seen her outside of his residence before. He forgot to swing the handset, and it clattered to the carpet at the end of the cord.

"That's my cat," he said.

In the electric silence Charlotte relaxed her spine and curled slowly around herself, trotting towards the other end of the desk. She hissed at Paul as she passed, though not as murderously, more in the spirit of "What are you looking at?" Then, as the freezing cold prickled the skin of everyone in the room, she leapt at the window overlooking the courtyard.

The window disintegrated—the whole window, all at once— and an infinity of tiny, blunt fragments like windshield glass sagged away from the frame and cascaded in a glissando through the branches of the tree to the courtyard deck below. Charlotte leaped straight through the glittering waterfall of glass and landed lightly on a large limb of the tree just below the window. The humid air of a warm Texas evening flooded through the wide gap, and Charlotte glanced back at Paul and gave him a curt little *mrow* like a command, then started down the limb towards the trunk.

Paul dropped the phone and lunged over the desk for Callie. He grabbed her by the wrist and practically flung her out the open window. She shrieked, but the limb caught her in the midriff and she clutched it with both arms. Paul followed an instant later, knocking himself nearly breathless, and the two of them swung for a moment by their fingers and then dropped the three or four feet to the deck, prancing on tiptoe among the atomized glass.

The three pale men who had cornered Preston backed slowly away, their goggling gazes fixed on the cat in the tree. Charlotte hissed again, and the pale man descending the tree scrambled back up towards the roof. Over his shoulder Preston said, "Get behind me." Paul and Callie trod carefully through the glass; Paul felt the stinging little pellets embedding themselves in his soles. He glanced up through the tree and saw Colonel and Olivia and the mob of pale men crowding to the edge of the open window; above them he saw Boy G peering out of the ceiling, warily watching Charlotte.

Then the cat, out of boredom or mischievousness, vanished, and the pale man in the tree started to descend again. Others leaped out of the office into the upper branches. Pale faces appeared over the edge of the courtyard roof again, and the three men around Preston started forward.

"Head for the stairway!" barked Preston, and he shot one of the pale men through the throat; the man fell gagging to the deck as the crack of the pistol reverberated round the courtyard. But the others kept coming, and several more dropped from the branches, plopping softly against the deck. As Preston slowly backpedaled behind them, Paul and Callie inched towards the stairs where the courtyard emptied into the parking lot, but more pale guys were crowding into the gap. Paul stopped and threw his arm across Callie, putting her between him and Preston. She glanced round at the pale men bobbing along the roofline and hanging from the tree and crowding closer along the deck, and she pressed Paul's back with the tips of her fingers.

"Where'd your cat go?" she said.

"What cat?" shouted Preston, as he backed into Callie and Paul.

"Here, kitty kitty kitty," called Callie, tremulously.

Preston fired another shot and missed, and the bullet whined around the courtyard. Everyone hunched their shoulders— Paul, Callie, Preston, the pale men all around—but as the ricochet died away more pale men jumped from the roof to the courtyard deck or dropped from the tree, chanting *"Are we not men?"* louder and louder. Paul glanced at the exit to the parking lot, but more pale men were swinging down from the pedestrian bridge and crowding the gap. Two of them were already grappling Preston for his gun. Paul reached back for Callie, and she wrapped her arms around him from behind, pressing her head against his shoulder. In the distance he heard the rising grumble of an engine, some late-night cowboy peeling rubber, no doubt, and as pale hands reached from the tree and pawed softly at his scalp and arms and shoulders, Paul thought, I wish I was that guy.

But the engine came closer, and through the gap Paul heard the piercing screech of tires, then a door opening, then the *ping ping ping* of a little warning alarm. "Your key is in the ignition," said a pleasant little recording. Paul heard the glide and thump of a sliding door, and he looked through the gap into the parking lot, over the heads of the pale men, and saw Nolene marching towards him, looking righteously pissed off. One of the pale men heard her coming, too, and turned towards her. Without ceremony she lifted her left hand and spritzed him point blank with a little canister of pepper spray, and he squealed and threw himself to the pavement. She was swinging something from her right hand—Paul saw it rise and fall over the heads of the pale men—and suddenly the knot of men in the gap under the pedestrian bridge tumbled out of the way like bowling pins. No-lene marched into the courtyard under the bridge, liberally pumping pepper spray in all directions, and, with her other hand, swinging a bulky child safety seat in a wide figure eight. The seat swung free at the end of its seatbelt straps, which Nolene had wound round tightly round her wrist, and she worked her massive arm up and down and over and under, clob-bering screeching pale men right and left.

"Out of my way," she hollered, "you self-pitying sons of bitches!"

"Go!" shouted Preston, and he took advantage of Nolene's distraction to pistol-whip one of the men struggling with him; the other let go of Preston's wrist and ducked away as Preston fired over his head. Callie shoved Paul from behind, and they skipped painfully over the broken glass towards the gap where Nolene swung the child seat to one side to let them pass.

"I ain't got all night, Preston!" Nolene barked. A pale man leaped from above, and she clocked him under the chin with the car seat, sending him flying backwards against the wall. "I told the sitter I'd be back in an hour."

"Yes'm," Preston called out, trotting across the littered deck, firing wildly back into the tree and up at the roofline.

In the parking lot Callie dived through the open sliding door of Nolene's minivan onto the backseat, but Paul hung back just outside the gap.

"Move your ass, Professor," barked Nolene, as she backed into the parking lot. "I ain't doing this for my health."

She dropped the empty pepper spray canister and marched towards the minivan. But Paul couldn't tear himself away just yet. Past the stairs and through the branches of the dying oak, where pale guys swung like pale, fat spiders, he saw Colonel in distress in the window. Plans A and B failed, Paul thought, and now they're moving to Plan C. The pale men were wrapping themselves around Colonel, sliding their hands around his wrists and ankles and over his nose and mouth. His frantic eyes darted everywhere. From above, Boy G swung upside down and caught Colonel under his arms, hauling him into the ceiling.

But Olivia, queen of the underworld, stood nearly unmolested in the window; one of the pale men curled his fingers around her wrist, and she slapped him. As he winced and slunk away, her gaze met Paul's, and the last he ever saw of Olivia Haddock, just before Preston caught him by the elbow and marched him into the minivan, she was standing, arms akimbo, in her ruined red prom dress, glowering at him through the branches of the tree.

FORTY-ONE

A FEW DAYS LATER, on a hot, sunny Texas afternoon, Paul Trilby—failed academic, former employee of the Texas Department of General Services, born-again vegetarian—was ferrying his last few remaining possessions into the hatchback of his battered old Dodge Colt. He had rolled down the windows of the car, and he kept the door of his apartment propped wide as he went back and forth; it wasn't like he needed to worry about the cat getting out. The parking lot was nearly empty; only a couple of his neighbors were taking their ease along the balcony, slouching over the rail and sucking back on long-necked bottles of beer. Mrs. Prettyman was watching from behind her curtains, he knew, but she had only come out once, her fingers twitching at her throat.

"You're paid up till the end of the month," she'd said. She almost sounded sorry to see him go. "I'm afraid the owner don't allow partial refunds."

"Tell him to keep it, with my compliments." Paul stood up

from laying the backseat of his car flat, his t-shirt already soaked through with sweat. "Get him to take you out to dinner."

As he went back inside, Mrs. Prettyman stepped under the balcony and peered into the dim recesses of his apartment, but she wouldn't come through the door. She pressed her fingers to her collarbone. "Where should I forward your mail?" she said.

"What mail?" Paul asked from the sink, as he slung his plastic plates into a box.

Finally she went away, and now Paul was almost done. None of the furniture was his, and he had already loaded his dishes and his clothes. He yanked out the sofa bed and began to strip the sheets off the mattress, stuffing them into a pillowcase. He hadn't slept in the bed since last Friday but had been staying in Preston's trailer south of the river. Paul, indeed, had not been in his apartment after dark since the week before, and even during the day, as now, he kept a weather eye on the grate in the center of the parking lot.

He slung the pillowcase into the back of the car and went back inside the apartment. He still hadn't made up his mind whether to take the TV or not. On the one hand, he was tired of cat shows, but on the other hand, if he ended up in the middle of nowhere someplace, Charlotte's programming might be preferable to whatever he could pull in from some podunk local station. So he tugged the plug out of the wall with the toe of his sneaker, lifted the set in his arms, and carried the TV out to his car. He tread carefully; it was still painful for him to walk, or even to stand for too long. Inside his sneakers, his lacerated feet were taped up in gauze, which he had to change twice a day at least. Preston had doctored him in the narrow living room of his trailer, picking the glass out of Paul's soles with a pair of tweezers and painting the cuts deep purple with Betadine. Friday night, as they had raced away down empty streets under traffic lights blinking yellow, Preston and Nolene had explained why they couldn't take Paul and Callie to the emergency room.

"The docs'd take one look at y'all," Nolene said, watching Paul in the rearview mirror, "and call the po-lice."

"Why the hell shouldn't they?" said Paul, still trembling from fear and exhaustion.

"And tell them what, chief?" Preston sagged in the deep passenger seat up front, daubing the sweat off his forehead with a massive red bandanna. He turned and focused his tired eyes over his shoulder at Paul. "Huh?"

"Shouldn't they know?" said Paul. Callie's palm lay limp in his, and he squeezed it, glancing at her for moral support. But she was crumpled against the door, taking shallow breaths and gazing at nothing out the window.

"*We* know," said Nolene. "And we know how to take care of 'em."

"But...," said Paul.

" 'Nuff said, Professor," said Preston.

In the end Nolene didn't even take him home but dropped him off a few blocks away from TxDoGS, where Preston had parked his truck in the empty lot of another state building. By now the adrenaline had worn off, and the walk across the pavement to Preston's pickup had been excruciating. Even so, Paul had shaken off Preston and limped back to the van to crawl back in next to Callie. He kissed her sweaty temple, but she said nothing. She didn't even look at him.

"Nolene'll look after her," said Preston, and Paul let himself be led away again, leaving bloody footprints on the asphalt.

"I told you, didn't I," Nolene called after him. "I *told* you not to go in that building after dark."

Preston took Paul to his small but fastidiously kept trailer in a little park tucked behind a taqueria and a boot repair shop, where he cleaned and dressed Paul's feet and then gave Paul his own bed while he slept on the sofa. Paul slept all day Saturday and into Sunday, waking up at noon to the smell of slow-roasted meat. He limped out of the cramped bedroom at the end of the trailer, past a row of framed commendations and pictures of Preston and other men in fatigues, and found his host in the kitchenette.

"Sit," Preston said, hooking Paul under the arm to help him into a chair. "I got you some 'cue."

But as soon as Paul popped open the large Styrofoam take-out shell and saw the barbecue steaming before him—a limp heap of crumbling brisket and bias-cut slices of hot sausage—he put his hand to his mouth and began to gag.

"Whoa there!" said Preston, whisking it away. "Sorry, bud, I wun't thinking." He snapped the shell shut and buried it deep in his little dollhouse fridge, and then—rather expertly, Paul thought, once his stomach settled—steamed some vegetables for Paul, broccoli and peppers and squash. As Paul ate, Preston sat with him and nursed a cup of coffee, shooting concerned glances across the little table.

"Colonel approached *me* once," Preston said quietly, without any preamble, "back when I first came to TxDoGS."

Paul said nothing; he kept his eyes on his plate.

"Nearly took him up on it, too." Preston pushed his coffee cup to one side and rested his forearms on the table. "I was a career marine, a colonel by time I retired. A real one," he added, his eyes flaring. "I commanded men in battle, Paul, and now, here I was working as a security guard for minimum wage." Paul met his eyes, and Preston must have seen something in his look because he added, "Let's just say that from the bottom of a bottle, security guard looked like a step up." Preston held Paul's gaze. "But in the end," he said, "I couldn't stand that jumped-up little pastry chef. He was plenty pissed when I turned him down, but there wun't a whole hell of a lot he could do about it."

Preston explained how he had watched Bob Wier and J. J. fall into Colonel's orbit. "I didn't try hard enough to talk 'em out of it," he said with some regret. "The way I was raised, Paul, I don't hold with self-pity. You play the cards you're dealt. Like the man says," Preston went on, lifting his eyes to the ceiling as he quoted from memory, " 'I won't be wronged, I won't be insulted, I won't be laid a hand on. I don't do these things to other people, and I require the same from them.' "

"Who said that?" Paul looked up from his vegetables.

"John Wayne." Preston blushed. "In *The Shootist.* His last picture," Preston added helpfully.

Paul resisted the urge to smile or roll his eyes, but he couldn't help wondering how many East Texas platitudes he was required to endure. Still, it would be impolite to accept a man's generosity and then call him on his clichés.

"When you come in Monday morning," Preston was saying, "I think you'll be surprised at just how little has changed."

"You're kidding, right?" Paul said. "Why would I ever go back there?"

Preston opened his mouth, but then resigned himself to a smile. "I could tell you, but you wouldn't believe me. You'll just have to come in and see for yourself."

"I don't understand." Paul sagged in his seat. "I don't understand any of it."

"I wouldn't work too hard at it," Preston said, smiling.

"How can I go on working there?"

"You don't have to." Preston gazed hard at Paul. "If I was a young fella like you, with no ties, I'd come in, collect my pay, and take off."

"You stay, though."

Preston nodded. "Yeah, well, me and Nolene, we've sorta made it our business to keep an eye on things." He lifted an eyebrow at Paul. "You might say, I got myself a mission. More vegetables?"

That afternoon Preston offered to take Paul to his apartment to pick up some clean clothes and his car, but Paul wanted to see Callie first. He directed Preston up South Austin Avenue to Callie's complex, but her truck was not in the parking lot.

"Maybe she's at Nolene's," Paul said.

"She ain't," said Preston. "I talked to Nolene, and she said Callie insisted on coming home yesterday."

Even so, Paul made Preston stop. He got out of the truck and limped up the stairs to Callie's door. He rang the buzzer and knocked, and finally tried the doorknob. It was unlocked, so he opened the door a crack and called her name. Then he pushed it open all the way and stepped into Callie's empty living room. He limped to the window and looked down to see Preston walking across the lot towards the manager's office. Then

Paul made his painful way to the kitchen, where the cupboards stood open and bare. His heart began to beat a little faster, and he hobbled to the bedroom and propped himself in the doorway. In the glare of the overhead light, the bedroom seemed even emptier than the living room; the mattress and chair were gone, the closet was empty. Not a scrap of clothing remained on the floor. The only thing in the room, in fact, sitting square in the center of the floor under the overhead fixture, was Callie's copy of *The Norton Anthology of English Literature*. Fixed to the cover was a square, yellow Post-it, and Paul limped to the center of the room and stooped for the book. The only thing on the Post-it was a three-digit number, so Paul hefted the spine of the book in his left hand and thumbed through the tissuey pages to the number. It was *Love's Labour's Lost*, and one line of a speech was highlighted in bright yellow: "Love is a familiar; Love is a devil. There is no evil angel but Love."

"You find it?"

Paul turned to see Preston in the doorway. "Find what?" he said.

Preston nodded at the book. "Manager, he said Callie moved out this morning, just tossed her stuff in her truck and took off."

"Did he say where?"

"He don't know," Preston said. "She didn't say." He glanced round the bare room. "He did say that she said to tell you, if you came by, that she left a book for you." His eyes landed on the open volume in Paul's hands. "What's it say?"

"Nothing." Paul flipped it shut.

On Monday Paul called in sick and spent the day sleeping on Preston's couch. But he went to work on Tuesday, and Preston offered to walk Paul to his cube.

"Is it safe to go up there?" Paul said.

"Go see for yourself," Preston said, so Paul went up alone. As he came out of the groaning elevator, the first thing he saw was the broken chair with the note taped to its back, propped against the window. Paul drew a breath, then lifted the lid of the recycling box. It was full of cans, so he replaced the lid and tilted the box to one side to look at the dusty tiles beneath. They looked like all the other tiles.

Just inside the door to cubeland he paused and surveyed the ceiling. Every panel was in place, as far as the eye could see, especially over the library cube, where Paul was surprised to see no ragged hole, and no sign of repair. He limped around the corner into his own cube, switching on the monitor to watch the motto on his screen saver stream annoyingly by. There was a note on his chair, in Rick's vivid scrawl—SEE ME—so Paul started up the aisle, one painful step at a time. Even though he was walking like an arthritic old man, Renee glared at him as he passed her cube. Paul laughed. As he came to the junction of the two aisles, he saw nothing out of the ordinary—no broken glass, no fragments of ceiling panel, no litter of office supplies. The bookcase in the library cube stood erect as always, and the worktable looked positively dusty; the three-hole punch and the big stapler looked as if no one had touched them for years.

Then he hobbled past the three cubicles of J. J., Colonel, and Bob Wier. The personal effects of all three men still sat on their desks or along the shelves, but all three were absent. Paul paused the longest in the doorway of Bob Wier, where he gazed along the shelf above Bob's desk at the speed-reading manuals and the TexGro literature, his gaze coming to rest on the portraits of Bob's wife and children, arranged by height. Paul stared longest at the picture of Bob's wife, a scrubbed young woman with a helmet of blonde hair and the vacant look preferred by the Sears photographer. Paul felt a thickening in his throat.

"Rick's waiting for you, Paul," said Nolene from behind him, and Paul turned. She was gazing down at something on her desk and expertly twirling a pencil in her right hand. Paul stared at her until she looked up and met his gaze. Very slowly she shook her head, then lowered her eyes again.

"Paul!" cried Rick from inside his office. "Git on in here."

As Paul limped through the door, he glanced quickly round Rick's office. The ceiling was undisturbed; the chair was tucked neatly under the table; Rick's monitor and desk lamp and telephone sat where they always had. Not only was his window intact, there wasn't a scratch or a chip on it. Beyond the glass the thick limb of the dying oak seemed to cock its elbow at Paul.

"Way-ul, it never rains, but it rains," Rick said, as Paul propped himself against the table to take some weight off his feet. "Colonel, J. J., and Bob have jumped ship." He gestured at three letters laid side by side on his desk, each one on TxDoGS stationery, each one smudged in a different place. "They say they've quit to open their own pit barbecue establishment, can you believe that?"

Rick looked as flustered as Paul had ever seen him. He lifted his eyes beseechingly to Paul. "What the hell do these birds know about barbecue?"

Paul bit his lip and said nothing. Rick heaved himself back in his chair and linked his fingers behind his head. "Damnedest thing I ever heard," he muttered, addressing the ceiling. Then he heaved himself forward, shuffled the three letters of resignation together, and folded his hands.

"That makes you the go-to guy on the RFP," he said. "You're the lead honcho now, Paul. Well, truth be told, you always was, but now it's official." Rick's antic bonhomie seemed to founder a bit as he met Paul's steady gaze. "Unless you're leaving, too," he said, with a nervous laugh.

"Actually . . ." Paul shifted his weight to his other foot. The pain was a dull ache, but it never went away.

Rick's shoulders sagged, and for a moment Paul thought the man might actually cry. He'd never seen anyone look so crestfallen, and he took it as some kind of compliment.

"I just came in to say good-bye," Paul said.

"You got another job?" Rick said.

"Actually," Paul said, "I'm going back to school." Then he smiled and said, "I think I've had my fill of government work."

Paul took nothing from his cube. He even left behind his copy of *Seven Science Fiction Novels of H. G. Wells*, placing it on the desk next to his mouse pad for the next temp to find. Then

Preston walked him out of the TxDoGS Building to his car, and he helped Paul open the doors and the hatchback to let the heat out. As Paul settled behind the wheel and started the engine, Preston slammed the hatchback for him and came around to Paul's window. He tossed an envelope on Paul's lap, and Paul pried it open to find three hundred dollars in twenties.

"I can't take this," Paul said. He felt tears forming in the corners of his eyes.

"Son, you can't not take it," Preston said.

"I'll pay you back," Paul said, struggling to control his voice.

"Well." Preston squinted away towards the river, then peered through the window at Paul. "You pass that money along to somebody else someday, and we'll call it square." He stuck his big, rough hand through the window, and Paul took it. Paul didn't know what else to say, so he put the car in gear and Preston stepped back and crossed his arms. Halfway out of the parking space, Paul stopped and looked out the window and said, "Hey, Preston, you ever been to Beaver, Oklahoma?"

Preston smiled, thinking of the obvious joke, but he resisted the temptation. "Can't say that I have," he said. "What's in Beaver, Oklahoma?"

"I don't know yet," said Paul.

Now, two hours later, Paul was finished loading his car. The only thing of his left in the apartment was the *Norton Anthology*, resting on the kitchen table; the Post-it with the page number on it was folded over and tucked tenderly between the pages like a billet-doux. Paul pried the apartment key off his key ring and placed it on the table next to the book. Then he glanced around the apartment, even lifting his eyes to the ceiling.

"Charlotte?" he said, though he didn't expect any kind of answer. He hadn't seen her since that crucial moment in the tree Friday night, but then he hadn't spent any time in his apartment since then. He still could not puzzle out her presence in Rick's office on Friday night, nor could he make sense of what she had done there. Not only had he never seen her outside of his residence before, she had certainly never done him any favors. Yet she had saved his life and Callie's. That was what he couldn't understand. It was too much to hope, he supposed, that maybe her curse was broken, that he would never see her anymore, that somehow, by doing more or less the right thing— even a few seconds late—he had dispelled Charlotte's juju, repaid his debt to her, alleviated her feline rage. That would be too much to ask.

"Alright, I'm leaving now," he said aloud, lifting the anthology off the table. "Um, thanks, I guess."

He turned and carried the book out of the apartment, pulling the door shut after him and twisting the knob to make sure it was locked. Then he hobbled to his car, hauled open the screeching door, and settled himself behind the wheel. He turned to drop the book on the passenger seat, and there sat Charlotte, looking nearly as she had done when she was alive, her paws tucked neatly under her, her tail curled all the way around her. She looked up at him with her indifferent gaze.

"Well, this is new," said Paul. He tossed the book behind the seat, onto the heap of boxes. He glanced at Charlotte and shrugged. He started the car, and the engine clattered to life, the metallic banging from the undercarriage bouncing off the walls of the Angry Loner Motel. He laid his hand on the gearshift and looked back through the rear window, but then he sagged in his seat and sighed, the car vibrating noisily under him. He looked down at the ghost of a cat beside him.

"You still hate me, right?" he said. "So why didn't you let them kill me? Do you *care* if I live or die, or are you just being territorial?"

Charlotte did not move or make a sound, but she watched him steadily.

"Okay, I get it," Paul went on. "It's not that you don't *want* me to be tormented, you just don't want anybody else to do it." Paul narrowed his gaze at her. "Or is it possible you didn't want anything to happen to Callie, and I just rode along in her slipstream. Is that it? Do you love Callie? Is that even possible?"

The car chugged almost expectantly under him. Jesus H. Christ, he thought, I'm talking to a cat. Hell, I'm talking to a *dead* cat. He looked down at Charlotte, curled calmly on the seat. It occurred to him that she might even be purring, but he'd never be able to tell over the racket of the car. He wondered what she'd do if he touched her and decided that it probably wasn't a good idea to try.

"Never mind," he said, his fingers curled round the gearshift. "Forget I asked. Screw it. Because you know what, Charlotte?" He settled himself firmly in his seat and gave her a defiant look. "I don't care. You do whatever you want, and I'll do whatever I want. It just doesn't matter anymore. Whether you're real or imaginary, whether you haunt me in public or in private, I *just don't care.* You want to know why, Charlotte?"

She was watching him wide-eyed. Her tail had come uncurled, and it lashed back and forth across the worn corduroy of the seat.

"Because in the last four weeks, Charlotte, I have *seen it all.* Of all the strange things that have happened to me in my life, you're not even at the top of the list anymore. Okay? Got that?"

He leaned towards her, brandishing his index finger.

"Whatever you do," he said, "wherever you follow me, there's not a single goddamn thing you can do to surprise me anymore. Not one."

Charlotte yawned, splitting her sharp little muzzle nearly in two. She blinked up at Paul.

"Shut up and drive," said the cat.

AUTHOR'S NOTE

THE AUTHOR IS GRATEFUL TO H. G. Wells for the Morlocks and the Beast Folk; to Henrik Ibsen for the Boyg and a few lines from *Peer Gynt*; to Lady Mary Wroth (1587?–1651?) for her "Crown of Sonnets Dedicated to Love"; and to Edvard Grieg for the incidental music to *Peer Gynt*, especially "In the Hall of the Mountain King." He's also extremely grateful to Neil Olson, Mimi Mayer, Keith Taylor, John Marks, Gretchen Wahl, Becky McDermott, Martin Lewis, Ross Orr, and Josh Kendall. And it wouldn't be a proper Author's Note if he didn't thank his two cats, Conrad and Hobbes, who carry on the spirit of Charlotte, sprawl across his keyboard, and (lucky for him) keep their opinions to themselves.